By Emmanuel Dongala

Jazz and Palm Wine

Little Boys Come from the Stars

The Fire of Origins

Johnny Mad Dog

Johnny Mad Dog

Farrar, Straus and Giroux | New York

Johnny Mad Dog

Emmanuel Dongala

Translated from the French by Maria Louise Ascher

FARRAR, STRAUS AND GIROUX
19 Union Square West, New York 10003

Distributed in Canada by Douglas & McIntyre Ltd.
Printed in the United States of America
Originally published in 2002 by Le Serpent à Plumes, Paris,
as *Johnny Chien Méchant*
Published in the United States by Farrar, Straus and Giroux
FIRST AMERICAN EDITION, 2005

Library of Congress Cataloging-in-Publication Data
Dongala, Emmanuel Boundzéki, 1941–
[Johnny chien méchant. English]
Johnny mad dog / Emmanuel Dongala ; translated from the French by Maria Louise Ascher.—1st American ed.
p. cm.
ISBN-13: 978-0-374-17995-3
ISBN-10: 0-374-17995-6 (alk. paper)
I. Ascher, Maria Louise. II. Title.

PQ3989.2.D6J6413 2005
843'.914—dc22

2004062606

Designed by Gretchen Achilles

www.fsgbooks.com

10 9 8 7 6 5 4 3 2 1

The author gratefully acknowledges the support of the Simon Guggenheim Foundation, which afforded him the time to write a major part of this book.

To Philip Roth

To C. H. and Mary Huvelle,
with gratitude

If suffering is human, we were not born humans merely to suffer.

—**GEORGE SEFERIS, "An Old Man on the River Bank"**

Pity the planet, all joy gone
from this sweet volcanic cone;
peace to our children when they fall
in small war on the heels of small
war—until the end of time . . .

—**ROBERT LOWELL, "Waking Early Sunday Morning"**

Translator's Note

The CFA franc is the unit of currency in fourteen Central and West African countries. In 2002, when this book was first published in French, 1 U.S. dollar was equal to about 625 CFA francs. Thus, 500 CFA francs is about 80 cents (this sum is mentioned in Chapter 4) and 15,000 francs is about 24 dollars (Chapter 19).

The pagne (pronounced *pahn*-yeh), a brightly colored length of fabric approximately one meter by two meters, is a traditional and universal item of clothing among Central and West African women. It is wrapped around the lower body to make a long skirt, which may be paired with a loose-fitting long-sleeved embroidered tunic called a boubou. A pagne can easily be made into a sling for carrying a baby or a bundle on one's back, and has countless other uses—as a ground cloth for eating or sleeping, a privacy screen, a tablecloth, a bedsheet, a dustcover, a window shade, a towel, or, as seen in this novel, a shroud. The pagne is a symbol of women's strength, resourcefulness, and creativity.

Johnny Mad Dog

Chapter One

Laokolé

General Giap proclaimed a period of looting that was to last forty-eight hours.

Instantly I switched off the radio. I took the hurricane lamp and ran toward our little storage shed, to make sure the wheelbarrow was there and in working order. Yes, it was there, lying upside down. I spun its single wheel. The wheel turned smoothly but squeaked a little. I went to the kitchen to find the bit of palm oil we had left. I oiled the wheel and tested it again. It didn't squeak anymore. Despite the rust that had begun to corrode the body, the barrow was in good repair and both of its handles were steady.

I returned to the house. I raised the pagne that served as a curtain between my room and Mama's. She was still asleep. Wake her, or let her sleep awhile longer? I hesitated briefly, then decided to wake her only at the last minute. She'd had a very difficult night, unable to fall asleep until three a.m., when the two water-soluble aspirin I'd forced her to take had dulled the pain of her injured legs and allowed her to get some rest. I would leave her in peace for another half hour. I lowered the pagne and went over to Fofo, my little brother, who shared the room with me. He was still snoring, sprawled comfortably on his foam mattress, which lay on the floor next to my bed. I shook him roughly. He was almost twelve now, no longer a small child, old enough to help the family.

He awoke with a start. I told him that another round of looting would begin in a few hours and that we had to hurry—we mustn't be taken by surprise, the way we had been last time. Panic in his eyes, he began to cry, his whole body trembling. He was terrified, I knew, because he was dreading a repeat of the day when members of the first militias—the men who, back then, were fighting against the troops gearing up for the looting today—had killed Papa right in front of him. It would be a disaster if he had another of his breakdowns now. So I had to shake him, had to impress on him the urgency of the situation in order to prevent him from dwelling on its gravity.

Raising my right hand in a threatening way, I told him to run and fetch two shovels from the shed where the wheelbarrow was stored, then wait for me behind the house. He understood right away that I wasn't joking; he calmed down and went out into the darkness. I was afraid I'd woken Mama by speaking so loudly to Fofo. I raised the pagne once more; she lay undisturbed. It had been a long time since I'd seen such tranquillity in her face. She was sleeping so peacefully!

I followed Fofo outside. He was already waiting for me in our little garden behind the house. He had only one shovel with him; the handle of the other, he said, was broken. I told him to go fetch a hoe instead. When he came back, I handed him the shovel and took the hoe. I marked out a rectangle on the ground and we began to dig a large hole by the light of the moon. Since it was garden soil—lucky for us—it was easily worked. Imagine if we'd had to dig in sand or packed ground! After ten minutes or so, the hole was deep enough.

I looked at Fofo. He was sweating profusely. Poor child! I'd gotten him up at five in the morning, threatened him, made him work like a dog, and he hadn't even had breakfast yet. A twelve-year-old doesn't deserve that. I told him to go wash up and then have something to eat. "Remember to brush your teeth and comb your hair. And be quick about it! Don't dawdle, or I'll come looking for you." He went without a word. How I wished I had a treat to give him, if only a piece of chocolate!

I picked up the shovel Fofo had been using and moved the heaped-up soil farther from the edge of the hole, so it wouldn't fall back in. Now I had to attend to Mama.

Chapter Two

Johnny, Known as Lufua Liwa

Giap authorized a period of looting that was to last forty-eight hours. You should have heard him, squawking away on the radio.

> *"This is General Giap speaking. Our brave freedom fighters have fought like lions, like buffalo! They've struck fear into the hearts of our enemies, who have fled with their tails between their legs. Victory!* La luta continua! *We are afraid of nothing! We will pursue them to the depths of the ocean—we will cling to them like lice! To celebrate this triumph of a liberated people, I, General Giap, together with our new president, give you full authorization to take anything you want for a period of forty-eight hours. Whatever you wish is yours! Confiscate what you please! To the victor go the spoils—this is one of the benefits of war. So help yourselves until Monday . . ."*

"Help yourselves until Monday . . ." Who the fuck did he think he was, with his "forty-eight hours"? Did he really think we needed his okay? We were going to loot until there was nothing left to be looted, whether that took twenty-four, forty-eight, or seventy-two hours, or as long as a week. Even the VIP we were fighting for, the guy who'd been president of the country for the past few hours, ever since we'd captured the city—even *he* couldn't stop us. He knew that of all the militias who had fought and were fighting on his behalf, ours was the best. It was no accident that we were called the Mata Mata—the Death Dealers—for we were completely fearless when killing others or meeting death ourselves. In fact, it was our commando unit that had secured his power, because we'd been the first to enter the city and had taken over the radio and TV stations. And when the city was cleansed and the entire country was under our control, the government would have to integrate us into the army. Otherwise, there'd be hell to pay! I myself would be integrated with the rank of lieutenant colonel. Giap had been promoted to general because he was already old. He was twenty-five.

It was thanks to me that he was called Giap. His *nom de guerre* was Pili Pili, because he liked to torture female prisoners by rubbing their eyes with pili-pili, the little red pepper that, when made into a sauce, burned your mouth so badly you'd swallow the entire Congo River trying to put out the fire. Unlike us, he didn't screw the pretty girls we captured. He said that if he did, his fetishes would be robbed of their power—that, for example, he'd lose his ability to become invisible to the enemy and that bullets would no longer turn into clumps of dirt as they approached him. Actually, I was the only one who knew his secret: his piston was dead, and he could no longer pump the women the way we could. His thing got really stiff only with women we didn't want, those that didn't excite us. He would take them, would douse their eyes with pepper sauce or powder that he'd made himself, and would tear their clothes off. And while the women screamed, rubbed their eyes, and writhed from the burning pepper, he'd howl with laughter, laugh till he cried. When he saw them rolling on the ground, twisting and jerking, and wriggling their bare asses as if performing some devilish dance—well, then he got a hard-on like a bull's. His eyes, the bulging eyes of a pot smoker, were even redder than the pepper-filled eyes of his victims. He'd feel gay and happy, and would come without any inhibition. I knew when he'd shot his wad, because a dark stain, round and wet, would appear on his khakis right below his fly. Once, when he was all played out, I saw his banana droop and go soft, then shrink away and vanish into the folds of his belly. Amazing! But you had to pretend not to see that, or else he'd go crazy, like a bitch in heat when she's been denied a male. Once, Smoking Cannon, on seeing Pili Pili's thing shrivel up and disappear, had dared to say, "Hey, it looks like a worm crawling back into its hole!" And Pili Pili had blown him away with a burst from his Kalashnikov. Ever since then, we all watched our step and averted our eyes when he was like that. Even Rambo, our previous leader, had been afraid of him. Yeah, Pili Pili was a good name for him.

When Major Rambo was killed in an argument over some stuff we'd looted from the home of a rich Mauritanian shopkeeper, I'd had the feeling the guys were going to ask me to take his place. I was all ready to refuse. I would have said that Pili Pili was the oldest and that he was the one who should take command. But the truth was that I was afraid of his fetishes, because I'd seen them in action. One day, when he'd forgotten to put on the fetish that made him invisible, he'd been captured by the Chechens, allies of the militias we were fighting. He'd managed to escape, and by the time he'd gotten back to our camp his clothes were so wet you could have wrung them out like a mop. All of the bullets that hit him had been transformed into drops of water! No shit, he was one powerful guy. So I would have let him lead the group. Apparently this was precisely what he was expecting, since he accepted without batting an eye, and said that his name from now on was General Pili Pili.

We all thought it was ridiculous for a general to call himself "Hot Pepper." The other militias made fun of us and disrespected us for being led by a guy who got a hard-on staring at the twitching asses of women with spices in their eyes. Then he looked at us while flexing his biceps and said that since Rambo was dead, *he* was now General Rambo. I objected strongly. Since it was my bullet that had killed Rambo, I thought something bad might happen to me if the name Rambo stayed alive in our group. A name isn't just a name. A name contains hidden power. It's no accident that I've taken the name Lufua Liwa, which means "Kill Death," or rather "Cheat Death." So in order to stroke his ego, I told him that the name Rambo was too common, almost vulgar, and that in Texas there were more than three hundred Rambos in Dallas alone. The others, who considered me pretty smart (in fact, I was the only intellectual in the group), agreed. We all began to think hard, very hard. We came up with "Godzilla" and "Orangutan"; then "Khaddafi," "Saddam Hussein," "Milosevic"—all the strongmen whose names we'd heard on the radio. But I wasn't satisfied. Those names were too well-known, and, like daylight, names that are too well-known contain no secrets and thus no hidden power. The light of day is transparent; it has no secrets, no mystery, the way the night has. And then, *bang*, he came up with "Grenade"—"General Grenade." He was hugely proud of himself. The others had begun saying: Yeah, that's perfect, that's a great name, a name that scares you shitless, a name that explodes like an armed grenade.

Pili Pili had his fetishes and his pectorals going for him, but I had my brains and I wanted everybody to know this. Maybe someday the others would choose me as leader. So I said it was nothing for a general to pop off like a grenade. That wouldn't scare anybody. A general should make a horrendous explosion and a vast fiery cloud—like a bomb, not like a stupid grenade. He hesitated a moment and saw that there was some truth in what I was saying. He looked at me, his eyes red from the weed he'd been smoking, and asked me to think of a name that sounded good. And think of one fast. Since I'm an intellectual—I've completed second grade, while Pili Pili never even finished first grade—my brain is always working even when I haven't put it in gear, the way you breathe without knowing it but you're breathing all the same. So all of a sudden, *bang*—I myself exploded like a grenade: "Giap!" I don't know where or when I'd heard this name, or who Giap was, but this was what I came out with: "Giap." Pili Pili seized on it right away. "Yeah, General Giap—I'm General Giap!"

And instantly Pili Pili was transformed. He straightened his spine and gazed at us with the look of a true leader. I saw the power of a word, of a name, and I regretted what I'd done. I should have taken the name myself. A name is never innocent. "Lufua Liwa" doesn't inspire fear. Someone who cheats death is certainly crafty, sly, cunning, and shrewd, but he has never struck terror into the enemy's ranks. From now on, I'd call myself Matiti Mabé—"Poison Weed." Poison like *diamba*, the powerful hemp that grows around here and that makes your head spin, drives you crazy. Poison like the deadly mushroom. Matiti Mabé!

But *fucking hell*—of all the guys there, it was me he singled out when he gave his first order as General Giap. A humiliating order: he told me to go fetch his boots. Matiti Mabé, ordered to bring him his shit-kickers! And why not polish them too? I was on the verge of saying it was thanks to me that he'd become a general. And not just any general—a general named Giap! But the look he gave me, and the power of his fetishes and his abdominals, were so strong that I obeyed right away. I hustled off to fetch his boots.

Chapter Three

Laokolé

I went back to the house. Fofo had finished washing and was rummaging through the little bamboo cupboard to see what he could find for breakfast. I told him to take the two eggs that were left and make himself an omelet.

I headed to Mama's room to wake her up, and lifted the pagne that served as a curtain. Incredible! This woman who hadn't had a good night's rest since her husband's murder, who was continually being awakened by the pain in her legs, was sleeping peacefully, her face calm. Despite the urgency of the situation, I didn't have the heart to drive away the fleeting smile I thought I saw on her lips. Right away I found a rationalization: waking her five minutes later would hardly affect our escape.

Fofo called out from the little galley kitchen, saying the groundnut oil had been used up—there was only palm oil. I don't care for palm oil and think that eggs fried in it are inedible. I told him to hard-boil the eggs; there was kerosene in the portable stove we'd bought to replace the stolen gas cooker. And above all not to dawdle! We had to be out of the house in half an hour at the latest. This time, we wouldn't let ourselves be taken by surprise.

I went over to my bed. I knelt, bent down, and pulled out the large metal trunk we kept hidden beneath it. I opened it. Inside were three dead cockroaches and their dung. How had they gotten into a closed trunk? A mystery. Quickly I cleaned it out and started filling it with the important things we had to save at all costs. The choice was difficult, even though I'd devoted much thought to it since the last round of looting. I began with the big cardboard folder that contained all of our official documents: birth certificates, my parents' marriage license, report cards, diplomas. Then I put in my textbooks, and Fofo's as well. I wished I could take with me the large *Encyclopedia of Space* that I'd received as a school prize the previous year, but it was too heavy and bulky. As for the photo of Papa and Mama holding hands, I slipped it into the little purse where I'd also stored our money. In situations like this, I would keep the purse tucked inside my dress, my pants, or my pagne while carrying a decoy—a larger bag—which I wore openly, slung bandolier-style across my front, making sure it always contained a few coins and bits of cheap jewelry. A ruse like that can save your life. Then I filled up the trunk with Mama's three superwax pagnes, my two prettiest dresses, and my new pair of shoes. I asked Fofo to make sure I hadn't forgotten anything that was important to him. At last, I went to wake Mama.

I approached her bedside, averting my eyes from her face, and put my hand on her forehead. I called to her softly, as if nothing were wrong. She opened her eyes and smiled at me.

Visibly happy but with a touch of regret, she said: "Oh, Lao, I was having the most wonderful dream! I was strolling by myself through the city zoo, and I stopped to watch some little girls who were playing *ndzango*. They were skipping about, clapping their hands, laughing—"

"Mama, listen, you can tell me about your dream later. We have to leave now."

Quickly I told her that the government troops, those who had ransacked our house the last time, were fleeing the city, while the rebel troops were entering it at that very moment, which meant that another round of looting would begin shortly. Her eyes grew wide with shock, fear, rage, and determination. She made me tell her again whether it was the government soldiers or the rebels who were fleeing. I repeated that those who had been the government forces were now the rebels, and those who had been the rebels were now the government forces. She knew as well as I did that for us it made no difference. All of the warring factions claimed to be fighting in the name of the people, so it was up to the people to pay the expenses of both those who were winning and those who were losing. And we, of course, were "the people."

After hearing what I had to say, she once again became the mother she'd always been before losing her legs—the tower of strength who ran the household, sold goods at the market, fixed our meals, saw to our clothes, our health, and our schooling, while Papa spent long hours away from home, pushing wheelbarrows full of cement and sand, mixing mortar, hauling bricks, and climbing walls so that he could bring home the money to support us. She sat up straight on the bed and berated me for not waking her as soon as I'd heard the news on the radio. I explained that I'd taken care of the most important things—the wheelbarrow, the trunk, Fofo's breakfast —and that there was no time to lose. This calmed her. She pointed out two or three other things to be placed in the trunk ("and above all don't forget to add your father's photo"), then quickly began to wash and dress.

I called to Fofo to come and help me carry the trunk to the hole we'd dug. It was heavy, but the two of us managed to move it. We then slipped two ropes underneath it (I'd learned this technique from watching Papa's coffin being lowered into his grave), but before we could maneuver it into the hole, Mama began calling to us and waving the hurricane lamp. She was trying to come toward us by hitching along on her backside with a halting, crablike movement. She was holding some of Papa's tools—his level, his T-square, his folding ruler. If I hadn't had firsthand experience with looting, which in our country always marked the arrival of victorious or fleeing troops, I would have laughed out loud and told her that nobody would ever dream of taking those old tools—a T-square whose right angles had been warped by the tropical rain and sun, a level whose little glass window was so dirty you could barely see the air bubble inside, and a ruler that splayed out like a fan when you tried to fold it. But in our country there was no longer any logic: soldiers destroyed for the sake of destroying, killed for the sake of killing, stole for the sake of stealing—even the most improbable objects. And then, suddenly and unexpectedly, a wave of affection surged up from the depths of my being, and my body began to vibrate in synchrony with those instruments. Those old mason's tools had not only fed us and clothed us and enabled us to buy medicines that had kept us healthy up to that point, but they had also given me a certain advantage over my fellow students. They had provided me with a quick, thorough grasp of the concrete reality that lay behind abstract concepts; and, conversely, they taught me the way in which concrete, real things could engender abstract, conceptual forms. Thanks to that T-square, I had seen and comprehended the reality of a right angle, which we'd learned about in geometry class. Thanks to that level and its air bubble, I had easily been able to conceive of an inclined plane or a perfect, frictionless surface on which a ball could roll indefinitely. And last but not least, thanks to that folding ruler—which Papa had me fold and refold, that ruler with which he'd measured everything measurable in the world around him—my dream had been born: my dream of graduating from high school and becoming an engineer, so that I could construct buildings even bigger than the ones Papa had built. I took the tools from Mama and put them in the trunk.

Using the shovel and hoe, we buried our treasure—everything that was most precious to us in the world, apart from our lives.

The sky was beginning to brighten in the east. Dawn would soon come, and at any moment the troops would descend on the city. It was time to leave.

Chapter Four

Johnny, Known as Matiti Mabé

Before we hit the road in preparation for the attack, Giap, like a true leader, assigned each of us a share of the gear. In addition to my own weapons, a load that already felt like a sack of stones, he told me to carry the rocket launcher, which was almost twice my size and weighed a ton. "Okay, the rocket launcher—today it's your turn, Lufua Liwa," he said. Hold on a minute! Just as he was no longer Pili Pili, I was no longer Lufua Liwa but Matiti Mabé. I realized I hadn't told him my new name. At this point, everyone had a stake in knowing it and remembering it, even him. I looked him in the eye and said: "Matiti Mabé. My name is now Matiti Mabé!" He laughed. The others, seeing him laugh, began to laugh, too. "Poison Weed—like grass? Like a lawn? Okay, I'll call you Turf." The others laughed some more. I was boiling with rage. I thought of killing Giap, and I imagined my hand reaching stealthily for my AK-47. But my quick mind realized that he'd already attached his bullet-shield fetish to his biceps. This fetish, at its weakest, could transform bullets into clumps of wet dirt, and at maximum power could make the slugs ricochet off his body and whiz back to strike whoever had fired them. At such times, only a blade could penetrate his body and kill him. I thought of the knife I had in my belt. I would leap on him like a panther and stab him in the heart! But no, I kept my cool—not because I was scared at the sight of his well-muscled chest, but because I understood he hadn't meant any harm by what he'd said. Since he wasn't very bright, he didn't know that grass isn't a poisonous weed. Goats eat grass, soccer players love to play on grass, and poor people cushion their beds with it because they don't have enough money to buy foam mattresses. He couldn't know that. So I said to Giap for his edification, without losing my temper, that grass wasn't a deadly weed like me. Ignoring what I'd said, he repeated: "Turf, for tonight's attack, you'll be the one to carry the rocket launcher." Well, okay, I'd let Giap call me Turf—but the others had better call me Matiti Mabé. Wherever I tread, the grass is dead! If they didn't, they'd be goddamn sorry.

But there was no way I was going to carry the rocket launcher. He could damn well get Idi Amin to lug it. Idi Amin was always bragging that he was stronger than me, and it was true the guy was a fucking ox. I'd once seen him lift a refrigerator all by himself and put it in the truck we'd requisitioned to haul loot from a Mauritanian-owned shop—while three of us were struggling to lift a freezer. Of course, he'd kept the fridge for himself; no one had dared to argue with him about this, except me. Normally, we had to divvy up what we looted. He'd gotten mad and started cursing me. I'd appealed to Major Rambo, who was our leader at that point. He hadn't wanted to reprimand Idi Amin; maybe he was afraid of him, I don't know. Instead he'd started bawling *me* out, and Giap—who in those days was still calling himself Pili Pili and whom I'd looked to for support—hadn't even taken my side. On the contrary, he'd started laughing, with his big stupid guffaw. Only Gator, who was my buddy and who respected my intelligence, had backed me up. Well, now I was Matiti Mabé, and I was going to let it be known that I was already carrying a shitload of weapons in my gear. Once again, I wanted to look Giap straight in the eye and tell him there was no way I was going to haul that rocket launcher and he could damn well get Idi Amin to do it. But once again I saw the fetish on his upper arm—that fetish in its little bag of tanned saliva-brown leather, dyed with chewed and spit-out kola nuts. It not only protected him against bullets; it also filled his head with rage and made him as vicious as a gorilla. When he was wearing it, he didn't listen to anyone, wasn't afraid of anything, could climb a coconut tree in a split second—and you'd be crazy to try talking sense to him at such times. An intelligent man knows you've got to pick your battles; only women and weaklings act any old way and argue over trivial stuff. As for me, I was no weakling and was the smartest of the group. Not only had I made him leader, but it was thanks to me that he was called Giap. He owed everything to me. So I thought it would be better if I took the rocket launcher without griping and without losing my cool. That was how I'd impress him—and not only him but the whole unit, including Idi Amin. I'd show them that I, too, had muscles—biceps, pectorals, abdominals, quadriceps. Giap would understand he could count on me, and the others would understand they had to reckon with me. So I lifted the rocket launcher without protest and heaved it onto my shoulder. We set off. Dusk was falling.

I don't know whether we'd attacked at some arbitrary time or whether Giap had received precise instructions, but in any case we were the first to arrive in front of the compound that housed the radio and TV stations. I fired my first rocket at one of the two armored vehicles that flanked the entrance. It practically exploded, and the other one caught fire as well. The enemy soldiers got off a few rounds, then took to their heels. Gator turned his flamethrower on the panicked men—transformed them into human torches shrieking with pain and writhing on the ground. It was pretty funny. They squealed like stuck pigs.

We advanced on the buildings. Giap led the way. Whatever else he might be, when it came to the crunch he was a true leader. If he were ever killed in battle, and even if I were the one who killed him in order to become the new commander, I would always maintain that he was the bravest of the brave. The manager of the radio station came out, along with a few journalists. They held their hands high in the air to show they were unarmed and to signal, too, that they were merely civilians, poor wage slaves who were just doing their job, and that they were surrendering. Giap went for the manager, grabbed him by the chin and the top of his head; there was a *crack!* and the manager went down. Wow! I'd seen that trick in *Mission Cobra II*, but I never knew Giap could do it. The guy was a fucking giant! I'd have to learn the technique, if only to use it on Idi Amin. The other journalists threw themselves on their knees, pleading for mercy, begging us to spare their lives. I didn't bother to listen. Two or three of us emptied our clips into them at the same time. They shouldn't have spread propaganda for the previous government and its leader, enemies of the people and of democracy, a genocidal regime with contempt for human rights. I think that's what we'd been told to say. They shouldn't have treated us like rebels and bandits. I put a new cartridge in my gun and continued walking toward the buildings on my right.

* * *

I found myself standing before a double door labeled STUDIO B, with a red light above it. The light was on. I emptied my cartridge at the lock and gave the door a kick. The wings of the door burst open and I rocketed into the room, Kalashnikov at the ready, a grenade in my other hand, and . . . *Shit!* I almost blasted myself to Kingdom Come when I dropped the grenade out of sheer surprise. Thank God I hadn't pulled the pin. But as surprises go, this one was a whopper. Tanya Toyo! Yeah, in the flesh. I won't lie to you: I've always admired that woman from afar—her beauty, her eyes, her lips, her everything. My finger immediately relaxed on the trigger. Quickly I bent down to pick up the grenade, and I looked at her. To see if she remembered me. If she recognized Matiti Mabé, I'd spare her life even if she didn't ask me to. We'd met and had a conversation two or three years before. Of course, back then I hadn't been Matiti Mabé, or even Lufua Liwa. I'd been only twelve or thirteen. But so what? If I remembered that unforgettable encounter, she ought to remember it too.

She had come to the market in our district to buy a twenty-kilo sack of rice from a Malian shopkeeper. I'd been in the middle of cleaning the gutter for that same merchant (a job paying five hundred CFA francs), when, raising my head to toss a shovelful of muck onto the pavement, I'd seen her come out of the little shop. I'd recognized her right away.

Who wouldn't have recognized Tanya Toyo—"TT," our star journalist and celebrated television news anchor? The most stylish and elegant woman in our country, who, according to rumor, was often invited to Paris, Rome, New York, and Ouagadougou by Pierre Cardin, Paco Rabanne, and Chris Seydou for fashion shows. The woman who would have been crowned Miss Universe on the spot, if she'd deigned to enter the competition. It was even said that the president of the republic (the one who'd been ousted from power a few minutes ago, when we entered the city), a man whose fly was famous because it opened all by itself for every beautiful woman who wiggled her ass and wore a bra, would often invite her to his palace by inventing phony interviews, just so he could have the pleasure of looking at her. Rumor also had it that the president's wife was insanely jealous of her . . .

And there I was, watching her come out of that shop.

"You, boy! Come take this sack of rice and put it in the trunk of my car."

"Yes, ma'am," I answered promptly.

Unfortunately for me, it had rained that day, which meant that my shorts, my legs, my arms were all wet and covered with mud. As I stepped onto the edge of the concrete sidewalk, one of my plastic sandals remained behind in the gutter, stuck in the mire. I had to come out of the gutter in my bare feet to carry the sack. She was waiting for me near the open trunk of her car—one of those big Japanese 4×4's that you couldn't have bought even with ten years' salary but that all of the politicians and military brass in our country owned. The sack on my back made me stoop a bit, since twenty kilos was no feather, but I managed to carry it because I was already big for my age. I trembled as I approached her, because of her beauty, because of that form-fitting silk blouse. I trembled because of her tight pants, which shamed my mud-covered shorts; because of her high-heeled shoes, which mocked my bare feet; because of her perfume, which my gutter-smell overpowered. But I trembled above all because there before me stood Tanya Toyo, TT, in the flesh—that dream woman fallen from heaven, who was projected into every home in the country on our television screens.

"Thank you," she'd said, and had tossed three hundred-franc coins into my open palm, which I'd hurriedly withdrawn for fear of soiling her fingers, with their polished red nails.

And now before me stood TT, in the flesh, surprised, scared, unsure whether this was reality or a dream. She was holding the pages of the news bulletins she was preparing to read on the air. Closeted in the soundproof studio with two technicians, she hadn't known that the building was being attacked.

I ran my fingers through my hair, to give myself a quick sprucing up; I told the two technicians to get down on their knees; I smiled my handsomest smile; and I gazed at her ardently, the way a man gazes at a woman. A woman you love, not the sort of woman you take prisoner and then hop on, just like that. Still, she was afraid—that was obvious. She was trembling. But I had no intention of harming her. She was my star; I was her fan.

"Remember me, TT?"

"N-n-no," she stammered, shaking her head.

It was then that I saw how beautiful she really was. Three years before, when we'd met at the Malian shop, my fondest dream was that she'd take me in her arms and comfort me like a big sister. Because at the age of twelve you think of a beautiful woman as being like a mother, the only difference being that the beautiful woman is nicer and you can tell secrets to her that you'd never share with your mother. Now I was no longer a kid; at almost sixteen, I was a man. I knew what you could do with a chick, what you *ought* to do with a beautiful chick, even a chick two or three times older than you, like TT.

"Don't you remember me?" I repeated.

"N-n-no," she said again, glancing at one of the technicians with a look of desperation.

I could tell instantly, from the way she looked at him, that the guy had slept with her. He must have forced the poor woman to do it, perhaps even raped her. He had sullied my beautiful TT. I glared at the traitor; he was still on his knees. He wasn't even good-looking. And *bang*! A single bullet, right between the eyes. He went down. Yeah, they didn't know I was quicker than greased lightning. Rambo knew a bit about it, from where he was at the moment. TT threw herself on the floor screaming.

The other technician, who was still alive, opened his mouth and eyes so big they got stuck, and he froze like that, as if he were dead too. A tear ran down TT's cheek and dripped onto her front. Then I noticed the shape of her breasts, which swelled beneath her loose-fitting boubou. My little guy immediately began to get stiff, not like the prick of that idiot Giap, who couldn't do anything, but like that of a man who wanted to go all the way. All the way with TT.

I told her to take off her boubou, her pagne, and her bra, because I wanted to see her breasts. She looked at me without moving. Then I lost my patience. I ripped off her boubou and her bra. She no longer resisted; she let me do what I wanted. That's what's so terrific about a gun. Who can resist you? We'd been told that power lies at the muzzle of a gun, and it was true. Finally I took off her panties and went at it right there in the studio, before the eyes of the technician, who was still paralyzed, openmouthed and wide-eyed, next to his colleague's body. I pumped and pumped the beautiful TT. I even think she liked it—she was weeping with pleasure, was no longer struggling, was looking at me without emotion, her eyes wide as if she were in another world. Yeah, she *was* in another world, as cold as a fish, skillfully concealing the heights of pleasure I'd taken her to with my thrusts. I turned her over and rode her from the rear. With her, it wasn't like doing it with the others.

She was classy; I respected her. I'd never dreamed that someday I'd be doing this with her. I wished the TV cameras had been on, so that all my buddies, even Giap, could see that I'd really done it with TT. They'd die of envy—maybe they'd even kill me.

When I'd finished, I wiped myself with her pagne. Then I dug around in her handbag and found a photo of her, which I kept as a souvenir. I also pulled off the jewelry she was wearing and put it in my pocket. As I was about to leave the studio, it occurred to me that I should kill the technician in order to protect TT. Guys like him were all spies for that elitist, antidemocratic government we'd just driven from power. Besides, if TT hadn't dared to reveal our liaison, it was because she was afraid the technicians might betray her to the secret service of that evil regime. She would have been tortured and perhaps executed. That was obvious. I understood. If I'd been in her shoes, I would have done the same thing.

But at the very moment I was squeezing the trigger, I had second thoughts. If I killed him, there'd be no witnesses left to prove that I'd done it with TT. Giap, Gator, Idi Amin, Hurricane, and the others—no one would believe me. As a witness, he was essential. So I merely shot him in the right leg to prevent him from escaping, and then I left.

Chapter Five

Laokolé

As soon as we came to the main street, we were caught up in a maelstrom, a seething mass of panic-stricken humanity. The crowd had inundated the pavement and was advancing with difficulty, fifteen or twenty people abreast, raising a cloud of ocher dust and thundering over the ground like a herd of stampeding elephants. The movements of the individuals in this mass were so chaotic that it took me a while to realize the crowd was actually moving forward. Those who wanted to hurry were blocked by the slower ones and brought up short; people who slowed down felt the pressure of those pushing from behind; still others were zigzagging, with the hope of finding a gap they could slip through.

Everyone had had the same urge that we did: flee, with whatever belongings were most highly prized. People were carrying their cherished possessions on their heads, on their backs, in wheelbarrows, in basins and baskets. Swaying to the rhythm of people's steps were demijohns, straw mats, plastic jugs. I understood completely why these destitute people forced to take to the road were hauling so many miscellaneous objects. Whereas rich people all prized the same things, for us, who had so little, identical objects did not have identical worth. A pair of slippers was less valuable to one person than an old plastic bag was to another; a bar of soap was worth more to one person than a liter of kerosene was to another. But for everybody, these objects were as precious as a diamond necklace was to a rich person; the most important thing was that they could help you survive. And since women were the ones who were the most skilled in the art of surviving, I took to observing them while I was walking.

All of the women had enormous bundles balanced on their heads. As if that weren't enough, they also had heavy loads or babies tied to their backs. Their children who were old enough to walk followed in their wake, the littlest ones attached to their mother by a cord. An ingenious way of preventing them from getting lost in the confusion. I suddenly realized why a woman should limit the number of children she has. It wasn't only for the reasons we were always given—namely, that the fewer children you had, the better you could feed and educate them. It was also because the fewer children you had, the more easily you could flee in times of war and looting. These children, some of whom were scarcely old enough to walk, were not suffering lesser torments commensurate with their age; no, they were paying the same price but at a higher rate than the adults. They, too, carried burdens—small bottles of oil or water, woven mats, little bundles—as they toddled along, unsteady on their feet. Silently I swore that I would never have more than two children.

It wasn't only children who were paying the price of the suffering that those politicians and their armed supporters were inflicting on us. There were also old people. I saw many—hobbling along, sometimes with the aid of canes—who were likewise trying to escape with us, for one is never too old to flee death. But at the snail's pace they were going, I doubted they would get very far.

The men were not like the women. They didn't know the difference between what was essential for survival and what was not. The things they were carrying were extremely varied and sometimes surprising. Several were wheeling heavily laden bicycles. I saw one man laboriously pushing a bike that bore a trussed-up pig squealing plaintively on the baggage rack and a demijohn of palm wine suspended from the frame's horizontal bar with lengths of vine. Surely the dowry of his daughter or niece and the remains of a ruined wedding. Another man, in contrast, had taken practically nothing. He was fleeing at a jog-trot, carrying only an enormous radio–tape player blaring at full volume, and he made dancing movements in time to the music, as if he were off in a different world. That radio was doubtless his most cherished possession. My own most cherished possession was the wheelbarrow holding Mama.

Fofo was pushing the wheelbarrow. I'd tried to make it as comfortable as possible for Mama. The acrid dust that rose from the ground made her cough badly, more so than it did us. I'd put a pillow behind her back and, underneath her, a blanket folded in four. Since her legs were nothing more than stumps, there was room for her to cross them and even to stretch them out if she wished.

It hadn't been easy. At first, she hadn't wanted to go with us at all. She'd ordered us to leave her behind, saying that she was already an old woman and that nothing would happen to her. I pointed out to her that in this country age was no longer a protection, as it had been according to the African traditions of her day, and that in any case, at thirty-eight, she was still young. She replied that even if something happened to her, it couldn't be worse than what she had already lived through—namely, the day they'd murdered her husband. She mustn't delude herself, I retorted; if she stayed, those men wouldn't hesitate to use her cruelly before killing her. Well, she answered, since her husband was dead, she had no further reason to live; life had lost its meaning for her.

At that point, I pretended to get really angry. I said that Fofo and I had thought she loved us, her two children, but now I realized that she didn't love us at all, that we didn't count. That hurt her, and made her very unhappy. She choked up and found it difficult to restrain her tears. In a voice full of affection, but also of sadness and helplessness, she swore that she loved us very much, loved us terribly, and that after Papa's murder she had stayed alive solely for our sake. If she didn't want to leave, it was precisely because of her love for us. She would be a burden to us, would slow us down in our flight; and she wanted to spare us the trouble of hauling her along in a wheelbarrow. I was speechless when I heard this. Never had it occurred to me that my mother could be a burden. It was my turn to be unhappy, even desperate. I didn't know what to say that would persuade her to leave with us. And leaving was absolutely essential. General Giap's troops would soon overrun the town.

It was Fofo who hit upon the perfect argument. Dear Fofo! He told her that we, too, loved her very much, and that if she didn't want to come with us, we wouldn't go at all. Period. He started to undo the ties on his baskets. The argument shook Mama—she wasn't able to find a retort. I seized the opportunity to add that it was better to die like that—all together, as a family. She gazed at us both, and the tears she'd been trying to hold back spilled down her cheeks. Mothers are like that. They can fearlessly contemplate their own death, but cannot bear to see their children die. The only thing left for her to say was, "Let's go."

I asked Fofo to push the wheelbarrow while I carried on my head the large bundle that held two days' worth of food, a few kitchen utensils, and some spare clothing (as well as some cotton cloth for me, since my period, always quite painful, was due very soon). Fastened close around my waist and hidden beneath my pants was the little purse that held our money and the photo of Mama and Papa. I'm not sure why I put the photo there—perhaps it might bring me luck. In any case, one would have to take off all my clothes to find the little purse. In contrast, my large leather bag hung openly across my front like a bandolier—the decoy purse to fool people. Into this I had put the things we would sacrifice, the ransom that would save our lives if we ever came to one of those barricades that the militias were always setting up along the roads.

The crowd of refugees was moving more slowly, often by fits and starts. Someone ahead of us would stop short; Fofo would bump the person with the wheelbarrow; there would be shouts and insults, which I tried to calm as best I could.

A car horn sounded behind us and I turned to look. Unbelievable—a vehicle was trying to get through the crowd. It was inching forward, honking furiously, and actually making some headway. People would reluctantly clear a bit of space for it, and then close up behind it once it had passed. I helped Fofo move the wheelbarrow from its path, and when the car came up to us I recognized the Japanese 4×4 owned by Mélanie's family.

* * *

Mélanie was my best friend. We were both in our senior year at school, but I was two years younger. I'd done well in my studies and the principal had allowed me to skip a grade, whereas Mélanie had had to repeat one. We'd become friends when her father had hired my father to build a large wall that would surround their house and screen it from the street. Since my father could use an extra pair of hands, he often took me along to help on days when I didn't have classes. It was hard work sometimes, but I enjoyed the role of mason's assistant when, from his perch on the scaffolding, he would call down to me to hand him his folding ruler, or the trowel, or a pail of water.

One day when it was extremely hot and I was sitting in the shade of a badamier tree, tired after helping to mix the cement, Mélanie brought me a glass of lemonade. While I was drinking it, she looked at my raggy sneakers, which I always wore when I was working on-site with Papa; she looked at my old jeans, covered with cement dust; and she looked at my hands, not callused but slightly hardened by the loose stones I often had to pick up and by the buckets of water or sand that I hauled for Papa. And she asked, "What would you like to do when you finish school?" And I answered right away that I would become a mason or an engineer, so that I could construct large buildings. She gazed at me sympathetically and said that hauling wheelbarrows full of sand or cement, climbing scaffolds, and pulling tape measures were not women's work. You didn't go to school for that. You went to school to become a doctor, like Mélanie's father, or a judge, like her mother; you could also become a businesswoman and earn lots of money, or a TV journalist and be a celebrity.

It had never occurred to me that there were professions reserved for women. I hadn't dared to tell her that although I was a woman, I loved to measure things with a contractor's ruler; loved to see how bricks were laid at the intersection of two walls to create a perfect right angle, and how little taps with the handle of a trowel or hammer could adjust a brick so as to make a wall as straight as a plumb line. To fasten the rectangular iron-cable armatures to the vertical rebars before pouring the cement into the forms, we used steel wire; for that, we had to cut long steel wires into lengths of fifteen or twenty centimeters, and often I was the one who did this. I particularly liked to hear the steel wire break with a snap between the beveled blades of my shears from nothing but the strength of my left wrist, for I was left-handed and it wasn't always easy for me to use some of those tools. There were no problems when the tools were symmetrical, like the pliers, the hammer, or the plane. But when there was a break in the symmetry, the asymmetry was always biased in favor of the right-handed, who had built a world that operated the wrong way around. They'd made it difficult for you to use a pair of shears with your left hand; forced you to screw a lamp to a wall by turning the screwdriver clockwise, though the most natural thing for a lefty is to turn it counterclockwise. They had even skewed the neutral orientation of a saw blade by shaping the handle for righties, making it more receptive to their grip. Yes, it was hard to live in a world of right-handed people, but eventually I'd gotten used to it.

I hadn't said any of this to Mélanie; I'd merely told her that I would think it over. Little by little, we'd become close friends, and since I was better at math, she would often invite me over to her house so we could do our homework together and watch TV on her color set, especially the evening news presented by the beautiful journalist Tanya Toyo, whom we both admired.

* * *

Immediately I saw through the window that the entire family was in the vehicle, all six of them: Mélanie, her sister and brother, her parents, and her elderly grandmother, who lived with them. I couldn't tell if they'd seen me. I would have liked to ask them to take my mother along—Mama, who was riding so uncomfortably in the wheelbarrow. But they had already passed us, and the only thing still visible in the distance, through the mass of people, was the big blue tarpaulin covering the baggage piled on the vehicle's roof. They, at least, were saved. They had a car; and once they'd gotten beyond the crowd that was hindering them, they could step on the accelerator and leave behind the anarchy and chaos in which we were mired. Life was like that. Some people were lucky; others weren't.

Mama asked me whether that was indeed the 4×4 of Mélanie's family. I answered yes. She said nothing, but the look of sadness that flickered across her face did not escape me. The feeling that she was a burden to us was doubtless still weighing on her. She was surely thinking that were it not for her—a cripple confined to a wheelbarrow—her two children would already have made their escape. You had to understand her point of view. The poor woman had been through a frightful time.

When rumors of the first round of looting and violence had begun, she'd kept insisting that it didn't concern us, that it was the work of a bunch of politicians and their henchmen who were settling scores and jockeying for power. "Your father's a mason—he's not mixed up in politics. And I run a stall at the market." Furthermore, what did we own that was worth stealing? A few sticks of furniture and an old gas stove? Well, she was wrong.

They had savagely kicked open the door and invaded our

little living room. It's true we didn't have anything worth stealing, with the possible exception of the cheap gas cooker that Mama had bought the previous month, to relieve us of the irritating smoke and hot embers of the wood fire. That made no difference. They still took the rickety table, the four chairs, and the old sofa that served as Fofo's bed. In the kitchen they found Mama trying to hide a sack of rice. Furious, the leader of the unit attacked her and began to tear off her pagne. Hearing her cries, Papa and Fofo ran to the kitchen. Everything happened very quickly after that. Papa, blazing with anger, grabbed the soldier by the collar, threw him to the ground, and began to kick him. At that instant, one of the militiamen shot him in the head at point-blank range. Fofo, spattered with his father's blood and brains, began to scream hysterically. They shoved him roughly into the living room. The leader of the commandos got up off the floor, beside himself with rage, and dealt Mama two violent blows with the butt of his gun, breaking her legs. Then he stripped her, just to humiliate her, to display her naked before his men.

I wasn't at home when all this happened; I was at school. Unfortunately, it was the first day of our high school exams, and there had been no warning of the chaos that was to descend on the town. Of course, the examinations came to a halt amid the general panic. I returned to the house through streets filled with gunfire, looters, and burning buildings. Utter chaos. I found Mama moaning in pain; there was nothing to assuage her suffering. We didn't know where to take her for treatment, in a city that was no longer functioning. Some of our neighbors came by after the marauding soldiers had left the house, and were weeping next to Papa's body, which was wrapped in a sheet. Later, when we were able to get Mama to a hospital, there was nothing that could be done to save her legs. Thus, in a single day, this woman who, regardless of the season, would get up every morning at five to wait for the trucks bringing vegetables from the countryside so she could buy produce for her stall; this woman who would elbow rivals on the docks in order to buy boxes of trinkets from Europe or America so she could resell them and provide clothes for her children; this woman who risked her life in old jalopies on rutted roads to hunt for groundnuts or cassava roots; this strong, dynamic woman had, in the space of a few brief minutes, been transformed into a cripple, simply for trying to keep a few grains of rice to feed her children. For her, this was a fate worse than death. It was certainly for our sake that she had not let herself die.

I looked now at Fofo. He was beginning to get tired. It hadn't been easy for him, either. Arriving home on the day Papa was killed, I'd found Fofo lying in a corner of the living room, completely silent, staring into space. The boy once so lighthearted and always happy to see me, his only sister, the big sister to whom he confided all his secrets, hadn't even raised his eyes to look at me. It took us three days to coax him out of that state, only to see him go immediately to the opposite extreme—a state of severe agitation in which he babbled feverishly and incessantly. Eventually the crisis passed. He relapsed only once, on the day we were looking through Papa's things and found his hat. I never allowed Fofo the time to feel sorry for himself, for our survival depended on it, the survival of two fatherless children with a helpless mother; we still had to eat and go to school. Yet one mustn't think that we were unhappy.

Despite the loss of her legs, Mama continued to run her stall at the market, thanks to her best friend, Auntie Tamila, who would come to the house every morning to pick up Mama in her old secondhand car, which she also hired out as a taxi. The driver would drop them off in front of the stall they jointly owned; would help them to get out and set up their merchandise, stored during the night in a little locked shed that the two women rented by the month from a West African; and then would begin his day as a taxi driver. During this period, Fofo and I would divide up the household chores when we came home from school. He would do the dishes and, if necessary, his laundry (he washed only his own clothes, because I didn't want him washing my underthings, or Mama's), while I would sweep the house and the courtyard and prepare dinner. In the evening, after Mama returned, we would eat dinner together and I would do my homework, unless Mélanie came to pick me up so we could watch TV together at her house. On days when there weren't any classes, and since Papa was no longer around to take me to construction sites with him, I would earn some extra money by selling ice in plastic bags. All things considered, we managed to get by. Fofo was growing up normally—the way trees grow, without being aware of it. I dreamed of becoming a master mason or an engineer; he dreamed of becoming a great soccer player and spent his weekends watching matches at Auntie Tamila's house, where there was also a TV; and the two of us dreamed of buying a wheelchair for Mama as soon as we'd saved up enough money.

I'd given him the wheelbarrow to push because I'd thought it would be easier for him. But I soon realized this was too much to ask of an eleven-year-old, even if he was almost twelve. I asked him to stop. Despite the crowd jostling around us, I managed to open a bit of space between me and the wheelbarrow. I lightened the bundle I was carrying by unloading the bag that contained the food, and I gave it to Fofo. I tied the rest firmly to my back, so that I was carrying it the way other women were carrying their babies. I grasped the handles of the wheelbarrow and began pushing it through the dust, the crowd, and the cries. In the distance, we could hear the first bursts of gunfire. The victorious soldiers and militiamen had begun laying waste to the town.

Chapter Six

Johnny, Known as Matiti Mabé

That moron Giap—he started yelling at me as if I were a piece of shit. "Move your carcass, you lazy jerk! Think we're planning to sleep here?" he shouted, staring at me with his evil owl-eyes. I felt like giving him a bullet in the ass, but I only muttered, "Fuckhead." The guy not only had owl-eyes but hawk-eyes as well, since he must have seen my lips move.

"You said something?" he yelled even louder.

"No, sir," I answered, pretending to stand at attention.

"Good—otherwise I was going to lay you out flat, Turf of My Ass."

He called me Turf. Me, Matiti Mabé. And in front of everybody! All because I was the last to arrive.

It's true, when I came out of the studio the others were already gathered in the courtyard in front of the buildings and Giap had launched into a harangue. He was saying that our side was stronger, that we'd taken the radio station, that he'd met face to face with our new president, and that he, Giap, would soon be speaking on the radio. An announcement had to be made. A military victory was never complete until the winners had seized the radio and television networks in the nation's capital. That's what we had done, and that's why Giap was a true general. If someone had asked him to say a few words on the radio in the name of all the combatants, this was a sure sign he was going to be promoted and—why not?—become a member of our president's own bodyguard. Well, if that happened I wouldn't do the same stupid thing I'd done when Major Rambo had been killed and I'd urged that someone other than me—namely, Giap—fill his shoes. This time, *I* would take control.

A man of action is stingy with words and moves ahead quickly to practical matters. This is what Giap did. He said that the battle was not yet over, since there were still rebels hiding among the people. We had to hunt them down and exterminate them like vermin. At this point, being an intellectual who values clarity, I felt the urge to help Giap out of his mental confusion. I told him that the rebels were actually us, because we were fighting against the established authorities, and to say that we were going to hunt down the rebels was tantamount to saying we were going to hunt down ourselves.

"Idiot," he said curtly. "We're the established authorities now, and the others are the rebels." Everyone laughed, even that clown Twin-Head. He was another guy who owed his name to me. I'd explained to him one day that a little snake found around here called an amphisbaena could move in one direction and then in the opposite direction without turning its body, because it had a head at each end. He'd liked this idea so much that he had immediately adopted Amphisbaena as his *nom de guerre*, then shortened it to Amphi. And then, thinking he was being smart, had changed it to Amphi-Amphi, wanting the name itself to illustrate the double movement of the snake.

I'd told him a name like that was ridiculous, and in any case "amphi" was short for "amphitheater"—an enormous hall where people gave political speeches and which had nothing to do with a snake. He'd gotten mad and threatened to kill me, and said he no longer liked the name Amphi-Amphi after all. He wanted to be called Twin-Head, because in battle he could see what was happening in front of him and in back of him at the same time, as if he had two heads. After that argument, I hated him.

Well, even that moron laughed! I didn't see what was so funny. Anyway, how could an illiterate like Giap know how to use the word "rebel" correctly when he couldn't tell the letter *u* from the letter *n*? But I didn't give a damn. I was Matiti Mabé, the deadly plant that contains curare—the demon weed whose smoke is so strong that when the merest puff penetrates your brain, it can transform the cold white moon into a fiery sun dripping with blood.

Giap continued his speech after my interruption. Now that we'd taken control of the capital, we had to change tactics in order to hunt down the rebels who were hiding among the population. He divided our unit into four fifteen-man squads and designated a leader for each. The first one he named was Idi Amin. I don't know why, when Gator was in the same group, he chose that stupid Idi Amin—who'd be a great leader the day pigs grew wings. Gator was my buddy and, after me, was the most brilliant of the bunch; next to him, Idi Amin was a shit-brain. But what could you expect from Giap, a man who couldn't tell the difference between the letters *p* and *q* because he hadn't even got halfway through second grade? He was bound to favor abs and biceps over brains. Idi Amin was not only the biggest and strongest of us all, but he had the courage of a bull and would often charge ahead without thinking. This limited side of his nature was combined with a brutally efficient side—we all knew he never sweated the details. Depending on what he had in his hands, he'd toss a grenade or fire a flamethrower into a crowd, and off he'd go. I wasn't happy with this choice of a leader, and I had a feeling that Gator wasn't either. For the moment I wouldn't say anything, but I'd give Giap a piece of my mind when the time came.

Then he picked Snake to head the second group. Snake was a good guy. He never bad-mouthed anybody, always kept to himself; but when it came to spotting and dodging the enemy, there was no one like him. Cunning, evasive, slipping through the enemy's traps like an eel through your fingers, leaving no trace in the grass—that was Snake.

Giap then turned to the third group, my group, which included that retard Twin-Head. If Giap picked him as leader, I'd quit the Mata Mata and go join our rivals the Chechens. And after that, I swore, I'd come back when Giap was least expecting it and blow his brains out. He surveyed the group with his druggy glare, and his burning eyes caught mine, and he said: "You'll be the leader." Did I hear him right? "You'll be the leader." No, I must have imagined it. Me? "Well, Turf, get a move on. You're the leader of Commando Unit Three."

"Yes, sir," I blurted.

He was stupendous, Giap—a terrific judge of men! He knew what you were worth and what you could do. Those eyes of his, which fools thought were clouded with pot smoke—in reality their mysterious veil protected people from the lethal, unearthly fire that burned in them. With a single glance, he had immediately understood that if anyone was a born leader, it was me. Yeah, me! No doubt he remembered that I was his godfather, the one who'd baptized him Giap—a name rich with hidden power, a name that had transformed him and made him what he was today: a man who no longer enjoyed rubbing pepper in the eyes of naked women and getting a hard-on watching their asses twitch as they writhed in pain. This name was the spirit that had enabled our leader to take power by seizing the radio and TV stations.

My spine immediately straightened, adding two inches to my height. I felt taller than Idi Amin—taller, in fact, than anyone else except maybe Giap. I didn't wait to find out who would be named leader of Commando Unit Four. Already, from the loftiness of my new stature, I was surveying my troops the way every general does before a battle. And while all of my attention was focused on this visual inspection of my unit, I heard shouts and realized right away that trouble was brewing.

"We want our hundred thousand francs now!"

That was Gator's voice. He was angry, no shit. We were each supposed to get a bonus of one hundred thousand after taking the capital. Well, here we were and we'd taken the capital. Gator was right—we ought to be paid our money. Anyway, if he hadn't demanded it, I would have. Giap kept his cool and tried to explain that we'd only just captured the city and that he hadn't yet had a chance to meet with the higher-ups to collect our bonus. There was a general uproar at this. No one believed him, not even me. It would be a dumb move to take us for idiots—because if he cheated us out of our money, we'd raise hell! I know how our leaders behave. Whenever there's a bit of money, they grab everything. Some of them even think themselves generous when they toss us a few coins, the way you'd throw scraps to your dog. No, Mister Giap! This time it wouldn't work! We'd taken risks, and every risk ought to be rewarded with a bonus, and we wanted our bonus now.

"You must think we're stupid, Giap!" Gator shouted, as if a geyser of long-stifled resentment were erupting from his mouth.

Gator is my buddy. He always backs me up in a tight spot, and I do the same for him—I'd never let him down. The first time we captured a chick, during a raid on the Chechens, he shared her with me: while I held down the woman's spread-out legs, he pumped her, and then vice versa—we took turns. This is to show you how well I knew him. But I'd never seen him in such a fury. He was yelling at Giap! He was standing up to him! That encouraged all of us, and the minor protest turned into a major rebellion.

"Giap, give us our dough! Giap, give us our dough! Giap, give us our dough!"

At that point, Giap flew into an infernal rage. He touched his fetish and his neck immediately swelled; his biceps, pecs, and calf muscles tightened involuntarily, as if seized with spasms. He glared at us, and with a sudden movement he grabbed Gator by the neck and threw him to the ground. He took his own backpack and hurled it at Gator.

"There's my pack!" he shouted. "Look inside! If you don't find any money, I'll kill you!"

Giap was serious—he never kidded around. He always kept his word. Gator's anger evaporated instantly. He looked at me, appealing for backup as usual, like the time the three of us (he and I and Pili Pili, who hadn't yet become Giap) had shot Rambo. But Giap wasn't Rambo.

"So, have you found that money I was going to steal? Yes or no, shit-head?"

"I didn't say you were going to steal it. I only said—"

Blam! A single round from his gun. My friend Gator was dead.

"Who else is demanding money?"

Nobody said a word. Nobody moved a muscle. Giap continued as if nothing had happened.

"Commando Unit One, you'll be operating in the Kandahar district. Commando Two: the Kuwait district. Commando Three: the Huambo district. And Commando Four: Sarajevo. All unit leaders should keep their ears glued to their cell phones for instructions. And you soldiers—you damn well better obey your new leaders, understand? If not, I'll shoot you myself. You saw what happened to that asshole Gator. Dismissed!"

He walked up to Gator's body sprawling in the dust, turned it over with the toe of his boot, pointed at the four unit leaders he'd just named, and ordered curtly:

"Idi Amin, Snake, Turf, Savimbi! Take this subversive element away and chuck it in a ditch!"

That "element" was my friend Gator. I almost cried. You don't kill someone's friend like that. Really, people are awful. They have no heart.

Chapter Seven

Laokolé

There was a pause—a moment when, like a wave at its crest, we were neither advancing nor retreating. Then, suddenly, the crowd turned back in great hubbub and confusion. We were caught between two opposing masses in which those who had already managed to turn around and begin retracing their steps collided with those who were still moving forward. And in the collisions, those who fell had little chance of getting up again, since they were immediately trampled underfoot.

I didn't understand what was happening—all I knew was that we were making an abrupt about-face and fleeing in the direction we'd come from. I panicked, for people were pressing so densely around me that I couldn't turn the wheelbarrow around. Dismayed and desperate, I shouted for Fofo, who was being driven farther and farther away from me by the spasmodic movements of the crowd. Panic-stricken, he threw down the bundle he was carrying on his head, and by shoving his way through the crush with his elbows and shoulders he managed to get back to me. "Turn the wheelbarrow around!" I shouted to him, while I shielded him with my body and made a bit of space around him so that he could move the vehicle. He grasped the handles of the wheelbarrow and succeeded in giving it a quarter turn, but just at that moment several people fell against me. I was unable to keep my footing. Pushed over by the force of the impact, I knocked Fofo down as I fell, and he in turn collided with the wheelbarrow. There was a scream of pain from Mama.

I've no idea how long it took me to extricate myself from that tangle of legs, elbows, and feet, but when I was finally standing again I saw with horror that one of Mama's stumps was caught under the wheelbarrow, which had borne the weight of all our bodies. The agony she must have been feeling pierced me like a knife, and I uttered a loud cry. Quickly I righted the wheelbarrow. Then Fofo and I lifted our poor mother and gently laid her down in it once more.

The stump had a large wound and was bleeding—an awful sight. I couldn't tell if the bone was broken. What to do? Again, there was no emergency clinic where we could take her. Why was Fate pursuing this unfortunate woman so relentlessly? Seeing her like that, her battered body lying in a mason's wheelbarrow, I don't know why but I thought of Mélanie's mother. I wasn't envious. I just thought that Mélanie, my best friend, was very lucky. Thanks to their 4×4, she'd been able to save her mother without difficulty.

Mama's sufferings must have been dreadful, but she didn't say a word, didn't moan. Tears flowed down her cheeks—that was all. And again, I suspected she wasn't shedding tears for herself. I think, rather, that she was crying for us and in frustration at herself. Doubtless she was cursing herself for being there, preventing us from escaping more rapidly, already feeling guilty should something happen to us. Mothers are like that; they never think of themselves. How could I tell her that she was in no way responsible? That we loved her and that it was inconceivable we would ever try to escape without her? No, I couldn't cry—Fofo mustn't see me crying. At sixteen, a girl is already a woman. I was now the mother of my mother, and the mother of my brother. I had to go on.

I put the pillow under Mama's back, and made sure the bundle on my own back was still firmly tied. Then I took hold of the wheelbarrow's handles and began pushing ahead as quickly as my arms and legs would allow.

It didn't take me long to realize why we'd made our about-face. There were troops (whether winners or losers, we had no way of knowing) attacking from that direction. When we'd left our house to escape the looting, we had simply let ourselves be carried along by the current in the sea of humanity we had joined. This human flood was fleeing toward the city center, and unfortunately that was the wrong direction: we had come face to face with the troops who were now moving toward our home districts, and we had to retrace our steps.

The sound of gunfire was growing louder. People were no longer walking—they were running, and almost all of them were passing me. Most of those who were rushing past had dropped everything they were carrying in order to move more quickly, so that they could save the only precious things they had left: their lives. Or the lives of their children. Like that woman who had just passed me as soon as she'd caught up with me: she had no possessions left, neither the bundle on her head nor the one on her back, but carted along four children she was intent on saving, bearing one on her back, holding another in her arms, and towing the last two in her wake by means of cords tied around her waist. Only the man who was pushing his pig-laden bicycle still clung to his worldly goods—I saw him go past me, his breath coming in audible gasps, the pig and the demijohn of palm wine still firmly attached to his vehicle. As for me, I was struggling and sweating, despite the fact that I'd hauled many a wheelbarrow of sand in my time!

I glanced behind me to make sure Fofo was still following us. He no longer had the bundle I'd given him to carry, but he was there, and that's what mattered. Turning my gaze forward again, I noticed that Mama, who'd been silent all this time, had raised her head to give me a searching look while I checked on Fofo; and though we'd been doing everything we could to avoid looking at each other, our eyes suddenly met. She could no longer restrain herself.

"I beg of you, Lao, I implore you—leave me here! Run! Save yourself! At least save Fofo!"

I pretended to be angry, saying that if she continued to talk like that, I was going to stop in my tracks, sit down by the side of the road, and wait for the soldiers. Hearing the determination in my voice, she said no more and again lapsed into silence.

I wonder if there are degrees of fear. I mean, when you're already afraid, is it possible to be even more afraid? When you're already afraid of being killed by a stray bullet because bullets are whistling all around you, can you be even more afraid when you see who is shooting those bullets? I don't know. All I can say is that the shooters had now caught up with us. People scattered into the side streets; others were struck and fell to the ground. I couldn't continue straight ahead. That would have meant sure death, since the soldiers were firing directly at us, or would simply have run us down—their vehicles were like machines gone haywire. I was on the left side of the street, and the only available opening was on the right. So I darted across at the very moment a 4×4 full of armed men was barreling by. A gun was pointed at my face, bullets whistled past our heads. I gave the wheelbarrow a violent shove and plunged behind a lantana hedge; my green kerchief (tied over my hair to protect it from the dust) sailed into the air like a kite; the vehicle was gone like a gust of wind. The whole episode had lasted only a few seconds—but in those few seconds, Mama, the wheelbarrow, and I could have been reduced to a pile of mangled metal, bone, and blood.

I found myself lying facedown behind the hedge. Then, I don't know how, I was sitting on the ground next to the wheelbarrow, which miraculously had avoided tipping over. My strength was gone, my will had vanished. I was no longer afraid, no longer trembling—felt only a vast weariness, and a total emptiness in my head.

How long I stayed that way, I have no idea. But suddenly my ears began listening, my body began trembling, and my brain remembered that my primary goal was to flee with Mama and Fofo. I stood up to see whether people were still running in the same direction, but when I peered over the hedge that screened our hiding place, I saw my green kerchief hanging from a post and fluttering in the breeze. I felt a sudden stab of joy, and without hesitating I dashed out to recover it. At that moment I heard the soldiers driving back at top speed.

They'd nail me the second time for sure. I had to get out of sight, and fast. I dove behind the hedge again. Immediately I heard the vehicle that had just passed our hiding place come to a screeching halt and then accelerate like mad in reverse. No doubt about it—they'd spotted us. They must have seen me trying to recover the kerchief that had flown from my head, and were coming back to finish us off. This was the end. I couldn't look at Mama, couldn't bear to read the anguish in her eyes. They would kill me—fine. But only over my dead body would they harm Fofo and Mama.

All was not lost, though. I heard them jam on the brakes—the 4×4 came to a stop about ten meters from us. They got out, slamming the doors. One of them ran a few paces, stopped, bent down, picked up something that appeared to be a gun, and shouted:

"Mad Dog, I was right! Come take a look!"

Mad Dog walked forward. He must have been their leader. He came up to the man who had called to him, accompanied by two others, one of whom was carrying a long tube with a bulge at the tip: a rocket launcher, flamethrower, or grenade launcher—I can't tell the difference. They all examined the object that had been found. If they stopped there and came no closer, they wouldn't spot us, since the lantana hedge we were hiding behind was extremely thick. In contrast, we could see and hear them quite well. They didn't come any nearer.

Judging from their motley attire, I knew they were militia types, adjuncts to the so-called regular army. They weren't foreign mercenaries, since they were speaking one of the languages of our country. Why were some called "regular army" and the others called "militias"? I have no idea—they treated us exactly the same. They were equally cruel. Perhaps the difference lay in the way they dressed. In any case, I'd never seen any outfit as bizarre as the one worn by this Mad Dog. He sported a baseball cap worn backward, a sleeveless T-shirt, and a cowrie-shell necklace hung with two or three little pouches. A bit of red cord was tied around his right arm, above the elbow. He wasn't very muscular or even very tall, and his olive-drab pants looked too big for him. In contrast, the two ammunition belts that were slung crosswise over his chest Zapata-style gave him a soldierly air. The machine gun in his hand and a long knife suspended from his belt completed his warrior's arsenal. Dark glasses hid his eyes, and—even more strange—from time to time his T-shirt gave off flashes of light.

"Shit!" cried Mad Dog. "It's an Uzi!"

"Chinese-made?" asked the man who had called to Mad Dog.

"No, it's an Israeli gun. If the Chechens have Israeli mercenaries with them—well, guys, we're in for a rough time. I saw a movie, *Raid on Entebbe*, where the Israelis transported a commando unit more than a thousand kilometers in order to free some hostages. Now we've really got to watch our backs. If you capture a Chechen, don't be Mr. Nice Guy. Send him off to join his ancestors pronto."

He took the gun in his hand, examined it, checked the clip, and began spraying bullets haphazardly around him—fortunately not in our direction. When he stopped firing, I heard someone call from the other side of the vehicle:

"Mad Dog, I've captured one of those subversive elements!"

The "element" was a boy who was being shoved roughly forward, a gun at his back and a booted foot jabbing his rear. On his head he was carrying a small rusty basin, which he made efforts to steady with one hand every time a blow made him stagger; with the other hand, he was trying as best he could to hold on to his belt and keep his pants from falling down. No sooner had he come up to Mad Dog than the latter gave him a vicious kick in the stomach. He fell and let go of his basin. Oranges and papayas went tumbling all over the ground. A few bananas too. "Get up!" shouted Mad Dog. The boy got to his feet, still holding on to his pants with one hand. He was just a youngster. One of the countless kids who were part of our everyday landscape, urchins who hung around in our marketplaces and streets and peddled things illegally—

single cigarettes, pieces of fruit, cookies, candies—in order to scrape together a few coins for their daily bread. He was probably Fofo's age. No, not that old—around ten or eleven. He was terrified.

"It was you who threw down this Uzi as you were running away, wasn't it?"

"No, I swear . . . I . . ."

"And what are you doing here? Why are you hiding? Were you planning to take potshots at us?"

"No! I was hiding on account of the oranges and bananas. Mama told me not to let anyone steal them from me, like last time."

"Where is she? Show us where she's hiding."

"I don't know! We were all running away, and I got separated from her."

"Liar!" said Mad Dog, hitting the boy in the face with the butt of his gun. "Nobody runs away for the sake of a few bananas. You think I'm an idiot?"

The boy was howling with pain. He let go of his pants and brought both hands up to his face. He had no underwear on. Blood was running from a gash over one of his eyes.

"Tell us where you got this gun!"

"It isn't mine! I only had Mama's oranges and bananas—"

"Shut up, liar! You're a Chechen, I can tell—you speak with a Chechen accent. We'll kill you if you don't tell us where the others are hiding. So, are you ready to talk, you little shit?"

He pointed the Uzi at the boy.

At that moment, a voice came from the 4×4. "What's going on, Stud?"

"We caught an Israeli spy," replied one of the militiamen.

The owner of the voice got out of the vehicle. A girl with short hair, dressed in pants, wearing an orange bandanna around her head. I didn't know they let girls join. Aside from the belt around her waist, the only military-style things she was wearing were the boots on her feet. She slung the strap of her AK-47 between her breasts and strode over to her confederates. As soon as she joined the group, the boy seemed to recognize her and threw himself at her feet.

"Big sister! You know me—I'm Pepa, Mama Mado's son! Mama Mado—the one who sells oranges, bananas, soursops, and mangoes, and hot donuts in the evening in front of her garden. You know me! Lékana Street—we live in the same neighborhood! I'm not a spy, big sister! Big sister—"

"Go on! Get away!" said the girl, giving him a push with her booted foot. "We know your type—kids working as spies, always acting so innocent."

The boy fell on his back, but got up immediately. On his knees he pleaded with them, repeating over and over that he had only his mother's oranges and bananas. Then he began to cry, wailing, "Mama! Mama!" and "Big sister, don't kill me! Don't kill me, big sister!"

Mad Dog looked at him for a moment. Holding his Uzi with one hand, he fired. The boy collapsed but did not fall full-length on the ground. He remained on his knees, while his head pitched forward and hit the ground. It looked as if he were praying to Allah. I covered my mouth with my hand, to stifle the cry that rose in my throat. I didn't know there were people who could murder a child.

"Finish him off, Little Pepper—a present for you."

"Thank you, sir," said Little Pepper, who wasn't little at all but a huge fellow, much more solidly built than Mad Dog. The most striking thing about him was that he wore a large red wig.

He walked up to the motionless boy, who was still on his

knees, his head resting on the ground. He pushed him over with his foot and, raising his machine gun, fired a number of rounds into his body. Pointless, since the boy was already dead.

Mad Dog picked up a banana, peeled it, and tossed the skin onto the corpse.

"These bananas are good—very sweet," he said, enjoying the taste.

They all set about gathering up as many bananas, oranges, and papayas as they could carry. All except the girl, who had taken the Uzi from Mad Dog and was admiring it. Abruptly she fired a volley into the air.

At last I saw them walk back toward their 4×4 and only then did my rigid body begin to relax. The one they called Stud reached the car first. He opened the door, but for some reason slammed it shut and retraced his steps. Like Mad Dog, he was hiding his eyes with dark glasses; but in contrast he sported a metal helmet, weirdly adorned with two red feathers, and was wearing a military jacket and a backpack. A gourd was attached to the left side of his belt, and an empty holster swung from his right hip, as if he were in some cowboy movie. He wore brass knuckles on both hands. His movements were clumsy. Perhaps the name Stud came from the way he walked—he had the macho strut of a male gorilla, pitching from side to side with every step. No doubt about it this time: he'd spotted us and was coming to wipe us off the face of the earth.

But no. He stopped next to the corpse and gave it a savage, thudding kick in the genitals, then went back to the 4×4. A single kick—that was all. Why? *Why?* His buddies obviously found it terrifically funny, since they burst out laughing. The girl punctuated their laughter with another burst from the Uzi. I saw their mouths open wide soundlessly before their guffaws reached me, over the sound of the gunfire and over the child's still body. I shuddered.

The girl got behind the wheel of the 4×4. So she'd been the insane driver who had nearly crushed me and the wheelbarrow! Mad Dog sat in the front seat, too. Just as he slammed the door shut, a light went on in my brain. I nearly fainted. There was no mistaking it: that was the 4×4 belonging to Mélanie and her family! I hadn't noticed the fact until then, perhaps because of my panicked state. Despite its broken windows, I recognized everything now—the make, the color, the license plate, the blue tarp that covered the luggage they'd stowed on the roof. For sure, they'd killed Mélanie and her family in order to take their vehicle. They must have fired through the windows. Mélanie, my best friend; Mélanie, who wanted to become a wealthy businesswoman. Or a TV news anchor, like Tanya Toyo. Or a judge, like her mother. A brilliant career destroyed. Yet again, our shitty country had killed one of its children. I wept uncontrollably, with convulsive movements and loud hiccups, now that the militia fighters had disappeared down the road in a cloud of dust. Mama tried to calm me and console me, but my tears continued to flow. I'm not sure whether I was crying for my friend or for that boy, whom I didn't even know. I think I was weeping for both of them. What kind of country kills its children in cold blood? How can you kill a person's best friend? Really, people are awful. They have no heart.

Chapter Eight

Johnny, Known as Matiti Mabé

We buried Gator behind Studio B, in a small hole that we dug hastily in the sand, scarcely a meter deep. One tropical downpour and his body would be prey for stray dogs. While Idi Amin, Snake, and Savimbi began to head back to the meeting place, I fired three volleys into the air as a last homage to my friend, to show he had died like a brave fighter and not like a coward, and I put some bullets and empty cartridges on his grave to protect him. As we were walking back to join the others, we passed by the door of Studio B and it suddenly occurred to me that Tanya Toyo must still be inside. She was no doubt thinking of me, too, and was secretly wishing I'd return; no one had ever taken her to the heights of pleasure the way I had, and, knowing chicks the way I did, I was sure she was still fantasizing about me. But then I heard Giap hollering. I couldn't make out what he was saying, but I increased my pace anyway and avoided dawdling. Now that I was a leader, I didn't want to get bawled out in front of my troops by that fathead. Tanya would just have to wait—we'd play leapfrog some other time.

"Was it you I heard firing?" Giap said in his stupid but authoritarian voice as soon as he saw me.

"Um . . . yeah," I answered, not knowing the reason for his question.

"Why?"

Okay, then I got it. Giap took me for an idiot, but he was forgetting that I'm an intellectual and that I can spot traps and evade them even before they're set. No, shit-brain, I'm not going to tell you those gunshots were in honor of my friend, because you'll get mad and might kill me.

"I saw something move behind the studios and I thought it might be an enemy, so I fired. Turned out to be nothing but a bird."

That must have satisfied him, since he didn't press the point. In his general's voice, he told all of the units to leave the radio-TV compound immediately and set up their command posts in the districts they'd been assigned. My own assignment was Huambo, and my mission was to flush out the Chechen militia fighters who were hiding among the population. Not an easy task, because Huambo was their stomping ground. Giap repeated that he wanted us to keep our ears glued to our cell phones and wait for instructions.

"I'm counting on you. Above all, don't let the soldiers beat you to it."

By "soldiers" he meant the forces of the "regular" army. Our guys were called militia fighters, or backup troops, or were designated by the *noms de guerre* the squads had chosen for themselves—such as Mata Mata, the name of my group. Actually, apart from their uniforms, I didn't see what made them any more "regular" than we were. If they were so powerful, they wouldn't have come to the districts to hand out weapons to us and forcibly recruit young boys and girls who were reluctant to join up. We were fighting the same enemies they were; we believed in the same fetishes; we did the same things to the men and women we captured. Plus, we looted the same territory—though I must admit they were better at it than we were. They had a lot of heavy ordnance we didn't have: trucks, large-caliber guns that could breach the walls of a house, and even cranes to remove roofs. While we were fighting unaided, they had reinforcements—foreign mercenaries who backed them up with planes and armored helicopters. It wasn't really clear to me why they were "regulars" and we were "irregulars." But for the moment I didn't give a damn, since I had to take command of my unit and show them that, as a leader, I was just as effective and tough as Giap, not to mention more intelligent.

*

So my unit was being sent to the Huambo district. Knowing Giap, I realized that this was no accident. He knew I was very familiar with the district because my girlfriend Lovelita lived there. And he was familiar with it, too, since before the war started he'd had a market stall where he sold fish he caught with his partner Dovo, who lived in Huambo. Those guys were two of a kind—a pair of crooks who didn't hesitate to double the price of their merchandise when they saw they were dealing with a sucker. Since the district was inhabited mainly by Mayi-Dogos (the adversary of our great leader was a Mayi-Dogo) and was a stronghold of the Chechen militias, it was essential to send someone with a thorough knowledge of the terrain. And that someone—Giap had hit the mark here—was me.

For our headquarters I chose a large building at the edge of the district, on its main street. The only thing that hadn't been stolen from the structure (because it couldn't be torn away) was a blackboard painted directly on the wall; and from this I deduced that the place must have been a school. Everything that makes a school a school—tables, benches, books—had been looted. Who had been there before us? I took the principal's office all to myself, and I sent the others to camp out in a huge room that had no doubt been a gym at some point. There I had them all line up and stand at attention, so I could give my first orders.

"We're no longer the Mata Mata. Our unit has to choose a new name. Any suggestions?"

Actually, I already had one in mind, but I wanted them to rack their brains so I could get an idea of their abilities. It went without saying, of course, that I would reject all of their suggestions, even the good ones. I'd tell them that the names they came up with weren't worth shit, and then I'd announce, in a commanding way, my own unarguable and definitive choice as leader. As I expected, they came up with nothing but vulgar, banal names they'd seen or heard on TV—stupid names like the Ninjas, Cobras, Zulus, Mambas, Sharks, Condors, Falcons, and so on. No one hit on anything worthwhile. So then, in a voice full of authority, I announced:

"The Indomitable Lions! That's your new name."

To my great surprise, I heard chuckles. They were laughing! They never did that to Giap. Even before I had time to react, I heard Little Pepper burst out in an indignant voice:

"No, no! Not that, sir!"

"And why not?" I asked, trying to keep my voice firm. "Have you got anything against the king of beasts?"

"We're not a soccer team."

Shit—*shit!* I'd forgotten that the Indomitable Lions were the national soccer team of Cameroon. How could I get myself out of this?

"So what?" I demanded. "Where's the shame in being named after a great soccer team?"

"No, that's ridiculous, sir. We're not soccer players, and we're not here to play a game. We're soldiers. How about the Black Panthers? A panther doesn't play around—it leaps straight onto its prey."

This was said not by Little Pepper but by Exocet. For a long time the asshole's name had been Missile, but one fine morning, as he was waking up, he heard a radio report on a war taking place somewhere in the Gulf, in Iraq or Iran, and he'd suddenly announced to everyone that from then on his name was Exocet. What a shit-head. But I had to come up with something quickly—a leader should never let himself be outflanked. Giap would have put a stop to all this nonsense with one of his mystical looks. So I adopted the pose of a man who was deep in thought and whose brain was revving like the engine of a warplane:

"Panther . . . panther. No—too common, too vulgar. Jaguar! That's it—jaguar! It's the most dangerous of the panthers, and it doesn't even live here in our country." (I was remembering an Indian or Brazilian film in which a man had been torn apart by a jaguar.) "We're the Jaguar Commandos!"

Not at all a bad name. On balance I was satisfied, even if it wasn't the name that I'd first proposed. The important thing was that I'd been the one who'd finally thought of it.

"Okay, let's move on to something else."

A finger was timidly raised, and behind it I recognized Piston's head, bald as an egg. Piston was our specialist at hot-wiring vehicles—an essential skill when we were looting. The little guy could get a tank started with nothing more than a screwdriver.

"A jaguar isn't a panther—it's a car."

Well, that floored me. Jaguar, a brand of car. Of course, I knew that. Shit! A leader must assert his authority from the outset. I shouldn't have asked them for suggestions. Pili Pili, as soon as we'd named him Giap, had been instantly transformed into a leader and had sent me to fetch his boots, whereas I couldn't even manage to impose a name on troops that were under my command. I wanted to be a democratic leader, but what do you expect—this wasn't a democracy. Leaders didn't get any respect in our country anymore. So, not knowing what to do to shore up my crumbling authority, I looked Piston in the eye while tilting my head back slightly, to show that I was gazing down on him from a height, and said:

"Yeah? So what?"

"Well," he said, "we're not cars."

"Cars or not, we're the Jaguars. Or the Tigers. See, we're tigers—tigers that not only leap on their victims but roar in order to terrify them. Roaring Tigers. We're the Roaring Tiger Commandos! Understand? Good, let's move on to something else."

Period. Over and out. End of sermon. And God help anyone who tried my patience with any more comments. But all of a sudden I thought: A tiger doesn't roar. A lion roars, a dog barks, a cat meows, a sheep baas, but I didn't know what a tiger says, and I was afraid one of the men would remark on this. Furious, I seized my Kalashnikov and cried:

"Like it or not, we're the Roaring Tiger Commandos! Let's move on to something else!"

Evidently there would be no further challenges to my authority, since nobody said a word. They had realized that a leader is always right, even when he's wrong. But I couldn't let it end there. I had to leave them with a strong impression.

While they continued to stand at attention, I took the Kalashnikov I was holding and, keeping my eyes on the men, I removed the clip, pulled the cover off the breech block and the repeater mechanism, and then—still without looking at my hands—removed the action and separated it from the housing. Immediately after dismantling the gun, my expert fingers re-assembled it, and I concluded by tripping the release twice to make sure it was working properly. At last I fired a volley into the air. The whole maneuver hadn't taken me more than ninety seconds. They couldn't help applauding. Our leader—he can handle his gun with his eyes closed! That's what they'd be saying over and over. And that would mean one thing: respect. They were going to respect me, even though some were older than me or had bigger muscles. And then I looked at them. I pointed at Twin-Head:

"Hey, Twin-Head, go fetch my boots!"

He stared at me as if he hadn't understood.

"My boots! On the double! Don't make me say it again!"

I think he must have silently called me a son of a bitch, since I saw his lips move but didn't hear him say anything. He left the room and came back with the boots.

"Don't forget to polish them before you give them to me!" I snapped, and returned to my office—with chin high, chest out, and a military gait, just like a general.

At that moment I heard Giap's voice on the radio:

"This is General Giap speaking. Our brave freedom fighters have fought like lions, like buffalo! They've struck fear into the hearts of our enemies, who have fled with their

tails between their legs. Victory! La luta continua! *We are afraid of nothing! We will pursue them to the depths of the ocean—we will cling to them like lice! To celebrate this triumph of a liberated people, I, General Giap, together with our new president, give you full authorization to take anything you want for a period of forty-eight hours . . ."*

I headed immediately for the room where my men were hanging out. In fact, they had already heard Giap on their own radios. A leader should always be a step ahead of his troops, and I wanted to show them I had more information than they did: I explained to them that the looting was a compensation for the bonus that had been promised us but not paid (the money that had caused the death of my friend Gator). And as for Giap, whether he liked it or not we were going to loot as much as we pleased. I made a big hit when I stood up to Giap like that—the men all applauded me. Some of them wanted to start right away. There were so many militias let loose on the town—aside from the regular soldiers and foreign mercenaries who'd come to help us win this war—that if we didn't hurry, the city would be picked as clean as an elephant carcass after an attack of army ants.

I told them they were right: it *was* important to get there first—for just as when an elephant is killed on a hunt, the first men on the scene would get the best parts. But there was a cardinal error to be avoided at all costs: one must never attack the Chechens by night, for they had owl-eyes that could see in the dark, and one was liable to be neutralized on the spot before even having the chance to lob a grenade or cock a machine gun. Of course, the darkness is an ally, but it can also be the worst of traps. The best way to take an enemy by surprise is to attack at first light, between darkness and sunrise, when no one really knows whether it's still nighttime or already morning. That's when people and animals are the least on their guard. It wasn't Giap who had taught me this, but Major Rambo, our previous commander. That's also the best time to begin raiding a town, because the people are taken by surprise and haven't had time to conceal their money or their valuables. Some of them even bury their possessions before they flee. Once, Gator and I had surprised a guy who'd already buried his bicycle and was in the process of digging a hole to bury his fridge. So the best thing to do is wait until the crack of dawn—then descend on the houses without warning, chuck a few grenades, kick down the doors, roust the women out of bed naked without giving them a chance to put on their pagnes.

I don't know why I said all this to a bunch of guys who knew everything there was to know about looting, since they'd already done it a thousand times and since it was the main reason we were fighting. To line our pockets. To become adults. To have all the women we wanted. To wield the power of a gun. To be the rulers of the world. Yeah, all of these things at the same time. But our leaders and our president had ordered us not to say this. They insisted that when people asked us questions we should say that we were fighting for freedom and democracy. By saying this, we'd win the sympathy of the outside world.

Maintaining my military posture, and holding my cell phone to my ear as if I were listening intently to an important message, I went outside.

The sky was beginning to brighten in the east. Soon daybreak would come, and in the blink of an eye the Roaring Tigers would descend on the town.

Chapter Nine

Laokolé

Mama gave me a stinging slap.

"Laokolé!"

I started as if I were coming back from another world, and the violent sobs that were racking me ceased abruptly.

"Fofo—where's Fofo?" she asked, panic-stricken.

With a shock, I realized that Fofo wasn't with us. Where could he be? In the madness of our flight, we'd lost him. Or rather, he had lost us. But where on earth should we begin looking for him?

"Fofo! Fofo!" we both cried, appalled, desperate, not caring that our shouts could give us away to the militia fighters if they returned, or to others who might come by.

The echo of his name, the echo of the sound *oh*, rebounded from the walls, circulated through the streets nearby, and like a magical summons drew forth as if by enchantment—from behind hedges, walls, and trees, from behind anything that could serve as protection or hiding place—dozens and then hundreds of people. They wasted no time; all resumed their headlong flight, a flight with no object, unless it was that of simply continuing to move forward. I had to face facts: we weren't going to find Fofo by sitting there on our behinds. He was young and wasn't carrying anything, so he obviously had been running faster than us and must surely be far ahead. We had to get going. I didn't ask Mama what she thought. I grasped the handles of the wheelbarrow and we once again began walking, in the wake of the others.

Dust, jostling, cries, sobs. We were fleeing, but why? What had we done? Why did we have to suffer in a power struggle that meant nothing to us? What would change in our lives if the Chechens ruled the country instead of the Mata Mata? Nothing. Absolutely nothing. Yet that's the way it was: we were the grass on which two elephants were engaged in combat.

Mama was now obviously in great pain, but let no sound escape through her tightly compressed lips. Only the tension in her face betrayed her agony. The stump of her leg was swollen and turning black. I feared that gangrene was setting in. How much longer could I cart the poor woman around like this, without finding a doctor for her, without any idea where we were going? I was afraid to answer my own question.

At that moment, from some unidentifiable source, a shout arose and spread through the crowd: "The embassy! The embassy!"

I don't know which embassy they meant, but all of a sudden it was like a password—a word that for us opened the door to hope.

I realized we were in the neighborhood where nearly all of the diplomatic missions were located. I'd always been taught that embassies were inviolable domains: if we could get into one, we'd be protected from the hordes of militiamen who were trailing us. I'd also heard people speak of the "International Community"—in particular, the fetishistic phrase "aid of the International Community." Along with those words, I'd learned that this International Community was the enemy of barbarism, and that never again would it sit with its hands folded and witness the massacre of a people, of a community. *We* were a people, a community, in the process of being massacred, so it couldn't let us down. But who represented that much-vaunted Community? I had never thought to ask myself this question. Were our heads of state members of it? Those leaders who marched heedlessly to power on roads paved with corpses—were they members, too? And was I myself a member?

I lifted my gaze and saw the row of embassy buildings in the distance, their flags rippling in the wind. I saw the flag of the European Union, blue with yellow stars. I saw the red, white, and blue flag of France. I saw the star-spangled banner of the United States. I saw the red maple leaf of Canada. On the flag of the United Nations, in front of the UN compound, I saw the two olive branches cradling all of the earth's continents, set off on a pale blue ground. The flags flapped in the breeze like a humanitarian call, a call to safety. For the first time since our departure at dawn, I felt that our flight was no longer a blind haphazard effort but that it had a direction, a goal: to reach one of those diplomatic missions, break through the metal barrier at the gate or scale the wall, and on the other side find—sanctuary. Safe harbor. I no longer felt the weight of Mama's body in the wheelbarrow or that of the bundle I bore on my back. My feet had wings. We were no longer walking—we were running. My anxiety about Fofo eased. I was sure he was safe and sound behind the walls of one of the embassies. In a few minutes, when I'd covered the fifty meters that separated us from those flags, Mama would be in the care of a physician from Doctors Without Borders. And we would be under the protection of the International Community.

Chapter Ten

Johnny, Known as Matiti Mabé

We fell upon the city the way roaring, bounding tigers attack a herd of antelope, except that those weren't antelope we were aiming to massacre but Chechen bandits who were preventing our leader from assuming power. And except that we had a surprise setback—for even before we entered the district, long streams of refugees were already flowing into the main boulevard of Huambo, streams fed by a continuous human flood that poured from the adjacent streets like tributaries joining a great river.

The fleeing people were transporting an incredible array of bric-a-brac in wheelbarrows, basins, demijohns, baskets, plastic bottles—all this junk, in addition to the babies the women were carrying. A cloud of ocher dust rose from the ground.

We hadn't expected such floods of people. For a moment, I didn't know how to proceed. My commandos were already at fever pitch, like a pack of hunting dogs poised for the chase—and then: *ratta-tat-tat*. The troops had begun firing volleys into the air, without waiting for my orders. This infuriated me, and I wanted to rip the head off the guy who'd sparked the shooting, so they'd understand that I was the boss and that nothing could be done unless I gave the go-ahead. But how could I find the guilty party when there were a couple of dozen men all firing at the same time?

In contrast, the refugees had been thrown into a panic. Those at the front of the crowd had stopped abruptly, while the ones coming up behind had collided with them as if running into a wall. A hellish confusion resulted among those who were trying to turn around and escape the gunfire, those who had tripped over abandoned bundles and were being trampled, those who were shouting, those who were weeping.

"Plug it up, guys! Plug it up!"

I was giving the order to plug up the street—that is, to put up barricades. Barricades to block the stream of people, and also to filter it. That would allow us to spot the enemies hidden in the crowd. We also had to search the people to see who was concealing weapons and who was carrying money.

The staccato noise of the gunfire ceased. We began dealing out kicks and blows to control the people and make them stop in their tracks. Yet while some of them had halted, the majority had managed to turn around in the chaos and were fleeing in the direction they'd come from. But it was no accident that Giap had made me the leader. He knew I could size up a situation quickly, and this situation demanded that we immediately barricade the main street leading out of the district—the exit toward which some of the refugees were now heading.

Scarcely had I finished reflecting on the situation when I heard a car horn honking and a motor revving, emitting a high-pitched whine as if the driver had one foot on the clutch and was having fun pumping the accelerator with the other. Looking for the source of the racket, I saw a vehicle whose luggage rack, covered with a blue tarp, was clearly visible above the stream of people. I craned my head a bit and made out a large Japanese 4×4. The driver was evidently having trouble turning around in the dense crowd. He had already managed a three-quarter turn; he needed only to back up slightly and he'd take off in the opposite direction.

Why was he running away? And what did he have beneath the blue tarp? Weapons, no doubt. A man with a clear conscience doesn't run away.

Since you must never hesitate when you're in enemy territory, I fired—or as former leader Rambo liked to say, "squeezed off a round"—into the vehicle. I think the bullets must have claimed some victims in the crowd nearby, but as I've learned from the Europeans and Americans, this was known as "collateral damage" and you can't have wars without collateral damage. Every innocent person killed was an unfortunate mistake or collateral damage. My shots must have hit the driver at the moment his foot finally released the clutch, for the car made a quick swerve before stalling. In the blink of an eye, the people around the vehicle scattered.

I approached the scene. I looked through the shattered windows. Five bodies: a girl, a boy, three adults, including an old woman, all covered with blood. An elite marksman like me rarely misses his mark. Yet the left-hand door of the car was open—one of the passengers had no doubt pushed it open in an attempt to get away, before being cut down by my shots. Tough luck. You can't run faster than a bullet from a Kalashnikov. There's no escape from Matiti Mabé, the leader of the Roaring Tigers.

I pointed my gun at two men in the fleeing crowd. Immediately they threw down what they were carrying and raised their hands in the air.

"Get over here! Move!"

They came toward me, trembling. They thought their last hour had come and that I was going to send them into the Great Beyond, to the fair land of their ancestors.

"Take those bodies out."

They dragged out the five corpses and laid them on the pavement. Then they stood looking at me. I had a gun in my hands. They had nothing. I had life-or-death power over them, and they knew that I knew it. The slightest pressure on the trigger would spell the end for them. I was so glad to have a command vehicle that just then their lives weren't worth the honk of a car horn. So I told them to get lost. I'd never seen guys take to their heels so fast.

Right away I began an inspection of the overhead rack by lifting a corner of the blue tarp. A quick glance showed that there was no trace of weapons. I did, however, spot a leather sofa, a large television, and a fridge amid the pile of stuff. Funny how people always manage to cling to their possessions even in times of crisis. Then came the inspection of the interior. There was blood everywhere, especially on the driver's seat. I found a blanket under the tarp and covered the seat with it. I told four of my commandos to get in the car with me, and the instant they jumped in I took off like a rocket, tires squealing. We had to bottle up the enemy with all possible speed, which meant barricading the other exit from the Huambo district.

*

I don't give a damn whether anyone believes this or not—but from the height of my new command vehicle, despite the immense crowd of fleeing refugees, I recognized her right away. Lovelita! Lo-Ve-Li-Ta! A name that I had given her, a name I'd stolen from a song on the radio, a name more beautiful than the too-common "Lolita," a name that sings all by itself. And to pronounce it, ah—the tip of the tongue just touches the ridge of the palate for "Lo," the teeth press firmly on the cushion of the lower lip for "Ve," the tongue tries to push its way past the teeth for "Li," and finally the tongue strikes the ramparts of the teeth, "Ta"! Lovelita—my doll, my sweetheart, the girl I love the most out of all the ones I've loved. Of course she's a Mayi-Dogo—that is, from the same ethnic group as our enemies the Chechens—but that doesn't prevent her from being beautiful and from being loved. Besides, she didn't choose to be born a Mayi-Dogo. Do you know anyone who chose the hour, the tribe, and the village in which he was born? Lovelita! I recognized her first by the way she held her head, then by her favorite red bandanna which was tied around her short hair. She was wearing the jeans I'd given her. There was no doubt she'd been walking for a long time, since at this point she was very far from her house.

She was fleeing like all the others, a large bundle on her head. Fleeing from what? Fleeing from us, the Mata Mata, who were going to wreak devastation in her home district of Huambo. I had to rescue my girl.

I braked abruptly, and when the refugees saw us come to a halt they began to run away because they thought we were going to fire on them. Lovelita threw down her bundle so she could run more quickly. I honked loudly several times, but she didn't understand that the signal was meant for her. I had to jump from the vehicle and clear a path for myself by firing a few rounds into the air. I must confess she didn't recognize me when she saw me approach. She was afraid, I suppose—she thought I was one of those brutes who wanted to rape her. Come on, Lovelita—a guy doesn't rape his girlfriend! I could understand why she didn't recognize me. I was dressed in an outfit she'd never seen before.

Admittedly, I cut an impressive figure. I wasn't wearing the leather jacket that I put on every time I went into battle and under which I hid my fetishes. On the contrary, I wanted to display them so the guys under my command would clearly see that I was armored against the enemy just as effectively as Giap. Accordingly, I'd chosen the most powerful of all my T-shirts—the one that bore an image of Tupac Shakur and that I'd enhanced in a special way. I'd glued and sewn onto it numerous bits of mirror, not only because the tiny mirrors would blind the enemy troops by reflecting the sun into their eyes, but also because they would deflect the oncoming bullets. I was wearing my cowrie-shell necklace, to which I'd attached three little sacks containing various fetishes; one of these had the power to make me invisible. I wish I owned a fetish that, like Giap's, could transform bullets into drops of water—but that would come someday; you can't have everything all at once. Oh, and I'd also tied a red cord around the biceps of my right arm. I topped off the outfit with a dagger, a pistol, and two grenades, firmly attached to the belt that held up my olive-drab military pants. Of course she could never recognize her boyfriend dressed like this.

"Lovelita, it's me—don't be afraid!"

She didn't seem to get it. I turned the visor of my cap around so she could get a good view of my face, and repeated:

"It's me!"

She recognized me then. Her fear changed into boundless joy. I pulled aside the two ammo belts I wore across my chest, to make a space where she could hug me and press her tits against me.

"Let's go," I said.

No time to look for her bundle of things. We ran back to the 4×4, whose motor was still running.

I told Stud to move to the back so Lovelita could sit next to me. I'd already asked her to put on combat fatigues. There was only one spare pair of boots, which luckily fit her. She put them on, and fastened a wide belt around her waist. I gave her one of the two extra Kalashnikovs we had, and showed her how to fire it. The first time she let off a round she nearly fell over backward and dropped the gun, because she hadn't expected such a strong recoil. But after several volleys she felt reassured and confident—in fact, she was as excited and happy as a child. I was proud of her. She fired one last round and we got into the car. There were several cassettes in the glove compartment. I chose one by Papa Wemba, and we set off again just as the music began drifting from the speakers.

Little Pepper and Stud, sitting on opposite sides of the 4×4 and leaning out of the broken windows, kept firing into the air to clear a path through the crowd as fast as possible. We'd gone no more than a hundred meters before we were in fifth gear and the speedometer was up to a hundred kilometers per hour—so quickly did the refugees make way for us, despite the welter of those who were falling down, those who were trying to get up, those who'd been cut down by stray bullets, and those who were seeking refuge in side streets.

The road chose to curve slightly at the precise moment I floored the accelerator. Instinctively, I stomped on the brake and the car began zigzagging dangerously. It was the end—we were dead. A rollover, and we'd be nothing but a heap of bloody metal and bone. But no, all of a sudden the 4×4 just began ambling along like a horse, its rear wheels lifting off the road a few centimeters. They came down with a thump as soon as I—still in a panic—took my foot off the brake and accelerated, again instinctively. The vehicle shot forward.

Suddenly, a mind-boggling sight: a girl pushing an older woman in a wheelbarrow. Stupid cunt! Instead of using her head and staying where she was, on the left-hand side of the street, she decided to run out in front of my command vehicle at the very instant it was bolting ahead. You think I'm going to brake for you? What an idiot! Again I hit the accelerator. She shoved the wheelbarrow into a thorny lantana hedge and threw herself after it, probably taking a few of the bullets that Stud fired in her direction, while the wind tore the kerchief from her head and made it twirl through the air like a great green snake. We laughed and sped past.

"Wait! Stop!" yelled Stud abruptly.

Without thinking, I braked as hard as I could, though I had no idea why he wanted us to stop. The brakes made an infernal squealing.

"Back up—back up quickly! I saw a weapon lying in the street. I think it's a machine gun."

I threw the 4×4 into reverse and we shot backward like an arrow. Stud jumped out. I told Piston and Lovelita to stay in the vehicle and I jumped out, too, followed by Little Pepper.

"I was right—it's a gun!" shouted Stud excitedly.

I came up to him and took a look. Incredible. From its squarish lines and curved stock, I could tell right away it was an Uzi.

"That isn't a Kalashnikov," said Stud. "Must be Chinese."

"It's an Uzi," I said, "a Mini Uzi. An Israeli gun. If the Mayi-Dogo militias, the Chechens, have Israeli instructors, we'll really have to watch our step."

I explained to them why we needed to be even craftier than the Chechens. In *Raid on Entebbe*, the Israelis had successfully carried out a commando operation on a target located more than a thousand kilometers from their home base.

Stud handed me the gun and I set about examining it, first of all pulling out the cartridge. In contrast to our good old AK-47s, the Uzi had its cartridge in the grip. The thirty-two bullets were all there. Whoever had tossed away the gun had been in such a hurry he hadn't even taken out the clip. I replaced it, released the safety, and fired off a volley. That first round threw me off balance, and if I hadn't been so experienced I would have fallen over. Didn't know Uzis had such a kick.

It was then that Little Pepper, expert tracker that he was, flushed out a Chechen spy. Was this perhaps the one who'd thrown down the weapon before running away and hiding? Little Pepper brought him to us. Actually, he was just a kid. He carried an old rusty basin filled with fruit that he insisted he was planning to sell. He was weeping, begging, crying, "Mama! Mama!" Those charades don't work with me—kids are often used as spies. He was a Mayi-Dogo spy, probably trained by the Israelis or the Palestinians. I whacked him with the butt of my gun and he went down. The little weasel then turned to Lovelita, who had joined us, and tried to play on her tribal sympathies by telling her in heartrending tones that he knew her, that they were from the same neighborhood, that she was his big sister, and other bullshit. But my Lovelita isn't a tribalist and refused to fall into the trap. I was proud of her. The kid didn't catch on and continued to pester her with his whining. I'd had enough of it, and taking up my Uzi with one hand I fired two bullets into him—without killing him, though. I let Little Pepper finish him off, as a reward for flushing him out. I picked up a banana, peeled it, and ate it. It tasted good. The others set about gathering the rest of the fruit, while Lovelita, fascinated by the Uzi, amused herself by firing off volleys.

"We've wasted enough time. Let's go," I ordered.

We headed back to the car, Stud in the lead, followed by Little Pepper. I brought up the rear, just behind Lovelita. She'd given me back the Uzi and had only the Kalashnikov, carrying it easily, the strap slung between her breasts as if she'd been doing this all her life. Stud reached the 4×4, opened the door, then closed it again with a slam. He went back to the corpse of the little street rat and gave it swift kick in the balls. Just a kick. The act was unexpected and made no sense. He came back laughing, and the whole bunch of us burst out howling, unable to contain ourselves. I started shaking with hiccups, while for some reason Lovelita's laughter turned into racking sobs. Only Piston, who'd stayed in the car, didn't laugh. He gazed at us with a puzzled air, as if we'd suddenly gone mad.

We calmed down. I wanted to please Lovelita, so I told her she could drive. She got into the driver's seat and asked me to change the cassette. I took out the cassette of Papa Wemba and put in one by Koffi Olomide. She said she didn't want to listen to Koffi, and I suggested Tshala Mwana. She was going to say yes when she saw a cassette by Mbilia Bel. "Play that one for me," she said. A guy ought to know how to satisfy his girl. I immediately put the cassette into the machine. We slammed the doors and she took off, singing the lyrics in Lingala along with Mbilia Bel as if she were singing them to me:

Yamba ngaï
Na yi maboko pwelele
Motema na ngaï ya pembe
Yamba ngaï na marriage.

Receive me
I come to you with open hands
With a pure heart
Receive me in marriage.

*

I hadn't been mistaken. When we got to the end of the avenue, a large number of people—surely including some Chechen militiamen—were fleeing toward the river. We had to stop them. Quickly we got out of the car. Lovelita remained at the wheel.

"Back up!" I shouted at the crowd.

We fired into the air to get the hordes of refugees to turn around and head in the opposite direction. This was tougher than we expected, and we were afraid of being trampled. There's a strange phenomenon that often occurs: when people are *too* frightened, they actually lose their fear and can behave with an audacity that even the boldest of men would consider suicidal. Like that runty fellow whose muscles were a joke but who refused to obey our orders. "Turn around!" Piston yelled at him. Instead, the man continued to run forward, wild-eyed, as if he hadn't heard.

Piston got mad and was on the verge of clobbering him with the butt of his gun. With surprising quickness, the guy grabbed the weapon from Piston's hands and hit him on the head with the strength of an ox. Since Piston had no hair to blunt the effect of whatever might fall on his head, he crumpled under the force of the blow. The incident galvanized the crowd, which came rushing at us. At that moment, I think Stud and Little Pepper panicked. They began firing on the refugees. For good measure, I tossed a grenade. Boom. Screams of pain and panic. Only then did the crowd begin to back up and flee in the opposite direction. It was a horrendous stampede.

I felt my hands trembling with rage, or perhaps with retrospective fear. Then I calmed down. Piston wasn't dead, and his head wasn't cracked, either, as I'd thought. Hardly surprising, since as a result of being exposed to the worst sorts of weather without the protection of a thick mat of hair, his bald head had become harder than a coconut. As leathery as a tanned hide.

But there was no time to lose—we had to pursue the refugees in order to drive them toward the barricade where the rest of the unit was waiting.

My cell phone rang. I jumped.

"Hello?" I said, bringing the phone to my ear.

"Turf?"

It was Giap. Now, this is what modern technology is all about. You can't wage war without good communications. A leader must be reachable at every moment. I was the leader, so it was important that I be consulted on the current status of operations. Giap was fully aware of my importance and especially of my intellectual gifts—my ability to come up with winning strategies and devise the most cunning traps. All the same, I wished he'd stop with the "Turf" business, which lowered me in the eyes of my troops. I wished he'd call me by my real *nom de guerre*, which was Matiti Mabé, the evil weed that can mess up your head with a single puff of smoke, transforming the stars in the sky into millions of glowing, menacing owl-eyes in the darkness.

"Turf!" thundered the voice, impatient because I hadn't responded immediately.

"Yes, sir," I said, to placate him.

"What the fuck are you doing? I hear there are hundreds of people fleeing toward the embassies. What are you waiting for? Stop them! Don't you know that once they get there, we can't neutralize the militia fighters that are hiding among them?"

"No one's fleeing toward the embassies—they're heading toward the river or toward the forest. That's why I'm setting up barricades here to—"

"You got shit for brains, or what?"

His anger made the phone vibrate in my hand.

"But . . . but . . . what did I do?"

"What did you do? You're incapable of controlling your zone, stupid! Go immediately to the other end of the district and neutralize those refugees. Let them run off into the woods, for all I care, but keep them away from the embassies! You got that? What on earth made me choose you as a leader? Turf—ha!—I should have given you a lawn mower, or a bunch of sheep to graze on you, rather than give you command of a unit! Who's there with you?"

"Uh, Little Pepper, Piston, and Stud."

"Stud is with you? He's the one I should have chosen to head the unit! Go on, get to work and prevent those refugees from reaching the embassies. Move your ass!"

And *bam!* he hung up. The village idiot.

Chapter Eleven

Johnny, Known as Mad Dog

He treated me like a goddamn simpleton, a retard. Who did he think I was? Had he forgotten that he owed everything to me, and that if he was now the commander, it was because I myself hadn't wanted to be? I knew people were ungrateful, but this was the limit!

He'd risen a few notches in the world since those days, the jerk—a guy whose only pleasure until then had been to come in his pants while watching women writhe in pain from the pepper he rubbed in their eyes, because he couldn't fuck them normally the way we did. Now he wasn't only the leader of our little group, the Mata Mata, but after the capture of the radio and TV stations he'd been promoted by our new president and had been made commander of all the militias. Really, you should never be surprised at anything in life, for that's often the way things turn out—the nonentities become leaders, and the most intelligent ones are always ignored. And he was a nonentity, Giap—a real zero. He wasn't even clever enough to think of a good *nom de guerre* for himself, and if it hadn't been for my brilliant suggestion, which had transformed him into a new man, he would have been stuck forever with that ridiculous name Pili Pili he'd thought was so cool. It was even thanks to me that he'd been recruited in the first place.

When the fighting had started, it was the usual story: all we knew was that two political leaders were struggling for power after a round of elections, which one guy claimed were rigged and the other guy swore were democratic and transparent. We didn't give a damn, because we knew what the politicians in our country were like. Con men all. They got you drunk with words that were sweeter than fresh palm wine, and just as you let yourself be lulled by the soothing purr of those fine words, they leaped on your back to shinny up the greasy pole they valued so much—and once they were at the top, rich and well fed, they treated you like shit. In this particular battle, the two camps had mobilized their supporters, who'd progressed from shouting insults to exchanging punches, then to throwing rocks, then to shooting at each other with pistols. Finally they wound up trading heavy-arms fire.

It was at the height of these disputes that one fine morning we saw newcomers in our district—young men, heavily armed, who obviously weren't messing around. They rousted us out of our homes; they closed down the marketplace; they raided the school and brought the little kids—frightened, confused, some of them crying—to the spot where they'd gathered everyone together. They told us they were with the Movement For the Democratic Liberation of the People, the MFDLP, and that they were fighting against the partisans of the Movement For the Total Liberation of the People, the MFTLP. They asked us to take up arms and help them. MFDLP versus MFTLP—to us, frankly, it was six of one and half a dozen of the other. Why should we take sides?

Then they explained things to us. The leader of the MFDLP was from our region, so his party was automatically our party and any man or woman who was against him was a traitor. Be on the lookout for traitors in the region! This great party that apparently was ours had won the elections—but the MFTLP, which was then in power, refused to abide by the results. Its members wanted to stay in office forever so that they could continue to pillage the national treasury, gobble up the income from the country's oil and diamonds, and above all bully us. The situation was dire, we were told: it was essential that everyone who was a native of our region—and this meant the majority of the residents in our district of the city—take up arms to chase the president out of office and give his tribesmen, the Mayi-Dogos, a lesson they'd never forget.

I'm sure the militants weren't expecting to hear the response they got. Speaking in our name, a number of elders from the district, both men and women, refused to believe the tales told by these individuals, rabble-rousers who'd come from god knows where. The elders told them in no uncertain terms that they didn't like being taken for idiots and that they were familiar with political tactics: when all was going well for the politicians, they ignored the people and no one ever saw them, whereas when they were in trouble they came and stirred up ill will among the ethnic groups to keep themselves in power.

"We're sick of your nonsense—it's nothing but a pack of lies. Go away and leave us in peace! We don't want to see you in our district anymore!" one woman had finally shouted. All of us applauded.

Hearing this, the young militants—zealots all—became angry. They clubbed four people with the butts of their guns and threatened to kill two others, among them the woman who'd shouted the words we applauded. Since this big mess of a civil war had done away with the national army that could have protected us, the people who felt like objecting were cowed. They swallowed their protests and said nothing.

Taking advantage of our silence and the relative order imposed by the militants, a man I'd never seen until then came forward. He was older than most of the commandos, had a serious air, wore a suit and tie, and so on. He must have been their leader, for as soon as he made a signal someone handed him a bulging briefcase. He pulled out a bunch of color photos and shoved them under our noses. They showed mutilated corpses, people with frightful machete wounds, skin festering with burns . . . unbearable things. I closed my eyes, didn't want to see any more. Then the guy started to speak.

The photos, he said, were of people from our ethnic group and our region who'd been attacked by Mayi-Dogo bandits in the pay of our current president. These thugs captured pregnant women and dismembered them alive; they crushed babies to death; they ran red-hot irons over the backs of our men; they chopped off noses, ears, and arms—committed countless atrocities. It seemed incredible that anyone had managed to photograph all that, but we shuddered in horror.

"We have to avenge our people!" the man said over and over. "For if we do nothing, the Mayi-Dogos (those stinking rats!) will kill us all—our women, our children, our chickens, and our goats."

I must admit that, like the individuals who'd protested aloud and been beaten for their words, I didn't believe what he was saying, and for a very simple reason: until that day, until the very moment he'd shown up to tell us these things, we'd never had any problem with the Mayi-Dogos. Moreover, among the young people our age, no one even knew who was a Mayi-Dogo and who wasn't. Most of us had been born in the city; we'd never set foot in the native regions of our parents, and very few of us spoke the tribal patois. Our language was that of the city—a lingua franca, often coded, which we spoke among ourselves and which our parents, whether they were from the north, south, east, or west, couldn't make head or tail of. We had our neighborhood soccer teams, and if there was any rivalry or fistfighting, it was with guys from other districts when they beat us at soccer, or won prizes for their elegant clothes in SAPE competitions, or stole our girlfriends. We'd never lived our lives in tribal terms. Besides, wasn't my current girl a Mayi-Dogo? I adored her. And I called her Lovelita, a name I'd taken from a romantic song I'd heard on the radio.

And now, all of a sudden, these militiamen were revealing that we were two different peoples, that we were enemies. We didn't know it, but in reality there were secular hatreds between us, hatreds that were just waiting for an opportunity to flare up. The proof? That they'd been so well hidden, of course! Hard to believe, right?

But that wasn't all. We were also told that because a party leader was a native of the same region our mother or father came from, we automatically owed him our support; his party became our party, and refusing to join it was tantamount to betraying our native region. This was pretty hard to swallow. What was so special about being from the same village, the same region, or the same tribe? For me, nothing! At least until I heard that man speak.

He began his talk by introducing himself as a native of the region. That didn't impress me much, since we were all natives of the region—or rather, of our country. It didn't impress me, because even though all of us had roots in the same region and the same tribe, our parents' generation had been rife with thievery, betrayals, jealousies, and feuds. I even knew of two guys who'd killed each other over a stolen rooster—a petty quarrel that had gotten out of hand. And not only had they been from the same village and the same tribe, they'd even been from the same clan. So once again you'd have to point to something more than the hallowed tribe if you wanted me to swear blind allegiance to a politician.

And then suddenly everything got turned around: the man said he was a doctor of something or other, a professor at some university. At that point I pricked up my ears. He was an intellectual! In our country, the people who were widely admired, especially by kids, were politicians, soldiers, musicians, soccer players. No one looked up to intellectuals, and certainly not to professors. But I had great respect for them. They had impressive diplomas and spoke flawless French; they were more intelligent than politicians because they'd read a great many books on politology, polemology, pharmacology, phrenology, phenomenology, topology, geology—too many things for me even to mention (since I can cite only the disciplines I've heard of, and I'm sure they'd read books in fields I've never heard of). Some of them had libraries where the books were piled up to the ceiling and spread all over the floor for lack of space; yet this didn't prevent them from continuing to buy more, so that they could keep nourishing their brains already saturated with knowledge. That's what an intellectual is. So believe me, if I were asked to take the word of a soldier, a businessman, a magician, or an intellectual, I wouldn't hesitate to put my faith in the intellectual. With so much knowledge in their heads, people like that couldn't possibly lie.

In any case, I myself was already a bit of an intellectual, and if anyone in this district could understand what our countryman was saying, it was me. I had completed fourth grade, after all! So my mind immediately felt an intellectual rapport with the mind of this doctor of something or other, and I realized that the Mayi-Dogos were actually our secular enemies and that we had to kill them. I applauded. That must have pleased him, and I was the first to be recruited. It wasn't Giap.

*

Right away I was assigned an important, even preeminent role in the cell that our party, the MFDLP, wound up organizing in our district. The leader of the cell was a young man who'd come with the organizers and who called himself Major Rambo. The name Rambo wasn't typical of our region, and I knew immediately it was a *nom de guerre* he'd taken from some American film, since I'd seen dozens of them. I was the second in command, and was given the task of recruiting young people not only in the district but also in the surrounding villages—recruiting them by force, if necessary. Since charity begins at home, I decided to start by signing up my immediate friends, and it's a fact that the most difficult to recruit was the guy who just now was treating me like an idiot.

I've always said that it helps to be an intellectual, because then you can grasp things very quickly. This has been the case with me, for even if I did quit school after the fourth grade, I was actually at fifth-grade level. But Giap, whose brain was slow to catch fire, didn't always understand the need for the battle we had to wage.

"Why should I fight the Mayi-Dogos?" he snapped at me with a scornful expression. "They've never done anything to me. Tell me—you know me pretty well: Who's my best friend in the whole world? Even you aren't as close to me as he is. Who is it?"

"Dovo."

"And who's Dovo? He wouldn't happen to be a Mayi-Dogo, now, would he? Well, I'm not joining up with you. I don't get into fights with my friends."

"You don't understand anything! He's not your friend because he's a Mayi-Dogo. That has nothing to do with it. You're buddies because both of you are troublemakers—you can sell a rotten fish to someone and make him think you've just caught it. You've even tried to pull that trick on me! But at the moment I'm not talking about buddies or friends or fish. I'm talking about politics. Our current president is a Mayi-Dogo. He runs a corrupt and tribalist government that serves only the interests of his native region."

"Look me in the eye and tell me: Do you know anyone who chose his native region or his native village? Aren't we all born somewhere by chance? You could have been born a Mayi-Dogo, too."

"Yeah, but I wasn't. Do you like staying poor while your buddy is rich, or will become rich, simply because one of his tribesmen is in power? Because whoever's in power controls the country's oil income and—"

"That's not true," he interrupted. "I know a lot of Mayi-Dogos who are poor just like you and me. You think the president gives them a thought when he's raiding the coffers? He thinks first of his own pockets, then of his children and nephews, and then of the bootlickers that hang around him. Don't be taken in by those politicos, my friend—let them fight it out among themselves, and let them kill each other if they want to."

"You don't understand. If you found out they were doing something shady, you'd take up arms against them right away!

They're arrogant, they think they're smarter than we are, and above all they're always insulting us. What's more," I flung at him, "they're threatening our power—and that's worse!"

He laughed at me, the shit.

" 'Our power'? I didn't know you had any power. How come you're not tooling around in a Mercedes, instead of pushing a broom for a bunch of Malian and Lebanese shopkeepers?"

At that point I almost lost my temper, but with an effort I controlled myself and kept my cool. I said, confidently and enthusiastically:

"You'll see. All of that will change when we return to power."

"Who's 'we'?" he demanded. His sluggish brain still didn't understand what I was talking about.

"Well—us," I retorted. "If one man from our region has power, it's *our* power."

He laughed sarcastically.

"So if a guy from our tribe becomes president, the mosquitoes will respectfully avoid us and will sting only the people from tribes that aren't in power? No more malaria for us, right? All of a sudden we'll be able to stuff our faces every day while other tribes are dying of hunger. Plus, overnight I'll acquire enough money to buy the multisystem VCR I've been dreaming about for the past two years. Paradise, huh?"

Honestly, I nearly wept at his crass stupidity. I couldn't understand him at all. What did power have to do with mosquitoes and malaria? Or with the fact that sometimes we didn't have enough to eat? He was always earthbound, Giap. He saw only what he encountered in daily life, and not the ideals that ought to guide us. It wasn't worth the trouble—I decided to let the matter drop. Too bad for him. Impossible to get anything out of that ignoramus; yet he would have made a great soldier, with those bulging calf muscles and biceps (even though he couldn't get a hard-on like a real man). Perhaps he'd closed his mind because he thought all those ideas were my own? So then I tried a sledgehammer argument, the one that had toppled me. Or rather, I invoked the imposing authority behind the argument that had led me to support going to war with the Mayi-Dogos, those Mayi-Dogos who up till then had successfully made us believe we were all brothers and sisters sharing one country.

"Did you see the guy in the suit and tie who came to speak to us the first day? Well, he's a doctor."

"So why didn't he give us medicines to help the sick? All he did was wave those horrible photos around, and then he left."

"No, no," I said patiently. "He isn't the sort of doctor who takes care of sick people. He's the kind who has diplomas and who has read half of all the books in the world."

"You mean even books written in Chinese?"

"Yes."

"In Kikongo?"

"Yes."

"In Kpellé?"

I'd never heard of that language, much less of any books being written in it, but I responded with the confidence proper to an intellectual:

"Yes."

He remained silent for a moment. Then, with a triumphant air, as if he'd hit upon an insuperable difficulty for our doctor:

"Does he have his elementary school diploma?"

"Of course! Ten times more than that. He has two doctorates."

"What does that mean?"

"It means he's intelligent and an intellectual."

"And what's that, exactly—an intellectual?"

Just as I'd suspected—he didn't even know what an intellectual was.

"An intellectual is a man who's extremely intelligent and who has read a great many books. Even when he's asleep, his brain keeps working away, finding solutions to problems that don't yet exist."

"Aha!" he exclaimed triumphantly. "You see? He creates problems! Where there aren't any, he creates them—and then he finds solutions. He creates false problems so that he can find false solutions. Like this business with the Mayi-Dogos. You know there have never been any problems between them and us. Besides, your girlfriend, Lovelita—isn't she a Mayi-Dogo? Are you going to kill her, too?"

My god, his mind was a mess! And he was always so flat-footed and unimaginative. What did my girlfriend have to do with it? Instead of conceiving of the situation on a higher level, as a battle for power—power that we ought to win and keep—he was unable to think of anything but our personal lives. He continued to speak, and got more and more heated. To hear him, you'd have thought that he was the intellectual and I was the village idiot.

"Do you really believe that because a guy has an elementary school diploma and knows how to read Chinese, Kikongo, and Kpellé, he knows what people's lives are like? That he knows how much suffering we all endure? I bet he doesn't even know whether the rooster or the duck covers its female longer when it mates. And you're going to kill Lovelita for a guy like him? I thought you were smarter than that."

"You leave Lovelita out of this!" I warned. "Nobody's asking us to kill all the Mayi-Dogos. We're only being asked to fight some of them—the ones who blindly follow the current president just because he's from their region or a member of their ethnic group. That's called tribalism, and we should resist tribalism because it's bad for our country. It has nothing to do with Lovelita."

"So when they support a leader who's from their region, they're being tribalists—but when we support one who's from our region, as you say we ought to, we're *not* tribalists?"

"It isn't the same thing!" I shouted. "It's . . . it's . . . How can I explain? With us it's . . . it's a *positive* tribalism! . . . Meaning that when our group gets to power, we're going to stamp out tribalism! We're going to give great jobs to everyone, even the Mayi-Dogos!"

"And what if *they* want to do that, too?"

Exasperating. Hopeless. Demoralizing. No sense wasting my breath—his skull was thicker than a coconut. I gave up.

It was the unexpected appearance of Major Rambo that saved him. Just as I was about to turn my back on him and walk away, leaving him to his dreary future as a good-for-nothing, we saw a car pull out of a nearby side street and pass the corner where I was trying to convert him to our cause. The vehicle came to a screeching stop next to me. Major Rambo was at the wheel. Three kids jumped out, brandishing guns. I knew them well because they'd been recruited at the same time as me, or shortly after me, and they served as Rambo's bodyguards. One of them fired his Kalashnikov into the air, just to show off. It was Smoking Cannon, a guy who was slightly crazy and unpredictable—he could go from extreme gentleness to the most uncontrollable rage with no warning at all. A psycho with a machine gun in his hand. The two others were also in a state of great excitement. They had two girls in the car, as well as a stereo, an impressive number of CDs, and a giant television.

"We were just at Hojej's place—the Lebanese guy. We knew

he had a big photo of the president tacked up on the wall in his store. It proved he was in league with the government. We beat him up and looted the store."

Actually, every merchant licensed to run a business was required to display a picture of the head of state—this rule had been established by the Ministry of Commerce. So according to the way these guys were thinking, all the businessmen in the country were supporters of the current government. But right now we were the ones, machine guns in hand, who were rewriting the law. There had to be a reason for looting, just as there had to be a reason for drowning one's dog; well, instead of saying we were eliminating rabies, we had decreed that every person owning a likeness of that "tribalist" and "regionalist" president was a traitor. Especially if the person had valuables worth looting.

"We're heading over to Tomla's now—there's good stuff at his place, too."

Tomla was a well-known merchant in our district, the only one of our countrymen who could compete with the shopkeepers from Mali and Lebanon. But before I could say anything, our future Giap—the guy for whose sake I'd been wasting my precious time—exclaimed, his eyes glittering with barely concealed greed:

"To Tomla's! Hey, he sells multisystem VCRs!"

"So come with us and get yourself one!" said Smoking Cannon, who knew him well, since they were both from the same district.

The car door opened. A Kalashnikov was tossed to the future Giap, who seized it and jumped into the vehicle. Slam went the door, and there was just enough time for my question:

"But Tomla's one of us! He's not a Mayi-Dogo!"

"He's got a photo of the current president in his shop—he's a traitor to our region!"

This was shouted from the window, with the car already far away, wrenched from a standstill with a squealing of tires as Rambo floored the accelerator . . .

So that's how, thanks to me, the guy who would return from Tomla's shop with a multisystem VCR, dozens of videocassettes, and the nickname Pili Pili had been recruited into our group, the little band that would soon become the Mata Mata commandos, fearsome enemy of the Mayi-Dogo militiamen known as the Chechens. And this was the guy who had dared to treat me like an idiot on the phone!

*

I turned off the phone and stuffed it in my pocket. I was furious. Little Pepper, Stud, and Piston were watching me in silence, as if they'd guessed it was Giap I'd just been speaking with. I hoped they hadn't heard him treating me like a dummy, calling me Turf and suggesting that Stud should have been made head of the unit instead of me. I eyed Stud closely.

One thing sure: from a physical standpoint, he was completely unlike me. He made people quake in their boots with nothing but his gorillalike size and strength. Between him and Idi Amin, I'd say he was the more impressively muscled. He wore only one fetish, which consisted of a couple of red parrot feathers stuck in his hair. Since these feathers were inserted through two holes in his cap—which he never took off, even when sleeping—he looked as if he had antennae on his head, like a wasp or a grasshopper. His thing, unlike Giap's, worked perfectly. I'd even heard that when it was excited, it grew as big as an elephant's trunk and would become so heavy that he had trouble hoisting it all by himself—which is how he got the name

Stud, allegedly given to him by the women who helped him lift it. He loved boxing with his American brass knuckles, which he would slip onto his fingers like gloves, one set on each hand. Last but not least, Stud had it all in his fists, his cock, and his calf muscles—nothing above the neck. Looking at the guy, I came to the conclusion that Giap didn't have an ounce of common sense. The fact that he'd even considered appointing a Neanderthal with such a stupid name to the post of unit commander proved that his powers of judgment weren't worth five CFA francs. A real leader would never have screwed up like that . . . But all of a sudden I realized that if anyone had screwed up, it was me and not Giap. It wasn't his fault if he continued to call me Turf—I'd never let him know that I'd changed my name!

I'd adopted a new *nom de guerre* just after debaptizing and rebaptizing my Roaring Tiger Commandos. Changing names hadn't been easy, since the guys in the unit had no imagination whatsoever—almost none of them had been to school, the way I had. Their brains could come up with nothing but ordinary names that had no warlike punch. Some of them had even suggested that the unit should take the name of a soccer team! I'd had to exert all of my authority, intelligence, and dexterity—breaking down and reassembling a Kalashnikov in ninety seconds with my eyes closed—to get them to accept my choice.

To have confidence is good, but it's always wise to tether your goat when it's grazing. So before we swooped down on the city like a flock of falcons, I wanted to get the men's blood up by making them chant our slogan, our new name.

Holding my head high and straight, with my cap turned backward to display my commanding gaze, my chest giving off flashes of light from the dozens of mirror fragments I'd glued to my combat T-shirt to deflect bullets, I surveyed my men lined up at attention and shouted at them the way Giap had taught us:

"What's our name?"

"The Roaring Tigers!" they yelled in unison, without the slightest hesitation.

I felt as proud as a rooster who's beaten all his rivals in a race to mount the finest hen.

"What?"

"The Roaring Tigers!" they repeated.

Seized with euphoria at this new demonstration of my authority, I hurled at them like a roaring tiger:

"And what's the name of your leader?"

There was a silence. The men stared at me as if puzzled by my question. Then, timidly, Little Pepper said:

"Matiti Mabé."

"Turf!" Twin-Head shouted triumphantly with a big smile, as if he'd drawn the winning number in the national lottery. Seeing that happy, imbecilic grin on their buddy's face, all the others thought they'd made a blunder and yelled with one voice:

"Turf!"

Was I angry? I was fucking furious! I seized my gun to blow Twin-Head away, just like Giap had done with Gator—but when I saw how they were looking at me, I had second thoughts. To begin by eliminating one of my men was perhaps not an intelligent thing to do, since I hadn't yet fully established my authority. Moreover, it wasn't their fault—it was the fault of that idiot Giap, who in front of everyone had called me Turf, harmless grass, when my real name was Matiti Mabé: evil, poisonous, deadly weed; the mushroom that kills, that sends you *ad patres*, to the land of your ancestors; the cannabis whose smoke makes your head explode into a thousand psychedelic pieces; the beautiful, mysterious, yet carnivorous flower that feeds on live animals . . . But since my brain was capable of doing more than one thing at a time—talking and thinking simultaneously, for example—I said to myself that maybe it was a bad idea for a military leader to adopt a name like that. After all, a plant, even a poisonous one, won't scare the shit out of an enemy. With a pair of good boots, you can safely walk on it, trample it. Even piss on it. Cat piss, sheep piss. Bush-pig dung, dog shit. No, it was a stupid name—I had to change it. And I had to think of something quick, because all eyes were on me.

And *wham!* a name exploded in my brain, which is always working even when I'm not paying attention, running all by itself like an idling motor that needs only a touch on the accelerator to come roaring to life. A strong, powerful name. A name that inspires the same gut-wrenching terror that a condemned man feels before the firing squad, a name that makes people tremble when they see it on a sign.

"Forget Turf and Matiti Mabé. From now I'm MAD DOG!" I shouted. "What's my name?"

"Mad Dog!" they answered all together.

"Twin-Head, I couldn't hear you very well. What's my name?"

"Mad Dog!" he yelled, with an expression that showed he understood completely.

Then, convinced that I'd reestablished the natural order of things, I gave the command for them to fall upon the city like roaring, bounding tigers.

*

Now I realized I'd never told Giap that I'd changed my name. I'd do it for sure the next time we talked. I was angry with myself. And with Stud, Little Pepper, and Piston.

"Change of plans. We've been ordered to go to the other end of the district, where we were before. Seems the guys we left there have been unable to maintain the blockades and many of the refugees are fleeing toward the foreign embassies. Understood?"

"Yessir," said the three of them.

"And what's the name of your leader?" I asked, before giving the order to get back in the vehicle.

"Mad Dog, sir!" they repeated once more.

Satisfied, I gave the order to get in the car and head back the way we had come.

Chapter Twelve

Laokolé

The armored gate of the first embassy remained stubbornly and hopelessly shut.

The heavy metal panels shook but did not give way before the dozens of weary fists that pounded it like clubs, accompanied by cries of anger and fear. The crowd then broke into smaller groups, and two, three, four other embassies were besieged, likewise without success. It seemed that all of them had received the same warning: Don't open your gates.

Abruptly, like a leaden pall, complete silence descended on that welter of people. A strange phenomenon, as if those thousands of individuals had suddenly exhausted the energy of their despair and had decided as one to pass without transition from chaotic Brownian movement to utter inertia. As if a raging ocean, seething with thousands of foaming waves and whipped furiously by the wind, had suddenly become a calm, flat, glassy sea.

One by one, the people sat down. First the women. They

began by spreading a pagne on the ground and thus staking their claim to a bit of space amid the tangle of feet and legs; they consolidated their occupation of the conquered territory by placing on it the bundles they'd been carrying and then sitting down themselves, along with their children and relatives. Within a few minutes, men, women, children, virtually everyone in the crowd was sitting down. Bodices were promptly opened and breasts were slipped into the mouths of hungry infants; wet and soiled diapers were removed from babies' bottoms and replaced with dry, clean ones; cups of water, which was now tepid from the heat, were passed from hand to hand. Those who'd brought something to eat took out their provisions, from a motley assortment of containers—plastic bags, cassava leaves, sheets of paper torn from bags of cement. The stores included bread, boiled cassava, fried dough, corn mush, bananas, raw and roasted groundnuts. One man who probably had nothing to eat made a general offer to the people around him: five chloroquine tablets in exchange for a baguette of bread or ten fingers of banana. As if that had been a signal, other voices piped up and offered various other objects for barter. Thus, a refugee camp formed spontaneously in front of the diplomatic missions, beneath the sweltering sun of Central Africa, where men and women had been turned into refugees in their own country. The heat was indeed oppressive, and there wasn't a single tree to protect us from the sun, though the city was famous for its greenery.

I was exhausted. After lowering the wheelbarrow onto its supports and helping Mama to get out, I shed the bundle I'd been toting on my back, rubbed my palms against each other, flexed my fingers several times to ease the stiffness and get the blood flowing again, and sat down. Mama crawled over to sit on the mat I'd spread on the ground, and looked at me. She wasn't crying, but I knew that her sufferings were not merely physical. There comes a moment in every daughter's life when she becomes a mother to her mother. For me, this was that moment. I knelt so that I was on a level with her and tried as best I could to assuage her bodily pain, if only by finding a slightly more comfortable position for her wounded, swollen stump. I examined the bit of her leg that was left below the knee. I was afraid that gangrene was setting in, and, not knowing what to do, I turned my eyes away and began rummaging in the bundle I'd been carrying on my back. I pulled out a bottle of water and handed it to her. She barely wet her lips and handed it back. I took a good swallow, and as I was unwrapping a bit of dried fish, I heard:

"Do you think Fofo will be able to find something to drink?"

Fofo! My god, where was he? I was overcome by a wave of anguish. I had pushed the thought of his disappearance to the back of my mind, consoling myself with the fervent hope that he was safe and sound in one of the embassies. Now their firmly closed gates brought me face to face with the stark reality. What should I do? Begin searching? But where? And should I abandon Mama to go look for Fofo, or stay with her and abandon him? My god, what should I do?

Heat. Cries of babies. Sweat. If we didn't die from the militias' bullets, we'd surely be baked to death by the sun. Mama had to be protected from sunstroke. I took out a pagne and draped it over her head. Look, there was one of Fofo's caps! The orange one. Since I'd lost my green scarf, I put on the cap to protect my forehead and neck from the intense rays of the sun. I must have looked like an American tennis player. But I couldn't avoid answering Mama's question. Where was Fofo?

I told Mama that I wanted to take advantage of this brief

respite to begin looking for her child. I wouldn't go very far, and I'd come back to check on her every fifteen minutes. She acquiesced with a nod. Perhaps she thought that if she said anything, I'd put off leaving or would change my mind.

I started wending my way through the crowd. Moving about was difficult because many other people were also walking around, looking for a child, a sister, a parent. Names and cries flew back and forth and blended with each other. "Lolo!" on one side, "Milete!" on another; "Michel!" over here, "Mandala!" over there. I tried to make myself heard above all these noises by emphasizing the two *o*'s of "Fofo" and producing the sound from my diaphragm like an opera singer. I looked everywhere. A head of hair that I thought I recognized made me run in one direction; the color of a shirt drew me in another. Then I'd return to the wheelbarrow to see if Mama was still safe . . . I was going to die of sunstroke . . . Scant mouthful of water, bottle handed back to Mama, and I was once more wading into the crowd, searching ever farther, toward the place where I thought I'd heard a "Lao-o-o!" echo in response to my "Fofo-o-o!" Alas, still no Fofo on the horizon. Was he perhaps farther away, with the group that was besieging the fifth embassy? I decided to cover more ground on my next foray and leave Mama for a full hour. I knew she wouldn't object. With Fofo's cap firmly on my head and my eyes shaded from the sun by its visor, my leather bag still slung like a bandolier across my front, I began to elbow my way through the crowd toward the fifth embassy. I hadn't gone very far, ten meters perhaps, when I heard the first gunshots.

No doubt about it—the militia fighters who'd been pursuing us had come back and were beginning to fire on us. The refugees, just settling into the routines of their life as survivors, again rose to their feet in panic and prepared to flee. Quickly, children were tied onto backs, bundles replaced on heads. People gathered up what they could and left the rest—this was no time to dawdle. In fact, though, we were trapped. The gunfire was coming from the south, behind us; we had nowhere to go but forward, yet ahead of us were only the walls of that International Community that had let us down. As for me, I had only one thought: Find Mama!

I set about forcing my way diagonally through the dense crowd, which was moving in a direction parallel to mine. It wasn't easy. I was hemmed in, buffeted, jostled, knocked this way and that, at the whim of its movements. I no longer knew if I was going the right way, but I continued moving, and by a lucky chance I fell over the wheelbarrow. It was upside down; the mat that I'd spread on the ground for Mama was in shreds, as if it had been trampled by a herd of elephants. Miraculously, the bundle containing our things was still intact after being kicked and stepped on by thousands of feet. But Mama was nowhere to be seen. I looked around frantically.

When the ocean tide recedes from a beach, fish are often left stranded. Torn from their natural environment, exposed to the sun and the wind, they thrash desperately on the sand as they die. This was the impression I had when I looked toward the south, toward the area that the human tide had just abandoned in its chaotic flight. Shoes, pagnes, plastic bags and bottles, great quantities of dust—and here and there, amid the unidentifiable flotsam and jetsam, forms lying on the ground. Human forms. And on one of them I recognized the color of the camisole, the color and pattern of the pagne knotted around the waist. I recognized the . . . "Mama! Mama!"

Mama lying in the dust, Mama trampled, Mama crushed, Mama dead . . . No, she wasn't dead, she was breathing. I spoke to her; she didn't answer. I patted her cheeks. Her eyes opened but didn't focus. Could she hear me? Could she feel me? The wheelbarrow—put her in the wheelbarrow and save her! I burst into sobs. All at once, a great weariness settled on my shoulders. I collapsed next to Mama. Never had I felt so alone in the world. I'd lost all hope.

"Come on, move! Now! Or you'll get yourself killed!"

A voice came from above me, a voice from the clouds, a voice from heaven. Arms gripped me, raised me, pulled me.

"Get up! Quick!"

I found the strength to murmur:

"Mama—the wheelbarrow."

The arms let me go. They lifted Mama, who suddenly appeared to be as light as a feather, and in three or four steps had placed her in the wheelbarrow, seized the handles, and begun pushing it at a rapid pace. I quickly tied the bundle to my back, the way one would carry a baby, and I followed.

We could go no farther, because of the crowds massed before the walls of the embassies. The blows of fists on the closed gates became increasingly violent as the gunshots of the militias grew louder. In front of the second embassy, where we had somehow wound up, appeals for help were being shouted over the wall at those who were keeping the gates locked, and these appeals were growing ever more desperate.

After gazing so long at that colossal, unfriendly, inviolable wall, I reached a point where I ceased to notice its repellent features and found myself admiring the solidity and professionalism of its construction.

As the daughter of a mason, I knew a fine wall when I saw one. I'd built a number of them with my father. Though the walls I'd constructed had been fairly simple, made out of concrete blocks or terra-cotta bricks, my familiarity with my father's profession had taught me about the techniques used for constructing large buildings. Looking at the pilasters that strengthened this wall, each anchored to its own footing, I knew that these were not made of ordinary poured concrete;

they were reinforced with steel cables. When we'd built our own house out of hollow concrete blocks, we had used a simple method: wooden braces had supported the formwork around the lintels, and we'd removed the forms merely by tapping them on the outside with a hammer or a mallet to make the concrete vibrate. Seeing this embassy's imposing lintel, which topped the enormous opening that held the two large metal wings of the gate, I wondered what kind of bracing they could have used to hold the formwork in place. A wall so sturdy, though it was three meters high, could only have been made of cinder blocks strengthened with interior rebars and concrete. Or was it made entirely of steel-reinforced poured concrete? The people who'd had these walls built were obviously very rich. Cost was no object for them.

Mama had often said to me, when she returned home exhausted after selling her wares at the market all day, that she felt instantly soothed and relaxed as soon as she came through the door of our house, for the walls of a house enclosed a space of peace, security, and tranquillity. What she'd never said was that the reverse was likewise true: a wall could also be a barrier. In history class, I'd learned that in medieval times the Africans of the city of Great Zimbabwe had built high walls of enormous stone blocks around the town's center, as protection against local invaders and Arab conquerors from the East. Similarly, the rulers of China had constructed a wall several hundred kilometers long, to defend themselves against the barbarians who roamed the border regions of their empire. Now we were the ones who were facing a wall. Were we the new barbarians, assailing the fortresses erected by the world's current rulers?

I've no idea how long my mind wandered like this, before being yanked back to reality. A young man had gotten a boost and had managed to reach through the strands of barbed wire that bristled at the top of the wall. With an effort he hauled himself up, and I saw him standing there, his shirt torn, preparing to jump down on the other side. Then came gunshots, followed by a silence. The young man flung his head back, remained motionless for an instant above the barbed wire, then toppled over, and was snagged for a few seconds on the barbs of the coiled strands before falling heavily onto the crowd.

All hell broke loose. The guards in the embassy compound were shooting; the militiamen coming up behind us were shooting. Trapped between two lines of fire, we could do nothing but run, run, even without knowing where. Staying put would have meant sure death. And stray bullets were already claiming victims. Mama's rescuer had once again seized the handles of the wheelbarrow. I was following. I don't know how long we ran this way through the confusion; I don't know how long I could have kept up such a mad pace. My breath was coming in gasps, and I had a pain in my side.

Suddenly, ahead of us—a miracle! A metal gate, its wings outspread like the wings of an angel, wide open. We threw ourselves toward it, were entering, were inside. My legs gave way beneath me. First I fell on my knees next to the wheelbarrow, which the man had just set down—that unknown and generous man who'd saved Mama's life. Then my head sagged and I toppled over on my back. I made an effort to keep my eyes open. As if through a fog, I saw the man's lips move but no sound came out, as if he were speaking in a silent movie. Beyond his face, at the top of a long pole, a rectangle of pale blue cloth was undulating in the breeze. On the blue background, in white, were two olive branches cradling and supporting a number of concentric circles on which were depicted all the continents of our planet. Higher still was the sky, an immense blue sky. Then nothing more.

Chapter Thirteen

Johnny, Known as Mad Dog

We had to hurry, so I took over the wheel from Lovelita. Sitting next to me, she watched everything elatedly. She was no longer afraid, and even felt a certain pleasure at being able to participate in our operation. Here was something that Giap really ought to see. If we were tribalists, would we have had a Mayi-Dogo chick with us? I came up with a neat idea—took off my cap and put it on Lovelita's head, over her red bandanna.

"Now you're a member of the Roaring Tigers!" I announced solemnly in a loud voice, so that Piston, Little Pepper, and Stud could hear me clearly. She smiled and adjusted the brim of the cap. I gave her a sideways glance. The cap suited her—she looked like a real fighter, and a *très* sexy fighter at that. If I wasn't a respecter of women, I would have fucked her on the spot, right there in the car, despite the fact that we were on an official mission and despite the perpetual ogling of Stud, who never took his prying eyes off us. No, I respect women, and Lovelita wasn't the sort you'd take for a quick lay, like some low-class call girl. She was a woman you had to honor at such intimate moments. But one thing was beyond doubt: the Roaring Tigers weren't tribalists. Didn't we have a Mayi-Dogo fighting in our ranks?

We drove back along the avenue at top speed to rejoin the rest of the unit and then head all together toward the embassy compounds. Giap had told us to use whatever means were necessary to prevent the refugees from the Huambo district from seeking refuge there. I don't know where Giap had got his information, but all the people we passed as we drove were running in the opposite direction, the one we were coming from. Some of them still carried a ridiculous array of possessions, while others were fleeing empty-handed.

"Look!" Lovelita cried suddenly, pointing ahead and a bit to the right. When we looked in that direction all of us burst out laughing, the scene was so absurd. A man—panting for breath, his shirt drenched in sweat—was struggling through the sand, trying to push a bicycle that had two flat tires. There wouldn't have been any difficulty if he'd had only the bicycle to contend with. The problem was that attached to the bike, firmly lashed to the luggage rack, was a big fat pig which was nothing but a dead weight. And that wasn't all: a demijohn of palm wine was hanging from the horizontal bar of the bike's frame, secured with lengths of creeper.

"Oh, look at that! Stop, Mad Dog, stop!"

I might have known—it was Piston who was now shouting and gesticulating behind me. He could never pass up a bit of pork. In his village, pork with bananas was the favorite dish of the menfolk. Furthermore, before getting married, a suitor had to prove his worth to his girl's family by bringing them a pig—and not just any pig, but a stolen pig. Piston's eyes were bright with greed. Hardly had I stepped on the brake when, quick as a squirrel, he leaped from the car and ran over to the bicycle. Obviously, the violent blow recently inflicted on his bald head had done no lasting damage and had failed to curb his aggressiveness.

"Hey, you! Gimme that pig!"

"It isn't mine—I'm just transporting it," the man pleaded. "I'm being paid to deliver it to someone on Lumumba Street."

"I don't care," Piston snapped. "Give it to me."

While Piston was speaking with the man, Little Pepper had noiselessly come up to the bike. Supporting the demijohn carefully with one hand to prevent it from falling and breaking, he cut the creepers that attached it to the frame. He stuck his knife back in his belt and, without a word, hoisted the large bottle on his shoulder, walked away, and put it calmly in the car. Lovelita and I watched him, vastly amused. Even Piston had temporarily forgotten his pig and was admiring the finesse of Little Pepper, who didn't give a damn about pigs. If offered a choice between a plate of pork with bananas and a plate of salted fish—preferably cod, lightly braised—he wouldn't have hesitated for an instant. With a bit of pepper, the little red pepper that burned your mouth as soon as it touched your tongue, and a small piece of cod, he could polish off a large helping of cassava and would even ask for more. That was actually how he'd come by his *nom de guerre*, Little Pepper. But I never knew he liked palm wine so much that he'd steal an entire demijohn.

Piston brought his gaze back to the man with the bicycle.

"So, are you going to untie that pig?"

The man looked at him stupidly.

"But what am I going to say to the owner? He'll take me for a thief! He'll make me pay him back, and I don't have any money—"

Piston raised his gun and pointed it at him. As soon as he

saw the weapon aimed at his chest, the man immediately let go of the bicycle and raised his hands in the air. The bike crashed to the ground and the animal squealed loudly from the impact. Piston bent over and untied the pig. He took hold of it and, with a clean-and-jerk worthy of an Olympic weight lifter, hoisted the animal onto his shoulders and walked back to the car with a triumphant air. "Bravo!" cried Lovelita. He quivered with pride and pleasure. If he'd been in his native village, he would certainly have won a bride.

The man with the bicycle, standing there dumbfounded, watched him walk away and kept repeating like an idiot, wild-eyed: "What am I going to tell the owner?" The dumb shit. He was still speaking of owners and private property—in front of us, the rulers of the world. Why were we holding guns in our hands, if it wasn't to have everything we wanted? He should have been glad we were letting him live.

Now we had to step on it, since we'd lost a lot of time. I didn't want Giap to start wondering where I was and realize that I hadn't yet arrived at the embassy district. We couldn't make any more stops. I floored the accelerator.

"Oh, look at the radio, honey! I want that radio!"

Lovelita, my girl. Lovelita, my love. The wife of a leader can have whatever she wants—you can't refuse her anything. This would be her first bit of war loot. Squeal of brakes. But I'd been preoccupied with my thoughts and hadn't noticed any radio.

"Back up," she said.

I threw the car into reverse and backtracked along the street. Yeah, it was some radio! A big one, with speakers that gave out a booming bass. I didn't know how I could have missed seeing the guy. He was young—one of those Chechen elements, without a doubt—but I was puzzled by the fact that although he had no gun, he wasn't the slightest bit afraid. He was striding along, swaying and bobbing in time to the music, which was amplified by the boosters.

"Hey, kid!" I shouted. "Gimme your radio!"

He looked at me as if I were a pile of dog shit and went right on past, swinging his shoulders and snapping his fingers to the rap song he was listening to. That wasn't normal. I honked the horn loudly. He turned around and stopped. Looking me straight in the eye, he turned up the volume on his ghetto blaster, set it on the ground, and began to swivel his hips and jump around to the rap song. For a moment, I didn't know what to do. Usually, when I didn't know what to do in a particular situation, I'd shoot. But this wasn't by any means a usual situation. It was easy to kill a guy when he was afraid. But this guy? He stared straight at you, looked you right in the eye, didn't give a damn. I felt Lovelita shiver.

"Let's get out of here!" she cried. "It's a devil! Some of the refugees are ghosts, spirits—people who are already dead. The Mayi-Dogos are like that—they're all sorcerers. I don't want his radio anymore. Let's go!"

I heard mounting fear in her voice. And I must admit that after her words, I, too, began to feel uneasy. A normal guy couldn't have managed such contortions. He writhed and twisted; his head would disappear entirely between his shoulders, then suddenly pop out on a neck longer than a heron's; the next instant he was lying huddled on the ground; then he would leap up like a jack-in-the-box, his limbs all going in separate directions, and when they reconnected they formed a shape that was only outwardly human. This was definitely no human being! No one could ever break-dance like that. And he kept shouting the words of the rap songs the whole time he was gyrating so weirdly.

I almost panicked when I realized that none of the fetishes I was wearing could help me in such a situation—that is, in a duel with the undead. I had gleaming bits of mirror to deflect bullets, I had a fetish that could make me invisible, I had plenty of other things to protect me—but I had nothing, absolutely nothing, to ward off a demon. Incredibly stupid of me, especially since I knew that the Mayi-Dogos were the greatest sorcerers and fetish makers in our country. But maybe the pieces of mirror on my T-shirt would blind those owl-eyes of his and drive him away. Or maybe my red cord . . . I touched the strip of red raffia that I'd tied around my upper arm. It reassured me a little. I reached for the Uzi, and as I did so I heard Stud say urgently behind me:

"Those undead, the ones like him—you have to kill them with a knife. If you try to shoot one, the bullets will be absorbed into its boneless body and someone you're fond of—your father, mother, brother, or girlfriend, for example—will feel a sudden pain in exactly the same place where the bullet hit the phantom, and that person will die instead. There's only one way to kill them: by stabbing them in the heart."

I lowered the gun and cast a sideways glance at Stud. He'd pulled the two red parrot feathers out of his cap and was pressing them feverishly between his fingers. Little Pepper, hearing Stud's thoughts on the matter, had unsheathed his knife and was offering it to me. Who asked him to do that? The asshole was putting me in a difficult situation: either act like a leader and take the knife—or don't, and lose face in front of Lovelita. I began to sweat. The guy continued to jump around to the jerky rhythms of the rap music. I had to do something. It was Lovelita who saved me. Knowing the evil power of her tribespeople, she begged me to get going. I seized the opportunity, and pushing away Little Pepper's knife I said with all the wiles of a true leader:

"This phony human takes us for idiots. He thinks Mad Dog and his team are going to swallow his line and fall into his trap. The best way to throw him off balance is to ignore him. Come on, let's go. He'll understand that we . . ."

My cell phone rang. I pushed the talk button.

"Turf?" the receiver crackled impatiently.

I didn't want to answer until I'd finished my sentence.

". . . don't have time to waste on shit-heads like him."

And I stepped on the gas.

"Turf, are you calling me a shit-head?"

Giap! He'd heard me.

"No, no—not at all, sir. I was talking about a Chechen dead guy—undead, I mean—who thought he could trick us. I was speaking to the men in my unit."

"Undead? You talking crap to me about goblins? Listen, don't fuck around with me. Where are you?"

"Almost at the embassy district."

"*Almost?*" he shouted. "You're not there yet? What the hell have you been doing all this time? You a snail or something? Good thing I told Idi Amin and his unit to get over there, too—I think they've already arrived. If it was up to you, the whole country would've taken refuge in the Western embassies by now. And the Chechens with them!"

"No problem, Giap—I swear! I'll be there in five minutes. Less than five minutes!"

"You'd better! Come on, move your ass! Can't believe it—dragging your feet like a slug. Over and out."

"Giap! Giap! Don't hang up yet! I've got something important to tell you!"

"What?" he barked.

"Well, it's . . . I mean . . . it's just that Matiti Mabé . . . Turf . . . I'm done with those names. I've decided to call myself Mad Dog."

"What?" he guffawed.

"From now on, my name is MAD DOG!" I practically shrieked.

"Okay, okay. Grrrr! Woof-woof! I'm scared shitless of those fangs."

And he hung up.

I looked at Lovelita out of the corner of my eye, hoping she hadn't heard Giap's last onomatopoetic words. Apparently not. And the other two hadn't heard him, either—Kalashnikovs in hand, leaning out of the car's broken windows, they were surveying the crowd. I gave a final glance in the rearview mirror. With impossible agility, the man with the ghetto blaster was continuing to fling his arms, legs, and head in all directions like the loose pieces of a disjointed puppet. Then, focusing my thoughts on the nature of my mission—to prevent people from taking refuge in the embassies of the Western nations—I put the pedal to the floor.

Chapter Fourteen

Laokolé

The stars had come loose from the sky and were floating in space, chaotic and unfettered, dappling the shadows with myriad pulsating lights. Or could it have been a swarm of fireflies making those glowing, flickering sparks in the nighttime fog? Silence. I couldn't hear a thing. Then I picked up a sound. First a distant rustling, as when two angels cross paths and their wings brush against each other. Then the sound of the stars. Finally those indistinct noises changed little by little into sounds that my memory recognized. I was in the marketplace of my home district, the great marketplace of Huambo. Amid the hubbub, I heard the sales patter of the merchants, the cries of the street peddlers, the wailing of hot, thirsty infants tied to their mother's backs in large pagnes, the disputes of the idlers. I could discern the odor of strong spices over the smell of rotting meat and fish that had been lying in the open too long, exposed to the sun's rays and the hairy feet of flies. I heard these things distinctly, but could see nothing. A damp coolness on my forehead. Eyelids heavy. I attempted to open them. With great effort, I succeeded. Everything was hazy and shifting. I closed them, then opened them again. The universe continued to pitch and toss for a moment, then stabilized as the mirage-like shapes moving around me became solid and distinct. But nothing looked familiar. This wasn't the marketplace; I wasn't sitting with Mama at her stall. Where was I? I felt as if I were emerging from a long, deep sleep. How did I come to be lying on this camp bed, and who was the woman bending over me with a kindly smile?

This couldn't possibly have been a marketplace, though it was filled with people and as noisy as a carnival. The crowd overflowed from the large room in which I'd awakened and spread across the enormous courtyard outside, under the sun. I couldn't have said whether there were two hundred, five hundred, or a thousand people. They were in every sort of position—standing, lying down, squatting on their heels, sitting on their backsides on the ground. The personnel in charge, greatly overburdened, could be identified by their clothing. People in blue berets were trying to bring some order to the confusion; they were asking new arrivals to line up and be registered before allowing them to settle in. Men and women wearing armbands emblazoned with a red cross were transporting the wounded on stretchers, setting up intravenous equipment, or tending to people who, like me, were lying on cots. With a sudden shock, I remembered.

"Mama! Fofo!"

"There—she's coming around," said the mouth of the woman bending over me.

I tried to stand, to get up from the camp bed. Her hands firmly restrained me. While she was holding me back, another woman arrived.

"Where am I? Where's my mother?"

"Easy, now," said the woman. "There's nothing to be afraid of. You're under our protection."

In her face I saw calmness, serenity, and what I can only describe as goodness—all of which immediately reassured me.

"My name is Tanisha," she continued. "What's yours?"

"Laokolé, but everyone just calls me Lao. Where is my mother?"

"Your mother's here?"

She turned her head and looked around as if trying to find Mama. Her braids followed the movement of her head with a slight delay. Two little iridescent points on her pierced earlobes drew one's eye to the only jewelry she wore. Her gaze again came to rest on me.

"You think she's here? Did you arrive together?"

"We all fled together," I said. "She could no longer walk—I was wheeling her in a wheelbarrow. At the last moment, someone came along to help me. Her leg is infected. It has to be treated, or she'll die of gangrene."

"If she's here, we'll find her. In any case—"

"Tanisha! Tanisha!" someone called in an urgent voice. "They've broken into the compound! They're threatening the refugees!"

"What!" she exclaimed. "But they have no right! They must be stopped!"

She sprang up, threw me a glance as if to apologize for leaving, and said hurriedly to the woman who was restraining me:

"Take care of her, Birgit—I'll be back!"

And out she went, raising a great whirlwind that made pagnes, bedclothes, and all the curtains in the room flutter in her wake.

Birgit asked one of her colleagues to register me. I gave my name, age, and address, and told them I'd fled with my little brother, Fofo—who had disappeared and was perhaps in this very place, lost in the crowd—and also with my mother, who was certainly here somewhere.

"There's nothing seriously wrong with you. You fainted when you arrived. Doubtless from exhaustion. Here, drink something. And then you'll be able to free up the cot."

Scarcely had she handed me a plastic cup when we heard shouts and a commotion outside. Birgit went immediately to find out what was going on. I followed, and through the window I saw a group of blue berets confronting a dozen militia fighters. Right away I recognized the group that had killed the boy on the road. Their leader was speaking. I think I heard them call him Mad Dog. He was no longer wearing a baseball cap turned backward, or dark glasses, but he still had the ammunition belts crisscrossed over his chest and the fetishes hanging around his neck. Now he was armed with two guns, one of which hung from his shoulder and rested on his right hip. I also recognized the fellow with the big red wig. The heartless girl who had kicked away the boy kneeling before her and begging for his life wasn't with them.

I couldn't hear much from where I was watching, but the discussion was obviously heated. At one point in the face-off, Mad Dog put on his dark glasses and aimed his gun at one of the blue berets. A moment later, he changed his mind and turned the muzzle toward Tanisha. She promptly leaped at Mad Dog and his gun like a raging panther, but one of the blue berets held her back. The dispute went on awhile, and then the militia fighters decided to leave. The crowd of refugees broke into spontaneous applause and began yelling insults at Mad Dog and his men, as a group of armed blue berets escorted them to the gate.

As soon as they'd left, Birgit and the other staff members hurried to join Tanisha and her companions. I watched them gesturing but couldn't understand what they said, so I left the window and returned to the camp bed to wait—worried, impatient, hoping their discussion wouldn't last too long, since the two women had to come back quickly if we were to begin looking for Mama before nightfall. The day was already waning. Perhaps these foreigners didn't know that here in the tropics there was almost no such thing as dusk—that we went from daylight to complete darkness, without transition, in a matter of minutes. My one consolation was knowing that the compound had electricity.

While waiting for them to come back, I took stock of my possessions. My bundle was there, and so was the leather bag I wore bandolier-style. Slipping my hand discreetly under my clothes, I verified that the little purse I'd fastened around my waist was still in place. Then I replayed all of the day's events in my head. Early that morning, along with thousands of other residents from our district, we'd fled the bombardments and the subsequent looting and killing by the soldiers and militias of the various factions battling for power. In the confusion of our flight, I'd lost my little brother, Fofo. With my mother, helpless in a wheelbarrow, I'd eventually found myself outside the fortified walls of the Western embassies, which had refused us their protection. A man had tried to climb over the wall of one of the compounds, but the embassy guards who were fending us off and the militias who were hunting us down had both begun shooting, at the man and at us. Panic, flight. Out of nowhere, a man had appeared and had helped me to get Mama and the wheelbarrow out of the line of fire. With luck on our side, we'd barely made it to this compound, which belonged to the UN and its High Commission for Refugees. I'd fainted on arrival, and when I'd regained consciousness the man and the wheelbarrow had disappeared.

At Birgit's request I repeated all of this when she returned, though I'd told the whole story to the agent who had registered me. When I'd finished the account I asked to see Tanisha, since her presence had reassured me and given me confidence, despite the fact that we'd spoken only briefly. Birgit said that Tanisha was the director of the center—she had to coordinate and supervise everything, and thus was extremely busy. Moreover, there was an immediate threat to the safety of the refugees, who were being hunted by rogue militias. At the moment, Tanisha was working with other UN and HCR representatives to contact the local authorities, or what remained of them. Birgit then told me that she herself was in charge of my case and that I could rely on her. She'd been in Africa for a long time, working in civil war situations, and had a lot of experience with problems like this. When she said she was Swedish, it took me a moment before I believed her. I thought all Swedish women were blond (I'd never met one before), but Birgit's hair was light brown. I then realized I'd been an idiot to use such absurd logic. An entire country can't be blond, just as an entire country can't be right-handed. Anyway, I hesitated only a few seconds—the warmth of her voice and her words quickly reassured me. When she asked me to come with her to the reception desk, I promptly followed her, my leather bandolier bag slung across my front.

*

The register contained no mention of a crippled woman in a wheelbarrow or a twelve-year-old boy named Fofo. Birgit told me not to get discouraged. "If she indeed came in with you, there's no way she could disappear without leaving some trace." She headed toward the emergency area and I went with her.

Just as we were entering the large tent that served as the

emergency ward, two stretcher bearers were coming out, carrying a body covered with a sheet. Already people were dying, I thought.

"How long have you been here?" Birgit asked them.

"Since the crowd of refugees came in this afternoon," answered one of them.

"Do you by any chance remember carrying or helping a crippled woman? She arrived in a wheelbarrow."

"I don't think so . . ." said one of the stretcher bearers, searching his memory.

"Crippled, did you say?" volunteered the other. "Both legs? Yeah . . . I think she died. We carried out the body of a crippled woman around midafternoon."

"No!" I cried. Birgit put her arm around my shoulders. I began to sob. She tried to calm me.

"There's no proof it was your mother. Only the list of the deceased can confirm that."

We went into the tent. If the compound had been a regular hospital, this would have been the intensive care unit. There were so many sick and wounded that many of them were lying on the bare ground. IV bottles and tubing were hanging here and there on improvised supports. The air was thick with the smell of disinfectant, along with the moans of adults and the wailing of children.

The first thing I recognized was the pagne. Then the kerchief on her head. "There she is!" I cried, and rushed to the far end of the tent. She was lying on the ground but at least had a cloth under her. No sign of the wheelbarrow. I immediately sat down beside her. To my great surprise, she was asleep, but I couldn't tell if it was a peaceful sleep. The marks of suffering were apparent on her face—lines, creases, dried tears. It was a face only barely illuminated by the few electric lights that had been hastily installed under the tent. Bare bulbs assigned the Herculean task of driving back the thick darkness that relentlessly encroached on the twenty meters of space between them. Mama was perspiring heavily in the heat. I gently raised her pagne to look at what remained of her legs; the wounded stump was obviously still infected, but I couldn't tell if the inflammation had worsened or not. As my gaze returned to her face, I saw a mosquito, swollen with blood but evidently not yet sated, land on her forehead and plunge its stinger into her skin. Furious, I crushed it with a light slap and it burst, spattering my palm with blood. Disgusting. Mama must have felt the slap, for she stirred slightly. But she didn't wake up.

Birgit arrived, accompanied by a doctor—a Frenchman, I think. He explained to Birgit that the woman had arrived in a wheelbarrow, aided by someone who hadn't left his name. She had been in a great deal of pain, so the doctor had given her a strong sedative to ease her suffering and help her sleep. She'd also been given an anti-inflammatory. For the moment, that was all he could do. The two of them went away and left me alone with her.

I took off Fofo's cap, which I'd been wearing all this time, and used it as a fan. And while I was fanning Mama, I thought of Fofo. How could a boy of twelve, deprived of everything, survive alone amid such chaos? I couldn't sit still—I had to get up, had to look for him. I immediately justified my decision by telling myself that Mama was now safely in the care of a large, well-known, highly respected international organization and one of its specialized branches, the HCR. So I could leave her to go in search of my little brother.

Outside the tent there was no electricity, but the moon's glow revealed that the courtyard was teeming with people, their features indistinguishable in the faint light. I could see isolated forms moving about, or groups silhouetted by the few scraps of light coming from candles and storm lanterns. In contrast, off toward the right were two brightly lit buildings with real walls and real roofs. They were the refuge of the white foreign nationals and their families, those who had been unable to reach the protection of their embassies or consulates in the general panic. I felt discouraged. I couldn't go around calling, "Fofo! Fofo!" through the compound, where so many sick and injured were sleeping and so many people were working. They'd think I was crazy. There was only one thing to do: wait for dawn. In the meantime, I had to go back and find the bundle I'd left by the camp bed when I'd gotten up to follow Birgit. Then I would return to Mama's side and watch over her. Early the next morning, at first light, I'd begin the search for Fofo.

Chapter Fifteen

Johnny, Known as Mad Dog

The area around the embassies was in chaos when we arrived. Clusters of people who had come to the various diplomatic missions were pounding ceaselessly on the gates, no doubt with the hope of seeing them magically open, despite the shots being fired from inside to dissuade them. Giap had been mistaken: the Western embassies had done our work for us—they'd shut their doors to our enemies, the people who were seeking refuge. So here we were, coming to the aid of our unexpected allies and likewise firing into the air to disperse the crowds and drive them back toward the Huambo district, which was now completely under our control. But our gunshots had the reverse effect. With a mass change of direction, the crowd turned to the east, fleeing toward the Kandahar district—a neighborhood that was largely Mayi-Dogo, a Chechen fiefdom.

Kandahar was the area Giap had assigned to Idi Amin. Under no circumstances could the people be allowed to flee there.

This would be a strategic mistake that that sicko Giap would never let me get away with, even if I still accomplished my primary mission of preventing the refugees from taking shelter in the foreign embassies. With half of my unit crammed into the 4×4 like sardines, I raced off to set up a roadblock on the main street leading into the Kandahar district. I hadn't gone three hundred meters when disaster struck: the gate to the enormous compound of the High Commission for Refugees swung open and, like a vacuum cleaner, sucked in children, women, and men—some of whom, despite the chaos, were still carrying bags in their arms, bundles on their heads, sacks on their backs. I even saw a few who were pushing wheelbarrows. They were shoving, bumping, trampling one another. Too bad for those who fell. I'd never seen anything like it before in my life, not even in a soccer stadium, not even the time the Brazilian team came to play in our city and there was a stampede that killed twenty-two people. When I die and am whisked off to heaven with the rest of the righteous, I hope the Good Lord will have better crowd control outside the Pearly Gates.

We jumped out of the vehicle. Clearing a path for ourselves with blows from our gun butts, we made our way to the gate and tried to close it. Impossible. Whenever we managed to move one of the two wings a few centimeters, it was immediately pushed back again, forcing us to give way like a dam yielding to the pressure of the water behind it. If we didn't do something to get the situation in hand, the wild mob would overrun us—would trample us to a pulp, including our family jewels. There was only one thing we could do to save our lives: start shooting. At first we merely fired into the air, but that didn't stop those people desperate for asylum. So then I fired squarely into the crowd, and immediately the rest of the unit followed my lead.

The people didn't understand right away what was happening. Driven by their urgent need, they continued to rush forward, trampling those who had been cut down by our bullets and were already lying on the ground. When the people up front finally realized what was going on, they tried to back up, but the ones behind them kept pressing ahead. I began to be seriously frightened—even though I had a machine gun in my hand! I'd always thought that power lay at the muzzle of a gun, that with a weapon you could do anything, you were master of the world. But here I could fire away, we could all fire away, and the people would still keep coming. I started to panic. Where was Idi Amin's unit, which Giap said he had posted here? In a few minutes, in a few seconds, we'd be underfoot, squashed like bugs. It was time to clear out . . .

All of a sudden, for no apparent reason, the crowd changed direction like a herd of sheep and headed off in the direction of Kandahar. Man! About time. With trembling hands, I wiped the sweat dripping from my brow and armpits. We'd won. We were the stronger. After all, we had the machine guns. But that wasn't the end of it. We still needed to chase away the people who'd managed to get into the compound. I immediately told the commandos to make a sweep through the courtyard and the buildings, and roust out the refugees.

At that moment, three people came out of one of the buildings and walked toward us: an Indian or Pakistani, and two whites. They were all wearing blue berets. They weren't carrying guns. The Indian or Pakistani—or maybe he was a Bangladeshi—seemed to be the leader, and he was extremely angry. He spoke very quickly, as if trying to confuse me. But since I'd been to school, I knew he was speaking English. Amid all the gobbledygook he was spewing out, I recognized the words "you," "international," "out," "refugee," "help," and especially "crime," which figured in nearly all the sentences he uttered. (I should mention in passing that I also know Spanish. For example, "I love you" is "*Te quiero mucho muchachita amor de mi corazón*," and "To dance the rhumba you have to look good" is "*Para bailar la bamba se necessita un poco de gracia.*" It was while listening to one of those Spanish songs that I'd picked up the beautiful name Lovelita.)

So by putting together and properly arranging all the English words I recognized, I understood he was trying to tell us that he was offering us his international help to chase out, expel from the compound, all of those refugees, who in fact were nothing but criminals. That was precisely what I wanted, so he had no reason to take such an angry tone with me. He could certainly speak in a calmer and more civilized way, especially since those two whites were observing us and might think that we Third Worlders—whether Indians, Bangladeshis, Congolese, Yemenites, or Uighurs—were uncivilized. But before I could explain to my commandos what he'd just said, one of the whites wearing a blue beret began to shout at us in French, one of the languages of our country:

"You have no right to come in here! This is the property of the United Nations, an international zone! You can't shoot unarmed people! You've committed a crime! We're going to write up a report!"

The guy hadn't even finished speaking when a woman appeared—so suddenly that it seemed she'd been blown toward us on the winds of a hurricane. She'd come out of a building that was flying the HCR's flag. And she was in a raging fury.

"You realize what you've done? Have you seen all those wounded? All the people you've killed for no reason? You're murderers! Criminals! How could you shoot at defenseless men and women? And children! Children—do you realize that? You're a disgrace to us! A disgrace to Africa and to all Africans! You have no right to be here—this is UN property! Get out!"

Taken aback, I stared at her. She wore her hair in something like dreadlocks, but fine, clean dreadlocks that swung freely as she shook her head in anger. No jewelry, except for two little earrings that would have gone unnoticed if they hadn't given out flashes of light with every movement of her head. I don't know why, but I thought she looked like Lovelita. Why was she so angry? And how dare she tell me—me, Mad Dog!—that I had no right to be there? Didn't she know that we'd won the war and that our leaders had assigned us the task of tracking down Chechens, wherever they might be? Hey, beautiful, I don't take orders from any chick!

"You can't order me to do anything, and I don't give a shit what you think, no matter how beautiful you are! This is my post, and I'm the commander of this unit. Beat it! Go back to the building you came from and let us do our work! If you don't—"

She interrupted me again:

"*You're* the ones who are going to beat it! You and your gang of killers!"

"We're UN staff—that's what our blue hats mean. You're in the compound of the High Commission for Refugees, and this lady is the director of this branch of the HCR, which shares the premises with us." One of the two whites said this very quickly, as if to take the words out of the fury's mouth and calm things down a bit. (He, at least, had realized that it wasn't smart to mess with me.) "It's our responsibility to protect the men and women who seek asylum here," he continued impassively. "In addition to the refugees, personnel from the International Monetary Fund, the World Bank, some charitable organizations, and various development projects have also taken shelter here. It's our job to protect them."

The problem for me was that up to now, my business had been solely with the Mayi-Dogos and their militia fighters, the Chechens. And here I was, trying to cope with foreigners, with an international organization, the UN, and last but not least with a woman who hadn't the slightest fear in her eyes. But since I was an intellectual, I knew what the UN was—yeah, I'd heard people speak about the organization and its soldiers. They were neutral. They didn't make war; they kept the peace. But when things got hot and their lives were threatened, or if they simply thought they were in danger, they took to their heels and left you all alone in the shit. That's what happened in Rwanda. So I decided to follow the same strategy—to threaten them, so they'd go away and leave us all in the shit, and then we could settle accounts with the Chechens.

I assumed my most commanding expression. I frowned and knit my brow, and with a menacing glare I put on my dark glasses, which I'd slipped into my pocket so I wouldn't lose them in the stampede. And I pointed my gun at the Bangladeshi leader. When you want to terrorize a village, you should always start by humiliating the leader.

"That's my last word," I said. "Go back to the buildings immediately, or we'll kill you, beginning with your commander."

To my great surprise they didn't run off, the way they had in Rwanda. On the contrary, their Pakistani leader began to shout in English—and even if you didn't understand a single word, it was crystal clear that the guy who was erupting like that was mad as hell. I was caught up short. I didn't have any backup plan, for it had never occurred to me that they wouldn't just turn tail and run. Maybe the Indian guy hadn't understood because I hadn't spoken in English? You know, to terrorize a village, you don't always have to humiliate or kill the leader. You have to begin by threatening the weakest, the women and children in particular. After that, the ones who are supposed to protect them, namely the leader and his men, will obey you pronto, for fear of seeing their precious little ones molested or their dear wives raped. A small arc, and the barrel of my Uzi was pointed at the woman from the HCR.

"This is my final warning. Go back to your buildings immediately, or I'll shoot the woman."

I shouldn't have said that.

"Get out of here!" she shouted.

With one bound she was practically on me, whether to hit me or grab my gun, I'm not sure. My god! Women these days are no longer women. She was restrained just in time by one of the white guys in a blue beret. She was trembling, not merely from anger but from uncontrollable rage.

"We may be wearing the blue hats of the UN, but that doesn't mean we're sitting ducks!" said the other blue beret. "We can defend ourselves, and we will! And we're not alone. Go ahead, shoot—we'll see if you get out of here alive!"

He didn't seem to be bluffing. With my attention focused on these four, I hadn't noticed that an entire operation had been mobilized. Blue berets armed with guns had appeared in the courtyard. I glanced toward the gate. They had managed to close it, and two jeeps emblazoned with the letters "UN" and sporting pale blue flags were posted there. One of them had a machine gun mounted on it, and the barrel was pointed in our direction. Even if Idi Amin and his commandos arrived, they wouldn't be able to help us. I glanced at the Bangladeshi leader. He didn't look like the weak-kneed type. He was saying something, but my mind was so preoccupied with the tight spot my commandos and I were stuck in that my brain couldn't recognize any of the words he was shouting in English. So I said:

"I'm going to call my commanding officer and tell him you refused to obey the forces of order and that you—"

"Who's your commander?" cried the Pakistani, and the sentence was translated immediately.

"Giap," I said. "General Giap. And he's a man who never kids around."

"Giap, my ass!" snorted one of the two whites, who no longer hid the fact that he, too, was angry. "You want to know the name of my grandfather who fought in Indochina? Ho Chi Minh!"

"Just get out!" yelled the Bangladeshi in English.

"Out!" cried the woman.

"We're going to arrest your superiors, and you'll be punished!" added Ho Chi Minh's grandson, who didn't look the slightest bit Chinese to me, though his grandfather had been a companion of Mao Tse-tung and must have been Asian. Maybe the guy was lying, or perhaps there was another Ho Chi Minh—a white European I'd never heard of. You never know. Whatever the case, now was not the time to reveal my ignorance. And besides, in life you have to know when to retreat, all the better to attack.

So I decided to return better prepared, with Giap, Idi Amin, and all the Mata Mata, to teach the UN's blue berets a lesson like the ones they'd been given in Somalia and Sierra Leone. And to accomplish this later, I had to beat a tactical retreat now, especially since more blue berets were approaching us in response to the Indian's orders. Without asking for my opinion, they escorted us firmly to the gate, with the machine gun on the jeep aimed at us as we walked. The entire crowd of refugees watched us in silence. There were a lot of them, and they seemed even more numerous if you counted the number of eyes that were fixed on us. I felt my skin burning from the heat of those gazes charged with hatred and fear. I was glad they weren't hurling laser beams—we would have been fried to a crisp. When they saw we were being shown to the gate, they began to yell, "Murderers!" "Thieves!" "Rapists!" and shouted cheers and other crude insults. Like the captain of a sinking ship, I was the last to leave. But even before the massive wings of the compound's gate had clanged shut behind me, I heard the crowd's applause and the cries of victory and joy.

Let them mark my words, those refugees, bandits, killers, tribalists, Mayi-Dogos: we'd be back, and we'd teach them a lesson they'd never forget! Let them mark my words well: we'd give them no quarter! No one humiliates the Roaring Tigers and gets away with it! If Giap had been here instead of me, they certainly wouldn't have done what they did. For that reason alone, my revenge would be all the more terrible. So much the worse for those UN employees, and so much the worse for that beautiful woman. She asked for it.

So we left. An eerie silence now filled the city, replacing the bedlam of grenades, Uzis, Kalashnikovs, and human cries. The silence was so profound you could have heard a flea fart. My commandos, too, were strangely quiet. I looked up and saw our 4×4 in the distance. Lovelita was still there, waiting for us. She was bobbing her head, *a priori* for no apparent reason, until the melody of a song—an incongruous, even unearthly sound in that ghostly silence—came drifting from the vehicle and reached our ears. I recognized the refrain and the voice. Lovelita was still listening to the tape of Mbilia Bel, and Mbilia Bel was taunting her ex:

Ozali ko loba que ngaï na bala te
E swi yo epaï wapi e

You tell everyone I'm not getting married.
So what? Why should you care?

It was beginning to get dark. Night would soon come. All of a sudden, I was ravenously hungry and dead tired. It had really been a long day.

Chapter Sixteen

Laokolé

It had really been a long day. I walked back to Mama's tent beneath a great big round moon. I'm very fond of the moon, especially when it's full. It looks like a large motherly eye watching over us, pouring out its smooth, milky light to calm our souls, which have become overheated from the violent solar eruptions of the daytime.

I thought I would collapse from fatigue and sleepiness as soon as I sat down next to Mama to begin my bedside vigil. But that wasn't what happened—quite the contrary. My mind went wandering about in all directions, caught up in the kaleidoscopic welter of experiences I'd had that day. One moment, there was an image of Mama in the wheelbarrow; next, an image of that young fruit-seller callously kicked away by the female commando before being shot; this immediately gave way to an image of the fellow wheeling a pig on his bicycle; which in turn yielded to the memory of the young man snagged on the barbed wire atop the embassy wall.

Then a different sort of image suddenly filled my head—a vision of the man who had appeared out of nowhere to seize the handles of Mama's wheelbarrow—and only then did my brain cease playing hopscotch. I tried to summon up his features, to remember the color of his clothing, to recollect if he'd worn a hat, if he'd had a beard. Nothing. I'd retained not a single specific trait of that person who had revived my hope when I was on the verge of letting myself fall into the black abyss of despair. How is it possible that I could recollect in minute detail all the scenes of cruelty I'd witnessed, even from afar, yet remember so little about a generous act that had such immense significance for me? Does this mean that evil leaves a deeper impression on our memory than good? It disturbed me even more to think that someday I might cross paths with the man without recognizing him, though I wanted so much to offer him something important in return for the life he had saved—to offer him the only thing in the world that could convey my profound gratitude: the word "thanks."

I must have fallen asleep without realizing it, for when Mama's groans awakened me, the sky was already beginning to brighten. The sedative had doubtless worn off long before—and if I knew her, she had surely done everything she could to avoid waking me, despite the pain in her infected leg. Actually, it wasn't even groans that had roused me but rather the sort of breathing—uneven, tense, controlled with an effort—that causes you to prick up your ears. The strain apparent in her face, the sweat glistening on her skin, the force with which she clenched her teeth—all showed how hard she was trying not to moan or cry out.

"Mama, I'm here!" I said, bending over to wipe her brow. She opened her eyes and looked at me, and the first thing she said was:

"Is Fofo with you?"

"Don't worry—he's here in the HCR compound. I'm going to speak with the doctors, and as soon as you're taken care of I'll go looking for him. Don't worry."

I got up and went to find a doctor. In a place like this, every case was urgent and there was no guarantee that anyone would be able to tend to Mama immediately. But I had to try, for I couldn't just sit there and watch her suffer so terribly. I had two great strokes of luck: not only was the first person I encountered the French doctor who had accompanied Birgit to Mama's bedside, but by some miracle he actually remembered me and my poor mother, despite the countless people he'd attended to since the day before.

"The woman in the wheelbarrow," he said. "Of course—how could anyone forget her? I'll come right away."

And he came immediately, with his disposable syringes and his little vials. He lifted the pagne that was draped over the stumps of her legs and examined the one that showed signs of gangrene. He frowned alarmingly and said:

"It's serious. The only solution is to amputate the stump. I don't know if we're set up yet to do surgery here. While waiting, we have to ease her pain. It's all we can do, for the moment."

He gave her an injection of what I think was morphine, and promised to come back as soon as he could. As he was turning to leave, I asked him if he knew where we could find our wheelbarrow.

"Yes, I told someone to put it over there, behind the tent, so it would be out of the way."

"Thank you, Doctor! And—forgive me—one more thing: I know you were very busy, but do you remember the man who brought Mama here in the wheelbarrow?"

"Not really. He didn't even give his name. Now that I think of it—yes, he mentioned that the woman was accompanied by her daughter, who had fainted on arrival and who was in the reception area. But your mother's condition was so urgent that we unfortunately didn't request any more information. Careless of us—but in all that confusion, there were many things we ought to have done and didn't."

"Could you describe the man? I'd very much like to find him, so I can thank him . . ."

"Honestly, I don't remember anything about him. Now I really must be going. I'll come back as soon as I can. Perhaps we can find some alternative remedy in the meantime, before the amputation."

Amputate a leg that had already been amputated. What would she have left? This was what I was thinking as the doctor walked away.

I dug around in our bundle of possessions and pulled out something to eat. Mama barely tasted the food but drank a good deal of water, which reminded me that the first thing I ought to do was replenish our stock of water, since we were down to our last few drops. The morphine soon began to take effect. The tension drained from Mama's face, and she gradually dropped off to sleep. The time had come to look for Fofo.

I went off in search of my little brother, taking along a plastic jug—which I tied to my back with a pagne, the way one carries a baby—in case I came across a source of water. I began, quite naturally, at the registration desk where Birgit had taken me the day before. Once again the UN workers looked through their lists of names, but there was no record of Fofo. I didn't know what else to do except crisscross the compound, look through the various rooms and tents, check the many clusters of people, make inquiries wherever I went. In the end, the camp wasn't as big as all that—within an hour, I had visited and revisited every inch of it. As I was walking past our abandoned wheelbarrow for the third time, I realized I had to face the truth: Fofo wasn't here. What was I going to tell Mama? For a long time, I sat by myself on the upturned body of the wheelbarrow so I could think. But think about what? I'd lost all hope.

I decided to fill the water jug before returning to Mama. There was a crowd around the two faucets that dispensed water for the camp. Things would have moved much more quickly if everybody had lined up and taken their turn—first come, first served. But if you'd expected that, you obviously didn't know my countrymen. No one was willing to yield to anyone else, so there was a general free-for-all in which only the biggest and strongest could get near the faucets. Our solidarity as refugees melted away before a few drops of water. Well, war is war. Mind your manners and you're dead. I untied the jug from my back, knotted my pagne tightly around my hips (just as I used to do when there'd been fights outside the schoolyard, often over trivial things), and waded into the melee.

I shoved, pulled, and stepped on people; I was shoved, pulled, and stepped on in turn. If anyone had bitten me, I would have bitten back. A woman stuck out her foot and tripped me; I got up immediately and gave her a jab in the ribs with my elbow. "Help!" she cried. "I'm dying!" A man was furious when I got ahead of him by shouldering him aside. "Cunt!" he yelled at me. "Asshole!" I shouted back, and thrust my jug under the spigot. I'd done it! I filled my jug to the brim and left the fray. Whew, it had been worse than a rugby match. I wasn't eager to repeat the experience.

I balanced the jug on my head, and as I turned to go I noticed a frail, elderly woman holding a five-liter plastic container in her unsteady hands and gazing hopelessly at the scuffling crowd. The old woman hadn't the slightest chance of getting near the faucets. I thought of my mother, who probably wouldn't have gotten any water either, if I hadn't been there. I lowered the jug from my head and set it down next to the old woman. I took her five-liter container, and with the determination of an American football player I again plunged into the scrimmage.

The second time was more difficult than the first, and when I finally emerged my clothes were soaked. She looked at me without speaking. I placed her jug on her head before doing the same with my own, and then I walked away as fast as I could. She still hadn't said a word, but I saw tears running down her cheeks.

I'd scarcely gone ten meters when I stopped in my tracks. No—it couldn't be! I must be dreaming! It was a vision, a ghost! But yes, it was really her—it was Mélanie! Mélanie my classmate, Mélanie my best friend! Mélanie who I'd thought was dead, killed, murdered in her car with her entire family!

She saw me at the same moment, and ran toward me. She had a small, one-liter bottle of water, which she dropped when she opened her arms and fell into mine—which I'd already opened wide to embrace her, after quickly setting down the jug I was carrying. Both of us broke into sobs.

When we'd calmed down, Mélanie helped to balance the jug on my head again, and decided to accompany me to Mama's bedside. In any case, she wanted to stay with me because she was all alone, lost, and knew no one else here. She was not only my friend—now she was my sister. I had never seen her in such a voluble state. She talked incessantly as we walked along, and never even paused to listen when I replied to her questions. It seemed as if long-repressed words had suddenly torn open the locks of her memory and were surging out like water through a dam that had burst in the face of a torrent.

"Yes, I have a vague recollection of seeing a wheelbarrow in the crowd when we passed—but it never occurred to me that it might be you transporting your mother! The first gunshots caught us by surprise. Papa braked suddenly and tried to turn the car around. A bullet hit him. He cried, 'Aaah!' and slumped over the steering wheel. The car jolted forward and then stalled. Mama cried out his name, and at that moment a second bullet struck my sister. My grandmother, who was sitting next to her, screamed and automatically threw herself on top of her. Suddenly, there we were, like prisoners in a sardine tin. And then Mama leaned back, opened the door on my side, and gave me a push, shouting, 'Run! Run!' I fell hard on the ground"—Mélanie showed me the bruises—"just as Grandma, too, cried out. All I could think of was what my mother had said: 'Run! Run!' I picked myself up and began to run. I ran and ran, until I noticed there were no more gunshots. When I came to a stop, I no longer knew where I was, since I'd been swept along in the chaos. I wanted to retrace my steps and get back to the car, but then a second wave of panic seized the crowd. When everyone stopped running, I found myself at the HCR, and have been in the compound since yesterday. My parents are dead, my grandmother is dead, my brother and sister are dead. I have no one. I *am* no one."

She wept with great racking sobs, hiccuping and sniffling. Mélanie, the girl who had been so full of confidence, whose future had been so bright, who had wanted to become a judge like her mother or a doctor like her father or a famous journalist like Tanya Toyo—my friend Mélanie was there before me, fragile, shaken, uncertain. Once again I set down my jug of water and took her in my arms, so that the warmth of my affection could envelop her and penetrate deep into her heart.

Just then, Tanisha walked by. When she caught sight of the two young women weeping in each other's arms, she ran to us, worried, leaving behind the person who was with her.

"I know you—you're Laokolé. What's the matter?"

I gestured toward Mélanie.

"This is Mélanie, my classmate and my best friend. We've just found each other by accident. Her parents were killed, along with her grandmother, her brother, and her sister. She's all alone."

"Poor child!" said Tanisha. She stroked Mélanie's cheek. "Don't worry—we'll take care of you."

"I'd like it if she could stay with me," I said. "She has no one else."

"Of course—I, too, think that would be best. Birgit tells me you've located your mother. Is that true?"

"Yes, thanks!"

A woman with short blond hair came up to us—the one Tanisha had left behind when she ran toward Mélanie and me.

"This is Katelijne, a journalist from Belgium," said Tanisha. She explained to the woman who we were.

"Hello," said Katelijne. "May I interview them?" she asked Tanisha.

"You'll have to ask them."

"I'd like to interview you," said Katelijne, turning to us. "I'd like to give a face to the suffering and misery I see here. This is really important."

Mélanie and I looked at each other, then nodded.

"Thank you! I'll go fetch my cameraman."

And off she went. Tanisha stayed with us a moment longer. She assured us that although there were still a few security problems to be worked out, she hoped to be able to distribute some food to us that evening. She left with a promise to come by and visit Mama. Her presence had comforted me. I appreciated it even more because I knew she was overwhelmed by the hundreds of people in the compound, yet she still gave me personal attention. A boundless generosity flowed from her entire being.

I stood and watched her go, the way a little child watches its mother go. And as soon as she disappeared in the distance, a phrase she'd uttered—which I hadn't noticed at the time—came back and struck me with all its force. She'd said she hoped to be able to distribute some food to us that evening. All of a sudden, I felt small, diminished. Never had it occurred to me that someday I'd be standing around idle, waiting for handouts like a beggar. We had always earned our daily bread through our labor. Papa had fed us with the aid of his ruler, his trowel, his T-square, and his level, tools that he'd used to build houses and walls, septic systems and flagstone terraces. Mama, for her part, had gone to her stall in the market every morning, and nothing had stopped her—not the humid heat of the rainy season, or the endless downpours, or the chill of the dry season. They had to work so that the family could be fed, and we all pitched in, even as kids. On days when there was no school, or after school was out, I would go help my father wherever he was working, while Fofo would lend a hand around the house. If it happened that one day there wasn't anything to eat—well, so what! Some citronella with a bit of sugar or honey would tide us over till the next day. It was out of the question that we would beg for anything from anybody. And here I was, waiting around for someone to give me food! I wasn't sure I'd have the courage to accept.

I bent down to pick up the water jug, but Mélanie insisted on carrying it, and so I helped her balance it on her head. Once again we set off toward the tent. When we got there, Mama was already awake and was sitting up on her mat.

"Mélanie, my child!" she exclaimed as soon as she saw us, a smile lighting up her features.

No doubt about it—she was happy to see Mélanie. At last, a familiar face in this human wilderness! Mama knew her well, since Mélanie had often come by to pick me up so we could go to her house and do our math homework together. And I'd taken advantage of those visits to watch programs on their color TV and see Tanya Toyo present the daily news. Sometimes, too, Mélanie would accompany her father when he gave Papa and me a lift home after a day spent working on their property.

Mama seemed to be feeling less pain now—the sedative was evidently still working.

"Where is Fofo?" she asked, after greeting Mélanie.

"I haven't yet found him, but I'll keep looking. There are so many people in the compound!"

"Fofo is here, too?" said Mélanie. "We'll look for him together!"

Deep down, I was sure that Fofo wasn't in the camp. If he had been, I would have come across him during the methodical search I'd just made. But I couldn't have said that to Mama—she was in enough pain as it was.

The Belgian journalist and a cameraman arrived while Mélanie was telling Mama everything that had happened to her since she'd fled with her parents. I remembered the woman's name, Katelijne, so I introduced her straightaway to Mama. She seemed quite moved and impressed at the sight of that crippled woman sitting on a mat on the ground, holding her spine so erect.

"The world is completely ignorant of the tragedy unfolding here. An appalling civil war that has caused nearly ten thousand deaths, half a million displaced persons and refugees, a humanitarian catastrophe—and not a single word in the American or European media. Obviously, this isn't Kosovo or Bosnia. Africa is far away, right? Who cares about Africa? Tantalum—okay. Oil, diamonds, hardwoods, gorillas—yes. But the people don't count. They're not whites, like us.

"We mustn't let this scandal continue, or let the arms dealers get richer and richer on the blood of Africans! It's a disgrace to all of humanity! We've got to bear witness! I want to interview you so the world can find out about the tragedy that's taking place here."

When people speak from the heart, there's something in their voice and expression that makes you feel their sincerity. That something was evident in the voice of this middle-aged woman. I listened to her closely, because I was learning many things I'd never suspected—for example, that the West valued our gorillas and oil more than it did our people, and also (I should have figured this out for myself, it was so obvious) that in killing one another, we were making the arms dealers rich. On the other hand, I couldn't see what the exploitation of diamonds had to do with the cruelty of that militia fighter Mad Dog, who had coldly shot a little kid kneeling in front of him and begging for his life, or how the looting of our country's mineral wealth related to the brutality of the soldier who had killed Papa and broken Mama's legs, or least of all how the silence of the Western media was responsible for the murderous pursuit of the Mayi-Dogos. I'd have to think long and hard about all that.

Katelijne began by having Mélanie speak. My friend gave a detailed account of her misfortunes. She got so wrapped up in her memories that she seemed to forget we were there. Katelijne didn't interrupt her with questions. But the cameraman kept moving around, trying every angle, shooting close-ups of Mélanie's beautiful face streaming with tears. When Mélanie had finished, Katelijne began interviewing me. Like my friend, I told my story—how we'd fled our home, how we'd encountered the militias, how Fofo had disappeared, how the embassies had refused to let us in, and how we'd wound up at the HCR center. At the end, she asked Mélanie and me to express our hopes for the future so that the whole world could hear about them in her film. Mélanie was silent. I said that it was impossible to have any hope in a country where the road to power was littered with corpses, where you were hunted down merely because you were a Mayi-Dogo, where children were murdered in cold blood. Katelijne looked at me, very troubled, and asked again:

"Isn't there anything you can envision for the future? A glimmer of hope?"

"Yes," I said at last. "If it weren't for this war, I'd be graduating from high school next week. I'm always fascinated when I see an abstract idea transmuted into visible reality—for example, when two perfectly perpendicular walls enable you to grasp the abstract beauty of a right angle, or when a mathematical expression is transformed into concrete reality, as when the equation $E = mc^2$ made it possible to convert nuclear mass into energy. The opposite fascinates me just as much—that is, when a bit of reality separates like a precious metal from the worthless ore surrounding it and is purified, to become something abstract and perfect. My father and I built perfectly vertical walls with the aid of a plumb line, and using a level I was able to make a perfect horizontal. Ever since, I've dreamed of becoming an engineer and constructing large buildings."

When I finished speaking, I saw that Katelijne and her cameraman were looking at me as if I'd come from another planet. I could hardly blame them. As if emerging from a dream, I wondered why I was saying all these things when here I was, weary and famished in a refugee camp with my poor helpless mother. Fortunately, the interview was coming to an end. But when the cameraman began folding up his tripod, Katelijne asked him to wait. Turning to me, she asked if she could interview Mama as well. I looked at Mama and could tell she was exhausted, so I said no. In any case, I explained, she couldn't add anything to my account, since we'd been through exactly the same experiences, which I'd already described.

"No, no!" said Katelijne. "It's not at all the same thing! If people could see your mother speak, the psychological impact would be enormous! Viewers always like strong images and emotions, you know. While your mother is speaking, we'll get a close-up of her haggard face. Then we'll pull back and focus on her in medium close-up for a moment, to show her sitting so fine and straight. Then we'll zoom in on her legs and end with a close-up of her stumps. It'll be dramatic! American journalists have a saying: 'When it bleeds, it leads.' In other words, the bloodier the image, the more visually compelling it is and the better it works. And when it comes to images, those stumps are unbeatable!"

At that, I almost lost my temper. Mama's stumps were *our* suffering, *our* pain. Katelijne saw them only as something that would attract the attention of an audience. Was she completely heartless? No, I don't think so—she simply lived in another universe. She didn't understand that poor people like us didn't make a display of our misery. We had the right to keep it private.

"No," I said firmly, "my mother's misfortune is not going to be turned into a spectacle."

Katelijne saw that I was displeased. She apologized and said she hadn't intended to make light of our suffering in any way. She thanked us, and before leaving she reminded us that her documentary would be shown on Belgian TV. That didn't give us a thrill, as it would have in the old days. Those insane militiamen might very well massacre us long before the broadcast.

As soon as Katelijne and the cameraman left, it occurred to me that this would be a good time to eat something, because Mama's pain was still under control and also because I was sure Mélanie hadn't eaten anything since the day before. I rummaged through our pack to find the food that remained. Tanisha had said that food would be distributed that evening. Despite my initial reluctance, I was hoping she'd keep her promise, since we had very little left. Mélanie suggested that we make a tour of the camp to see if there wasn't some sort of little market where we could buy something to eat. A good idea. Markets always sprang up spontaneously when there were communities of people, no matter what the circumstances. I'd already noticed this in our short-lived encampment before the embassy walls, and again near the spouts where I'd fought to fill my jug and where people were trying to sell the water they'd just obtained.

At first, Mama didn't want to eat anything more than a banana, but when Mélanie and I insisted, she agreed to eat a hard-boiled egg and a bit of bread.

All of a sudden, while I was eating, I felt a sharp pain in my lower belly. Oh, no—that was all I needed. I was getting my period, and it couldn't have come at a worse time. My cramps were always bad, especially during the couple of days before the bleeding started. Sometimes the pain was so severe that I was forced to lie still for hours. It was awful, because I couldn't go to school or help Papa with his work. Fortunately, Mama was able to make me an herb drink that not only soothed me but also took away the pain until my period arrived. I knew which plants she used, since she had taught me about them. She'd also taught me about many others, because, according to her, girls were better than boys at preserving a mother's knowledge, especially traditional lore passed down through the generations. But where in the camp could I find the plant I needed? If worse came to worst, I could endure forty-eight hours of physical pain, but I dreaded the way it would incapacitate me—I'd be stuck in one place, unable to move, unable to do anything to help Mama. I hoped we could stay in the compound at least until my period was over.

With the fingers of my left hand, I massaged the two spots that hurt, pressing hard. I was doing this when a visitor came by. It was Birgit, the only Swede I knew of who wasn't blond. She said she had come to fetch me—Tanisha wanted to see me right away, to discuss my mother's case and ask me some questions. Leaving Mama in Mélanie's care, I followed Birgit.

Chapter Seventeen

Laokolé

"Do you have any idea what's going on? There are women and children who have been here for more than ten hours, in need of everything, and you haven't helped them at all! It's unconscionable!"

"Calm down, sir. We're doing our best. A few hours ago, you weren't expecting to be here in an HCR refugee camp. Well, we weren't expecting you, either—we had no idea there'd be such masses of people coming through our gates. The good news is that a shipment of food was flown in this morning, and in a few hours, before nightfall, everyone will be fed. So please be patient. Meantime, we've at least been distributing bottled water."

"You think fresh water and sympathy are enough for people to survive in this hellhole?"

"Sir—you, your wife, and your children are lucky to have been granted the privilege. Other refugees haven't been so fortunate."

" 'Privilege'? No, madam—it's a right! And if by some stroke of ill luck we're still here when the food arrives, I'll make sure we're the first to be served."

Tanisha looked at him for a moment, and the fire I saw in her eyes indicated she was more than just annoyed—I thought she was going to give him a scorching reply. But she took a deep breath and kept her composure. Birgit and I had arrived at her office in the middle of the conversation, and we had no idea what they were talking about or why the three men in front of Tanisha were so angry.

"Pardon me, sir, but we at the HCR do not make distinctions among refugees. All are treated the same. Everyone is in an emergency situation."

"Don't be irresponsible! You intend to treat us like those people? We're foreign nationals, madam—high-ranking international officers, with our families. If this isn't enough for you, let me say that I'm head of the regional division of the nation's largest oil company and that I have unrestricted access to the country's president, or at least I did when this country had some semblance of a government. We're European citizens—some of us are even Americans. So show us some consideration! We're not begging for food like those people over there—because this food, this aid, comes from our own countries! It's been paid for by taxes on our citizens! So when I say that we've got priority, we indeed have priority, HCR or no HCR!"

He was extremely angry—his face was as red as a brick. Immediately his associate picked up where he'd left off.

"We must be evacuated! It's urgent! You say that you've contacted our embassies, but we've heard nothing so far."

"We've alerted the embassies of France and Belgium, and I'm sure they're in the process of negotiating with the present authorities for your evacuation. You must realize that the logistics are quite complicated. I've also informed the secretary general of the UN and the ambassador of my country."

"And your country is . . . ?"

"I'm an American."

"Ah," said the oil company executive. "I took you for an African."

"And how does that change things?" Tanisha wanted to know.

"Well, you can understand better than an African that our evacuation should be given top priority. We want nothing to do with the mess in this godforsaken country. If those tribes want to slaughter each other, we don't give a damn. We're not humanitarians."

These words succeeded in enraging Tanisha, who had thus far managed to stay calm. Her blood began to boil.

"You have no right to take that tone with me, sir! Keep it up and I'll throw you out of my office! You think I'm impressed that you're the regional director of the country's largest oil company? I couldn't care less! I have a lot more concern and respect for the other refugees than I do for you, if you want to know. So you don't give a damn about this country? As if that weren't obvious! Money, money, money! Oil, oil, oil! Diamonds, diamonds, diamonds! I never for a moment thought that a businessman like you was a humanitarian. Get out of here and let me do my job! I've contacted your diplomatic representatives and they're taking steps to save your precious hides, which are so much more valuable than those of the native people. That's all I can tell you. Allow me to get back to work!"

She nodded in the direction of the door, and her braids emphasized the movement of her head. The oil executive was incensed. The officer of the International Monetary Fund spoke sharply:

"What you say is racist, ma'am—discriminatory against whites! You can be sure we'll report this to the HCR administration and the consular authorities, and they'll hear about your unfriendly, uncooperative attitude as well! Believe me, you'll be disciplined and relieved of your position!"

"I'm trembling in my boots! The difference between you and me, gentlemen, is that I'm a kind person. Go tell your families not to worry—you'll be evacuated. When the tribes have stopped killing each other, you'll be able to return to this 'godforsaken country' to pump its oil and have fun drawing up pie-in-the-sky plans for economic restructuring!"

At that moment we heard gunshots, which ceased almost as soon as they'd begun. The three white foreigners immediately forgot their anger and hurried away. For a moment Tanisha looked weary, as if the confrontation had depleted her stores of energy. But she took a deep breath, shook her head (making her braids fly), and in a minute was her old dynamic self.

"Birgit, the food situation and the security situation are both seriously compromised. The leaders of the faction that apparently controls the city have given us an ultimatum: if we haven't driven the refugees from the compound by fifteen hundred hours sharp, they'll enter by force and there's no telling what will happen to employees of the UN and the HCR—they're accusing us of harboring criminals. The deadline is only three hours away. After numerous tries, I finally reached our supervisors at the HCR regional office—they assured me they were in the process of negotiating with the authorities, but I wonder what authorities those could be. There's no longer any government; there are only warlords. As for food supplies, the regional office also assured me that a convoy of trucks loaded with provisions had left the HCR's storage depot near the airport and was heading toward the compound. That was more than two hours ago and the convoy hasn't yet arrived, though the depot is only half an hour away. We have children here who are on the verge of starvation. It's maddening—all we can do is sit and wait! We're completely dependent on decisions made elsewhere. As if that weren't enough, all the foreign nationals are getting into a panic, as you've seen. They can't understand that the situation is difficult for everyone—they're convinced they have special privileges because they're white and because they're Westerners. Such arrogance! They think the whole world revolves around them!"

She leaned away from the desk, resting her long straight spine against the back of her chair.

"We're an international relief organization," said Birgit. "The Geneva conventions will protect us."

"Go tell that to those armed thugs! I repeat, Birgit—we're not dealing with a government. The warlords are in control."

"But who will protect these people if we don't?"

"That's the problem. The blue berets here aren't trained for armed combat—that's not their mission. Besides, Captain Iqbal has just informed me that the UN is planning to evacuate them. We've got to stay here, Birgit! Our presence is the only thing that can prevent the refugees from being massacred!"

It seemed to me she'd flung out these words as a desperate act of faith, in the teeth of a situation that she felt was slipping inexorably from her control. Then her gaze came to rest on me, as if she'd only just noticed I was there.

"Ah, Laokolé! I asked you to come so that you and I could discuss your mother's case. We thought we could perform an emergency operation with the equipment we had on hand, but at the moment things are becoming complicated. I don't know what to tell you."

I didn't answer, because I didn't know what to say. She looked at me, her face full of sadness. I thought the conversation was over, but as I made a movement to leave she stopped me.

"Katelijne, the Belgian journalist, was very impressed with you and your friend. So you want to become an engineer and build skyscrapers? Good for you! I, too, would like to be an engineer and build things, but in the field of the new communications technologies. I'm just coming to the end of a two-year stay in Africa that has taught me a great deal. I'm actually a doctor. After practicing for two years in the United States, I dropped everything and joined the Peace Corps, then the HCR. When I get back to the States, I want to set up a foundation or NGO that will build a satellite communications system for exchanging health services with Africa. That will be my contribution to the continent we all come from. Well, you'd better return to your mother now. The camp is being threatened—we're working to stave off a catastrophe."

Just as I was getting up to leave, a searing pain shot through my pelvis. I winced and clenched my teeth, but couldn't repress a small cry. I doubled over, my arms crossed over my belly.

"What's the matter?" asked Tanisha, jumping up from her chair. Birgit was already by my side.

"It's nothing. Just my period—always painful."

"Poor thing! I know how it is—I have the same problem."

She opened a drawer and took out a small bottle of pills.

"Here's some acetaminophen. It's an anti-inflammatory and analgesic. Take two tablets now—they'll make you feel better—and take two more whenever the pain gets bad."

She handed me a glass of water. I swallowed the two tablets and looked at the bottle.

"Thank you so much! I'm very grateful."

"Wait," she said.

She hunted around in another drawer and handed me a packet of twelve sanitary pads.

"Take these—you'll need them."

I didn't know how to thank her. Tanisha had become a mother to me. No, she was too young to be my mother—she was my big sister. Having left home without any supplies, I'd been intending to tear a pagne into strips and make pads out of it, with a bit of cotton.

"Here's a magazine, too. I've finished reading it, and it'll be a good antidote for boredom. Has lots of articles worth reading. You'll learn about Mae Jemison—she'll be an inspiration to you."

When you've thanked a person once, and then twice, the third time you're left with nothing to say, for the words "Thank you" seem to have lost their force and even their sincerity. I'd also learned that if you can't precisely express what you feel deep down, it's better not to say anything. I was silent, and tears welled up in my eyes. Tanisha hugged me.

"It's all right, Lao. Go back to your mother now, and I'll come to see you as soon as I can."

When I reached the door, I turned to look at those two women, the black American and the white Swede, and I mentally added the image of Katelijne the Belgian. Three women providing humanitarian aid in a camp in Central Africa. Three fragile beings who refused to stand idly by in the face of the world's indifference. Why were they doing this? Why had they come to risk their lives in this country, where the people were so stupid they could find nothing better to do than kill one another for the sake of power and prevent their own children from going to school? Obviously, Tanisha hadn't come seeking glory or personal gain, since she'd given up a prestigious and highly paid profession. How was it that despite the cruelty humans were capable of, there were still people who sacrificed themselves for others? To put this another way: given all the evil that human beings strive so hard to perpetrate, the good ought to have been driven out of existence. Yet it exists. Why? Who knows!

As I was hurrying through the camp to get back to Mama and Mélanie, gunfire broke out. I even heard the dull roar of heavy weapons. The camp was thrown into turmoil. People were running about and had ceased listening to the UN medical personnel and blue berets, who were appealing for calm. Near Mama's tent, I saw two people snatch their bags of IV solution from the hangers and rush away with them. I stuffed the bottle of acetaminophen into my pants pocket. Tanisha's other presents—the sanitary pads and the magazine—went into the large leather bag. Above the sound of the shooting I heard a droning noise, which grew steadily louder. I looked up.

Three helicopters appeared in the east, moving very rapidly. First they flew over the camp; then two of them landed near the buildings to our right, where the foreign nationals were being housed, while the third continued circling above our heads. Eight white soldiers jumped out of the two helicopters and took up defensive positions. Almost at the same time, intense gunfire erupted at the entrance to the camp, and then, with a deafening noise, the gate burst open and a tank followed by three huge military trucks rumbled into the compound. More white soldiers jumped out and headed for the buildings guarded by the helicopter troops. Out of the buildings came white men, their white wives, their white children. They were shouting in every Western language—French, Dutch, English, Portuguese . . . The soldiers loaded them into the enormous military transports. All of this happened very quickly—a real commando operation.

Soon hundreds of refugees were milling around the trucks, crying out to the soldiers, beseeching and imploring, often on their knees. Some were begging, "Don't go! Stay with us! Defend us, or they'll kill us!" Others were shouting, "Please, please, take us with you! Don't leave us! We'll be murdered!" I heard one man call out, "I've worked for your embassy for fifteen years! How can you abandon me and my family like this? Take us with you! Save us!" The trucks were completely surrounded, as if the refugees were capturing the foreign nationals and their rescuers and taking them hostage.

The wheelbarrow! We had to get ready. I ran to fetch it, and Mélanie followed. She stopped for a moment to look at the people the soldiers were loading into the transports. And we saw Katelijne moving toward the next-to-last vehicle.

Impulsively, Mélanie ran to her and caught her by the waist. "Katelijne, take me with you! Please don't leave me! They killed my father and mother, and my brother and sister—I'm all alone! They're going to kill me, too! Don't leave me! Take me with you, and I promise you can show me on television as often as you like!"

The two women gazed at each other. Katelijne didn't know what to do. She'd come to a halt, frozen in her tracks, and was stroking Mélanie's hair and cheeks. I saw Katelijne's lips move, but was too far away to hear what she was saying. I thought her eyes looked shiny. With tears?

The encounter was cut short. A soldier came up to them, roughly elbowed Mélanie away, and pushed Katelijne toward the truck. Mélanie caught her by the arm and Katelijne almost fell. At this, the soldier drove Mélanie away with a violent kick and shoved Katelijne into the transport. Mélanie fell. The three trucks began honking to clear a path through the crowd, but when the people didn't move aside the soldiers fired shots into the air and the vehicles began rolling forward. Too bad for the two people who were clinging to the fenders of the first vehicle. Mélanie ran after the truck Katelijne was riding in and managed to catch hold of it, but one of the soldiers gave her a blow on the fingers with the butt of his gun and forced her to let go. At the same moment, the third vehicle, following close behind, struck her full force and carried her along on its bumper for several meters. Then she fell under the immense wheels of the heavy military transport. It was horrible. I closed my eyes and screamed. I couldn't look—I couldn't look.

The vehicles picked up speed and headed for the gate. Wild with panic, not knowing what to do, the image of Mélanie's broken body seared into my brain, I ran to find my mother. I was interrupted before I could get very far. Soldiers from the helicopters, whom I recognized by their uniforms, were accompanying Tanisha toward one of the vehicles. I don't know how she spotted me in all the confusion.

"Lao!" she cried, running up to me and putting her hands on my shoulders. She spoke very quickly. "I had people looking for you everywhere—thought I'd never find you! I've appealed to the HCR authorities and they've agreed to let me take you along. Come with me—there's room!"

My head swam. To leave, to get out of this godforsaken country—this was the dream of every young person of my generation.

"Come on!" she begged. "I'll get you a scholarship, definitely! You can become an engineer. You've got a future!"

No, I couldn't go. I couldn't leave Mama by herself, or Fofo either.

One of the soldiers escorting Tanisha said, "We have to move quickly, ma'am—we absolutely have to take off in three minutes!"

"Lao, there's no time to hesitate! Come on!"

The soldier grabbed my arm and pulled me toward the helicopter. No, I didn't want to! I didn't want to leave the country if it meant leaving Mama and Fofo behind!

"Let me go!" I shouted. Since he didn't release my arm, I kicked him in the leg. He pushed me away angrily, and I fell. Tanisha looked at me with eyes full of sadness: "I understand, Lao." She dug around in her bag and handed me a card, then began walking mechanically toward the helicopter. A moment later, it was rising into the air.

I got to my feet and looked at the card I was holding. She had written down her home address, two phone numbers, and an e-mail address. I tucked the card securely into my pocket and once again set off in search of the wheelbarrow, to rescue my mother, whom I'd left all by herself. There was no doubt in my mind: we had to get out of the camp as fast as possible, now that there was nothing here to protect us.

For some reason the convoy with the white evacuees had halted suddenly just before reaching the gate. The last truck, the one that had hit Mélanie, was backing up at top speed, followed by the tank. Did the soldiers know they had run over a young woman? No. While I was watching them back up, someone behind me fell, probably because of all the pushing and shoving, and brought me down, too, just as the vehicles were passing us. As I got to my feet—infuriated, especially since I'd lost my cap—I was just in time to see the tank and the truck roll once more over Mélanie's shattered body, before coming to a stop in front of the second building.

Two soldiers got out of the truck, supporting a woman who was on the verge of hysteria. "My little one! My darling! I have to find him!" In the general confusion, the soldiers had no doubt forgotten to take her child, a baby who was probably sleeping blissfully in an improvised cradle. The three of them went into the building. They wasted no time, and came out again almost immediately. They were no longer supporting the woman, who was holding a little poodle, its curly coat neatly manicured. Escorted by the two armed soldiers, she walked out the door caressing the animal and murmuring, "There, there, don't be afraid, my precious! You're saved." When she reached the truck, the soldiers helped her get in, along with her dog. The vehicles took off like a shot, rolled over Mélanie's mangled body for the third time, and rejoined the others. Led by the tank, the three military transports and their white passengers left the HCR compound. They were saved.

Run to get the wheelbarrow. Find Mama. Lift her into it. Tie the large bundle firmly to my back. Sling my leather bag across my torso. Raise the handles of the wheelbarrow and push. Leave—flee with all possible speed from this camp which had become a trap, where no one and nothing remained to protect us.

I couldn't find the wheelbarrow! Yet I had put it there myself, after the interview with Katelijne. With growing alarm, I went through the entire large shed that had served as the camp's emergency center and that now looked like a ruined warehouse. Gone! Someone had borrowed it—no, someone had stolen it. My alarm turned to panic—a panic that had contrasting effects. On the one hand, it threw my mind into a state of extreme agitation just when I needed a cool head to cope with the situation; on the other, it paralyzed my body, impeding my movements just when I had to hurry as fast as possible to leave the compound. How could anyone have stolen the wheelbarrow of a poor crippled woman? Human beings had fallen really low, if they'd stoop to that. Well, you'd have to be completely naive to think that the world was good, that the world was beautiful. I was angry at myself for not having learned, despite all I'd been through, that faith in people was a fine thing, but it was even better to tie up your wheelbarrow the way a trader tethers his camel in the desert, though he knows there isn't a single other person for a thousand miles around.

My mind had calmed down, but not entirely; my body could move, but only slowly and hesitantly. I was a zombie when I finally rejoined Mama. I sat down heavily by her side while the rest of the camp seethed with activity, people rushing in all directions, commotion everywhere. She looked at me with questioning eyes. How could I tell her that our wheelbarrow had been stolen, and that if we were to flee the compound I'd have to carry her on my back?

Chapter Eighteen

Johnny, Known as Mad Dog

Obviously, things were more complicated than I thought. After those UN soldiers threw us out of the compound, I figured I could simply call Giap and explain the situation. Giap in turn would call our new head of state; the president would send troops to back us up; and in the blink of an eye we could empty the compound and at last root out the Chechens who were hiding among the refugees. Well, it didn't work out like that.

First, it wasn't easy to reach Giap. When I finally got hold of him, he told me to hang up and he'd call me back right away. A quarter of an hour later, he still hadn't called. I waited another ten minutes while my anger mounted. The asshole! What did he take me for? If he didn't get back to me in five minutes, *I* was damn well going to call *him* so he could hear what I had to say, and I wouldn't mince words! We couldn't stay here indefinitely, cooling our heels in front of the compound where those Mayi-Dogo killers were sitting around so peacefully . . . Five minutes passed . . . Okay, I was going to call him. I stepped away from the others so they couldn't overhear the conversation. I checked again to verify that five minutes had passed. They had—six whole minutes, in fact. I punched in the number but hung up before it rang; you should always give people a second chance. I would allow him five more minutes and then I was going to— My cell phone rang. I jumped and pressed the talk button. It was Giap.

He sounded preoccupied. He explained that the city had not been entirely pacified and that there were still pockets of strong resistance. It was thought that the Chechens had foreign mercenaries fighting with them and that the mercenaries' planes might even bomb the city. Our job was to surround the HCR camp to make sure that no one came out and, at the same time, that nothing—no food, no medicine—could get in.

My unit consisted of only about fifteen commandos. I didn't see how we could prevent armed men, like the UN soldiers I'd seen inside, from entering and leaving the compound whenever they pleased. I needed reinforcements. I told Giap that I hadn't seen anything of Idi Amin and his commandos, though he said he'd sent them to help us prevent people from taking refuge in the embassies. Giap replied that he couldn't reach Idi Amin—maybe the guy's phone was broken or the batteries were dead. Instead, he was going to tell Savimbi to leave the Sarajevo district and come to back us up. I would have preferred him to send Snake instead, but it made no difference. I didn't have anything against Savimbi. We'd been Mata Mata together in the old days, under the command of our great leader Giap.

I thanked him, and said that of course I'd be in charge of both units, mine and Savimbi's, and that he could rely on me—we'd keep the compound sealed as tight as a drum. Giap laughed. He said I hadn't understood a word he'd said. The blockade was of such strategic importance that it would be carried out by soldiers of the regular army, with the aid of heavy weapons. We'd be there only as adjunct forces. Still, our presence was important, since there were things we could do that the regulars couldn't. These last words eased my disappointment, but not completely. I hung up.

Yeah, the world was full of injustice. We'd shown our stuff by carrying out our assigned mission, and we'd taken the Huambo district without encountering any resistance. Then we'd been told to prevent people from taking refuge in the embassy compounds, and we had again been the first ones on the scene. And now they were laughing in our faces, telling us we weren't even capable of mounting a simple blockade. I was pissed off. There was nothing for us to do but spend the night here, out in the open, and wait for the army instead of routing out the enemy ourselves. I summoned all of the Roaring Tigers, including our new recruit, Lovelita.

"In cooperation with Giap, we're going to set up a blockade around the HCR compound to prevent anyone from entering or leaving. Food and medicine, too. Understood? The army is coming to lend us a hand."

"But you said we were going to punish those UN soldiers and their Pakistani leader for kicking us out," said Stud.

"They didn't kick us out," I said, annoyed because that shit-head Stud wanted to humiliate me in front of Lovelita.

I know what men are like, and seeing the way his bug-eyed gaze slithered over Lovelita's ass when she was walking ahead of him, I suspected he was feeling her up on the sly. I said in a firm voice:

"They didn't kick us out. It was I who decided to make a tactical retreat."

At that precise moment, Piston's pig—which I'd forgotten about—squealed loudly. I don't know why, but that squeal brought my irritation to a peak, and suddenly it occurred to me that the pig's filth was beginning to stink up my command vehicle.

"Piston, you've got to slaughter that animal!" I snapped, turning my gaze away from Stud.

"Not yet, Mad Dog!" Piston protested.

"And why not?"

"Well, because . . . because we're on a mission and . . . Let's wait till we have some bananas, so we can cook up a nice dish . . . And we need a good knife, because to kill a pig and do it right . . . you don't kill a pig the way you kill a man—that is, any old way . . . you have to do it properly, with respect . . ."

I'd had enough of his hemming and hawing. In a split second I'd reached the pig, whose legs were tied together. I dumped it on the ground and drew my pistol.

"Let's see if this doesn't do the job as well as a good knife!"

Blam! Blam! The creature gave an agonizing squeal, twitched two or three times, then lay still. No one said a word, but I sensed that Piston was angry. He would have murdered me if he could. But since he couldn't do anything, he stalked away, then came back after a few minutes, walking slowly and calmly. I was sorry for what I'd just done—I don't know why I'd taken it out on Piston and his stupid pig when it was Giap and Stud who'd gotten me so mad. But that's the way things are—life is unpredictable.

We all realized, at one and the same time, that we were hungry. To my great surprise, after we'd rummaged around in our packs and looked through everything we'd looted, we found we had nothing to eat. Night had already fallen but we couldn't go till morning without something in our stomachs, especially if we had to stay awake and keep watch.

"Let's take the car and go find something to eat," suggested Lovelita.

That seemed like a good idea to me, but I couldn't leave my post. I was the leader.

"Who wants to go with Lovelita?" I asked.

I was sure that Stud would volunteer, if only for the pleasure of being with Lovelita when I wasn't there. But no, he didn't react. He must have known that I'd refuse. So I picked two other commandos, one of whom was Piston.

*

They weren't gone very long. I don't know how Lovelita, who was at the wheel, managed during the trip, but they returned with cassava, roasted chicken, tins of sardines and corned beef, several baguettes of bread, and some bottles of beer. A real feast. We had such a good time that for a while we forgot we were on a combat mission. Sometimes war can be a real blast.

After drinking two bottles of beer, I remembered we had a demijohn of palm wine, courtesy of Little Pepper. Since we'd left it out in the heat all day, it had fermented and, as the connoisseurs say, had acquired "body." I helped myself from the bottle several times. I was feeling good. I put some music by Papa Wemba on the cassette player and grabbed Lovelita by the waist. She, too, was in a great mood. We danced together while the others clapped, and then everyone began to dance. After a while my bladder felt like it was going to burst, so I left them dancing and went off to take a leak. As I was pissing, I gazed up at the moon. It was big and round—the eye of a spy, of a Judas, scrutinizing the world. I've always distrusted the moon. It throws a smooth, deceptive light that conceals snakes in the grass and makes dogs howl. I prefer the fiery rays of the sun.

I rolled a joint and took some long, deep puffs. Matiti Mabé, poison weed. I felt the warm smoke fill my lungs, spread through my blood, rise to my brain, exploding it into a thousand pieces. And then the foul moon turned blue and I began walking on air. The wind lifted me as if on pigeon wings and set me down amid my commandos. They were all dancing and having fun. I took another deep drag on my joint and the night began to glow. I saw what the darkness had been hiding. I saw Stud's hands reaching out toward Lovelita's behind as she danced. I drew my pistol and aimed it at that son of a bitch, yelling, "Hands off my Lovelita, you asshole!" and I fired. The shot missed. I hurled myself at him, but he began to run. I couldn't see him anymore, because the sky had spit out all its stars, and these, dancing about chaotically, had made the darkness dazzlingly, blindingly bright—which didn't prevent me from firing several more shots in his general direction. I was furious.

The others had stopped dancing, and Lovelita came toward me. Lovelita, my darling. I ordered her to smoke the joint with me. She took a few puffs, and I drew her far away from their prying eyes, into the high grass. My thing had gone all stiff, and like a heat-seeking missile it set about probing my Lovelita's mouth. Then I turned her around, so she was on all fours. I pulled down her jeans and panties, which fell around her boots. Bending over her, I slid my hands upward along her sides and cupped her breasts, like two oranges, which I'd been sucking a moment before. An electric charge ran the length of my spine and spread through my entire being. Finally the head of my missile and its long shaft penetrated the silky moist tunnel she offered me, her hips slightly raised and angled back. With violent thrusts I took her again and again, until, driven mad by the spurt of steaming lava ejected from the Nyiragongo of my loins, she uttered a cry of pleasure—a scream more heartrending than that of Piston's pig—and sank her teeth into my forearm. I cried out, too, but from pain. The bitch! She'd probably bitten off some of my flesh in her cannibalistic orgasm. Utterly spent, the two of us collapsed on the grass.

I'm not sure why—perhaps it was the coolness of the night—but I awoke with a start. I was sweating profusely, trembling all over and racked with nausea. I thought it was the end. I was going to die. When I got up to take a piss, a knife-like pain pierced my lower belly, rose into my chest, and stifled me. The next moment I was vomiting onto the grass with such violent spasms that I thought I was going to throw up my guts. Then everything subsided. I felt fine.

It was like emerging from a fog. I saw Lovelita sprawled on the grass under the pale, sly moonlight. Why was her crotch exposed like that, her beige panties and her jeans pushed down around her ankles? Oh, yeah, I remembered—we'd been screwing. I hadn't raped her. You don't rape a woman you love, especially not on the grass. I woke her. She squatted on the grass to piss, then pulled up her panties and jeans, a bit unsteady on her feet. We walked back to the car, where the rest of the commandos were gathered. I checked the time—it was four in the morning.

If Giap could have seen them! They were snoring away in a sea of empty beer bottles, after their blowout of a feast. The demijohn of palm wine was also completely empty. Their guns were strewn on the ground. I'd heard people speak of "warrior's repose," but I had no idea it turned guys into such shitheads. Piston was the only one who was armed and keeping watch, sitting up against the car, puffing on a joint. The anger that rose in me was directed not only against the others but also against myself. I began to yell, kicking and swearing at those so-called soldiers.

"Idiots! You're lucky the Chechens didn't come by, or you'd all be dead! You're not worthy of the name Roaring Tigers!"

They came to without really understanding what I was saying. Some of them were yawning during my tirade. Others unzipped without embarrassment and, in front of Lovelita, took out their things and began to piss, staring dully at me like a bunch of cows. Finally, after much shouting and cursing, I managed to haul them into reality and got them lined up and standing at attention. I inspected them the way Giap inspected us, with his evil eyes, and I noticed that one member of the unit was missing. At first I thought I'd counted wrong, since there couldn't be a deserter in our ranks. I tallied them again in my head, and in fact we were one short.

"Where's Stud?" I snapped. He was probably guzzling palm wine somewhere, or maybe he was still knocked out by the weed he'd smoked.

They looked at me with surprise. Then one of them said:

"He took off because you tried to kill him last night."

It was my turn to be surprised. Me? Kill Stud? Why would I want to do that?

"You thought he was trying to grab Lovelita's behind."

From the fog of memory, the scene came back to me. A jealous commander chasing after one of his men and trying to kill him! I felt sheepish, confused. If Giap heard about it, he'd certainly think even more highly of Stud! What should I do? What should I say?

"He must be found and brought back! In any case, you're a sorry bunch. Piston is the only true soldier here—he was the only one who remained on guard with his weapon. The rest of you ought to be ashamed of yourselves! I have more respect for him than for all of you put together! As for Stud—"

"Piston couldn't sleep because he was so angry," said Little Pepper. "You killed his pig."

My god! Echoing through the mist in my head came the grunts and squeals of the pig. Yeah, I'd shot the animal. Why had I done that? Piston had never done me any harm or shown me any disrespect. It had been a stupid thing to do. Piston looked at me without saying anything, his eyes completely blank. If he'd at least been angry, I would have known how to react. I, in turn, gazed back at him like a fool.

The sound of approaching tanks rescued me from an awkward situation. The troops that Giap had told me about were arriving. I led the guys over to welcome them. Actually, they weren't tanks but a couple of light armored vehicles escorting two transports filled with soldiers. In any case, they weren't militia fighters like us, since they wore real uniforms and were better armed than we were.

The commanding officer stationed his men around the compound without consulting me. I went up to him to explain that they were intended to serve as reinforcements and not to take our place.

"And who are you?" he wanted to know.

I told him that we were the ones who'd pacified the area, that I was in charge of the unit, and that Giap was our commander.

"Who's Giap?" he asked curtly.

Unbelievable! He'd never heard of Giap? The leader who'd captured the radio station and who'd been promoted by our great commander-in-chief?

"Giap is the head of one of those militias," said his lieutenant.

"And where is he?"

"He's with the other militia leaders—they've all been summoned to the central office. I think the authorities are going to give them military titles to flatter them and win their loyalty, and at the same time let them know that although their commandos aren't prohibited from looting, the government would like to see them devote their main efforts to combat."

The army officer turned toward me. "Okay. Stay here—maybe we'll need you."

They finished taking up their positions, aiming their vehicles' guns at the front of the compound so they were ready to fire on anything that came through the gate.

The first humanitarian convoy arrived at about eight o'clock. Three trucks, each emblazoned with a large red cross. The soldiers stopped them and made everybody get out. The leaders of the convoy explained that they were bringing in emergency medicine and food for the refugees, but it didn't do any good. On the contrary, the soldiers gave them a hard time—searched the trucks for hidden weapons, took the sacks of rice and crates of canned food for themselves, and refused to let the convoy pass. The army guy, the one who'd never heard of Giap, said that the HCR had been given an ultimatum: if the refugees hadn't been evicted from the compound by 1500 hours on the dot, local time, the soldiers would enter by force. The head of the convoy told the soldiers they had to respect the Geneva conventions on the treatment of prisoners and refugees, but the army officer told him this wasn't an international war—it was a war being waged within a sovereign nation and as such was not the concern of the international community. After much arguing, the humanitarians decided to make an about-face without even trying to reclaim the sacks of rice that had been confiscated.

My brain, which always thinks more quickly than other people's, understood right away that this officer from the so-called regular army was going to keep everything for himself and his men. The guy was a fox, but I was smarter. While the trucks were maneuvering to turn around, I jumped into my command vehicle with several of my men and hurried to set up a blockade a hundred meters farther along the convoy's route. We made them get out at gunpoint and then we emptied the trucks of all the sacks of rice, all the boxes of powdered milk—every bit of food and medicine. We took not only the supplies but personal belongings. In this way I acquired a small but powerful shortwave radio with a broad range of frequencies. Little Pepper got a watch that showed local time and Greenwich time and had a stopwatch function. Unfortunately, the convoy personnel had little money. Still at gunpoint we let them leave, having stripped them of everything of value. We transferred our loot to a warehouse we found on the outskirts of Huambo. It took three or four trips with our vehicle under the direction of Lovelita, the only one I fully trusted. If nothing else, selling the food and medicine on the black market would bring us a fair amount of cash. The day had gotten off to a very good start.

*

"The situation here is desperate. We could be killed at any moment. Yesterday the compound was invaded by a band of trigger-happy militiamen who were high on drugs. They were hunting for us, out to slaughter us. Fortunately, we were hidden in a spot where they couldn't possibly have found us."

"Do you think the danger is over now?"

"No, madam—they were extremely angry when they left. I saw them threaten an HCR employee at gunpoint, and I think they killed her before leaving the compound.

Believe me, they'll come back. Our governments must move with all possible speed to save us. Think of the women and children who are being terrorized!"

"How many of you are there altogether?"

"About fifty, perhaps a few more."

"Thank you. That was one of the European hostages, joining us by telephone. You're listening to BBC Africa."

If I hadn't had the radio on, I never would have known there were Europeans among the refugees at the HCR center. Where were they hiding? How had the BBC journalist managed to get their phone number? When we went back into the compound with our reinforcements, the Roaring Tigers would make it their absolute top priority to find those Europeans before anyone else could. It was always good to have white hostages. The Western embassies would pressure the HCR to give up the refugees so that no harm would come to their citizens.

After the world news and the sports results, there was nothing more of interest. I flipped through the stations to see if I could find something else worth listening to but didn't turn up anything, so I switched off the radio. There was nothing left to do but wait for 1500 hours. According to our ultimatum, that was when the refugees would begin leaving the compound, evicted by the HCR in exchange for the lives of the Europeans. Our plan couldn't fail—the UN was bound to yield to pressure from the Western governments. Those governments attached greater importance to the lives of their citizens than our African governments attached to the lives of their own people. Giap was a genius to have thought of this! So we had more than two hours to wait.

* * *

We waited barely half an hour. Three combat helicopters appeared on the horizon, and before we had time to realize what was happening they had dive-bombed us, and our two armored vehicles were nothing but a mass of flames. An attack! We'd been attacked! Panic all around.

I threw myself into a ditch with Lovelita. Two soldiers with rocket launchers were cut down while they were trying frantically to aim their weapons at the helicopters. A third managed to fire a rocket but it missed the target, whereupon the brave fighter dropped his weapon and ran like hell for cover, along with his buddies. The two trucks were incinerated in turn. The three helicopters zigzagged once more above our heads, then headed toward the HCR compound. Two landed within the walls, while the third kept circling above the camp.

We'd heard that the Chechens were being aided by Israeli mercenaries; I now knew that in fact they were Serbs. You didn't have to be terribly smart to figure this out immediately. During the battle of Kisangani, in the last days of Mobutu's reign, the planes that bombed the city had been piloted by Serbs. We even saw them on TV. Since the same things produce the same effects, the conclusion was obvious: these couldn't be Israelis—they had to be Serbs from Kosovo. Whatever they were, the raid had taken our soldiers completely by surprise.

Scarcely had the helicopters completed their assault when we heard a rumbling sound behind us. Turning around, we saw a column of military vehicles approaching, led by a tank. The tank didn't give us a chance. It fired without warning on the fleeing soldiers, and then, swiveling the barrel of its gun toward my command vehicle, which had miraculously survived the aerial attack, it fired again. The vehicle exploded in a gigantic ball of flame! If Lovelita hadn't restrained me, I would have leaped from the ditch to confront the tanks. After all, a lone man *can* stop a tank—I'm not saying anything absurd here. I once saw an old documentary on TV about a Chinese guy who single-handedly stopped an entire column. But Lovelita protested so strongly and gave me such imploring looks that I decided to stay put. Anyway, the battle was too one-sided. They were better armed than we were, and three-fourths of our men had been killed in that brief but violent exchange. The tank continued without stopping; it forced open the gate and entered the HCR compound, followed by the convoy of trucks loaded with soldiers. A second tank remained in front of the gate, preventing my commandos from rushing out of their hiding places and mounting a counterattack.

I heard screams and gunfire coming from inside the compound, and in less than half an hour the trucks emerged with the white refugees. Then the helicopters flew off in the direction they'd come from. The operation had been extremely quick and highly effective. We hadn't managed to kill a single enemy soldier.

Chapter Nineteen

Laokolé

"What's the matter, Laokolé?"

My expression no doubt betrayed the countless fears and worries churning in my mind. She must have noticed the heaviness that slowed my movements and must have seen, from the way I sank down next to her, that I was bearing an additional burden, beyond my usual physical weight. We can't hide things from our mother for very long—whatever our age, she can see right through us. After all, she's the one who made us. So I decided to tell her the truth.

"Someone stole our wheelbarrow."

Brief as a flash, the glimmer I saw in her eyes was not at all a look of dismay—far from it. It was more like the barely noticeable expression you see in the eyes of people who've been wandering in the dark for ages and who finally glimpse the end of the tunnel leading out. It was a glimmer of hope or solace. As if she'd always known this moment would come and had already prepared her response to it, she reacted to my admission without a moment's hesitation.

"So what are you waiting for? Get up! Get out of here! Run!"

Though I wasn't completely surprised by this—since she'd been reluctant from the outset to come with us, and Fofo and I had had to use blackmail to get her into the wheelbarrow—her words still threw me off balance, and for a moment I was speechless. She pressed her advantage:

"I'm nothing but a dead weight. Don't worry—no one will harm a crippled old woman like me. Go on! Move! If you save your own life, you can also save Fofo. See—it's not just a question of you and me!"

While she was speaking, people were rushing by us, jostling one another, almost trampling us in the dust that was rising all around—the familiar scene of a crowd of refugees once again taking to the road. Of course, I was silent only for a moment. Reviving my determination, I immediately focused all of my mental energy on getting her to accept the fact that from now on my back would replace the lost wheelbarrow and that there was nothing more to say on this point. I knew I could carry her on my back. I didn't think she was terribly heavy—I'd borne much heavier loads working on construction sites with Papa. She might have slowed us down if she'd still had her legs, for they would have dangled at my sides and made it more difficult for me to keep my balance as I walked. But her two stumps were shorter than a child's legs, and she'd be no more of a bother than the large bundle I'd been carrying thus far in our flight. We had to act—talking was a waste of valuable time.

I got to my feet. I emptied more than half the bundle, and told her she was going to carry what remained of it. She didn't ask me why—quite the opposite. Quickly she offered her back so that I could position the bundle, and then she helped me tie it on. I understood perfectly why she was in such a hurry. She thought that, as a good daughter who always obeyed her parents, I was heeding her words and giving her a share of the provisions before making my escape. I don't know if all mothers are like this, but mine could not get it through her head that her child would refuse to abandon her.

I again slung my precious leather bag bandolier-style across my front, and automatically checked to make sure the purse hidden under my pants was still securely tied around my hips. The fateful moment had arrived.

"Mama," I said, "I'm going to carry you on my back. There's no point in discussing it. Climb up and let's get going. We've wasted enough time—the militias will be here soon."

I knelt down and bent over so she could climb onto my back.

"What?" she gasped, as if I'd made the most outrageous proposal ever uttered by a child in her mother's presence. "No—leave me here! I'd rather die than be carried on my daughter's back! Don't be stubborn, like a badly behaved child. Your mother is ordering you to flee without her—you must obey!"

Naturally I wasn't taken aback by these words, and had already prepared an unarguable response—the one Fofo had come up with when she'd refused to get into the wheelbarrow. But this time I deliberately and unfairly added a sting of cruelty.

"Fine," I said. "We'll both stay here. I know you know I won't leave without you, and your refusal is just a ruse to get me to stay with you because you don't want to die alone. Yeah, you don't want to die alone—you want us to be killed together. Okay, I'm staying. They can kill us both. The only difference is that they won't rape you, but they'll probably rape me before killing me."

It didn't work. She stared at me in astonishment and horror when she heard these words, then burst out angrily:

"How dare you speak to me like that, Lao! You're wicked—wicked! My god, what has the world come to, that I should hear such words come from my daughter's mouth! . . . She insults me! . . . You want to stay? All right, stay! I'll kill myself before they come, and you'll be my murderer! Keep watch over my body, if that's what you want! I'll be dead already, and won't be here to see you get raped!"

Frantically, she hitched herself away from me with the painful dragging movements of a legless cripple, accosting all the people in the tumult around us and calling on them to take her side.

"Look at her! Look at that girl—she wants to die! She wants to stay here! . . . She's my daughter, sir! Tell her to flee! If she doesn't, the militias will kill her! . . . You're a mother just like me, madam! I see you have your two children with you. Tell my idiot daughter to stop wasting time and to follow you out of here! . . . Miss, you're the same age she is! You're fleeing, but she wants to stay! Tell her she must go!"

Using her arms as supports and jerking her hips, off she went, now here, now there, ignoring her swollen stump, which was scraped raw from being dragged over the rough ground. She began to laugh. She shouted appeals to everyone who passed. A man hurrying by shoved her out of the way with his foot when she tried to hold on to the leg of his pants. She fell on her side and laughed. My mother was going mad!

A man with a bicycle paused when Mama dragged herself in front of him and blocked his path. I ran to him.

"Please, sir! I'll give you money! . . . Let my mother ride on your luggage rack. We have no way to get out of here!"

The frown of anger that darkened his face disappeared—a miracle brought about by the desire for gain.

"How much will you pay?"

"Five thousand," I said.

"No."

"Ten thousand!"

"Child, you don't understand the situation! Hauling this old lady will slow me down and might get me killed. I could do it, but not for ten thousand CFA francs."

"Please! You know that nobody in this crowd fled with much money! Fifteen thousand is all I've got. I need to keep some to buy food!"

"Give me the fifteen thousand and I'll take your mother. If not, too bad for you."

"You're heartless! You're taking everything we have!"

"So? Is it my fault you're here in this camp? Decide—quick. Either give me fifteen thousand francs, or I'm on my way."

"Life is beyond price," I said. "I'll give you the money. It's over there, where we were sitting," I added, pointing to Mama's mat.

Actually, I didn't want him to see me take the money out from under my clothes. I ran to the spot where our things were lying. Turning my back, I discreetly unzipped my pants, reached in for my purse, withdrew fifteen thousand from the forty thousand it contained, and zipped up again.

I ran back to the man and handed him three five-thousand-franc bills. He grabbed them and stuffed them in his pocket.

Mama was calmer now—her fit of hysteria had passed, and she'd realized I was negotiating with the man with the bicycle. I knelt beside her and hugged her.

"I love you, Mama! I was only trying to get a reaction from you, to persuade you to come with me. You're the most wonderful mother any child could have!"

"Dear Lao—you and Fofo are all I have left in the world!"

She didn't break down, but two large tears glistened on her cheeks. She was ready for the torment of a mode of travel even more uncomfortable than the wheelbarrow.

The man who had taken our fifteen thousand francs asked me to hold the bike while he untied his canvas suitcase from the luggage rack, which fortunately was about the same size as the passenger seat on a motor scooter. He lifted Mama and placed her sideways on the rack. She held tight to the bicycle seat. Since he obviously couldn't abandon his suitcase, he asked me to carry it. I went to repack the bundle I'd half-emptied for Mama and tied it to my back. I returned to the bicycle, lifted the suitcase, and balanced it on my head. All set—we were ready to leave.

He pushed the bike and its passenger as fast as he could, and I strove to follow as fast as *I* could. There was no pavement, and the sandy soil made walking difficult, especially for anyone like me who was carrying a double load—a bundle on my back and a suitcase on my head. Pushing the bicycle wasn't easy, either. I found myself admiring the man's strength, and my admiration almost turned to gratitude—gratitude for having saved Mama.

But reason prevailed over my emotions. He wasn't doing this out of the goodness of his heart, like the fellow who'd appeared out of nowhere to help me with the wheelbarrow near the embassies. He was doing it for the money. If he'd known I had forty thousand francs on me, he would have taken the entire sum. He was the type who'd bleed you dry. He'd said that transporting Mama would slow him down and put his life in danger. But he'd wound up agreeing to do it for fifteen thousand francs. I began to despise him for that—for having valued his life so cheaply: three five-thousand-franc bills. To me, life didn't have a price. If he'd demanded all the money I had in return for taking Mama, I would have given it to him.

Still, when I saw the sweat running down his brow and the care he took to avoid jostling Mama's infected thigh more than necessary as we hurried along, my heart reasoned differently from my head. We were in a situation that benefited both of us—I had no cause to despise him. Without my money, he certainly wouldn't have taken us. But without him, my money wouldn't have saved Mama. I at least owed him some respect.

Getting through the gate was the hardest part. The HCR center had been designed to accommodate a diplomatic mission, not a great crowd of refugees. The massive wall that protected the compound had only one exit: the large double-winged gate through which we had entered. This was now the only way out. Imagine a giant soccer stadium during the finals for the Africa Cup, with panicked spectators rushing toward the only exit. We almost lost Mama in the crush as we tried to get through the opening—amid all the pushing and shoving, she momentarily lost her grip on the bicycle seat she was clinging to. Luckily she was able to regain her balance with a quick movement of her hips. If she hadn't, she would have been trampled under the countless feet that were pounding the soil like a herd of stampeding elephants.

At last we managed to get out. When we'd put some distance between us and the compound, I turned to look back. Waves of people were continuing to pour from the gate, as if expelled by violent spasms. But now we could walk much more easily, because once the people had gotten past that bottleneck, they spread out across the wide street that led to the

Kandahar district (toward which we were all fleeing), and also because the route was paved. Pushing on the handlebars, the man who was transporting Mama walked steadily forward. He never looked back, or even to the side—unlike me, who gazed at everything. I'd had no inkling of the battle that had taken place while we were in the compound. The landscape was littered with two burned-out tanks, the charred remains of a 4×4, and the corpses of a number of uniformed soldiers. Yet there was no trace of the militiamen who had pursued us and threatened the UN staff.

I knew that from here it wasn't very far to the Kandahar district. Rumor had it that the area was controlled by forces opposed to the ones that had been harassing us thus far, and that those other militias were well armed and would protect us. Why would they protect us? I couldn't say, for in my limited experience all militias behaved in the same fashion. But when your country is torn by civil war, you tend to put credence in rumors, since they help you to devise a strategy for survival—and at the moment, this meant heading toward Kandahar. But once we got there, what next?

An aunt of mine lived in the district and owned a large house, with ample room to accommodate us. Yet even though our situation was desperate, we would never have considered asking her for shelter. I don't think she would have chased us away—on the contrary, she would have been only too happy to gloat over our misfortunes. Solely to humiliate us, she would have been eager to offer us hospitality the way a lord scornfully tosses crumbs to the hungry servants kneeling before him. No, thanks—anything but that!

When families have a falling-out, the rift often begins with quarrels among the women, and often over quite trivial matters. In the days when Mama was dealing in waxes and superwaxes, those brightly colored pagnes of waxed cloth that were made in Holland and shipped in from Lomé or Cotonou, this aunt had bought a pagne on credit and promised to pay at the end of the month. After three months had gone by without payment, my mother sent me to my aunt's house to collect on the debt. My aunt was so offended by this that she descended on us one day around noon, when we were eating lunch, and began to call Mama names, saying idiotic things like, "Squandering my brother's money isn't enough for you? You have to insult me by sending your daughter to pester me for the sake of a mere pagne?" Papa had tried to calm her down, to reason with her, but she had no respect at all for her older brother—though in Africa it's customary to show respect to your elders—and had berated him as well, shouting, "You've always let her lead you around by the nose! She's the one who wears the pants in this house! Because of her, you've forgotten your own family! She's gobbling up all your money—she's taking advantage of you, but you don't see a thing!"

Papa had gotten angry in turn, and had shouted, "Whether that's true or not, you've no right to come into my home and insult my wife!"

"You see?" she shot back. "You don't notice what's right in front of you, because she's got you wrapped around her little finger! You've become weak and soft-headed from those fetishes the women of her region use!" She spat all this out with such hostility that it seemed to me she was using the incident as an excuse to release a lot of pent-up hatred and resentment. What made her even more furious was that in the face of her scorching rage, Mama responded with cold irony: "If *I* don't gobble up my husband's money, I know someone who *will*. Go squander the money of your own husband—if you can find one!" And: "A person who can't afford a superwax has to make do with local wares. If you can't even afford those, then you can just shop at the secondhand stalls where the stuff is spread out on mats on the ground. Maybe you'll find an old dress that'll suit you!"

Their voices rose, and for a moment I thought the two women would fling themselves at each other. Fortunately, Papa's voice prevailed. Mama fell silent but continued to look at my aunt contemptuously, while the latter never ceased her flow of invective. My father told her to be quiet or get out. She retorted that she was leaving and that she'd never set foot in our house again. And that she didn't want to see Papa at her funeral—as if she'd even know who would be there, once she was dead. Turning to leave, she bent over, aimed her rear end in Papa's direction, lifted her pagne, and gave us a good view of her naked behind. This meant she was placing a curse on us. So much for sisterly love. What a fine thing family is!

"Do you think we could go to Tamila's?"

Mama's voice tore me away from my thoughts and flung me back onto that street crowded with hurrying refugees. I was walking mechanically behind a man who was doing his best to push a bike over pavement that was as pocked with craters as the moon's surface seen through a telescope. A woman was perched rather precariously on the bike. Surprised by the unexpected intrusion, and not sure if I understood what I'd heard, I stammered:

"Wh-what did you say?"

"Do you think we could go to Tamila's house? It isn't very big, but there's a shed on the property. She could clear a bit of space to put us up. And who knows? Maybe Fofo had the same idea and is already there!"

Tamila was a good friend of Mama's. Their relationship

had begun long before I was born, so they'd been close as far back as I could remember. Throughout their lives, they'd worked hard together. When buying merchandise for their stalls at the market, they often got up at dawn to wait for the trucks bringing fruits and vegetables from the villages inland. Since that usually wasn't enough to make ends meet, they would visit the rough-and-tumble warehouses down at the docks to buy things they could resell, such as secondhand clothing from Europe and the United States. Sometimes they'd even risk their lives driving old rattletraps over storm-rutted country roads, filling their sacks with groundnuts and cassava they gleaned in the fields.

A friendship forged under such conditions can make people closer than kin. Our affectionate name for Mama's friend was Auntie Tamila. She had a crazy, impulsive streak, and I loved her for it. The day Mama had the terrific argument with my father's sister, Tamila came by our house in the afternoon, and when she heard what had happened she immediately offered to go box the ears of that shrew, without even bothering to find out whether her friend was in any way responsible for the rift. She was a "Shoot first and ask questions later" kind of person. And she'd helped us more than anyone else when Papa had been killed and Mama crippled during the first wave of looting. For nearly a month she'd sold Mama's goods at her own stall and had come to our house every evening to give us the day's receipts. And when the wounds in Mama's legs had healed, Tamila would come by every morning to pick her up and give her a ride to the marketplace. So we still had food on the table, and Fofo and I could keep going to school. When I needed to earn some pocket money in the heat of the summer, I'd use her freezer to store little plastic bags filled with water, which I'd sell when the water was ice-cold or frozen. In short, Tamila was a second mother to us.

Yet life had granted her a smaller share of happiness than her friend's. After several years of marriage, her husband had spitefully repudiated her and unjustly taken another wife, under the pretext that Tamila had failed to give him children. I'd learned later that her sterility was the result of a clandestine abortion she'd had when she was young, even younger than I was now. She spent her entire life paying for a mistake she'd made as a girl. But as the saying goes, every cloud has a silver lining. Since she lived as a single woman, without the burden of children or husband, the small business she ran with Mama enabled her to build a fairly large house that had running water and a kitchen, to acquire a television with its own dish antenna, and to buy a secondhand car that she also used as a taxi (unfortunately, the car had been stolen during the first wave of looting). Not bad for a small businesswoman—she did as well as the bureaucrats who depended on the government for their wages. While I went to watch TV at Mélanie's house, Fofo would spend weekends at Tamila's so he could watch the soccer matches. And he'd come home filled with dreams of becoming a star like Roger Milla. Thanks to his visits with Auntie Tamila, I knew that there were three teams of lions in Africa—the Indomitable Lions of Cameroon, the Senegal Lions, and the Atlas Lions of Morocco—as well as the Nigerian Eagles and the Malian Eagles, not to mention the Ivory Coast Elephants. But do you know what Congo had? Devils, of course!

We came to a decision. When we reached Kandahar, I would ask the man who was transporting Mama to leave us at Tamila's house.

I began to resent the weight of the suitcase on my head. Worse, I could feel a sticky wetness between my legs and knew that my period had arrived. Why hadn't I remembered to put on one of Tanisha's sanitary pads before leaving the camp? But even if I'd thought of it, I doubt that, with the crowds of people all around, I could ever have found the privacy to put the pad on. I felt soiled and uncomfortable, but we had to keep walking. Fortunately, I wasn't feeling the usual pain—the two pills I'd swallowed were still working.

Just as we came to Kandahar we heard loud gunfire. It didn't last long, but it nevertheless caused a fresh outbreak of panic among the already desperate refugees and forced us to hurry even faster, because we had to keep up with those who were less heavily laden than us.

We had just passed the first two or three houses on the outskirts of the district when the man wheeling the bicycle suddenly stopped.

"Okay, that's it. I've brought you to Kandahar—I've kept my part of the bargain. Take your mother off the bike."

"But—"

"Take her off or I'll throw her off!"

He couldn't just leave us there! What would we do? Tamila's house wasn't far away—it was down the street, opposite the two palm trees on the right. Not more than three hundred meters. I explained this to him, pointed out the palm trees . . .

"Don't you understand that I'm risking my life every second I spend with you?"

"But I paid you—"

"To take you to Kandahar, and this is what I've done. You heard those shots, right? The militias are coming, and I don't feel like getting killed. Come on, help me get her off the bike or I'll throw her off!"

"Listen!" I pleaded. "Just three hundred meters! It isn't far—it won't take more than five minutes! Wait—I've got a thousand francs left."

I set down the suitcase I was carrying, dug around in the leather bag slung across my front, and pulled out a thousand-franc note. The man looked at the bill, looked down the street, looked at Mama on the bike, and looked at the bill once more.

"Okay, I'll take you as far as the palm trees. But no farther!"

He pocketed the bill and began wheeling the bike again. I have no idea where money gets its vast powers of persuasion. Again, I balanced the suitcase on my head and trotted after him. Mama had observed the scene without uttering a word. What could the poor woman have said?

We made our way to the two palm trees, which I kept my gaze fixed on the entire time. Actually, you could see only their tops above the wall encircling the property. Papa and I had built that wall. It was enormous, and on the top we had embedded pieces of glass, sharp as razor blades, to discourage thieves from climbing over. Constructing its foundation had particularly impressed me, because for the first time we'd used a cement mixer, and also because we'd had to lay a stepped footing to accommodate the sloping ground. The owner of the property, Mr. Ibara, was so pleased with our work that he'd hired us to build a garage for him after he bought a second all-terrain vehicle. He always enjoyed watching as I pushed wheelbarrows full of cement and built forms for molding concrete. I suppose these weren't things he would let his own daughters do, since he was rich—very rich. He was a customs inspector, and in the entire history of our country there had never been a customs inspector of modest means. He was famous throughout the region for being the first person to have a Mercedes shipped to him directly from Düsseldorf by special cargo plane. People said he was as rich as the president, who controlled our country's oil revenues. Whatever the case, the home of this customs official was an opulent mansion that dwarfed Auntie Tamila's house across the way.

We reached the palm trees in record time. Immediately I set down the suitcase. The man and I helped Mama off the bike. He tied the suitcase onto the luggage rack and, with a look of relief, mounted the bike and pedaled away at top speed, without even wishing us good luck. He'd had a good day. The money I'd paid him was more than half of what he could earn in an entire month.

Chapter Twenty

Johnny, Known as Mad Dog

As soon as the enemy's tanks left the HCR compound, the large gateway in the legation's perimeter wall began to disgorge hundreds of people—wave after wave of them, an indescribable chaos. The gate, which had looked so enormous to me, now seemed very narrow in the face of this massive flood. What surprised me was that most of the people were still carrying personal belongings. I had the feeling that even if we looted them a thousand times, they would always manage to hang on to something.

My commandos and I watched the scene from our various hiding places—Lovelita and I from the ditch where we were lying on our bellies. If I didn't immediately order the men to attack, it wasn't because I was scared. It was because after the assault by the helicopters and tanks that annihilated the unit Giap had sent to back us up in our siege of the HCR compound, I thought the white attackers might have left soldiers behind to protect the refugees and the Chechens hiding among them.

I must admit I'd never experienced anything like this. We were prepared to fight the Mayi-Dogo militias because we'd been told their tribal leader had cheated in the elections and was organizing a genocide against our ethnic group—reports that were confirmed by intellectuals with imposing degrees and impeccable French. And finally we'd been assured that after we won the war, we'd get a share of the oil money and would be rich. Then I could order Fashion Fair cosmetics directly from America for Lovelita.

That was the deal. We had no idea our electoral dispute would turn into an international conflict, with foreign troops and planes coming in to drop bombs on our heads. At least, Giap hadn't said anything to *me* about this possibility. Anyway it wasn't out of fear that I continued to lie facedown in the mud at the bottom of that ditch, since the whole world knew that if you tried to prove you were tougher than me, you were dead. A true leader has to know when to attack. That's why I was keeping a low profile for the moment, just observing, taking note of small details—for example, a woman who was carrying two children, one tied to her back and the other on her shoulders; another woman sitting sideways on the luggage rack of a bicycle, which was being pushed by a man in the company of a young woman with a suitcase balanced on her head; a child tethered to his mother by a cord tied around his waist, trotting along while clutching a soccer ball to his chest; and, curiously, a man who—perhaps so he could move more quickly—was wearing a wheelbarrow like a helmet, his head disappearing into the hollow of the tray and his fingers grasping the handles. It takes all kinds to make a world, and when you're waging war you have to be a keen observer, because the detail that escapes you could be the detail that kills you.

I watched the crowd for more than a quarter of an hour, and then told myself it was time to do something. We couldn't just sit there with our arms folded while all the Mayi-Dogos and their Chechens slipped through our fingers.

After the assault by the helicopters and tanks, I'd tried several times to contact Giap on my cell phone to give him a report on the situation, but I hadn't been able to reach him. I didn't know whether this was because the enemy had destroyed all the relays or simply because Giap had lost his phone. I punched in his number again, twice, but each time the tones went out over the electronic network and then faded, with no result. I wasn't sure what to do. For a moment I felt at a loss, but fortunately an intellectual's brain is working away even when it doesn't seem to be, and I hit upon a good solution: flush the leopard from its lair. When you can't go hunt for an enemy, you have to make it come toward you, and that's what I did. I ordered my commandos to fire into the air—a sustained volley lasting several minutes—without giving away their positions. The enemy, hearing the gunfire, would either think they were being attacked and take to their heels, or leave their positions and come looking for us. Either way, we'd find out if the Western soldiers and the UN troops had left a rear guard to protect the refugees.

We fired into the air for a good three minutes. The shooting caused extreme panic among the fleeing people, some of whom threw down their cherished possessions so they could run faster. But for the moment we weren't interested in them. We were waiting to see if the foreign soldiers would come out and look for us when the volley was over.

We stayed hidden in our strategically chosen ditches and waited. The compound kept spewing out its contents for a while longer, and then the stream finally dried up. Four people straggled out, then three, then five, then two. That was it. We waited another fifteen minutes to be sure no one else was coming. If there had still been foreign soldiers or UN blue helmets inside, they would have come out with the last of the refugees. Reassured, I decided to go and check. We couldn't leave anything to chance.

I crawled out of the ditch and helped Lovelita out, too. I shouted to my commandos, telling them that the danger had passed and they should come out of hiding and join me. Well, I was disgusted to find that most of the men had run off. There were only three members of the unit left—Little Pepper, Piston, and Lovelita. But I wasn't discouraged. I ordered them to follow me into the HCR compound.

When you're on a reconnaissance mission, you have to be very clever. A general always leads his troops from the rear echelons. That's what I did. I sent the two guys in first, and then I went in with Lovelita. We jumped over a great many bodies piled up at the entrance, and then—darting skillfully here and there, from one section of wall to another, from one bit of cover to another—we made our way into the compound. There wasn't a sign of movement. The place looked as if it had been mauled by a hurricane. I fired several shots into the air to provoke a response from the enemy, if the enemy was still present. There was no response. The compound was empty—we could relax.

Piston and Little Pepper spread out and made a quick tour of the grounds, to see whether the refugees and the HCR staff had left anything worthwhile. I let them scout around. Giap had said—following directives from higher up—that we should authorize our soldiers to take whatever they wanted, since there wasn't any money to pay them. After a while I yelled for Piston and the two of us went to see if we could start up one of the vehicles abandoned by the UN troops. There wasn't an engine in the world that could resist Piston's screwdriver. But they'd wrecked everything, the scum! Not only had they removed essential parts from every motor, but they'd slashed all the tires as well. Our pickings amounted to a big fat zero.

Furious, I fired several volleys into the carcass of the jeep I'd wanted to requisition. Hearing the shots, Lovelita and Little Pepper came running. They'd turned up almost nothing in the way of loot. Well, if they'd asked the advice of an old hand like me, I could have told them they were wasting their time here. If you want to get rich, don't go looting a camp of African refugees. They're already poor when they flee their homes. What miracle is going to make them wealthy on the road?

We inspected every cranny and turned everything inside out. Night was beginning to fall. Now I was really at a loss, because I didn't know what mission to assign to my men. I couldn't reach Giap or any of our other leaders. I began to feel afraid, for I suddenly realized that we were only four individuals on the border of a largely Mayi-Dogo district, a Chechen stronghold, and that if the enemy decided to launch a counteroffensive, we were done for. So I immediately told everyone to leave the compound, which was liable to become a trap during an assault.

We left. A weird silence hung over the place. Thousands of people had been swarming around here only a few hours earlier, but now there wasn't a soul, not even a ghost. I would have been glad, as well as reassured, to see another living creature, even if only a dog (dogs, like hyenas, are always sniffing about places where the smell of rotting flesh hangs in the air). We couldn't stay here. One way or another, we had to rejoin the rest of the Mata Mata.

Lovelita, no doubt wanting to relieve the oppressive silence, said she felt like listening to some music. At that unbelievably stressful point—when I was at a crucial juncture with my troops and, as leader, was racking my brain for a plan that would get us out of this mess—Lovelita could think of nothing better to worry about than music. Shit, that bubblehead could probably live entirely on air, water, and music.

I handed her the little radio I'd acquired when we'd raided the humanitarian convoy and told her to keep the volume down, so the noise wouldn't disturb my train of thought.

I don't know if she increased the volume on purpose to attract my attention or if she simply turned the knob in the wrong direction by mistake, but all of a sudden I heard the name of our country. She immediately turned the volume down with a nervous look at me, thinking I was going to get angry and bawl her out. But on the contrary I shouted, "Turn it up! Turn it up!"

". . . special operation."

"And how did you go about preparing for this special commando operation?"

"We planned it very carefully. As you may know, we've had lots of experience in Africa with this type of operation—experience acquired in Congo, Zaïre (remember Kolwezi), Gabon, the Central African Republic, and so on."

"What did you need in the way of resources?"

"It was an armed air strike that required three hundred men, seven helicopters, and two planes. But this sort of operation doesn't depend only on matériel, you know. What's crucial is the caliber of the men—the deployment of specific types of expertise."

"The element of surprise must have played a role as well. Could you ever repeat this kind of operation?"

"If another threat were aimed at our countrymen and against citizens of the European Union—"

"Or against Americans, Russians, Serbs . . ."

"Yes, right . . . If any Europeans—any Westerners—were placed in jeopardy, no matter what their nationality, our paramilitary forces would be ready to intervene with the same airtight security and effectiveness."

"There are reports that those Serbs were mercenaries . . ."

"Listen, our mission was to save lives. When you're about to save someone's life, you don't stop to ask whether he's a mercenary or not."

"Still, there are reports that you refused to rescue Africans who were longtime employees of our embassies. Surely their lives were in danger because of their association with our country."

"Listen, we're soldiers. It's the politicians who decide such things. Our mission was clear: evacuate our fellow citizens who were in jeopardy. But let me say—if I may express my personal opinion here—that our country cannot solve all of the world's problems by itself. We aren't the ones who asked those people to go around killing each other."

"Thank you, sir. That was Colonel Jean Lagnier, commander of Operation Green Gorilla, which evacuated more than fifty Europeans trapped by the civil war raging in . . ."

"Mad Dog!"

Damn! Piston had just called my name, preventing me from hearing the rest of the broadcast. I was livid.

"Can't you wait a minute?" I yelled.

I turned my attention back to the radio, but it was too late. A stupid jingle, and then I heard: *"RFI Sports!"* I wasn't in the mood to listen to the sports news.

"So what was so important?" I said to Piston.

"I hear tanks coming! Listen!"

I listened. He was right. To judge from the racket they were making, there was more than one tank—it sounded like a whole battalion. What reassured me right away was that they weren't coming from the direction of Kandahar, which meant that they were from our own army. All we had to do was make sure they didn't mistake us for Chechens and fire on us. In any case, if they were coming to engage the helicoptered commandos mentioned on the radio a minute ago, they'd sure as hell missed the boat.

Apparently they didn't realize that the foreign commandos had been gone for some time, since they immediately began shelling the HCR compound with heavy artillery. They pounded it nonstop for nearly a quarter of an hour. By the time they ceased firing, the perimeter wall was a heap of rubble and not a single structure was left standing.

Taking advantage of the silence, I shouted at the top of my lungs that we were commandos from the Mata Mata, that we weren't Mayi-Dogos or Chechens, and that we were coming out from behind our cover. They understood what I was saying and told us to come out into the moonlight with our hands up. We immediately obeyed.

Though we were all fighting the same enemy, those guys had no scruples or any sense of honor. They grabbed us and began beating us up, as if we were common Chechen spies. What saved us was that two of them recognized us—they'd been with the men who'd come to help us set up a blockade around the HCR compound, and they'd managed to get away when the helicopters attacked. If it hadn't been for those two soldiers, we would have been killed.

The leader of the battalion, a colonel, asked us to give him all the information we had. Of course I readily complied, telling him how we'd surrounded the compound with the aid of backup troops and how we'd bravely fought the enemy. We'd put up fierce resistance, and if the attackers hadn't had helicopters, we would have neutralized them. After I finished my account, the colonel asked what we were planning to do now, since we didn't belong to his unit. I told him we were real fighters—that we'd captured the radio station and subdued the Huambo district, and that we were ready to join him in attacking Kandahar because Giap had given us orders to do so.

"Who's Giap?" he asked.

I was astounded. *He* hadn't heard of Giap either! Before I had a chance to explain that Giap was the commander of the Mata Mata, the brave militia fighters who had seized the radio and TV compound, I heard:

"He's probably the head of one of those militias we use as adjunct forces."

It was a junior officer who had answered for me.

"Okay," said the colonel. "You can come along with us as reinforcements, but don't be causing any trouble for my soldiers."

I didn't make a peep, for fear he'd change his mind.

Talking to one of the two soldiers who'd rescued us, I learned why Idi Amin had never arrived. His entire unit had been wiped out in Kandahar. According to information we'd gotten from our spies, said the soldier, hundreds of Chechens armed to the teeth were now in the district. They had heavy weapons, an entire battery of missiles, and were getting ready to attack. So this was no time to hesitate. We had to finish off the district once and for all—annihilate that Mayi-Dogo stronghold, rout the Chechens from their nest. Believe me, the guy wasn't just talking a lot of hot air, to judge from what I saw around me.

I haven't had a lot of experience with heavy weapons, but I do know a few. Right away I spotted a BM-21. Who in this country can't recognize a BM-21? A multiple-rocket launcher that's mounted on a Russian-made truck and that can fire twelve rockets in forty-five seconds. Turned out the soldier I was speaking with was also the guy who manned the BM-21. He told me proudly that each individual rocket launched a number of grenades when it exploded, so you could easily blanket an entire district. I was immediately sorry that I, too, wasn't a gunner assigned to an MRL. In addition to the BM-21, I saw two tanks, and two more pieces of artillery—howitzers—each mounted on a military all-terrain vehicle.

"Those are 105-millimeter howitzers," he told me as soon as he realized I'd noticed them. I wondered what would be left of the district once we'd finished shelling it. Well, too bad for the Mayi-Dogos. They shouldn't have killed my friend Idi Amin. They shouldn't have prevented our leader from taking power.

The colonel who was commanding the troops agreed to replenish our stock of ammunition, since we were beginning to run low. But it was the three tins of sardines and three baguettes of bread he gave us that really won my respect and admiration. A man who can find rations for his soldiers under such chaotic conditions must be a true leader. Giap couldn't have managed it, I bet.

I distributed three sardines to each member of my unit, beginning with Lovelita. We ate our meal and settled down to rest until dawn.

And at daybreak, a rain of steel began to fall on Kandahar.

Chapter Twenty-one

Laokolé

At daybreak, a rain of steel began to fall on Kandahar.

The first rocket startled me just as I was coming out of the latrine, a hole that had been hastily dug in a far corner of the yard to accommodate the large number of people who had unexpectedly sought refuge at Auntie Tamila's house. Privacy in the latrine was afforded by some old corrugated roof tiles, on which the current user would hang an object—pagne, towel, bit of cloth—to signal that the spot was occupied.

I'd gotten up at first light, before anyone else, to avoid the long line of people who went there to relieve themselves as soon as they awoke. I'd gazed around me. There was no one outside, and I'd wondered by what miracle Auntie Tamila had managed to find space for everyone in the house. I'd looked across the street at the wall that enclosed Mr. Ibara's property—the wall that protected him and his family in their secure existence, the wall that my father and I had built. A thrill of useless pride went through me. The construction of that wall had been a turning point in my life: for the first time, I'd had the experience of using a cement mixer.

Up to that point, when I'd worked with Papa on small jobs, we'd mixed the cement by hand, with a shovel, before loading it into the wheelbarrow. We would spread out a layer of sand approximately ten centimeters thick, distribute the dry cement more or less evenly over the sand, blend it all together with the shovel, and do this several times until we obtained a uniform mixture. Then we'd level it out again, as at the beginning. We'd dig a small hole in the center, pour in a little less water than we needed, and use the back of the shovel to push the mixture from the edges to the center, blending it with the water. Once it was thoroughly wet, we'd add the rest of the water and mix the whole batch one last time to distribute the moisture evenly. I assure you, it was a long and laborious process. And difficult.

Mr. Ibara, being rich, had leased a cement mixer for the extensive work on his property. I'd never seen one before—an enormous tumbler, more or less spherical, rotating on its central axis with the aid of a small motor. Once Papa had shown me how it worked, I thought it was marvelous. Making cement was now so easy! You loaded the barrel of the mixer first with the sand, then with the gravel, then with the cement; and finally you added the water. You let the barrel rotate for a minute and half (up to three minutes for large batches), and it was done! Cement or mortar in less than three minutes! Not only could we do the work in a fraction of the time, but we didn't even get tired. Yes, machines make a huge difference. Thanks to that cement mixer, I at last understood from personal experience what I'd learned in school—namely, why cultures that had machines enjoyed a decisive advantage over those that didn't.

Enough musing about Mr. Ibara's wall—I gathered my

thoughts and wished him good luck. He, at least, was safe and secure.

I set off toward the latrine.

*

We'd arrived at Auntie Tamila's house the day before, just as darkness was beginning to fall. We hadn't expected to find so many people there. They were milling around the courtyard, trying to get organized as best they could. Despite the crowd, Auntie spotted us as soon as we came into the yard, Mama hitching her way over the ground by sliding her hips forward, and me following with bundles on my head and back. Auntie ran to us, hugged us, carried Mama on her own back into the house.

"I thought of you and cried! I heard that your district had been attacked, but I didn't know what had become of you. I'm so glad you've come!"

"Is Fofo here?" asked Mama.

"No, I haven't seen him. Isn't he with you?"

"We lost him in the crowd."

"Poor child! Don't be too worried—I know Fofo. He's a clever boy, he'll manage somehow. Come, let's get you settled."

"There are so many people here!" I said. "Do you really think you can find room for us?"

"If there's no room for you, there'll be no room for anyone!" she exclaimed. "Do you think I'm friends with even half the people here? All I know about most of them is that they're refugees from the war and that they've lost everything. They have nowhere to go. How could I turn them away? So when it comes to you and your mother, Lao, how can you ask such a pointless question? You're like a daughter to me."

Yes, she was right—I shouldn't have said that. In Africa,

people shower you with kindness and generosity. Even if you were just the friend of a friend of someone who knew Auntie Tamila, you'd still be able to count on her hospitality. I think this was true of the majority of the homeless people there.

"But Auntie," I protested, "I only meant—"

"No need to say anything more. Your mother can sleep in my room—the bed is big enough for both of us."

And turning toward her friend: "You're covered with dust! And what's happened to your poor leg? You must be in terrible pain! Come—I'll help you get cleaned up, and then let's see what we can do for your leg. You're badly in need of rest."

She picked Mama up and took her into the shower off her bedroom. Meantime, I opened the bundle I'd been carrying since the start of our trek and tried to find some clean clothes for Mama. I needn't have bothered—when she came out of the bathroom she was wearing one of Auntie's dresses. Then Auntie Tamila massaged the stumps of Mama's legs with a soothing ointment she herself had made.

"You ought to rest now," Auntie advised. "A bite to eat, and then you can lie down."

No sooner said than done. For the first time since we'd left home, Mama ate with a good appetite.

Once Mama had been put to bed in her friend's room, my agitation and anxiety lifted—I was now free to tend to myself. Of course, what I most wanted to do was wash, since I was feeling unbearably dirty. For the time being, there was no shortage of water. The taps were all working, though no one knew how long this would last. Thinking ahead, Auntie Tamila had filled a number of large storage containers just in case. I filled a bucket with water and was about to take it outside to the improvised shower near the latrine, but Auntie stopped me. She insisted that I use her own private bathroom, the one Mama had used.

I let the water cascade over me, feeling it wash away the sweat and grime of the previous two days. What a relief it was to clean up after my period. When I'd dried myself off, I put on one of the sanitary pads Tanisha had given me. I changed my panties and washed the ones that I'd been wearing since we'd left home and that were now soaked with blood. At last I felt clean and comfortable. Then Auntie Tamila prepared a meal for me.

"Eat well tonight, my daughter, while we've still got something left. Tomorrow we start to tighten our belts."

Dear Auntie Tamila! If I'd known the way to Paradise, I would have shown it to you then and there. When I finished eating I took two acetaminophen, as Tanisha had recommended, since my menstrual cramps had returned.

Despite Auntie Tamila's efforts, it wasn't possible for me to sleep inside the house. Now that darkness had fallen, those who had arrived earlier were occupying every bit of space, spilling across the living room, packed so densely that you could barely walk without stepping on the mats and mattresses spread out on the floor. Tamila was distressed and suggested that if we could make do with a bit less room, the three of us could fit in her bed. I refused. The coming days, I knew, would be difficult ones, and the two women needed some good solid rest. I immediately thought of the shed, and asked if I could sleep there.

"No, no—I'd never let you do that! It's hardly more than a lean-to where I store bags of cement. How could you possibly sleep there?"

"Let me at least see what it looks like, Auntie!"

My efforts to convince her finally worked—she handed me a flashlight and said I could go take a look. Indeed it was a lean-to, built against the wall surrounding the property and located about ten meters from the main house. Thirty or forty sacks of cement were stored there, and at first glance it seemed there was no room to spread out a mat. But if the five sacks near the door were piled up on other ones, this would solve the problem. I asked two men to help me, since a sack of cement weighs fifty kilos. It wasn't difficult to clear a space measuring about three meters by one meter—three square meters—which was plenty for me. I still had to do something about the cement dust lying here and there on the shed floor. As the daughter of a mason and occasionally a mason's assistant, I knew that breathing cement dust was dangerous—the stuff was as toxic and dangerous as asbestos. So I sprinkled the ground with water and swept it twice with a broom. The surface was now clean enough to sleep on.

When I got back to the house, Auntie asked what had taken me so long. I described what I'd done and told her the place suited me perfectly. Then she invited me to stay and watch the news on TV before going off to bed.

Auntie knew that I liked to keep up with current events, and she and Mama often teased me about that. Fofo might know every important soccer team in the world and be able to reel off the most obscure statistics—such as the number of goals scored in a World Cup match that had taken place ten years before he was born. But I could give you all sorts of details on what was happening in the world right now.

In fact, I knew more about events abroad than I did about what was going on in our own country, for the simple reason that our national radio and TV networks told heaps of lies, all the time. I say this because if you listened only to what those networks said, you'd think that our country had no problems at all, that it was a veritable paradise. Everything was fine; the people were happy; the president was universally loved, since the peace that prevailed in the land was due entirely to his generosity; the public schools, like the hospitals and health care services, worked smoothly; and soon the country would have a system of highways and airports to rival that of Switzerland, if one could judge from the frequency with which such projects were inaugurated. But after I'd spent some time listening to our journalists, one thing became absolutely clear to me: the country they lived in was not the country we were living in.

Mélanie and I had tuned in to the national radio station only when we wanted to listen to music, and we'd watched the national TV station only to see the lovely Tanya Toyo present the daily news. Mélanie thought TT was very beautiful and had admired her elegant clothes. She'd tried to dress like TT as best she could, but it wasn't easy—even for Mélanie, whose parents were rich—because TT wore a different outfit for every show.

Out of necessity, we had turned to foreign radio and TV stations when we wanted to find out what was happening in our country. The news reported by the foreign media wasn't always accurate—sometimes we got the impression they didn't really know what they were talking about, because they often couldn't even pronounce the names of people and places in our country. But at least they alerted us to facts that our government was trying to conceal.

So I was very happy when Auntie Tamila invited me to watch the evening news. With her satellite dish, she could get channels from all over the globe. And even if there was only a single report on what was happening here, it would be worth it—for in the entire time since we'd left home, I'd heard nothing but the exhortations to looting that were being spewed out by a certain General Giap.

Although water still flowed from the faucets, electricity was no longer flowing from the sockets. But that was nothing new in our country, and Auntie Tamila, who was familiar with the problem, had long ago found a solution: her TV worked as well on batteries as it did on the main power supply.

Almost all of the refugees staying at her place had crowded into the living room to watch TV. I counted sixteen people—eighteen if I included myself and Mama, who had stayed in the bedroom. Everyone wanted to know what the news reports would say. I found a bit of space on one of the mats spread on the floor, and sat down.

CNN and TV5 made no mention of our country in their bulletins. So Auntie Tamila switched to Euronews, which was just beginning its evening broadcast. It was a good choice, since our country was mentioned in the titles at the beginning of the program. We had to wait ten minutes for the complete report. There was a rapt silence in the living room.

The story began with a sequence of images filled with refugees—long streams of men and women, their arms, heads, and backs laden with bundles, suitcases, countless miscellaneous objects, not to mention their children. In short, a sequence that seemed like a replay of old archival footage, images I'd seen a thousand times on programs about Rwanda, Angola, Sierra Leone, Liberia, the Central African Republic, and eastern Zaire. Images that gave the impression that Africa was nothing but a vast refugee camp. And not only Africa, for I'd seen similar images from Bosnia-Herzegovina, Kosovo, East Timor. But until that moment, they'd seemed not only very distant from my own life but a bit unreal, like scenes from a movie. I'd never imagined that one day I myself would be among those ragged, wandering hordes.

The voice-over informed us that the war we were experiencing on the margins—as looting, thievery, and rape—was actually much more significant, since a number of fighter jets, belonging to a foreign army allied with one of the factions, had bombed a section of the capital. The commentary stated that in view of the threat posed to citizens of the European Union—the looting of a humanitarian convoy, an ultimatum given by the armed factions—the EU had launched a rescue operation. And then came another sequence of images.

I recognized the HCR compound, the helicopters, the tanks . . . and I saw Mélanie. Oh, not for long—just a fraction of a second—but long enough to recognize her standing next to Katelijne. And there was Tanisha flanked by two soldiers, Tanisha boarding a helicopter. It was amazing! Television gave another dimension to reality, even though it was a reality I'd already lived. TV created a distance from the events, enabling me to see things I hadn't noticed or realized at the time—in particular, the chaotic and irrational way people behaved in an emergency situation.

For a moment the camera ceased roving about and remained focused on the scene as a whole. A tank entered the frame, backing up at top speed . . . The people were pushing and shoving to get out of the way . . . to avoid being crushed . . . A young man stood there, watching the tank come closer . . . I could see only his back—he was wearing jeans and a baseball cap . . . The tank was heading straight toward him . . . "Move, you idiot!" I shouted, as if he could hear me through the screen and as if I could alter the course of an action that, even if I didn't yet know its outcome, was already over and done with, irreversible, since it was on film . . . Move, you idiot! Throw away that bandolier bag and save yourself! . . . But he just stood there, hypnotized, frozen in place like an animal caught in the headlights . . . The tank was almost upon him . . . A woman standing behind him grabbed him by the shoulder and pulled him toward her. The two of them fell out of the way just in time. The tank thundered by them a fraction of a second later. His cap flew off—and lo and behold, he wasn't a young man but a young woman. She immediately got to her feet, shot an angry glance at the person who'd caused her to fall, and then turned to look at the tank. But . . . but . . . that young woman was me! That idiot, that blockhead who stood there so stupidly, like a cow watching a train go by—that was me, and I hadn't even recognized myself!

It was the weirdest feeling. I was simultaneously behind the screen and in front of it; I was shouting insults at myself; I was both actor and spectator in the life-or-death situation unfolding before my eyes; I was real yet at the same time imaginary, as in a painting that shows the artist himself in the act of painting. It was enough to make me schizophrenic!

Auntie Tamila called out my name. The others in the room did likewise. The entire incident hadn't lasted more than a minute, and the camera was once again panning across the scene, focusing on the white refugees, with many close-ups of their haggard faces, while a colonel boasted of his country's ability to deploy troops on the ground rapidly and effectively in a crisis.

"Were there any casualties during the operation?"

"No," he replied. "No one was killed, or even wounded. We even managed to save a dog," he said with a smile, as the camera panned to a woman cradling her precious poodle in her arms.

"No one was killed!" I exclaimed to myself. What about Mélanie?

"Mm-hmm! Well!" said all the women in the room, in a tone somewhere between approving and questioning.

I was surprised that the operation was considered so important. The eyewitness account was followed by two interviews—one with a European scholar from an International Center of African Studies at some French university, and the other with an African political analyst.

The interview with the European came first.

"Do you think," asked the journalist, "that this ethnic conflict—"

"Let me stop you right there, sir. We have to get beyond the distorted and stereotyped view that reduces all conflicts in Africa to tribal warfare, to a settling of scores between clans bent on avenging secular hatreds. Ethnic tensions are perhaps instrumental for the politicians—in fact, this is surely the case. But on the level of the ordinary person, of the poor farmer, there are no such conflicts, because everyone is living in the same poverty. In all those conflicts, if you look carefully, you'll find first of all the large petroleum companies and diamond producers, who manipulate the local politicians, and these in turn . . ."

The rest of his words were drowned out by a hubbub of voices in the room, retorting, commenting, protesting.

"What do you know about it? You're a white man! Just this morning I had to flee from the Manga district, hiding behind bushes the whole way, because gangs of youths were out to hunt down and kill all the Mayi-Dogos. And you say it isn't a tribal conflict!"

"Two blocks from here, they killed a schoolteacher. Why? Simply because he was a Mayi-Dogo. Isn't that tribal?"

"I saw something worse!" said another woman, outdoing everyone else. "When we came to this district yesterday morning, we saw that young Chechens had set up a roadblock where they were systematically shooting everyone who wasn't from their own ethnic group! They couldn't tell who was who just by looking, since we all have black skin, two arms, two legs, two eyes, and two ears—so they invented a language test. Anyone who couldn't speak the tribal tongue was automatically shot, as if all children in this modern world could still speak their tribal tongue. Isn't that tribalism?"

"When a Tutsi kills a Hutu just because he's a Hutu, and vice versa, when a Yoruba kills a Hausa just because he's a Hausa, and vice versa—"

"And when a Pashtun kills an Uzbek just because he's an Uzbek, and vice versa," I added—to show that, thanks to my keen interest in current events, I was up on what was happening in places other than Africa . . .

"Yes, that's right!" said Auntie Tamila quickly, continuing in the same vein. "And when a Sara kills a Yakoma just because he's a Yakoma, I don't give a damn for all your reasons and theories! I say that, manipulated or not, they're two tribes or ethnic groups that are killing each other!" She threw this remark directly at the European scholar, who was trying to camouflage the reality we knew firsthand.

Then, abruptly, as if someone had cast a spell, the people in the room fell silent. The young political expert had appeared on the screen.

"You know the country well. Can you explain to us what's happening? Is it true that the large oil companies and diamond producers bear some responsibility for this war?"

"Yes, I do know the country well, because I was born here. If you do nothing but lazily parrot the politically correct view—namely, that the war is the result of manipulation by large corporations—even if that's partly true, you'll never completely understand the reality of the situation here, and *a fortiori* you'll never find a way to resolve the crisis. In essence, it's a conflict between two of the country's major ethnic groups, the Mayi-Dogos and the Dogo-Mayis, a conflict that dates back half a century to a time when the groups' leaders began fighting for power after the colonial occupiers left. It's an ethnic conflict that disguises itself behind all these avatars. For instance, nowadays you won't find a single Mayi-Dogo living in a Dogo-Mayi district, and vice versa . . ."

"Ah, listen to that fellow! He's no better than the other one. What a bunch of lies!" exclaimed the first woman.

"He's eaten too many tinned sardines in Whitey Land and no longer knows what's happening in his own country."

"It isn't sardines that makes him so fat—he's been eating too much French butter!"

"I'm a Mayi-Dogo," said Auntie Tamila. "My niece Lao and her mother, who are in this house with us, are not Mayi-Dogos. But they're right at home here in this district!"

"Apologies for pointing this out, Tamila—but I've seen Mayi-Dogos killing Mayi-Dogos. They were shooting one another with Kalashnikovs in front of a shop they'd looted. Is that tribal?"

"Not at all!" chimed in another woman. "It's those politicians. They want to seize power, so they need militia fighters. But since they don't have any money to pay the fighters, they just tell them to go ahead and steal."

"I heard a general named Giap authorize forty-eight hours of indiscriminate looting," I said.

"But he gets his orders from people even higher up—from the president himself."

"Don't believe a word that fellow says, even if he *is* a black African, and even if he claims to have been born here. It isn't the tribes who are killing each other—it's the *politicians* who are killing *us*," concluded Auntie Tamila.

Expressions of emphatic agreement came from all sides: "That's true!" "She's right!" "Mm-hm!" And everyone nodded.

The newscast was over. It was followed by a program on the latest fashions—beautiful girls, beautiful dresses. We had to avoid running down the battery. Auntie switched off the TV.

I went outside for a few minutes to get some fresh air—to breathe some oxygen after the stuffy atmosphere in that living room, filled with carbon dioxide from all those lungs. I'd forgotten that outside, high in the sky, the stars were still shining. And, in turn, the stars above made me briefly forget my current situation: that of a young woman who for the past forty-eight hours had been fleeing a civil war together with her mother, and who had lost her little brother somewhere along the way. Even the peace and quiet all around—not a single gunshot could be heard at the moment—gave the impression that nothing was happening. Now it was time to go to sleep, to get some rest.

I went back into the house to tell Auntie Tamila I was turning in.

She gave me a small foam pad she had stored away, and a spray bottle of mosquito repellent. She lit a candle and asked if she could come with me. But before leaving the house, I wanted to say goodnight to Mama.

I went into the room where she was lying down. I raised the protective netting that hung down around the bed. She hadn't yet fallen asleep, and I could tell at a glance that her infected leg was once again throbbing, despite the ointment that Auntie Tamila had rubbed on it. And all of a sudden it occurred to me that if the medication Tanisha had given me could ease menstrual cramps, then it could also ease Mama's pain. To avoid giving Auntie the impression that I thought her ointment was useless, I assured her the doctor had told Mama to take two acetaminophen at bedtime. I made Mama swallow them. I wiped her forehead tenderly, and I hugged her with all my love. Such a brave woman, my mother! Tomorrow, at dawn, she would again be at my side and we would continue our struggle together. We had to survive—we *would* survive!

Auntie accompanied me to the shed, to see what kind of

lodgings I'd arranged for myself. She was quite pleasantly surprised. By the light of her candle she helped me to spread out the foam pad, and, leaving me a blanket, she wished me goodnight. I felt comfortable and safe, especially because the sacks of cement formed a protective wall around me. I tried out my improvised bed. The foam pad wasn't much—only about five centimeters thick—and I could feel the hardness of the ground as soon as I lay down. But that was nothing—I'd soon get used to it. And it was better than sleeping on a mere woven mat or cloth. I took the insect repellent and sprayed the exposed parts of my body—hands, arms, legs. The stuff was an olfactory disaster; it stank of fish. I sprayed some on my palms and rubbed it over my face and neck. Well, at least I'd sleep soundly. Before blowing out the candle, I removed the leather bandolier bag from my shoulder, as well as the purse concealed under my pants, and tucked them away between the sacks of cement.

An hour or two later, the sound of heavy-arms fire woke me. For a second I panicked, thinking that the district was being attacked. But when I listened carefully, I realized the noise was coming from the embassy district. I wondered who could still be fighting there, now that the refugees had left and the area was abandoned. After about twenty minutes, the firing stopped as abruptly as it had begun. I listened to the silence for another half hour, and then drifted off to sleep.

*

So it was at dawn, just as I was coming out of the latrine, that rockets began raining down on the district.

The main house was a scene of utter terror. Screams, shouts. Those who were inside wanted to come out, and those who were outside wanted to take refuge inside—both reactions being equally futile. I was among those struggling to get inside, not to seek shelter from the bombardment but to be near Mama. I found her with Tamila. They were clutching each other, huddled in a corner of the bedroom, which was roofed with a concrete slab. Their arms were so thoroughly entwined, I couldn't have said who was protecting whom.

"Go back to the shed, quick!" cried Auntie Tamila. "Get down between the sacks of cement. Don't worry about us—we'll be safe here under the concrete roof."

"I came to see how Mama did last night."

"I'm fine—the pain is gone. Tamila's ointment and the pills you gave me helped a lot. Now go! Get back to the shed!"

"Okay. I'll return soon—will bring you two more tablets when things have calmed down."

"All right, but get out of here now!"

I raced back to my little shelter and lay down on the foam pad, well shielded between the sacks of cement.

The shelling didn't let up. One, two, three, four . . . I counted a dozen rockets in one minute. It was always the same sequence, repeated over and over. A loud whistling noise, made even more terrifying by the Doppler effect, would rend the air, moving as swiftly as thunder; violent shock waves would emanate from the point of impact; there would be an enormous explosion; and everything would be reduced to dust, smoke, debris, and rubble. Every time I heard that whistling noise, I'd hunch my shoulders up around my ears, as if that could give me a bit more protection, and with muscles tensed I'd wait for the impact and the sound of the explosion. One, two, three, four, five . . . I gave up counting. Occasionally the shelling would stop, for minutes at a time, but it always started up again. I think those pauses were just a ruse, to get us to come out of hiding.

The brain is an extraordinary organ. After half an hour of fear and dread under the bombardment, mine adapted to the situation. It transformed the whistlings, shock waves, and explosions into routine sounds that were nothing more than familiar background noise. My terror faded and my body relaxed. I was able to think about other things, just as I'd done at home when I kept music playing in the background on the radio while I was doing my homework.

First I reviewed in my head all the images I'd seen on TV, particularly the sequence in which I was looking at myself but didn't realize it. If it hadn't been for the woman who'd grabbed me and pulled me back, out of the path of the tank, I'd already be dead. Saved by a total stranger, for no reason at all. She had no idea who I was. If our paths ever crossed someday, somewhere, she wouldn't recognize me and I certainly wouldn't recognize her. I couldn't figure out why—in this evil, disaster-ridden world I'd been living in for the past few days—people still persisted in doing good.

My wandering thoughts returned to the little shed where I'd taken refuge. I was being hunted by soldiers from my own country—militia fighters or regular troops, I didn't know which. I wondered why I had to die like this, senselessly, perhaps blown to bits amid sacks of cement. I didn't understand.

I didn't understand how a nation's army could attack a district of its own capital city and bombard its own citizens with heavy weapons. I didn't understand how anyone could launch rockets and deploy tanks against terrified unarmed civilians just because members of a rival militia had been spotted in the area. When we'd arrived in the neighborhood late the previous afternoon, I'd seen a few of them. Four men with shaved heads and one with short hair, faces whitened with chalk or blackened with charcoal, barefoot or wearing plastic sandals—swaggering show-offs with old Kalashnikovs. Were those the notorious Chechens? Or had the real fighters sensed a trap and retreated? Rather than protecting the population, they held it hostage; instead of reassuring people, they terrified them. And it was to eliminate those fearsome warriors that the entire district had to be brought down around our heads in this deluge of fire and steel? I didn't understand at all.

After Papa's death—after his murder—Mama always said to me it was politics that was killing the country and killing us. I think she was wrong. In Australia they have politics, in France they have politics, in Sweden and America, too, they have politics. Why doesn't politics kill those countries? Don't their children keep going to school? And eventually get their diplomas? Maybe politics was like a car moving along a road: everything depended on the ability of the driver. I'd never in my life met a politician, man or woman. But I swore that if I ever got out of this mess—if I wasn't blown to bits by a rocket, along with my sacks of cement—I was going to walk right up to the first one I saw and ask: Ladies and gentlemen of the political world, do you know what you're doing?

After you've spent a good long time asking questions that are never answered, you get the feeling you're going around in circles and racking your brain for no reason. I began to feel like this. So I decided I'd rather have silence in my head, because I've always thought that if you've got nothing worth saying, it's better not to say anything at all. So I told my brain to be quiet. To do something else. Read, for example. Read a book under the whizzing and whistling of the rockets the way you'd read a novel with music playing in the background. A book can make you forget about death. That thought made me smile.

I pulled the leather bag from its hiding place and took out the magazine Tanisha had given me. Scarcely had I hidden the bag again when my brain, like a radar system, detected something abnormal. On high alert, my muscles tense, I listened.

A whistling noise, far away at first, was growing louder and louder at horrifying speed. No doubt about it: a rocket was coming straight toward me. In the moment before the impact, I had just enough time to throw down the magazine, wedge my body between two piles of sacks, hunch my shoulders up around my ears, and brace myself for the explosion.

The rocket went over the roof of the shed, practically scraping the top, and slammed to earth about ten meters away. It struck with such force that the ground shook, and the sacks of cement, apparently so firmly stacked, came tumbling down around me. One of them landed on my right foot, pinning me down by the ankle. At the moment of impact, an enormous mass of dust and smoke, a flaming billow, a mushroom cloud, burst from the ground. Solar eclipse. Blackout. I couldn't see a thing. I was coughing. Then, through the cloak of darkness that blinded me, I heard shouts, wailing, screams of terror. They penetrated my dazed mind, which was jolted by the cries as if by electric shocks and finally made the connection: the rocket had struck the main house, where Mama was.

When I realized this, I panicked. I was desperate to get out, to run, to find Mama and Auntie Tamila, to help them . . . but my ankle was pinned under a sack of cement, and I couldn't even stand up. I shrieked, I yelled for help, for someone to come get me out—but the whole world was shrieking and yelling. I tried to move the sack with my other foot, but couldn't budge it. I began to feel a throbbing pain, and was afraid my ankle was broken.

The smoke and dust began to settle, and I kept calling out, to let people know I was there. At last someone heard me. Two men came into the shed. They were white with dust. They moved the sacks that were hemming me in, as well as the one that had fallen on my leg. I got to my feet. I flexed my ankle—it wasn't broken, but it was very painful.

Then I looked toward the house. It was gone. The rocket had smashed right into it. It was nothing but a heap of rubble, bricks, roof tiles, splinters. Part of it was in flames. Wild-eyed men and women were wandering aimlessly through this shattered landscape.

I rushed out into the courtyard, which was strewn with debris and wreckage. Limping because of my sore ankle, I ran as fast as I could to the ruined house. It would have been a miracle if anyone had survived. Mama was somewhere under all the destruction. I began to dig feverishly with my hands, clawing with my nails, heaving away bricks and boards, weeping. Other people came to help me. Using improvised levers, we managed to move the concrete slab that had formed the ceiling of her room and under which she and Tamila had taken shelter.

The horror was complete. Mama and Tamila, crushed, lying in each other's arms.

I shrieked. I wanted to hurl myself on the two bodies, but strong arms restrained me and pulled me back.

"No! Let me go! I want to stay—that's my mother!"

"Later, later," said a man's firm voice, while I was being led away. "You'll see them later. We have to get them out first."

Chapter Twenty-two

Johnny, Known as Mad Dog

So the bombardment of Kandahar had begun at daybreak. The artillery continued to batter the district all morning. The shells burst into the air at a rapid rate, full of thunder and force—a stupendous advance over our Kalashnikovs. I was elated. The shelling would neutralize as many Chechens as possible before our assault. Too bad for the other people in the district—they should have known better than to be born Mayi-Dogos.

Around midmorning, the racket from the barrage became so intense that I got a headache. I moved away from the guns, plugging my ears with my fingers. Lovelita followed me. Seeing that I wasn't feeling well, she dug around in the makeup bag she kept in the hip pocket of her pants, and from her assortment of beauty aids—eye pencils, lip gloss, a small mirror—she triumphantly produced a ball of cotton, which she offered me. I thanked her, divided it into two smaller balls, and stuffed them into my ears. My head immediately felt better—the din from the cannons and rocket launchers was muffled, as if it were coming from far away.

The artillerymen, in contrast, were firing without protecting their ears and had to be replaced every so often. They would become completely deaf and as a result would have trouble regulating the pace of the shelling. They staggered as they walked away from their posts, dazed and dizzy. Seeing how their legs trembled, I wondered what the noise was doing to their brains.

Oddly, after a while those explosions became our normal environment, and the silence that fell during the pauses in the shelling had something so harrowing about it that I couldn't wait to return to the natural order of things—that is, to the thunderous roar that accompanied the firing—even if the noise reached my ears only faintly through the cotton.

*

No one had given the order to attack. But we understood instinctively that the bombardment had ended and that the time to go for the spoils had arrived. What was surprising was that we, the Roaring Tigers, were no longer alone.

From the various districts loyal to our new president came a stream of armed men—militia fighters, soldiers from the "regular" army, and looters. But why bother saying "militia fighters, soldiers, and looters"? The phrase is redundant—I should have said simply "looters," because that's what they all were: jackals and hyenas coming out of their lairs, drawn by the smell of blood and plunder. Except for us, the Roaring Tigers.

This time we would put an end to the Chechens and to the arrogance of the Mayi-Dogos. We had entered their stronghold and were going to teach them a lesson they'd never forget.

They'd realize once and for all that they should have let our president, an army general, take control of the government.

Little Pepper, Piston, and I went into the yard of the first house we came to. It was just a tiny wooden structure, probably built very quickly by someone who was too poor to afford anything better. We were wasting our time there. But Piston pointed out that Chechens could use the place as a hideout, so it would be a good idea to destroy it. I agreed, and with one good kick I broke down the plywood door. I nearly had a heart attack—an old man dressed all in white was sitting calmly in an armchair, reading a book! He didn't even jump when the door was smashed open.

"On your feet! Now!" I shouted.

He raised his head and looked at me. Our eyes met, and then, without a word, he turned his gaze back to the thick volume in his hands, as if nothing had happened. I've often killed people at point-blank range, often threatened people with a gun, so I'm good at spotting the fear in their eyes—the terror that makes their pupils dilate—just before I pull the trigger. But I couldn't see an ounce of fear or a glimmer of panic in the eyes of this man. On the contrary, I saw complete serenity, as if he were living in some other world. It wasn't normal.

"D-d-drop the book, or I'll shoot!" I heard myself stammer, though usually I fired without warning. His gaze had numbed me—my finger was paralyzed, unable to squeeze the trigger. What the hell was happening to me?

I heard a shot—Little Pepper, standing next to me, had fired. All of a sudden, I felt released. My finger tightened on the trigger and I let loose volley after volley, as if I were taking revenge for that brief display of humiliating weakness. I think I must have emptied my entire cartridge into that demon—his body was reduced to a pulp. Out of curiosity, I picked up the book he'd been reading. It was a Bible.

The book was spattered with blood. I wiped it off. I'd never owned a Bible, and an idea came to me: I ought to acquire a personal library, like a real intellectual. This book would be the first volume in my collection.

Bible in one hand and machine gun in the other, I led my men out of that first house. The second was right next to it, and, stuffing the book into a canvas bag that I'd found and hung from my waist, I headed for the front door. I had to make my subordinates forget the momentary spell of weakness they'd just seen—a leader must never display cowardice. I broke down the door of the house with the butt of my gun, while my men covered me.

"Everybody out!" I yelled. They came out, one by one—thirteen terrified people with their hands in the air. Four men, five women, and four kids.

I went inside and searched the place. There are always idiots who think that hiding under a bed is a good idea. Understandable when you're ten years old. But if you're over thirty and you don't know that under the bed is the first place anyone checks when looking for a thief or a rival lover, then you've really got to have shit for brains. Well, this time was no exception. A guy had snuck under one of the beds—he was all curled up, trying to occupy as little space as possible, thinking he could become invisible that way. I drove him out with kicks and blows, while he squealed like a pig. I glanced in all the closets, to make sure no enemy soldiers were lurking there. There was no one else in the house.

Back outside, I pointed to the spots where I wanted them to go and shouted: "Men over here! Women over there!" And then: "On your knees!" They knelt down immediately.

We began searching the men, making them stand up one by

one. We patted them down carefully to make sure they had no hidden weapons, even a kitchen knife, and in the process we stripped them of whatever we felt like taking—watches, belts, shoes, you name it. They had very little money, though. Then we searched the women, squeezing their tits, stroking their bellies, feeling their asses. And we didn't forget to check between their legs—the wily creatures sometimes thought of the most unusual places to hide things. I ripped an earlobe snatching some pretty earrings off a woman so that I could give them to my Lovelita, who was waiting for me back in our district, as I'd told her to.

Little Pepper was furious at having turned up so little money. "*Somba liwa!*" he shouted, the locks of his red wig trembling. "Buy your death!" That was his way of saying, "Your money or your life!" I remembered back to a time in my military career when I'd been known as Lufua Liwa, or "Kill Death" (just hear my tread, and you were dead!). But now my name was Mad Dog.

Since no one responded to his commands, he doled out a kick to the oldest man in the group—a guy who must have been a grandfather.

"*Somba liwa*, or I'll shoot!"

"My son—"

Little Pepper shot him full in the chest before he'd even finished his sentence. He fell dead, and the women began to scream and cry. Little Pepper shut them up by threatening to kill anyone who wept. The sobs were instantly transformed into faint snifflings. At that moment, Piston—who had gone into the house to search for electronic stuff—came out the door, pushing ahead of him a boy of twelve or thirteen. The kid was crying. It was all an act, of course.

"I found him hiding above the ceiling!" yelled Piston, giving the brat a boot in the rear.

Shit! How could I have forgotten that people can hide in the crawl space above the ceiling? In retrospect I was scared, because if he'd been armed he would have killed us all, one by one, from his superior strategic position. From now on, I'd even check the trees to make sure there weren't any monkeys lying in wait.

"Why didn't you come out with the others?" I shouted at the kid, furious not because he'd posed a danger but because he'd shown he was cleverer than me, the leader of an elite commando unit.

He said nothing and continued to cry.

"You're a Chechen—that's why you were hiding! Get down on your knees!"

"He's my son! I swear he isn't a Chechen! He's only a child—he was just scared to come out! I swear he isn't a Chechen!" cried one of the women.

These people didn't know me. They thought I was a weakling whose heart would melt under the influence of tears and entreaties. But a Chechen is a Chechen—and a Mayi-Dogo kid, whatever his age, was a Chechen in the making.

"Shut up!" I yelled at the mother. And *blam!* I fired into the throat of the kneeling boy.

The horrified mother threw herself at the body of her child, but Little Pepper pumped a volley into her before she reached it. She fell to the ground, head first. Well, we'd wasted enough time and had to get going. We decided to kill all of the men. They were Mayi-Dogos anyway. Magnanimously, I spared the lives of the women, telling them to leave the district immediately and head for the areas we had already pacified. I know, I know—someday my kind heart is going to get me into serious trouble.

* * *

When we came out into the street, we saw some people wandering around the yard of a house about twenty meters away. It was pretty bold of them to have stayed there without taking cover, seeing as everyone knew we weren't going to deal lightly with those we found in the district. Were they trying to lure us into a trap? Advancing cautiously with our weapons cocked, we drew closer and saw the ruins of a large house that had been completely destroyed by the shelling. Dazed, hollow-eyed people were digging feverishly through the debris. For the most part they were silent, except for a girl with a bag slung bandolier-style across her front. She was crying hysterically and calling, "Mama! Mama!" while the others tried to restrain her. Still, there was no guarantee that Chechens weren't hiding among them—we had to secure the entire area.

We rounded the corner to the right, and I could scarcely believe my eyes when I saw what lay opposite the ruined house. There, intact and imposing, was a huge multistory residence—a fucking mansion. It was surrounded by a high wall, over which we could see the tops of two tall palm trees. The remarkable thing was that except for a big shell hole in the perimeter wall, the place was unscathed. Even more remarkable was the fact that despite the large hole left by the rocket, the wall was still standing! The masons who had built it must have been incredible—real masters of their trade. There was no doubt in my mind: they must have been experts from abroad.

I wasn't very familiar with the Kandahar district, and never knew that any of its residents had such fine villas. Whoever had built this one was surely a wealthy businessman, with millions of euros or dollars and not just paltry CFA francs. But if, like so many others, he was merely a bureaucrat on the government's payroll, then there were only two possibilities: either he had siphoned off large sums from the state treasury, or he was mixed up in politics and was an active member of the party in power (anyway, in our country the two always went hand in hand). I was determined to find out which. Luckily for us, the other militias hadn't yet come this way—we were the first.

We employed our usual tactics: volleys fired into the air, shouts and threats, kicks and blows with the butts of our guns against the front door and the windows, sudden and violent intrusion into the living room. I almost fell over when I saw the man who was cowering in a corner with his wife. Mr. Ibara! Ibara the customs inspector! The man who got a ten percent commission on all imported goods, the man who bought a new Mercedes every year, the man with the beautiful wife. People said he skimmed off more money from the nation's customs revenues than our president did from its oil revenues. There wasn't a soul in the country who hadn't heard of him. And I was the one who would have the privilege of looting his house!

I hadn't yet recovered from my surprise when Piston shouted from the garage: "He took the tires off the Lexus, and the Toyota is missing its battery!" Then he joined the rest of us in the living room, screwdriver in hand, and explained the situation to me. I turned to Ibara.

"Where are the tires for the Lexus and the battery for the Toyota?"

"I . . . I . . . They were stolen . . . Some militiamen came before you got here . . ."

"You think we're stupid? Militiamen came through here and instead of taking the Mercedes they just took the tires? Instead of stealing the Toyota . . ."

"Yeah!" said Piston excitedly. "A Toyota Hi-Lux Double-Cab!"

". . . they took nothing but the battery? You're a thief yourself, Mr. Ibara. Would you have done that?"

I raised the muzzle of my weapon and he immediately dropped all pretense.

"Take everything, but please—spare our lives! The tires and the battery are buried behind the garage. Here are the keys to the vehicles. I beg of you—help yourself to anything you want, but don't kill us . . ."

"I don't like it when people take me for an idiot!" I shouted, whacking him with the butt of my gun. "Who else is hiding in this house?"

"I swear there's no one here but us! Our children fled to the western districts. We stayed behind, just the two of us, to look after the house."

"We'll see about that," I said.

I wasn't about to be tricked again, after we'd found that kid hiding above the ceiling. Little Pepper and I fired a number of volleys into the wood ceiling, which wound up looking like a sieve. We checked under the beds, peered inside the cupboards and closets, poked into every nook and cranny of that huge villa. We didn't turn up any people, but you could hardly say we didn't find anything.

Two trunks filled with pagnes—waxes, superwaxes, batiks, java prints from Holland. Embroidered dresses from West Africa, a TV with a giant screen, a CD player, a DVD player, a computer. So many things, I can't remember them all. We helped ourselves, took everything we wanted, ransacked the entire house. The Toyota truck was piled to the brim with our loot. We went into the kitchen. The freezer was crammed with food and the fridge contained bottles of cold beer—not the cheap local brew, but the real stuff, imported from Europe and even from Asia! I didn't even know they *made* beer in China and Japan! No shit, that Mr. Ibara was rich. While we were dying of hunger, he could feast every single day. We went back to the living room, Piston knocking back a Tsingtao and me sipping Chivas Regal straight from the bottle. The only one who wasn't drinking was Little Pepper—he was still struggling to get the corkscrew into his bottle of Dom Pérignon. I immediately saw why he wasn't having any luck.

"You've got to take off the wire that holds the cork, stupid!" I said in my commando-leader's voice. He untwisted the wire and again tried to get the corkscrew in.

"A champagne cork will pop out, you know."

All three of us looked up. It was Mr. Ibara who had spoken these words, with a condescending smile. I didn't like that at all. He seemed to be looking down his nose at us, as if we were Pygmies who'd just stumbled out of the forest, or bushmen who'd just seen a bottle of Coca-Cola fall from the sky to land at their feet and didn't know what to make of it. Well, what the fuck! Did he take us for his Mayi-Dogos brothers—those village hicks who'd never seen a toilet and who pissed into the river over the sides of their canoes? Okay, so I'd never opened a bottle of champagne—but did he know how to dance the *ndombolo* like me? His scornful expression didn't sit well with the others, either. Little Pepper took the bottle of champagne and hurled it at him. It grazed his ear and exploded against the finely lacquered wall.

"Somba liwa!" shouted Little Pepper, and began beating Mr. Ibara, kicking him savagely and clubbing him with the butt of his gun. The poor guy had a split lip and was bleeding all over the place.

"Please, please, stop!" begged his wife. "I'll give you all the money we have, and all of my jewelry, if you'll go away and leave us alone!"

"Come on, hand them over!" ordered Little Pepper.

She took down one of the paintings and slid back a panel in the wall—perfect camouflage to fool the eye. The Ibaras had a safe! Never in my life could I have imagined that anything was hidden behind the wall. She opened the safe and drew out a large envelope, which she tossed over to me. It was full of money—bills of ten thousand CFA francs, as well as American dollars. Mr. Ibara was filthy fucking rich. And everything he had was ours. He didn't know that all his life he'd been working for *us*.

His wife handed me her jewelry box. Gold, diamonds, opals, rubies, and other precious stones I couldn't even name. I took a good swig of Chivas. Lovelita, you were going to be spoiled beyond belief! I'd give you superwax pagnes, diamond necklaces, gold chains. And my other girlfriends would be showered with gifts, too. Little Pepper and Piston watched me with big eyes, as if I were going to make off with all the loot. I reassured them.

The woman joined her husband on the sofa, where he was sitting with his shoulders hunched. There'd been a rumor in the city that Mr. Ibara had imported a set of furniture all in leather—some said it came from South Africa, others from the United States—in a special cargo plane. Well, it was true—everything was leather: the sofa, the armchairs. I dragged over one of the armchairs and sat down in it, facing the couple. It was cushy and comfortable. I lit up one of Mr. Ibara's cigars, a Davidoff. Being a militiaman was really nice—gave you a chance to sample the finer things in life.

"We've handed over everything—now please go!" begged the wife.

Despite the beating we'd given him, Mr. Ibara still radiated that sense of superiority he'd displayed when he realized we didn't know how to open a bottle of champagne. The guy didn't know that unlike Piston and Little Pepper, *I* had been to school, and he shouldn't make the mistake of lumping us all together. As for him, he might be rich but he certainly wasn't an intellectual, since the first thing you see in an intellectual's home is always books—books overflowing onto the floor and spilling out of a library too small to hold them. Now, I had counted and recounted, but he didn't have more than ten volumes (which I had immediately swiped for my own future library), a number far too paltry to make him an intellectual. I had to show him that he wasn't more intelligent than me just because he was rich and could guzzle champagne anytime he wanted. The best way to demonstrate this was to give him a test.

Through the fog and fumes of the Chivas, I thought back to the subject that had given me the most nightmares at school. And I decided that I'd ask him to state, right off the top of his head, the Pythagorean theorem. After slogging through many punitive exercises assigned by my teacher, I'd finally succeeded in memorizing that theorem, which says that the square of the sum of the hypotenuse . . . that the sum of the two sides of a triangle is the square . . . that the sum of the squares . . . Shit! I couldn't remember it! Fortunately, I hadn't yet uttered the question. Since I was a quick thinker, I instantly replaced the Pythagorean theorem with something more solid—a formula I knew like the back of my hand. Looking him straight in the eye, I asked him point-blank:

"Mr. Ibara, what's the area of a triangle?"

He stared at me, surprised. I'm sure he was prepared for anything from me, but he wasn't expecting this—a question of such high intellectual caliber. He no longer knew which of the two of us was off his rocker. Piston, who was uncapping a bottle of Sapporo, looked at me with his stupid cow-eyes. Normal for him. He'd never been educated and obviously didn't understand a damn thing—any more than Little Pepper, who'd been defeated by his inability to open the bottle of champagne and was making do with a bottle of Smirnoff's vodka.

But to tell the truth, as soon as the question escaped my lips I panicked—for all of a sudden I couldn't remember the answer. Such things often happen to extremely intelligent people, you know. Our brain works so quickly, performing so many operations per second, that sometimes the circuits become overloaded and information can no longer flow to the seat of our memory, the way cars are unable to move in a traffic jam. So I racked my memory in vain. I retrieved the equation for the area of a square, the area of a rectangle, and even the area of a complex shape like a cube—but for the area of a triangle, nothing! With all possible speed I had to deflect the missile I'd just launched, before it turned like a boomerang and exploded in my face with a thousand stabs of humiliation. Fire another question to make him forget the preceding one.

"Mr. Ibara, tell me this instead: What is ten to the third power?"

Here, at least, I knew the answer: one thousand. While he continued to stare at me, wondering what on earth was going on, his wife spoke up:

"Ten to the third power is one thousand. Ten to the sixth power is one million. And if you want to know, the area of a triangle is equal to the base times the height, divided by two. And now leave us in peace—we've already given you everything we have!"

People had always warned me not to trust chicks—I should have remembered. This one was dangerous not only because she had the balls her husband lacked, but also because she was more intelligent. There's nothing in the world more dangerous than a woman who's smarter than her husband. But how could she know the area of a triangle, while I, who had been to school, had forgotten it? That annoyed me, and I got angry.

Abruptly I got to my feet and stubbed out my cigar on the arm of the chair. Cloud of smoke, smell of burned leather. Mr. Ibara trembled as if his own flesh were burning. I couldn't see myself, but I knew that my eyes were madder than Giap's when he was in one of his rages. I grabbed the woman and pulled her roughly toward me.

"What do you do, aside from being Mr. Ibara's wife?"

"I'm a high school teacher."

Okay, now I understood everything. An intellectual. There was nothing in the world more dangerous than a woman intellectual.

"Whether you're a teacher or not, I don't like Mayi-Dogo women!"

I picked up my gun.

"No!" cried the husband. "My wife isn't a Mayi-Dogo! She's a member of your tribe—she's a Dogo-Mayi. Don't hurt her! I'm the one who's a Mayi-Dogo!"

When someone speaks to you in flawless French at the crack of dawn, before even drinking a cup of coffee, you have to take the person back to the village and pose a few simple questions, such as: Which one—the rooster or the drake—covers the female longer when he mates? Or: When growing on the tree, do the bananas in a bunch point up or down? Or, if you have no imagination, just ask the person to speak the tribal tongue.

I turned to the woman.

"Prove you're a Dogo-Mayi! Say something in the tribal language."

"I wasn't born in this country and I didn't grow up here. I don't know the language."

"Every good Dogo-Mayi was born in Dogo-Mayi Land and speaks the tribal tongue!"

"My father was the ambassador to Senegal, and I grew up speaking Wolof."

"I'm a kind person," I said. "I'll give you one more chance to make up for your mistakes and save your skin. Can you at least understand our language?"

"Yes."

So I asked her, "What's a *moughété*? Is it a fish or a bird?"

She didn't know—and small wonder! In our language, it was one of those rare words that someone who'd been born and raised in the city couldn't possibly know. A *moughété* was a fire-resistant tree. It was the proud, solitary form you saw on the savannah after all the other vegetation had been destroyed by a brush fire. I'd learned the word by chance, during a conversation in which my grandfather and his wife were lamenting the destruction of their fields.

"Too bad for you! Who told you to be born in a foreign country? Next time, you should be born here. And even if you're really a Dogo-Mayi, you're no longer one anyway, because you've let a Mayi-Dogo suck your tits. You're a traitor to your homeland and your tribe."

"I don't give a damn what you think! I love my husband!"

Furious, I shoved her away from me and she fell to the floor.

"Let's kill the pair of them and get out of here," said Little Pepper. "We've still got lots of houses to search."

I picked up the bottle of Chivas, brought it to my lips, and took three good gulps. Here I was, in the home of Mr. Ibara—one of those high-and-mighty types who would drive past us in their luxury cars and sneer at us, ignoring the misery around them. One of those bigshots who embezzled state funds to build their villas and support their mistresses; who had no need to build hospitals or schools in this country, because as soon as they felt the first twinge of a headache they could hop on a plane to America or Europe and get medical care. Yeah, I was in the home of one of those bigshots. I'd parked my ass in the armchair of a bigshot. I'd drunk from the glass of a bigshot. In a minute, I was going to take a piss in the toilet of a bigshot. And then, as I gazed at Mr. Ibara's wife sprawled on the floor, I had the urge to fuck the wife of a bigshot.

I threw myself on her, just like that, without warning. In no time, the only thing left for me to rip off was her panties. Mr. Ibara, who tried to come to her defense, got clubbed in the head for his pains. He fell back onto the leather sofa, firmly restrained by Piston and Little Pepper, who were snickering. He kept shouting, "Kill me if you want to, but don't touch my wife!" The woman fought like a fury, trying to kick me and bite me. I gave her a few slaps, and after a while she got tired and ceased to struggle.

I rode her good—I pumped and I pumped. I was fucking the wife of a bigshot! It made *me* feel like a bigshot. And for the first time in my life, I was fucking an intellectual. I felt more intelligent. Finally, I came. "My turn!" cried Little Pepper as soon as he saw me get up. But he was so excited at the thought of screwing the wife of a rich and famous kingpin that no sooner had he dropped his pants than he shot his wad, which spurted all over Lady Ibara's body. Immediately, his thing shrank and got soft. Piston, who was also looking on eagerly, cried, "Hey, let me have a turn!" Quickly he wiped away Little Pepper's mess with the woman's blouse and went at it, plunging his thing in the right place. Probably because he was so used to forcing in screws with his screwdriver, he didn't pump back and forth like other guys—instead, his buttocks bored in as if he were driving a corkscrew into the woman. "Okay, I'm ready!" cried Little Pepper, who was now less delirious at the thought of making it with the wife of a bigshot, and was easily able to do the job as soon as Piston had withdrawn his corkscrew. I wish Stud had been with us—I'd have liked to see how he went about it, with his thing the size of an elephant's trunk.

All this time, Mr. Ibara was literally weeping at his own impotence. Nothing humiliates a man more than seeing his wife violated before his eyes while he is unable to do anything about it. Mr. Bigshots of this world, don't forget that little guys exist, too! And know that they'll get you whenever they can. Remember this for your own good.

"I can't leave without having some champagne," said Little Pepper. "I've had a taste of a bigshot's wife, and now I want to know what champagne tastes like, too."

He was holding a bottle that Mr. Ibara had bought from a widow who'd written her name on the label—her name was Madame Clicquot. He handed the bottle to Mr. Ibara.

"Make the cork pop out, or I'll pop your brains out!"

Mr. Ibara took the bottle without a word. He was right—you didn't need a corkscrew to open a bottle of champagne, but what he hadn't told us was that the cork would explode from the bottle and fly through the air like a rocket. If I hadn't ducked just in time, it would have hit me in the eye—especially since Mr. Ibara had pointed it directly at me. Little Pepper grabbed the bottle, which was dripping with foam, and took a good swallow. He made a face, as if he didn't like the taste.

"Let me have some, too!" said Piston.

I, the leader, was content with my Chivas. Now that Little Pepper had finally tasted the famous drink he'd heard so much about, he was satisfied.

"Okay, so we kill them now?"

"No, I have a better idea," I replied.

A commander should always have better ideas than his troops.

"Mr. Ibara," I said, "if you want us to spare your lives, go over and fuck your wife."

A sudden resurgence of dignity and anger gave him spirit. He tried to get up, but Little Pepper beat him back onto his leather sofa.

"Kill me!" he shouted. "After what you've done to me, I'd be better off dead!"

He made a grab for Piston's gun. The shit-head. One good, well-placed kick and he collapsed again. He was lucky his daughters weren't around, or we would have made him fuck one of them—the way I'd once seen Giap force a young man to violate his own grandmother.

"We won't kill you, Mr. Ibara. We'll kill your *wife* if you don't fuck her—right now, in this living room, while we watch. Make up your mind! Either you fuck your wife or we kill her!"

Mr. Ibara, the Mayi-Dogo, looked at Mrs. Ibara, his Dogo-Mayi wife. She was lying on the floor in a miserable state, pressing her bloody thighs together and sobbing. Little Pepper pointed the muzzle of his Kalashnikov at Mrs. Ibara's crotch, ready to fire. Blubbering, Mr. Ibara got painfully to his feet, slowly unbuttoned his pants, and let them fall around his ankles. I was glad to see a bigshot humiliated. He walked forward in slow motion, with great effort, hollow-eyed like the ghost of a zombie, and when he was standing over his wife he lowered his underpants. His thing hung limply, wretchedly.

"Come on, let's get out of here," I said to my men.

*

We left Mr. Ibara's house, taking only the Toyota truck, since we didn't have time to dig up the tires for the Lexus and put them back on the car. We continued our raid through the Kandahar district, square meter by square meter, dynamiting the handsome villas, chopping down the fruit trees, killing the dogs, shooting every male individual between the ages of twelve and forty-five, and of course helping ourselves to whatever we wanted. For the entire rest of the day, we plundered, we killed, we stole, we raped. We were drunk with blood and sperm. From every direction you could hear cries of "*Somba liwa!*" along with gunfire, thundering grenades, screams, sobs, and the howling of dogs. Columns of smoke rose into the sky, twisted in the wind, and spread out over the city.

We had never suspected that the Mayi-Dogos, our countrymen, had so much wealth hidden away. No surprise that their leaders wanted to hang on to power at any price.

When we finally left the district at nightfall to return to our own neighborhoods, the scene looked like some vast carnival. Dozens of vehicles of every description—from huge military trucks to rickety old cars without headlights or license plates, from two-wheeled pushcarts to one-wheeled barrows—loaded down with the most motley array of items imaginable, all spoils of war—were streaming from Kandahar in a long, continuous file toward our own neighborhoods in the west of the city, their undercarriages scraping the ground because they were so heavily laden with CD players, DVD players, televisions, gas cookers, roof tiles, rafters, windows, sinks, toilets, mattresses, medicines, sacks of cassava flour, live chickens . . . Behind and alongside these vehicles trotted hundreds of other people armed with machetes, spears, automatic weapons, and, like us, gorged with blood and sperm—some of them brandishing pikes and bayonets topped with human heads, others sporting necklaces made of bloody human entrails, still others proudly flourishing genital organs, and all singing the war songs of our tribe. Finally came a long column of Mayi-Dogos made up largely of women, small children, and old people—a mass of lost, beaten, dazed refugees, carrying the little bundles of possessions that we, the conquerors, had been generous enough to let them keep.

Yeah, we had won the war! We'd proven that we were the stronger! In only a few hours, we had succeeded in emptying that traitorous district of its three or four hundred thousand inhabitants. Before taking us on, their puny, pathetic leaders should have remembered that *our* leader was an army general. You should always let sleeping generals lie.

Kandahar was devastated, bled dry, barren as a wheat field after a plague of locusts, bare as an elephant carcass after an attack of army ants. Once again, it was great to be on the winning side. That evening, our home districts would be alive with celebration. We would dance, we would make love, we would feast as we let loose our joy. We would organize one of those orgiastic revels whose meaning can be expressed fully, in all its nuances, only in the words of our tribal language. That evening would be filled with *lé dza, lé noua, lé bin'otsota.*

Chapter Twenty-three

Laokolé

My fit of hysterical grief must have lasted quite a while, for by the time it subsided the bodies of Mama and Auntie Tamila had been pulled from the wreckage. I was no longer sobbing, but silent tears still flowed down my cheeks. A woman led me to the spot where the two corpses lay. Mama a corpse!

The bodies were mangled and broken—a horrible sight. This was not a fitting death for a worthy woman who had never harmed anyone, a widow who had done the best she could to raise her children properly, a woman who had never stolen anything or killed anyone. To be crushed, along with her best friend, under the ruins of a house blasted by a blind mortar shell. Mama. Tamila. I had just lost two mothers in a single blow. I began weeping again, and fell to my knees beside the two bodies.

I wasn't given a chance to grieve. People helped me to my feet. They told me that Dogo-Mayi militias were prowling the district and were already across the street, in Mr. Ibara's house. I was a young woman and thus in as much danger as any of the young men, whom the militia fighters were killing simply because they suspected them of being Chechens. They would rape me, or else would kidnap me so they could rape me later.

"But what about Mama and Tamila!" I heard my voice say.

"We're going to bury them immediately. And then you'll leave with everyone else."

There weren't any shovels. Someone found a couple of hoes, and two holes were hastily dug in a corner of the yard, side by side, about knee-deep. The bodies were each wrapped in a pagne and then placed in the holes. I was asked to throw the first handful of soil on each of the two friends. As soon as my left hand had flung the second bit of earth, the people with the hoes began to fill in the two makeshift graves.

We had to leave. Someone gave me a push. I went a few steps and sank to the ground. I missed Mama. I couldn't accept the fact that after struggling so hard to get her this far, first in a wheelbarrow and then on a bicycle, I was being forced to abandon her in a little hole in a backyard.

"You must leave right away, Lao. They'll be here soon."

I looked up. I didn't know him—an old man whose white hair and deeply lined face bespoke weariness, pain, and resignation rather than the dignified coda of a happy, fulfilled life. I had no idea how he'd learned my name.

"If you stay here, they'll kill you—you won't have accomplished anything. I don't want to see what happened to my daughter happen to you. What she went through was so terrible she died from it. If you escape, if you survive, that will be one life those murderers won't get. It'll be like thumbing our noses at them—it'll prove that they'll never manage to kill us all. Go, my daughter, please! Go!"

His persuasive voice—warm, sincere, urgent—acted on me

like a stern command and got me to my feet. But I hadn't gone more than a couple of steps toward the departing group when he stopped me.

"Wait, my child!"

He opened his bag, which was lying on the ground, and handed me a small radio—one of those little transistors no bigger than the palm of your hand but capable of receiving an amazing range of frequencies. From the way he held it out to me, I was sure it was one of his most cherished possessions.

"Take this—it's my daughter's radio. So long as you have it, you won't be alone. Go now! The militias will be here any minute!"

He picked up his bag and turned away without saying another word. He rejoined the group of people who were continuing to dig through the wreckage and pull out bodies. Evidently, those people had chosen to stay and had decided that in every life there comes a point when you have to stop. When you have to cease running away and look squarely at your pursuers, whatever the outcome might be. That old man, whom I didn't know from Adam, had sensed that I hadn't yet reached this point and had urged me to flee because he fervently wanted me to survive. Why? How was it possible that good could still exist in this world? I've often asked myself this question, and to this day it remains a puzzle to me.

Before I, too, turned away, and set off down the road after the others, my gaze fell upon the wall surrounding Mr. Ibara's house. A rocket had blown an enormous hole in the middle of it, but despite this damage it was still standing. Any other structure would have collapsed. It was still standing because, after we'd laid the stepped foundation, we had decided to strengthen the wall with concrete pilasters reinforced with ten-millimeter rebars, instead of using a traditional vertical armature. And the result was before me—this wall that had defied the bombs. A wave of foolish pride ran along my spine and spread through my entire being.

At last I caught up with one of the groups of refugees and took my place in the procession. I felt lighter than usual. At first I attributed this to the fact that I was no longer pushing a wheelbarrow. Not until I'd been walking for about half an hour did I realize it was because I was no longer carrying the large bundle I'd borne on my head or my back ever since our departure. Not only had I left it under the ruins of Auntie Tamila's house, but I honestly hadn't given it a thought when I fled. The only bits of baggage that remained were my bandolier bag and, hidden under my pants, the little purse that contained all my money and the photo of Mama and Papa. What annoyed me the most was that I had only one pair of panties—the ones I was wearing—and I wondered what on earth I was going to do when they had become soiled and stained from my period.

Since all the routes leading to Kandahar were blocked by the army and their backup troops, we could flee in only one direction: toward the forest. And we had to proceed cautiously, for it was rumored that the first routes taken by the refugees were now being watched by the factions currently in power, which had set up patrols that would fire without warning. So we had to divide up into small groups and find alternate roads. By chance, I found myself with about twenty others in the company of a man who had generously offered to guide refugees to his village—anyone who wanted to come could follow him. The problem was that the village was located about a hundred kilometers away, deep in the forest. The trek would take at least a week. I knew nothing about the place—I'd never even heard of it. But that didn't matter. The important thing was to get away, to flee the bombs, the massacres, the rapes. At least he had a village. He wasn't like us, who had been born and raised in the city. We'd never had any desire or felt any need to go to the villages of our forebears, or to speak our tribal language. The city was sufficient for us. And now a political dispute was sending us back to our respective villages and our respective tribes. But the politicians who were forcing us to take to the road didn't know that most of us *had* no tribe or village. Our villages were the districts of the city where we had grown up, where we'd made our first friends, where we'd first fallen in love. The members of our tribe were the kids we'd played soccer or *dzango* with, running around barefoot in the dust; they were the friends we'd sat next to in school. And now all of that was being destroyed.

We walked and walked beneath the tropical sun, through the oppressive heat and humidity. I was perspiring so heavily that my damp clothes stuck to me, preventing the air from circulating over my skin and making it impossible to cool off even slightly. We were hastening toward that age-old refuge, the great forest, as fast as we could—for on the savannah we were crossing, amid the clumps of trees and the patchy secondary woods that had been thinned by agriculture and brush fires, we were exposed to view, and the sudden appearance of enemy helicopters or a militia patrol would mean the death of all of us.

Having climbed out of a valley to the top of a hill, we at last spied the forest. From a distance, it looked like an immense mass of solid greenery, but when we arrived at its edge I saw that the greenery was in fact a wall of trees—a twisted mass of trunks, limbs, leaves, vines, and shrubs that seemed all but impenetrable. I saw no way through, not the merest path. Born and raised in the city, I had never been in the forest.

This was not true of our guide. With a lithe movement, he ducked beneath a thick creeper and plunged into the dense undergrowth, vanishing into the depths of the woods. Like the others, I followed. I went into the forest. The true equatorial rain forest. I was sucked into a vaulted realm of shadows that, paradoxically, blinded me. I looked up toward the sky, but there was no sky—only a thick canopy that filtered the light and, with the stirrings of its leaves, imparted a rapid flickering to the few rays that penetrated it. At first, it felt good to be out of the scorching sun and in the relatively cool air under the forest canopy. But soon the muted light and the damp heat—all the more oppressive as it seemed to emanate uniformly from the surrounding atmosphere—in conjunction with the complete lack of any breeze, began to stifle me. All I could see were tree trunks, vines, leaves, ferns, grasses. How could you find your way in this seemingly endless ocean of plant life? I felt as if I'd been shipwrecked. I was suffocating, choking. I began to have difficulty breathing.

The woman walking behind me saw that I was gasping. She called to the others to stop. The leader of the group came up to me, and I admitted I was afraid. He thought that was funny, and laughed. He said I was afraid because I didn't know how to appreciate the forest. If I walked next to him, he said, he would teach my eyes to see.

And he taught them to see that each plant had its own shape, its own size, its own nature, its own shade of green; that you couldn't lump together this tree fern over here with the little phosphorescent frond over there; that if you thought this orchid was beautiful, take a look at that bird-of-paradise, which raised its petals proudly like the crest of a cock, and—

oh!—the flash of color down there wasn't the corolla of a blossom, but a butterfly; that amid the orchestra of diffuse sounds filling the air, not only could you distinguish the mocking screeches of the monkeys from the cries of the hornbills, but—listen!—you could tell the throaty plaint of a toad from the croaking of a frog; that over there—look where I'm pointing!—you've got to be careful: the thing you see wrapped around that tree trunk isn't a creeper, but a boa constrictor getting ready to pounce on you and strangle you . . .

My eyes worked perfectly well, but I hadn't noticed any of that. I realized then that, yes, whoever knew the forest couldn't get lost in it—there were so many markers and guideposts! My confidence returned and my distress faded away.

We continued to walk for a long, long time. The forest penumbra gave way to utter darkness. If we hadn't occasionally passed beneath one of the rare holes in the canopy, we wouldn't have known that a full moon was glowing in the sky. The people in the group who had flashlights got them out, and we followed the beams—which didn't extend very far, since they were blocked by the thick vegetation. At last we came to a halt. Our guide explained that the forest was dangerous at night—you could step on a snake or a poisonous spider without realizing it. He chose a spot where the undergrowth was sparse, and said that we would camp there.

I immediately sank down on the grass. I was completely exhausted and my feet hurt. Again I was glad that I'd decided to wear my old threadbare sneakers, which I'd often worn when I worked on construction jobs with Papa. I took them off and rubbed my toes. The people who were traveling with family sat close to their relatives, and the others sat apart or in groups, according to their inclinations. There were more of us than I'd thought when we set out—more than thirty, perhaps even forty. Small wood fires were lit, and people started cooking things to eat. Some began smoking wild tobacco, whose smell I found sickening. I had nothing to eat and was very hungry. My mother had brought me up to think that only a beggar would ask for food, and I told myself that going to bed hungry wasn't the end of the world. In any case, I was used to it.

I was sitting by myself off to the side, massaging my sore feet, when the leader of the group—the man who had generously offered to take us to his village—came over and sat down next to me on the grass. He asked me if I was feeling better. I expressed my gratitude and said that, thanks to him, I was becoming more familiar with the forest. I now understood how the Pygmies could live there all their lives: we had supermarkets, and they had the forest—which was stocked with more things and was less expensive. He asked, with great gentleness and tact, how a young woman like me came to be fleeing alone through the forest. I explained to him that in the space of forty-eight hours I had lost my brother and my mother, and that ten minutes before joining his group I hadn't known that I would wind up in the forest—which we city kids disdained, along with everything associated with it. I, in turn, asked about his situation. He was a retired nurse. Had come to the city to replenish the supply of basic medical supplies (aspirin, chloroquine, quinimax, common antibiotics, disposable syringes) for the small clinic he was trying to maintain out in the bush. It was heartrending to see a child die of malaria for the lack of a few tablets of chloroquine. He'd arrived at the height of the war. The pharmacy where he usually bought his supplies had been looted. Nothing left to do but head back to his village.

"And why this generosity?" I asked.

"What generosity?" he replied.

He urged me not to stay on the margins of the group, so far from the campfires. At night a fire would attract moths and other annoying insects, but it would keep away snakes and predators. I joined him and his companions around their campfire. They were welcoming and friendly. He offered me some water, as well as a piece of bread with sardines. Another person offered me a banana. I accepted. And then they all began talking about their flight, their sufferings, the horrors they'd seen or experienced, the atrocities committed by the two warring factions.

When someone mentioned the lack of news about what was happening in the capital, I suddenly remembered that I had a radio. It was too late to get the reports on the international stations, so we tuned in to the local station.

The leader of the faction currently in power, President Dabanga, was speaking:

> *"Congratulations to our brave fighters! They have routed the traitors who dragged our fair country down into the depths of anarchy, chaos, and senseless violence. We have taken power in order to reestablish peace and democracy. I have therefore instructed the troops charged with maintaining order to continue their occupation of the districts they have pacified. My fellow citizens, our country is too precious to be left in the hands of those genocidal villains, many of whom have fled into the forest. We will give them no respite! We will hunt them down! We will flush them out, village by village, and exterminate them, even if those villages lie in the depths of the jungle. I . . ."*

Someone asked me to turn it off. There was an odd silence, broken only by the throbbing sounds of the forest. I was a genocidal villain, and would be hunted down even if I fled to the farthest depths of the jungle. We settled down for the night with those menacing words in our heads.

Before going to sleep, I borrowed a flashlight and went off by myself into the darkness—not too far, though, for fear of meeting up with a panther, a boa constrictor, or some other dangerous animal. I changed my sanitary pad and buried the one I took off. I had no choice but to put my stained panties back on. Even though my cramps had subsided a bit, I took two acetaminophen before retiring.

It gets cold at night in the rain forest—I never knew that. Using my leather bag as a pillow, I curled up tightly, so that as little of my body as possible would be exposed to the air. I slept poorly. First of all, there were mosquitoes and gnats constantly buzzing in your ears; and then there were crawling insects, such as the ants, that suddenly bit you with their chelicerae. And there were strange noises and gruntings—quite alarming, since we were in a region inhabited by gorillas. I'd been afraid of gorillas ever since I'd heard that a woman at a banana plantation in the forest had had her baby snatched by one while her back was turned. Last but not least, I thought for a long time about Mama, weeping silently. I got up at dawn, with the first mocking laughter of the monkeys, and before the earliest birdsongs were drowned in the cacophony of the myriad species flourishing in that vast woodland aviary.

We broke camp fairly quickly. The coolness of the night had left the leaves and grass heavy with dew, so that my sneakers and the legs of my pants were soon soaked. We walked and walked and walked. We floundered through swamps. When there was no path, as was often the case, we cut our way through thick vines and underbrush with a machete. We ducked under low-hanging branches and clambered over the trunks of enormous trees felled by lightning or storm winds. From time to time, we were afforded a glimpse of the misty sky through a hole in the canopy that had been left by one of those fallen giants. My body was so weary that I no longer felt my weariness; I put one foot in front of the other, mechanically. When at last we rounded a bend in the path and caught sight of a village up ahead, I felt as though I'd seen the gates of Paradise.

The village was on a road, one of those thoroughfares that loggers had cut through the woods for their trucks. I never knew there was logging so deep in the rain forest. We arrived in the early afternoon. The men had returned from the hunt, and we came upon them as they were skinning a gorilla. They were surprised to see those forty-odd human animals emerge from the underbrush, and I got the impression they were briefly frightened when they caught sight of the first members of our group, for they hastily tried to conceal their prey. But the fact that we had women and children among us reassured them. Our leader explained who we were, why we were fleeing, and where we were going. He asked them if we could rest for a while in their village before continuing on our way, since the women and children were tired. They began laughing and confessed that they had just been poaching in the nature preserve, where they were forbidden to hunt even though the area was teeming with elephants, buffalo, and gorillas. Until they'd noticed the women and children, they'd taken us for game wardens.

The headman welcomed us and showed us to a large, open-sided, thatched-roof hut located in the center of the village. This was where the inhabitants always met to conduct their business. The women gave us water to drink, and a man brought us a demijohn of palm wine.

Sitting on a woven mat, I let my exhausted body relax. To see the sunshine again, after all that time in the chiaroscuro of the forest, lifted my spirits. I hadn't known I was so fond of the sun and its light. I drank only water, but the others—

women as well as men—indulged in the palm wine. I stretched out on my mat, overcome with fatigue, and before I knew it I was asleep.

Someone woke me up. The villagers were inviting us to share their meal, which consisted largely of gorilla meat. The women had cooked it into a stew, and it smelled good. Since nothing proved they had actually killed the ape, rather than finding it already dead, I declined to eat any of it—avoided even touching the bowls they served it in. I didn't want to risk catching the Ebola virus. To explain my refusal and avoid offending the villagers, I came up with a clever fib: I told them that in my father's clan, women who had not yet borne children were forbidden to eat gorilla meat. I almost said "women who were still virgins," but I decided this would sound too implausible. They believed the lie, and, continuing their display of generosity, a woman brought me a plate of *maboké*, a freshwater fish (catfish, I think) which had been seasoned with pepper, wrapped in banana leaves, and baked. It was delicious, and I ate every bit of it—even crunched on the bones. It was the first good meal I'd had in a very long time.

As the saying goes, newcomers bring the news. Our group told the villagers all about the latest events in the city—the fighting, the massacres, the horrors. They didn't understand in the least. "Well, we have our disagreements, too—but we don't kill each other!" declared one of the village elders, whose hair was completely white. I guess he was too old to comprehend the modern world, political matters, and the way politicians worked.

After the meal, to my great surprise, our guide thanked our hosts and said we had to take advantage of the three or four hours of daylight that remained in order to make progress before nightfall, since we were traveling far and needed to move on. With contributions from the group, he put together a gift consisting of four one-kilo bags of cane sugar, two 250-gram packets of salt, a large box of powdered milk, two small envelopes of ground coffee, and four large bars of soap. He himself added two packets of aspirin, and presented the entire collection to the chieftain as an expression of our gratitude. Sugar, salt, coffee—the villagers were delighted.

Our caravan prepared to set out, but my body refused to stand up, refused to leave. My brain as well. I couldn't see myself starting all over again—hunching and stumbling my way through the forest, tripping over roots, cutting myself on razor-sharp leaves, keeping a nervous eye out for poisonous snakes . . . No. The leader of our group tried to persuade me. He had brought me out of the city and felt responsible for guiding me to his village. I wasn't safe here, for this village was on a road. I told him he needn't worry—he shouldn't feel responsible for me at all, because I alone had made the decision to follow him and I alone had decided not to make the entire trek to his village—I was at the end of my strength. The others added their voices to his, urging me to come with them. But when I persisted, one of the women said: "Oh, let her do as she likes! Young people today, especially kids born in the city, never listen to their elders anymore. They've become so stubborn! Well, so much the worse for her." She was irritated. She attached her baby firmly to her back, placed her bundle on her head, and marched off into the forest.

So they left. I alone stayed behind in that unfamiliar village, whose name I didn't even know. I had no idea how long

I would remain there—a week, perhaps—hoping that peace would be reestablished in the meantime. Since we were on a road that was more or less driveable, a truck would eventually pass by and take me back to the city.

The warm welcome extended to us by the villagers had prevented me from noticing how poor they were. I watched as they divided up what the group had given them—they treated the items as precious commodities, picking up a crumb of sugar that had fallen to the ground, counting and recounting the spoonfuls of salt to make sure the distribution was fair, trying to cut a large bar of soap into eight equal pieces. Since there was no way all of them could have a bit of everything, some chose to have salt rather than sugar, or two little cubes of soap rather than four large spoonfuls of ground coffee.

A few scrawny chickens were roaming around, and two or three equally scrawny goats were grazing untethered just outside the village. Otherwise, there wasn't much. A field of cassava and some banana trees over here, patches of groundnuts and yams over there. With the exception of cassava leaves, which were available all year long, the villagers must certainly have known periods of scarcity between the growing seasons, for each crop has its season. And they certainly didn't feast on gorilla meat every day. It goes without saying that there was a shortage of medicines—the village didn't even have a clinic. You could die from just about anything there, even the slightest injury or ailment.

I didn't remain by myself very long. After the distribution of the sugar, salt, milk, coffee, and soap, a woman offered to take me into her home. She lived only with her daughter, whose sleeping mat I could share. Village people were like that—generous and hospitable. Things were different in the city.

We walked over to her house. I helped her carry her share

of the gifts. Her daughter, who was sweeping the front yard, gave me a warm welcome. Since the house was one of the largest in the village, with walls of brick and a tile roof, I wondered whether it wasn't the headman's house. When I asked my hostess this question, she looked at me as if she hadn't understood, and replied, "Why?"

"Because it's the biggest house in the village, and maybe the handsomest," I said.

With an expression that implied I was making no sense, she asked me in turn: "Why must the headman have the biggest house in the village? And," she said with a smile, "the most beautiful wife?"

Why indeed? I didn't know how to answer.

Her daughter asked me to sit in the living room, and disappeared into one of the bedrooms. I heard her rummaging about, moving things around, then sprinkling and sweeping the floor. At last she came out and, with great pleasure, showed me the bed that we would share. It wasn't a mat, as her mother had said, but a fine foam mattress large enough for two and a half people. Her mother asked if I needed anything. Water to wash with, I immediately replied—I hadn't washed for two days.

"That's not good for a woman," she said. "A woman should bathe every day. And she should tend to her intimate hygiene every evening before going to bed, and every morning when she gets up." She was already speaking as if I were her own daughter. "Asjha will take you to the river."

Asjha was her daughter, the young woman who had welcomed me. I told Asjha that I would like to bathe, and also to wash the few clothes I had. She asked, in turn, if I would help her fetch water to the house. With a yellow plastic jug on my head,

I followed her. The river wasn't very far from the village—half a kilometer, at most. We went upstream, to the spot reserved for the women. I took my clothes off, and then got rid of my sanitary pad. My panties—my only pair—were stained with blood despite the pad, probably because of all the arduous walking I'd done. The good news was that my period was over with. Asjha handed me the little cube of soap that she'd received as her share. I washed my panties, my bra, which was filthy with the sweat that had poured from my armpits, and the T-shirt I'd been wearing constantly for several days.

Then I turned my attention to my body. I poured water all over myself, rubbed my skin with the lavender-scented soap that Asjha had brought, and plunged into the cool, fresh water. Asjha disrobed as well, and, after soaping up, she joined me in the river. The water wasn't deep—it scarcely came up to my pubic hair, and came only up to Asjha's waist, since she was shorter than me. We paddled around in the water like happy ducks. Asjha splashed me in the face and ran away; I chased her, and caught her around the waist just as she was emerging onto the shore. The two of us fell. Trying to disengage herself, she turned to face me, and in a fit of high spirits we rolled over and over in the sand, one on top of the other, tangled in each other's arms, nude, her breasts and thighs pressed against mine. We were laughing like little kids. When we finally got to our feet, gasping for breath, she looked in frank admiration at my womanly breasts, the color of jujube fruit. To tease her, I turned my face to show my profile and struck a fashion pose: one hand behind my head, the other on my jauntily thrust-out rear, and one knee slightly canted forward. I arched out my bust and pulled in my stomach. A sudden breeze wafted over us. I felt good; I felt beautiful. Asjha laughed with delight. She came up to me and touched my firm breasts.

"How did you get such pretty ones?"

"You'll have them, too, when you're my age."

"How old are you?"

I lied, to impress her, and said I was older than I really was. "I'm eighteen and a bit."

I looked at her breasts, the two little buds of a girl just on the verge of puberty. I pinched them, and she trembled.

"How old are *you*?"

"Fifteen."

I was scarcely sixteen.

"You're going to have very beautiful breasts—you'll see," I assured her. "And just as many pubic hairs as me," I added, stroking the black hairs between my legs. She plucked one of the hairs with her fingers, stretched it out, and marveled at how long it was. We continued to compare and admire our bodies as the sun set, bathing us in its rosy light.

In contrast to the birds, which were returning to the forest in great noisy, disordered flocks, a swarm of butterflies emerged from the brush in silent procession. I didn't know what kind they were—all I knew was that they were magnificent. They had large blue wings edged with velvety black. They flew in a haphazard way, darting here and there, letting themselves fall briefly and then bounding upward again with a little jump, as if taking off from an invisible trampoline. It seemed that, just like Asjha and me, they were intoxicated with the sounds and scents floating on the evening air. One of them came to rest on Asjha's hair. She stood perfectly still, smiling with joy—and the butterfly, too, remained still, slowly fanning its azure wings like someone drawing breath, taking heart. A magical moment.

"Asjha, I crown you Queen of the Republic of Butterflies!"

She laughed gaily, a laugh full of starlight, and the butterfly flew away. The two of us ran to the river and plunged in, wading about, chasing each other, splashing each other—two young women, naked and happy in the soft tropical twilight.

"Big sister, it's time to go."

Asjha had never even asked my name. I was her big sister, and that was enough. I put my jeans back on without any panties, and to cover my breasts I took the pagne she'd given me and tied it around my ribs like a bodice. We walked upriver, passing the spot where the men went to wash, and came to a little cove where there was a spring with drinkable water—a clear, cool stream that welled up from the ground and flowed out over the sand and the fine white gravel. We filled our containers. I helped to balance hers on the cushion she'd placed on her head. Then I took up the plastic jug and we started back to the village.

Chapter Twenty-four

Johnny, Known as Mad Dog

I slept until noon. And I would have slept even longer if gunshots hadn't erupted near my window. God, what a night! We'd danced our legs off and downed whole pots of *cham-cham*, a liquor you extracted from raffia palms, then boiled and drank while it was hot. Not a cocktail for ladies—it went straight to your head and messed up the circuits in your brain. We'd started off dancing to rap, makossa, and funk, then moved on to rhumba, Franco, Papa Wemba, and Wenge Musica. Finally, carried away by the *cham-cham*, we'd taken our spears and assegais in hand, so that the rhythmic swaying of our bare torsos would harmonize better with the traditional rhythms of the tom-toms and tribal war chants. Every so often we'd picked up our machine guns and fired into the air, to enliven the festivities.

When I'd seen Abissélékou's tits bobbing free and unconstrained beneath her sheer blouse, I couldn't resist. Being a wily old veteran, I first checked to see that she was alone, or (if she wasn't) that her companion was unarmed—it's always wise to take precautions before approaching a chick. There didn't seem to be anybody hanging around her, so I asked her to dance. She didn't say no. From the way she was laughing and carrying on, I could tell she was already pretty far gone on *cham-cham*. I brought her over to my table and offered her some Chivas Regal, which she drank greedily, and a few minutes later we were behind the hut that usually served as the bar. At the moment, fortunately, it was deserted—everyone was gathered in the district's main square a few blocks away, celebrating the military victory.

I swear she was the one who made the first move. She pressed her body against mine, her tongue began exploring the inside of my mouth, and her eighty-proof breath filled my lungs. I dropped my gun, slipped my hand under her pagne, and pulled down her panties. My middle finger slid into the damp hole between her thighs. I wanted to fuck her right there, standing up, but this was difficult to manage, despite our athletic contortions. After a few attempts, we wound up on the ground. I gave one good thrust, and just as I was raising my hips to drive my piston in again, an enormous blow landed on my ass. I yelled bloody murder. A dark form swooped down on Abissélékou and pulled her hair—which came off. A wig. The fury tossed it away and began lashing out with kicks. "I'll kill you, you dirty whore!" I recognized the voice. It was Lovelita!

Lovelita whom I'd left back at the house, Lovelita whom I'd instructed not to go out, Lovelita whom I'd told to be extremely careful! Even though she was the girlfriend of Mad Dog, the great fighter, she was nonetheless a Mayi-Dogo and was in danger of being attacked by the idiots living in the district. She hadn't listened to my warnings—she'd followed me. No telling what a jealous woman will do.

"Lovelita!" I cried, trying to grab her by the arms. But she was nearly crazy with rage. She gave me a sharp kick, and I let her go. Abissélékou stood there for a few minutes, hurling insults.

"Filthy Mayi-Dogo! What the hell are you doing here? You coming to steal our men because you don't have any in that shit-hole you live in?"

"We don't steal them! They come looking for us because you Dogo-Mayi women are so pathetic in bed! You don't know how to move your ass, you don't know how to make them come, you don't know how to drive them wild with pleasure the way we do—"

"Lovelita, that's enough!" I shouted, slapping her across the face.

At that, she really went berserk, threatening to kill Abissélékou and then kill me. Meanwhile, Abissélékou snatched up the club that Lovelita had applied so vigorously to my ass. She provoked Lovelita, calling her every foul name she could think of. I was trapped between two chicks, and I didn't know who was to blame. Lovelita, for interrupting my fun? But she wasn't completely in the wrong—if I'd been the one who caught some guy fucking *her*, my Kalashnikov would already have blown him away.

Lovelita yelled another obscene insult, this one aimed at Abissélékou's mother. Abissélékou leaped at her furiously and tried to club her over the head, but because I was in the way, the blow landed on me and knocked me flat. Damn, those women could really hit hard. I heard Lovelita wailing, "You killed my man! You killed my man!" She picked up my gun over by the wall and fired. Abissélékou turned tail and ran for her life—naked tits bouncing, since I'd popped all the buttons on her blouse. Lovelita chased her, firing the whole time. I got to my feet, intending to run after Lovelita and stop her, but she'd taken my belt, and I couldn't very easily run and hold my pants up at the same time. The two of them arrived at the main square. I heard shouts and a volley of gunfire. It wasn't Lovelita who was shooting. When I finally made it to the square, clutching my pants and out of breath, I saw her body lying in the dust, riddled with bullets. Lovelita!

Everyone said she'd been asking for it—she should have stayed in her own district, instead of coming around to threaten our women. I had no idea those people could be so mean. She'd come to our district because I'd brought her there and because she loved me. Was there some law that said we couldn't love anyone but a woman from our own tribe?

"You're all assholes!" I shouted at them, as Lovelita's body was being taken away to the morgue.

The celebration was over for me. I went to bed, and I lay there thinking about Lovelita for a long time, a very long time, before finally drifting off to sleep at around three in the morning. And that's why I didn't wake up until noon, when two militiamen began trading shots over some loot they were trying to divide.

I turned on the radio to find out how the situation was shaping up. Our leader, the president, was in the middle of giving a speech. I'd missed the first part of it, but this didn't matter. I knew he'd repeat himself at least ten times.

> *". . . fellow citizens, our country is too precious to be left in the hands of those genocidal villains, many of whom have fled into the forest. We will give them no respite! We will hunt them down! We will flush them out, village by village, and exterminate them, even if those villages lie in the depths of the jungle. I assure you once again: this is not*

a tribal war—as some would like to believe, because this would confirm their fossilized notion that Africa is nothing but a bunch of tribes driven by hatreds they've been nursing for hundreds, even thousands of years. No, *we are waging our struggle in a larger context: that of democracy, the effort to build a better life, the restructuring of our economy to confront globalization and the challenges of the third millennium. Down with tribalists! Down with the perpetrators of genocide! Long live the people! Long live democracy!"*

Even though our leader was a military man, he spoke like an intellectual. I was happy. I looked around at all the fine things I'd acquired thanks to the war, and I was sorry that Lovelita was no longer around to share them with me. I would have to sell all the pagnes and earrings and necklaces that I'd been saving for her (assuming I didn't find another girlfriend). And there weren't only pagnes, jewelry, DVD players, and televisions—there were also the books I'd acquired with the help of the war. I now had enough to fill a library from floor to ceiling, and a good deal more. I was well on my way to becoming a true intellectual.

In the afternoon, I would have to round up the members of my unit. Then we'd go find our long-lost General Giap, so we could report on the battles we'd fought and he could assign us new missions. In the eloquent words of our president: now that we'd won the war, we had to continue it, in order to establish democracy and consolidate the peace. And for that, I was ready.

Chapter Twenty-five

Laokolé

When we got back to the village, I felt tired and rested at the same time—the kind of pleasant fatigue you feel after a few hours of playing sports. Asjha's mother asked what had taken us so long, and Asjha told her that we'd had clothes to wash and, above all, that we'd been having fun. Her mother looked at her with a broad smile and said:

"Yes, I haven't seen you looking this happy since we returned to the village."

At ease on the veranda of the house, sitting on a low, round-bottomed wicker stool and leaning against the wall, my face turned toward the setting sun whose rays had relinquished almost all their heat, I savored the colors of the equatorial twilight. I'd never had a chance to do this in the city, and the idea wouldn't even have occurred to me. I discovered that the sun didn't take leave of the world all by itself—the entire world around us went with it as it died, or at least paid homage to it, in a whole variety of surprising rituals. Flocks of chattering birds swooped high overhead, returning to their nests before darkness could lead them astray—the same darkness that, in counterpoint, drew swarms of insects of every species from the cool, shadowy places where they'd sought refuge from the pitiless star now fading. Bothersome insects, which penetrated everywhere and droned incessantly in your ears. But also beautiful creatures, like the moths that bothered no one, when their instinct for self-destruction wasn't driving them into the flames of the wood fire or candle that we lit to keep the darkness at bay. New sounds that didn't exist in the daytime could be heard on all sides, and the soft evening breeze drifting from the forest was imbued with complex fragrances, a blend of the myriad essences that inhabited the woods.

Asjha's mother prepared a fine meal. The three of us ate outdoors in the moonlight, sitting around the fire. There were fewer insects, perhaps because the wood smoke kept them away. In response to her questions, I told them all that had happened to me. As I spoke of Fofo's disappearance and Mama's death in the bombardment, my eyes welled up with tears. Asjha's mother comforted me, saying that she looked upon me like a daughter and assuring me that I was welcome to stay with her in the village as long as I pleased—she could see that Asjha was very fond of me and had adopted me as a big sister. No, I said, it wasn't possible. I wanted to leave as soon as I could, so that I could give my mother a proper burial. She understood, and declared that she would do the same thing if she were in my shoes. In any case, I could always come back whenever I wished.

She, in turn, told me about herself. "My husband is a noncommissioned officer in the national army. When the political situation became so unstable that he feared the worst, he sent us to the village, where we would be safe until things calmed down. But the worst in fact occurred: the army split into rival factions, each supporting one of the would-be leaders on the basis of tribal ties. Along with many others, he refused to ally himself with any of the warlords, saying that the army was supposed to defend the nation, not one man or one ethnic group. He and his companions were summarily denounced as traitors by both of the rival factions."

Since then, she'd had no word of him. She knew he'd been arrested by the militias fighting for one of the factions, but nobody could tell her which one. She didn't even know if he was still alive.

After dinner, we returned to the house. Asjha's mother went to bed. Asjha likewise retired to our bedroom, and I was left alone in the living room. I fetched my large bag to make an inventory of the contents, for I no longer remembered what it contained. Before going down to the river, I'd put my little purse inside it—the one that held my money and that I always wore under my pants. I took out the purse to count how much I had left. When I opened it, I found the photo of Mama and Papa in one of the pockets. I'd forgotten I'd put it there. They were holding hands and smiling, like every happy couple posing for the camera. I didn't want to start crying, so I quickly put it back. I had no picture of Fofo—could only hope there was one in the trunk we'd buried before we fled. Next, I took stock of what was in the large bag. A few bills and coins, some cheap jewelry, the remaining sanitary pads that Tanisha had given me, the bottle of acetaminophen, a magazine, and the little radio. Not a very impressive collection. I neatened up the contents of the bag and kept out the magazine, which I wanted to look at before going to sleep.

Comfortably settled in an armchair, I drew the storm lantern toward me and opened the magazine. On the fifth page, I saw the photo. She was wearing her orange NASA space suit and holding her helmet, her face lit by a radiant smile. Mae Jemison. That was her name. I knew there were women who had ventured into space. I even knew that one of them, a schoolteacher, had perished in an accident on one of the shuttles. But I never knew there were astronauts who had roots in Africa, like me. I read the article eagerly. She had been the Science Mission Specialist in the space laboratory of the shuttle *Endeavour*, launched in September 1992. She was a chemical engineer, a physician, and a university professor. But that wasn't all—she was also a dancer and choreographer. Everything I dreamed of being. Furthermore, as a doctor she had spent two years working in Africa and was familiar with our continent. How old had she been when she went to college? Sixteen—my age. If I'd gone to America, I would have been in college now, since my grades had always been good. But no—at sixteen, I'd had to flee the bullets on the very day I was due to take my baccalaureate exam, and here I was, shipwrecked in the middle of the rain forest, with no father, no mother, no brother. What had I done to deserve this? I cursed my country and its politicians. If I ever got out of this, I wanted to become an astronaut and fly up amid the stars, like Mae. But to do that, I'd have to go to a university in America; unfortunately, I didn't know anyone there. And suddenly I remembered that Tanisha had given me her card. Quickly I went through my bag and my little purse once more, but couldn't find it. Had I lost it in the confusion as I fled? My pocket! My pants!

I ran to the bedroom and grabbed my jeans, while Asjha, who was still awake, wondered what was going on. I searched feverishly, and exclaimed with joy when I found the card in my hip pocket. I returned to the living room. On the card were Tanisha's home address, e-mail address, and telephone numbers. So there I was, sitting by an oil lantern in the depths of the rain forest, dreaming of sending an e-mail to America. Again I looked at the photo of Mae. Not only was she smiling, but I was sure she was smiling at *me*. Asjha came noiselessly out of the bedroom; she must have been watching me for some time, without my realizing it.

"You look so happy!" she said. "What's making you feel so good?"

I showed her the photo.

"Do you know her?"

"Yes," I answered.

I wasn't lying, for I felt that Mae had been with me all my life, and that I'd always wanted to be like her even before I knew who she was.

"That's Mae Jemison," I continued. "She's an astronaut, and now a professor at an American university. I'd like to write to her."

"You want to become an astronaut?"

"Yes. Or else a great scientist, like her—it doesn't matter what field. An engineer, so I can build skyscrapers that will defy gravity and astound my father. Or the hard sciences—I'll make calculations and devise equations so beautiful that the stars will be envious and I can dance with the universe. Or a doctor traveling around the African countryside, developing medicines to fight diseases that everyone says are incurable. And in the evening, at home, I'll rest my mind and body by playing music, by dancing, and by making love with a man who pleases me."

She laughed, thinking that what I'd said was quite funny. And mischievously she asked:

"Have you ever made love with a man?"

"Shhhh," I said, putting a finger to my lips and widening my eyes mysteriously. "You shouldn't ask a big sister such questions."

She came over and snuggled into my arms.

"Let's go look at the stars," I said.

We went out into the darkness and gazed up at the multitude of luminous diamonds that shimmered in the sky. What would we do without the stars?

*

In rural areas, the day begins very early. I thought I was getting an early start, but Asjha and her mother were already up and doing chores by the time I awoke. Asjha was sweeping the yard, while her mother was grinding cassava leaves for our midday meal. Since my panties and T-shirt were dry, I put them on so I could give Asjha's pagne back to her. I picked up the magazine I'd left on the table the night before, intending to give it to my little sister as a present. When I came out into the yard, she stopped sweeping and ran over to me.

She asked if I'd slept well. "Like an angel!" I replied, and then said good morning to Mother—I mean, Asjha's mother.

"Asjha, I'm giving you this magazine because you don't have anything to read here in the village. It has some very interesting articles."

But before giving it to her, I opened it to the color photo of Mae and carefully removed the page.

"This is the only bit I'm keeping. There's another photo of her, a smaller one in black and white."

I folded the page in four and tucked it away in my little purse, in the same inside pocket that held the photo of Papa and Mama. And I slipped the whole thing into the back pocket of my jeans. Asjha took the magazine—she was delighted.

I filled a basin with water and washed up quickly, thinking I'd go back to the river again that afternoon. To brush my teeth, I used a root scented with citronella. Mother offered me breakfast, but I declined, saying that I'd wait until Asjha had finished sweeping and she herself had finished grinding the cassava leaves, so that we could sit down and eat together. I felt awkward, being the only one who had nothing to do, and I asked her if there was some household chore I could take care of.

"You can help us roll cassava dumplings after breakfast."

I was ravenous, and was hoping we would have a large breakfast. While waiting for them to finish, I decided to take a short walk around the village. It wasn't very big, but it was clean. The day before, when I'd arrived, my city-dweller's gaze had seen only poverty. I hadn't noticed the mango trees heavy with luscious fruit, the mandarin orange trees, the safou trees whose fruit was turning dark purple and almost ready to be picked. I strolled all the way through the village, to the edge of the forest . . .

No sooner had I heard the sound of an engine than the first helicopter was looming overhead. Another appeared on the opposite side, and the two of them began strafing the village. They swept from one end to the other, turned around, and came back. They had nothing to fear, since the poor villagers had no antiaircraft guns, not even a simple Kalashnikov. I heard shouts, screams. I don't know if we were being firebombed, but several houses were in flames. Then the helicopters flew off toward the east.

I ran back through the village, toward the house. Before I could get there, the shelling started again, this time from the direction of the road. Armored vehicles. And a military transport that unloaded a bunch of soldiers. They yelled at everything, fired at everything. I raced back toward the forest and hid in a spot where I could observe what was going on. I saw the headman pleading, explaining that his people had no weapons.

"You harbored Chechen militia fighters!" shouted the army commander.

"That's not true! We simply gave food to some poor refugees!"

"Shut up!"

And *blam!* he fired at the headman point-blank.

"We're not going to take any shit from rats like him," he said to his men. "Destroy all the fruit trees, the way we did in the other villages. We'll starve the traitors who are hiding in the forest."

While some of them began systematically chopping down the mango trees, safou trees, and orange trees, others trained their guns on the forest and started firing. I don't know what miracle saved me from being blown to bits by the first salvo, for it landed less than three meters away, throwing up an enormous quantity of earth. Wisdom told me to stay hidden, flat on the ground, but instinct was stronger and I lost my head.

I got to my feet, wild with fear, desperate to escape, and began running headlong into the forest. I stumbled over roots that tore open my sneakers; my legs got tangled in creepers that brought me crashing to the ground; thorns ripped my T-shirt and the supposedly rugged denim of my jeans; razor-sharp leaves slashed my arms, hands, and face—and still I continued mechanically to put one foot in front of the other, movement born of the instinct for survival. I was no longer thinking of the snake that could bite me, of the scorpion that could sting me with its poisonous tail, of the gorilla I might encounter in this forest teeming with great apes, of the panther hunting for prey nearby. I had forgotten all about the carnivorous flowers with enormous blossoms that could swallow me up and absorb me. I have no idea how long I ran like that—hours, maybe. At last I noticed that the forest had become darker than usual, and the air unusually cool. I collapsed against the trunk of a tree, gasping for breath, a sharp pain in my side. I had no time to feel sorry for myself—a rumble of thunder shook the world around me. A gigantic bolt of lightning lit up the forest penumbra for an instant, despite the thick canopy, and the heralded event came immediately. A violent tropical storm broke over the woods.

You really have to experience a storm in the rain forest to get an idea of the cataclysmic forces that, over the millennia, have shaped the surface of this planet. At first, you hear the thunder as a dull rumbling, like a drumroll echoing through the forest vault; then it suddenly explodes in a burst of sound and light. After a moment, you forget the celestial origin of the explosion, for the accompanying sounds—broken up by the forest's multiple echo points, which send them ricocheting back and forth in a welter of frequencies—are transformed into earthly forces that set the very foundations of the huge forest vibrating. As for the lightning, it isn't content just to expend its energy illuminating the forest twilight that even the sun can't penetrate—it strikes the tops of giant trees that dared to challenge the heavens, and those trees, mortally wounded, utter agonized cracking sounds and then fall heavily to the ground with a horrendous crash, to be slowly consumed by the flames of the lightning bolts.

I took shelter at the foot of a towering tree whose roots formed enormous buttresses near the ground. I huddled within the buttresses, curling up and making myself as small as possible to escape the fury of the elements. As I looked at those gigantic trees, and thought of the mastodons and scaly reptiles of prehistoric times, and witnessed the awesome force and incessant lightning of that storm, I felt as if I'd been transported back to the primeval age when the planet was being formed, millions of years before paltry *Homo sapiens* appeared on the scene—the age in which thunder and lightning, water and clay, nitrogen and oxygen all tumbled around in the primordial soup from which the first molecules of life ultimately emerged. I saw myself as small, insignificant, no bigger than a flea, a speck of atomic dust whose disappearance wouldn't alter the total mass of the universe by even a single femtogram.

And then I remembered that you should never take shelter under a tree during a thunderstorm. My fear returned. I got to my feet. The ground was a sodden mess of mud and dead leaves, and walking was difficult. I crossed a stand of bamboo, skirted tall thick prop roots that looked like stilts, and eventually found myself in a grove of wild banana trees. At least their broad leaves would provide some shelter from the rain, even if they occasionally sluiced water onto me and gave me a thorough drenching.

It seemed as if I'd spent forty days and forty nights in that deluge, when at long last the claps of thunder faded into the distance and the lightning flashes subsided. But although the water ceased falling from the sky, in the forest it continued to flow. It was running everywhere—pouring from the leaves that tipped it onto the vegetation below like tiny spouts, streaming down the smooth or shaggy bark of trees, murmuring in countless ephemeral brooks that splashed down eroded slopes and tumbled into ravines.

Night had fallen. I was soaked to the skin, and cold and hungry. Now I was sorry I hadn't immediately accepted the breakfast that Asjha and her mother had offered. What should I do? I couldn't risk walking around in the dark trying to find wild berries. If only my wandering steps would take me to where the Pygmies lived! With the confidence born of our superior stature (though we were Lilliputian next to a gorilla), we looked down on them as primitives, labeled them "forest dwellers." This now struck me as the rankest stupidity and arrogance, for what I wanted more than anything in the world right now was to be a little Pygmy woman gliding through the forest like a fish through water, as elusive as an eel, slithering among the leaves and vines like a serpent, endowed with night vision like an owl, turning to advantage all the tricks and snares of the forest.

I spotted another tree with huge spurs at its base and concealed myself there as best I could, fervently hoping I'd found a shelter for the night that would protect me from predators and, above all, from snakes.

*

Judging from the birdsong and the gentle light that suffused the undergrowth, I could tell that a new day had dawned and that it was time to get moving if I didn't want to die of stiffness. Adrift in that ocean of green, that trackless, featureless forest in which all directions seemed to offer the same risks and opportunities, I yielded to an atavistic instinct that human beings share with plants: I chose to head toward the sun, toward the light. I knew that the entire life of plants was nothing but a perpetual striving toward the light. So I looked at the leaves on the climbing vines and noted which way they were facing, and I decided to use them as a sort of compass. I set off toward what I reckoned was the east. I walked for a long time, squelching through the muck of dead and decaying leaves, slipping, sliding, falling. My sneakers were nothing but soles held on with laces—the canvas had been completely torn away. I was hungry. I had to eat, I had to survive. The Pygmies managed quite well in the forest. Why couldn't I? Okay, they were familiar with edible fruits I'd never heard of. For instance, that guava-colored berry over there, so plump and juicy. I reached toward it. But watch out! Poisonous plants, just like predators, often disguise themselves in attractive colors to lure their victims. You mustn't yield to temptation. I kept going.

Suddenly I emerged into a clearing. How could there be a clearing in the middle of the rain forest? Then I noticed the enormous stump of a mahogany tree sticking up like a headless neck, and I understood right away: I was in a forest-management area. I had no idea that logging operations extended so deep into our forests. The bright sunlight in the clearing dazzled me for a moment. I walked forward. In the hollow of a fallen tree was a little pool of rainwater, surprisingly clear. I knelt down, put my lips to the surface, and drank and drank. Then I sat with my back against the trunk. Hunger was gnawing at me. I wouldn't be able to go on if I didn't eat something soon. But what?

I heard gruntings and snufflings. A gorilla? Quickly I crouched down behind the fallen log. Not far away was a wild pig. At first I thought it was a boar, but it was obviously a female because three young ones were with her, now rooting around in the dirt with their snouts, now raising their heads and squealing. They were feasting on a large bunch of bananas. Bananas! Food perhaps fallen from heaven, like manna, but certainly fallen from a banana tree during the storm. I had to get hold of it!

I picked up a rock and walked toward the pig. I'd thought that since she was a wild animal with no knowledge of humans, she would scamper off and leave the rest of the bananas to this strange two-legged creature that had appeared out of nowhere. Not at all! She stood there and looked at me. We looked at each other. She still didn't move, and I got the impression she was challenging me. Maybe the poor thing didn't know that we were the superior species on this planet and that everything on it belonged to us. So what if she was the one who'd found the bananas? So what if she'd gone through all sorts of difficulties to obtain them? They were mine now—I had made that decision. But the animal didn't see it this way. I wanted the bananas for myself, while she, like any mother, wanted them for her little ones.

Force. Use force. With my left hand I got a good grip on the rock I'd picked up, and mustering all my remaining strength I hurled it at the pig. This did not have the desired result. The blow failed to make the animal run away—on the contrary, it made her angry. She charged straight at me. I snatched up a large stick that was lying nearby and I waited, ready to bash her over the head with all the strength I had left. Unfortunately, my foot slipped just as I was about to deliver the blow. I fell. The animal butted me so hard with her snout that I went sprawling in the mud. Still, I was lucky enough to grab her by the nose, and I tried to smother her by squeezing her nostrils and throat. But my muddy hands couldn't hold on for more than a few seconds—I was forced to wrap myself around the creature's middle, the way you grab your opponent in a wrestling match. The two of us rolled around in the muck, and at one point I found myself pinned under the animal's massive body. I thought all my ribs would break—I was suffocating to death. With the strength of desperation, I wrenched my body out from underneath and gave her a solid left uppercut to the eye. She squealed (from pain or anger?), raised her head, and—beaten at last—turned and ran toward her offspring, who were grunting with alarm.

I staggered to my feet, winded, furious, and ashamed. I grabbed the stick and chased after that goddamn stupid cunt of a pig. I wanted to kill her for refusing to let me have those bananas, kill her for having humiliated me—but she was quick on her feet, despite her bulk, and had already disappeared into the forest with her little ones, who continued to lament the loss of their meal.

I wiped my muddy hands on the inside of my T-shirt and pounced on the fruit like a wild animal. I tore off one banana, peeled it, and stuffed it into my mouth. Then a second one. Then a third. Barely stopping for breath, I ate them as fast as I could peel them. Full at last, perhaps too full, I got up to take another drink of rainwater from the hollow in the fallen tree. Since my hands were filthy, I plunged my mouth below the surface, just the way animals do. Once more on my feet, still dazed, I wanted to continue on my way—but despite my determination, I couldn't go another step. An immense weariness and despair overwhelmed me. I sank to the ground, closed my eyes, and wept.

Chapter Twenty-six

Laokolé

I was strolling through a zoo. All of a sudden, horrible noises started coming from the cages. Two male gorillas were challenging each other over a female—they were beating their chests, grunting, and howling. One of them managed to tear down the bars of his cage and escaped. He ran to break down the cage of the female who'd been the cause of the dispute, and in a fit of rage the two gorillas began destroying all the cages in the zoo. The animals were wandering around loose: lions, panthers, snakes, zebras, elephants. And then there were all the animals that had ever lived: kangaroos, bears, woolly mammoths, dinosaurs, countless extinct species—the whole mass of them fleeing with a deafening, apocalyptic clamor, the ground trembling from the stampede. The sky abruptly grew dark and reverberated with claps of thunder and forks of lightning. It was impossible to tell the humans from the animals in that world riven by unbridled forces. The panic was so great that even the trees, after much twisting and turning, managed to wrest their roots from the soil and began to run. I started running, too, but lost my footing in the mud. Just as a warthog was about to gore me with his curving tusks, a rumbling in the sky drove the animal away. The noise persisted and woke me up. I opened my eyes. It wasn't a dream—the noise was still there.

Obviously the sound of an engine. It was droning above the forest, about a kilometer from where I lay. For an instant I thought it was a logger's chain saw and my heart leaped with joy, for that meant I was saved. But when I listened intently to see if I could determine its location, I realized it was drawing closer—approaching so quickly that it was above the clearing before I even had a chance to get to my feet. A helicopter! It hovered in the air like a dragonfly, then began a slow, careful descent.

This was so unexpected that I remained frozen in place for several seconds. How could the soldiers have spotted me, a tiny speck in that vast jungle? I didn't come out of my cataleptic state until the moment the machine touched down and the change in the sound's pitch indicated that the blades would soon stop. I ran and hid behind a large tree. The engine fell silent. Two armed men in uniform jumped to the ground. Then a white man came out. A mercenary? A second helicopter landed near the first. Two more people came out, one of them a white woman. The woman began to speak into a two-way radio. I could hear what she was saying, but I didn't understand.

"We've landed . . . Yes, in the clearing—everything according to plan . . . Half an hour? Fine . . . Two? Terrific! . . . The male? . . . Yes, very effective as a sedative. The team's arriving. Okay. Over and out."

They headed for the trees at the edge of the clearing as if

they knew exactly where they were going, and left the two soldiers to guard the helicopters. One of the men was walking straight toward the spot where I was hiding. It was all over—they'd seen me. Five meters, four meters, three . . . He came to a halt scarcely two meters in front of me. I didn't dare breathe. I pressed myself to the tree the way lice cling to a scalp. He unbuttoned his fly, took out his penis, and began to urinate. I sighed with relief.

The men who had gone into the forest didn't stay there long. Three went in, and seven came out, struggling under the weight of two large motionless forms. When they drew nearer, I saw what they were carrying with such difficulty: two enormous gorillas!

The men brought the animals, each bound in a net, close to the helicopter, and the woman examined them. She asked that they be injected with another dose of sedative. Suddenly I realized these people weren't mercenaries but ecologists working to save endangered species. Well, by that point I considered myself an endangered species. If they could save animals, they could also save me.

I came out of my hiding place, my hands in the air to avoid any misunderstanding, and began running toward them crying for help. They turned toward me in surprise. The soldiers, who were already aiming at me, lowered their weapons when they saw me with my hands up and perhaps also noticed the condition I was in—a filthy, two-legged wild animal emerging from the woods. I rushed toward the one woman in the group, thinking I could count on female solidarity. The soldiers held me back.

"Please take me with you! I've been wandering in the forest, soldiers are chasing me, they're trying to kill me, I'm terribly hungry!"

They must have found my words incoherent—I couldn't manage to tell my story in an orderly, logical way. The woman interrupted me.

"Listen, we've got nothing to do with the war. We're from the International Institute for the Protection of Gorillas and Chimpanzees. We're here to evacuate as many of them as possible, because they're being endangered by this stupid war. The factions are killing even animals—poor innocent animals!"

"Why them and not me?" I pleaded.

"Because the extinction of the apes would be a great loss for humanity."

"Why them and not me?" I repeated.

"Because you're not an ape!"

"Yes, yes, I'm an ape!" I cried, and with legs bowed I began grunting and snorting, and mimicking the way a gorilla walks, and pretending to stuff my mouth with bananas. I was desperate.

"It's impossible to reason with her . . . She's crazy. We've got to get out of here—there could be dozens like her who might start pouring out of the woods any minute."

The soldiers were alarmed and began looking at me strangely, as if I were some outlandish creature—a faun with horns growing from my head and goat's hooves instead of feet. Keeping a close eye on me, they joined the others, who were laboring to attach the bound and sleeping gorillas to the helicopters by affixing the nets to hooks in the baggage compartments.

Since female solidarity hadn't worked, I tried my luck with the man who was keeping his binoculars trained on the spot where I'd emerged. "Please don't leave me here in the jungle! I'll die! I'll be devoured by panthers, strangled by boa constrictors, digested by giant carnivorous flowers, or simply shot by the soldiers who are destroying all the villages."

"Jane, what can we do for this poor thing?" he asked the woman, who must have been the leader of the expedition.

"We're not authorized to take passengers," said the woman. "Our insurance covers only animals. All we can do is notify the authorities of her whereabouts."

He looked at me and shrugged as if to say there was nothing he could do. I think I continued to speak, and to move agitatedly about, until the moment they got back in the helicopters. Before closing the doors, the woman gave me one last look—and then, just as she no doubt often did with her chimps or her pet dogs, she tossed me a packet of biscuits. Enraged, I crushed it into the mud with my feet. The blades and then the rotors of the helicopters began to turn. The first machine lifted off slowly, hovered a short distance above the ground, and began winching up the first gorilla.

When I saw that massive body disappear into the interior of the vehicle, I understood that I was truly being abandoned. But I could run to the second helicopter, cling to the gorilla, be drawn up with him . . . My fingers were unable to catch hold of the netting. The machine slowly lifted off, then began winching up the other animal . . . I made little jumps, trying to grab at the mesh, but in vain. Then the two helicopters were nothing but a droning noise that faded away in the distance.

If I fell, if I sat down, if I paused to rest, I would never get up again. Walk, keep moving, put one foot in front of the other, repeat this ad infinitum. Logging trails would certainly lead me to a road somewhere, since the timber had to be hauled out of the forest. And in fact I was on one of those trails. Walk, keep moving, put one foot in front of the other. Stagger but don't fall. Keep moving . . .

Chapter Twenty-seven

Johnny, Known as Mad Dog

We hung around for three or four days, strolling through our neighborhood with nothing to do. Our aimless existence was made even more unbearable by the savage storm that hit the city and kept us indoors for nearly two days. It had begun at midday and lasted all night, bringing great sheets of rain that transformed the streets into raging torrents. I was glad I didn't live in the Kandahar district. With the violent downpour inundating areas undrained by any sewer system, gouging out gullies, ripping roofs off buildings, and causing mud-brick houses to collapse, there was no doubt that many hastily buried bodies had been uncovered and were floating around in the water like dead dogs. The streets and yards were probably littered with corpses.

The end of the storm did not automatically mean the end of our confinement indoors. It was another day before we could go out. Deep pools and huge puddles of stagnant water prevented people from walking or driving around the city, and we had to wait until these had evaporated under the tropical sun.

I set out to look for Giap as soon as the streets were passable, because we needed new orders and I didn't know where else to get them. Most of the commando units had broken into smaller groups, which often wound up fighting one another. I attempted to bring the Roaring Tigers back together, but without success. It wasn't for lack of trying. When I began the effort to reunite my men, the first one I came across was Stud. I asked him to let bygones be bygones and join up with me. He replied scornfully that he was now his own boss and that he wasn't about to take orders from anyone, least of all me. As I was turning to leave, he said mockingly:

"So tell me—where's the famous Lovelita? The chick you nearly killed me for? Where is she these days, huh?"

I don't know how he'd learned of her death, but I suspected everyone in the district knew that Mad Dog's girl had been shot. Stud's words made me furious, and I told him his mother was a whore. I wanted to kill him right then and there, but he wasn't alone. He was surrounded by four heavily armed goons—probably members of his new gang. I swallowed my anger. He'd have to wait a while, but eventually he'd get what was coming to him.

I was able to find only two loyal members of the unit—Piston and Little Pepper. I invited them out for a beer, so we could discuss future operations. For me, there was no question about the first item on the agenda: destroy the bar where Lovelita had discovered me on that godawful evening, and ruin its owner. This was being generous on my part—I could have just blown the guy's head off. Because if the bar hadn't been there, I wouldn't have snuck off with that whore Abisélékou, Lovelita wouldn't have caught me by surprise, and she wouldn't have gotten herself killed.

We were sitting there knocking back a few cool beers in

that open-air bar when a truck filled with about twenty soldiers pulled up. It stopped and they all got out. Of course they didn't wait to be served. Brandishing guns, they seized entire cases of beer, which they loaded into their vehicle. The owner begged them to pay, but they beat him with the butts of their weapons and told him he was making a contribution to the war effort, and that if he didn't like it he could go complain to the president of the republic. It was hilarious. Inspired by this, my buddies and I decided we were going to contribute to the war effort, too, by not paying for our drinks.

Just as the soldiers were climbing back into their truck, I caught sight of Idi Amin. We'd heard he'd been captured, tortured, and killed by the Chechens—in fact, that was one of the reasons we had attacked Kandahar! He was holding a U.S.-made assault rifle, an M-16, and tied around his head was a scarf patterned after the American flag. Where had he gotten all that stuff?

"Idi Amin!" I shouted.

He saw me and wheeled his muscular bulk around, smiling broadly. We greeted each other like long-lost kin.

"Matiti Mabé! Great to see you!"

"I've changed my name to Mad Dog."

"Okay! Me, too. I'm no longer Idi Amin—that was a stupid name. Now I'm Chuck."

"Chuck?"

"Yeah, Chuck Norris."

"Okay. What's happening, Chuck?"

"We're on a mission. We're rounding up refugees and bringing them to the camps."

"Yeah? I'm coming with you."

Little Pepper and Piston joined me, and we climbed into the truck. Idi Amin, alias Chuck Norris, told us what he'd been up to, and then I understood why there were so many Russian-made MI-8 and MI-24 helicopters flying back and forth over the city. They were strafing villages they suspected of harboring Chechen traitors. After an intense four-day barrage, the villagers were streaming toward the city. We were to guarantee their safety in the humanitarian corridor that had been set up for them.

It was a spectacular reversal of the mass outflow of refugees who had fled into the forest. The crowds heading for the city consisted of long columns of gaunt women and children ravaged by hunger and disease, with a handful of men here and there. It's true these people were coming out of the forest because our new government had publicly assured the HCR and other NGOs that their safety was guaranteed, but this didn't mean we were no longer responsible for neutralizing the terrorists hiding among them. So we set up roadblocks along the route, to screen the new arrivals. We stopped all young people whose gait, posture, or rough hands betrayed the fact that they were used to handling guns. We'd shove them a few meters into the underbrush, and *blam!*—happy trails. We had to maintain national security. Some of them were let through because their parents offered us money and pleaded with us, but mostly we took both their money *and* the lives of their precious kids, if these young people looked or walked like terrorists. Others assumed we were idiots and told us they weren't Mayi-Dogos, but one glance at their ID card was enough to show that their names began with an *A*, an *X*, or a *T*—typical of the inhabitants of that region. We took care of them pretty quick.

We continued our work for two days, and then foreign radio stations, the international press, and local organizations claiming to be human rights groups but allied with the defeated factions began telling all sorts of lies about us—in particular, that we were terrorizing the civilians, holding them for ransom, and carrying out summary executions. With a little effort they would have learned that we were executing only Mayi-Dogo bandits, to prevent them from reestablishing their militias, and that the young men we were accused of frequently kidnapping from the refugee centers were all terrorists. But under the pressure of those cock-and-bull stories, our government, which had nothing to hide, agreed to allow teams from the Red Cross, Doctors Without Borders, and the UN High Commission for Refugees to accompany the refugees out of the rain forest. Since we could no longer do our job in peace and privacy, we were redeployed to other locations around the city.

During one of our patrols through the districts, by a stroke of sheer luck, we met up with Giap. I practically hugged him. We described how we'd been searching for him, and said that now that we'd found him we were at his disposal.

He told us not to call him "General" anymore—he had changed his rank. He was now a real soldier and had been integrated into the army as a corporal. Goddamn Giap! What a guy—full of surprises and always way ahead of us. When I remembered that he owed his prestigious name to me, that it was thanks to me he'd been recruited into the militias, that I was better educated than him (since he'd never got beyond first grade), and that now he was a soldier and I was nothing, I understood that life was truly unfair. But this wasn't all. He'd been given an even more spectacular promotion: he was now a member of the president's bodyguard. You know what that means? The fucking pinnacle! The president's life in your very own hands!

Our reunion couldn't have been better timed. Giap said he could use us in the security force at the refugee camp during the president's upcoming visit. After the grotesque campaign of lies mounted by the foreign press and its local lackeys, the president was coming to tour one of the camps. In this way he would undermine the propaganda that the former rulers, those genocidal murderers, were continuing to spread abroad via the Web and the international media, while they stewed over their defeat and dreamed of a coup d'état.

*

We were at the camp long before the arrival of the president and his wife, to prepare for the ceremony and set up the basic components of the security system. We'd spent hours ripping off the labels of the charitable organizations that had donated the relief supplies, and replacing them with tags that said "Children's Solidarity," the name of the nongovernmental organization headed by the president's wife. We'd chosen six refugees, three girls and three boys who clearly showed the ravages of hunger and malnutrition, and we'd given them new clothes. We'd made them repeat several times what they were supposed to say in front of the cameras and the president. Above all, they'd been reminded to convey a heartfelt thank-you to the president's wife, whom they were supposed to address as "Mama." Then we'd set up a security cordon around the dais where the nation's leader was to stand.

The excitement was at a fever pitch when we heard the sirens and spotted the surveillance helicopter that preceded the head of state on all his travels. The refugees were crowding so closely against the barriers that they risked endangering our beloved leader, and we were forced to drive them back with the butts of our guns.

Accompanied by his legitimate wife, the president finally arrived, shielded by a forest of machine guns. Giap, the point man, was wearing dark glasses and looked like an FBI agent. He no longer had his Kalashnikov, but was carrying a new automatic weapon—I couldn't tell where it had been made. The children of the Mayi-Dogo refugees began to sing spontaneously:

Papa a yo, nzala essili,
Mama a yo, nzala essili.

Papa is here, good-bye hunger!
Mama is here, good-bye hunger!

It was touching to see how deeply the people loved our leader! Although I was responsible for security, for staying calm and vigilant, I, too, was inspired—I couldn't help silently joining in as the crowd shouted its enthusiasm:

"Papa brought peace to our land! Long live Papa!"

"Stay on as leader! Complete the work you've begun! Without you, war will return . . ."

"You're like Muhammad Ali! The greatest! Unbeatable! You KO them all!"

The president was beaming with pleasure, and his wife was even more radiant. The children we'd selected were obediently lined up in front of the dais. The president's wife said a few words and offered the first bit of cake to a little girl of five or six, who was smiling in her brand-new dress, courtesy of Children's Solidarity. Then, with the gesture of a loving mother, she took the child in her arms, and in front of the cameras—not just our national network but media from all over the world—she hugged her several times to the cheers of the crowd. After a scene like that, I didn't see how the liars who were spreading disinformation could possibly go on saying that the refugees were being mistreated.

Then the president gave a speech, while the helicopter circled overhead and we kept watch on high alert. He began by thanking the refugees for their warm welcome, promising that they would be able to return to their districts as soon as vital services were restored and public health could be guaranteed. And here he thanked the international humanitarian organizations that had sent contributions. He expressed particular gratitude to France, which had been the first to come to our aid by sending six tons of lime and a thousand shovels. This was news to me. Our masons would certainly find the shovels useful for digging foundations and mixing cement when they were rebuilding the houses that had been destroyed, and the lime would come in handy for whitewashing the walls. It was a pity France hadn't provided us with sacks of cement as well, since I could have used a couple of tons to build a place of my own.

Finally the president left and the camp administrators got ready to distribute the food, as planned. But before they began, we decided we'd take ten percent for ourselves, despite the protests of the NGO representatives. What did they expect? A goat grazes where he's tethered, and a bellboy eats at the hotel. So it was perfectly normal that we should claim our share, and the money we got from selling the goods at the market would be our well-earned salary.

But as soon as the refugees saw us toting sacks of food to our trucks parked in front of the camp, a riot broke out. Those runty children who'd stared wide-eyed with fear at our guns, those mothers who'd been so passive just a few minutes before, threw themselves at the boxes of biscuits, the sacks of rice, the cans of beans, the containers of oil . . . They broke through our security cordon. So we began driving them back with kicks and blows.

Even the kid who'd been embraced by the president's wife, the little star of the day's festivities, the child whose image would soon be appearing on national news reports and on TVs all over the world—even she had lost every shred of dignity. She was a disgrace to our country and to the president's wife! She began by picking up the pieces of biscuit that had fallen to the ground and stuffing them into her mouth. Then she blatantly stole a whole packet. A thief at the tender age of five or six! Can you imagine? The nation was in peril! I unbuckled my heavy military belt and aimed a tremendous whack at her just as she was reaching for a box of powdered milk. The belt missed its target and hit the box, which flew apart and scattered its contents in the dirt. I raised the belt over my head, but just as I was about to give the little thief a blow across the back, someone came up behind me and snatched the belt from my hand. I whirled around. I was furious. In front of me was a young woman, likewise in a rage.

I glared, glowered, thrust out my chin—assumed the terrifying expression that Mad Dog used like a weapon to strike fear into the heart of the enemy. But she didn't even bother to look at me; she acted as if I wasn't even there. Shouting words that my brain couldn't register through the fog of my anger, she ran past me and shielded the child with her own body. My fury doubled, and seizing my belt again I began lashing out. Bending over the child's body, she completely blocked it from view. I took my rage out on her. I struck her on the back, on the ass, on the head, everywhere—but she never let go of the child, who was crying the whole time.

Someone dealt me a blow behind the ear. The men—who had thus far been slouching about with a shamefaced expression, like dogs that have been beaten—had suddenly joined the fray, as if bent on avenging all the humiliations that they and their wives had endured. I fell to the ground. They whipped me with my own belt; they struck me with the butt of my own gun. The riot spread through the camp. If the guards didn't fire soon, it would be the end of all of us. Then I heard gunshots, screams. And finally, after a while, calm was restored. The riot had been quelled.

We called off the food distribution, to punish everyone. And then, to stifle any further revolt, we made a sweep through the entire camp. We rounded up all the men between the ages of fourteen and forty-five, to take them to our military bases. They were terrorists bent on inciting rebellion among the refugees. And this time the women weren't going to get off so easy. Each of us chose a young and pretty female (except for Little Pepper, who chose two) to take away with him.

But I didn't need sex; I needed revenge. And you won't be surprised to hear that the one I threw into the truck was the bitch who was responsible for the beating I'd gotten. I could have been killed if the soldiers hadn't shot at the rioters. In any case, she would feel the heat of my revenge. She looked at me contemptuously in her ragged T-shirt, still holding the little girl in her arms, as if protecting her from the rest of the world.

Chapter Twenty-eight

Laokolé

So now I'm in a refugee camp. I don't really know how I got here. Only a few vague impressions—sounds, voices, colors, kaleidoscopic fragments—emerge now and then from the fog of my memory. A long walk through the forest. A road of blood-red laterite, so muddy that my shoes were soon covered with mire and every time I lifted a foot to take a step, I felt as if I were tearing a ton of earth from the ground. Legs weak and trembly. Body on the verge of collapse. The sound of passing cars. The words, "She's alive . . ." Cool water trickling down my throat. Then nothing more. I regained consciousness in a truck belonging to Doctors Without Borders that was returning from its rounds. A refugee camp. I was unloaded from the truck.

I found a bit of space beneath a tent made of orange plastic. All around me were emaciated children with swollen bellies, discolored hair, limbs puffy from edema, faces prematurely aged with malnutrition and hunger. It was hard for me to look at those girls and boys who had been robbed of their childhood.

A young woman arrived that morning, destitute, accompanied by a daughter who appeared to be about twelve. The woman was walking like a zombie. I made room for her next to me. She sat down without noticing that she'd sat down. She remained motionless for a long time, a handkerchief on her bowed head, her chin resting listlessly on the palm of her right hand. It was as if she were in another world. Obviously, she and her daughter were suffering from more than fatigue—malnutrition, no doubt, and some profound inner torment. The day before, I'd had my ration of beans boiled up with a bit of palm oil, to bring out the flavor and also to keep them from spoiling in the heat. Since some of the food remained, I offered it to them, as well as water to drink. I thought they would pounce avidly on the beans, the way I'd pounced on those bananas in the forest. Far from it—they ate slowly, like gourmets. The mother drank the water I offered her, and thanked me with the simple words: "I'd forgotten what salt tastes like."

That night, I offered my blanket to the little girl. She fell asleep immediately, and her mother began to confide in me, probably because I was the first person who had shown any compassion toward her since she'd first fled her home. Her husband was a senior manager in a bank. When she, her husband, and her daughter came out of the woods in response to appeals from the authorities, they were arrested at a checkpoint along the so-called humanitarian corridor set up by those same authorities. After they were robbed of all their possessions—money, watches, jewelry, cell phone—a soldier tried to force her into the bushes and rape her. Her husband, outraged, tried to intervene. The soldiers seized him, beat him savagely, and threw him into a large truck parked near the roadblock. Then they raped her, right there on the grass by the side of the road, in front of her daughter. Several times. And then they raped her daughter—a girl of twelve! She thought she would go mad. The arrival of a Red Cross team saved them, and that's how they wound up at the camp. Now she had only one thought: Was her husband still alive? She had no idea how to find out.

What could I say to someone in her situation? Nothing. Happiness may be collective, but suffering is intensely personal. No one but me could feel the almost physical pain that tore my heart whenever I thought of Fofo. I, in turn, could never feel the grief of this woman the way she felt it. My words could do nothing to assuage what she, in her own body, was suffering. In such cases, it's better not to say anything. I was silent.

The wonderful thing about children is that it takes so little to make them happy. They never put off their happiness till tomorrow. If it's there, they stretch out their little hands to seize it. In the camp, children were fluttering all around, laughing the buoyant laughter that takes wing as soon as it leaves their lips, trying to learn the songs I made up for them—songs about animals, flowers, and stars. They were running here and there, chirping like birds, capering like goats, meowing like cats, roaring like lions.

I had come up with a crazy idea and managed to make it work. Seeing all those children who were languishing from boredom, whose dejected mothers were at their wits' end and didn't know what to do with their offspring moping about the camp, where the only distraction came when the rations were doled out, I had made up my mind to do something. One afternoon, I gathered together all the children in the vicinity of my tent—about a dozen girls and boys. I asked them if they wanted to play with me.

We began with a game of *ndzango*, which the boys loved because it was usually reserved for girls. I didn't choose it at random. Two opponents facing each other, hopping on one foot, clapping their hands, finally raising one leg high in the air—the game was a good opportunity for the kids to get some exercise. After the *ndzango* and a few songs, I decided to play schoolteacher.

"Children," I said, "I've got something for you to recite. Repeat after me: '*The Hand*' . . . *This is my hand* . . ."

"*This is my hand,*" they chorused enthusiastically.

"Five fingers there be . . .
Five fingers there be . . .
Here are two of them, here are three.
Here are two of them, here are three.
The one at the end is a brave little man,
And the thumb's the one that says, 'I can!'
Watch my fingers as they do their work,
Each does its job and never will shirk!"

The hand. The head. One can't manage without the other. You should never say that one is more important than the other. This was a rhyme that my grandfather, my father, and I had all learned when we were small. And now I, in turn, was passing it on to a new generation. Doing this gave me great intellectual satisfaction—and suddenly my hope in the future revived, for the first time since the beginning of this stupid war. If the girls and boys remembered the rhyme, they would eventually teach it to their own children. And thus the chain of life would continue. All would not be lost. Since the dawn of humankind, knowledge had been transmitted this way: through the children and then the children's children.

I watched their lips recite, watched their fingers spring up one at a time and finally wiggle in sequence as if performing arpeggios on a keyboard. The kids had forgotten the dreary camp in which they were stagnating. They had become children once more, doing what nobody in the world does better: playing. With their little hands and their boundless imaginations, they built houses and trucks out of bits of bamboo; from empty sardine tins mounted on beer corks, they made cars that they raced in the sand; out of scraps of iron, they fashioned airplanes; using empty tin cans and pieces of plastic, they erected structures I couldn't even name. No sooner had their brains thought of an object than their nimble fingers would set about making it, their creativity finding abundant raw materials in the piles of trash that lay all over the camp. I was happy.

But if I was happy, their parents were even happier. My improvised classes combined games, songs, recitations, simple arithmetic, and drawings done with charcoal on a large piece of plywood (our makeshift blackboard), and my little school grew from a dozen students to more than twenty in just a few days. The entire time it lasted, parents who had nothing to do would come and gather around under the tarp I'd put up to ward off the sun. Often they would sing along with us, and sometimes, briefly forgetting their plight as refugees, they would even burst into laughter—gay, liberating laughter—at the antics of one of my students.

*

During one of those playful moments, I happened to look away from the blackboard and spied—Birgit! Birgit the Swede who wasn't blond, though I'd once thought that all Swedish people were blond. At first I assumed I was hallucinating because I'd eaten nothing but red beans for days, with not a bit of meat or fish. Unable to move, I called out to the apparition:

"Birgit?"

"Lao!" came the reply.

It was her!

We ran to each other, and she gave me a long, strong hug. I gazed at her face, while she did the same to me.

In the line of work that she'd chosen, Birgit had no doubt seen and experienced the worst kinds of human suffering. She had certainly witnessed the most extreme cruelties that human beings can inflict on one another, and so she must—I thought—have hardened herself against any emotion or sentimentalism that would impair her ability to do her job. But I was wrong. When she saw my T-shirt, the same one I'd been wearing the day the French army had evacuated her, except that now it was filthy and tattered; when she saw my shoes, which were nothing but a couple of plastic soles tied to my feet with two laces; when she saw my sunken cheeks and my tangled hair, wild and matted like the hair of a grieving widow—her eyes grew wet with tears. As for me, I was sobbing outright.

Class ended early that day, and I didn't know it would be the last one. I took Birgit back to my tent. She had arrived only that morning under a new mandate from the HCR, and she was making a quick inspection of the camp to get an overview of the living conditions before returning with a permanent team. She hadn't known I was there, and was completely astounded when her attention had been attracted by the laughter under the tarp canopy, and she'd seen a young woman teaching a group of little children. At first, she hadn't wanted to believe it was me. It's too good to be true, she'd thought.

"To come face to face, in the first camp I visited, with the very person I was looking for! It was unbelievable! You may not know this, but one of the reasons I was intent on returning to this country and searching the camps was to find you. Tanisha and I felt so miserable at not being able to rescue you. Of course, there are thousands of people we'd like to rescue—I mean, we wish we could rescue everybody! But sometimes, for some unknown reason, we become especially attached to one particular person. It isn't fair, I know, but we can't help it—you've become special to us. Oh, I'm so happy to see you, Lao! We'll get you out of here! This time we won't abandon you!"

She was doing all the talking. But that was okay—I was so choked up that I don't think my throat could have let out a sound.

"I'm going to send an e-mail to Tanisha and let her know that I've found you. She told me she was trying to get a scholarship for you and had some very promising leads. In any case, if she can't arrange something in the United States, I'll bring you with me to Sweden. You've suffered enough. How is your mother?"

"She was killed in a bombardment."

"My god. Oh, Lao, I'm so sorry! . . . Did you find your brother?

"No. But after what happened in Kandahar, I don't have much hope."

And I told her everything I'd been through since we'd last seen each other. When I finished, she said:

"You remember the Belgian journalist Katelijne? She came with me this morning to do a report on the refugees. I'm going to let her know you're here, so that you can tell her your story.

It's essential that the rest of the world understand what's happening. Katelijne was very impressed by your friend Mélanie, and told me that the last image she had of her has remained vivid in her mind. She'd like to do something for her . . ."

"Mélanie is dead," I said simply.

"Oh, my god!" she exclaimed.

We fell silent. I took out the little purse that contained all I had left in the world and that by some miracle hadn't gotten lost. Birgit watched me, wondering what I was looking for. I took out the photo of Mae, unfolded it, and showed it to her.

"When you send your e-mail to Tanisha this evening, please tell her that I read the magazine she gave me. And tell her that if she ever manages to bring me to America, I'd very much like to meet Mae Jemison."

"Who's that?"

"Tanisha knows, and she'll understand."

"Okay, I will! I have to go now. I'll give you Tanisha's response tomorrow afternoon, when I come to pick you up and take you out of the camp. You could use some new clothes and some shoes—I'll bring those as well. Is there anything else you need?"

"A fresh pair of panties, please."

"Of course!" She hugged me once more, then added before leaving the tent:

"Cheer up! Tomorrow you'll be getting out of here. Meantime, don't go away—I'll send Katelijne over."

Katelijne arrived soon after. She came with her loyal cameraman, and was delighted to see me. The first thing she asked for was news of Mélanie. Obviously, Birgit hadn't told her.

"Mélanie was run over three times by the vehicles that rescued you."

Katelijne was speechless for several seconds, as if she'd been punched in the stomach. Then, trying to hide her distress, she said that I absolutely had to repeat for the camera everything that I'd told Birgit.

When I saw the lens of the camera pointing at me, I was suddenly overcome with weariness. I felt as if I had told my story ten times, twenty times—and I couldn't bear any more. I didn't want to retail my misery before the world. No, at this point my personal history mattered very little, since I had already escaped from the mess. In a few hours I'd be leaving the camp, and in a few days or weeks Tanisha would send me an airline ticket and I'd finally get out of this godforsaken country that had murdered my father and mother, killed my Auntie Tamila, and wiped my brother off the face of the earth. Few people had my opportunities. I'd been rescued and was able to escape because I knew some people who had influence abroad. But not everyone was so fortunate, and in any case a country couldn't base its future on a mass exodus of its people. True, I was happy to be leaving—but I wasn't proud of it. For if everyone did the same, who would see to the future of the millions of children condemned to live out their lives here? Those children had as much right to a future as children in Europe and America, and the first thing one had to do to improve their lot was inform the world of their sufferings. And these began with the sufferings of their mothers. That's why the stories of *those* women deserved to be made known, rather than mine. So I ventured a suggestion to Katelijne: instead of me, she should interview my neighbor in the tent and her twelve-year-old daughter, since they'd been through a worse hell than I had.

Katelijne agreed to this idea, and the woman did, too. She sat in front of the camera and unhesitatingly gave the harrowing account she'd already given to me. Katelijne was amazed.

"Tell me . . . A woman who's been raped usually hides that

fact. She's ashamed to speak of it, or else speaks of it only if assured of anonymity. Why have you agreed to speak of it so openly, revealing your face to the world?"

"I wasn't raped in private—the crime was committed in public. Seven soldiers brutally violated me in front of about fifty people, including my daughter. I couldn't possibly conceal it. Look at my daughter. She's twelve years old. What man would want to marry her now? What diseases might those soldiers have given her? And who's to say that she isn't pregnant as well? For we've been utterly abandoned and have no access to a doctor—no one at all to help us, listen to us, care for us. We've got to make the outside world understand what's happening here! The whole world must be told that the people running our country are criminals, because they're the ones responsible for those soldiers—they're the ones who sent them. They can't go on claiming that those men are simply social misfits who have run amok. No! A responsible government can't expect to get away with such excuses and let such terrible crimes go unpunished. By remaining silent, we've become invisible. Well, I'm no longer hiding! I'm showing my face and declaring who I am: my name is Lea Malanda!"

She spoke her name emphatically, looking straight into the camera, as if flinging a challenge in the world's face. What was there to add after that? Nothing. Since Katelijne plainly could not find any words of similar intensity to comfort the woman who had just announced her name so publicly, she merely listened and nodded. I don't know if that was good television. Katelijne had told me viewers liked reports from Africa that featured scenes of blood and gore, starving children stretching out their hands imploringly, dramatic images like the ones she'd wanted to make of Mama. In this case, she had only the defiant words of a humiliated woman—one of a great many such women—who described her sufferings before the world without losing her dignity. I hope Katelijne wasn't disappointed.

We'd been listening so intently to Lea Malanda that we hadn't noticed the half dozen women who had gathered around us. They seemed liberated by what Lea had just said—seemed to realize that the true shame would lie in continuing to keep silent about what they had endured, and that their freedom was beginning with this effort to make their voices heard. Only minutes before, they had been reluctant to display their humiliation before the world, but now all of them were eager to speak.

"I wasn't raped, but I want to tell you about another sort of shame. I sold myself. Yes, look at me, listen to my words: I sold my body for four tablets of chloroquine to save the life of my child, who was dying from malaria. The child is alive today because I spread my legs for a price. When will we be done with such humiliations? Even in this refugee camp, there are still people who force us to pay with sex for a box of powdered milk, a bit of space under a plastic tent, a bowl of rice. Some of the staff ask us for money before they'll give us rations cards."

"And since I didn't have any money, I agreed to sleep twice with a man just so I could get that stupid card!" exclaimed another woman angrily, brandishing a rations card—which, thanks to Doctors Without Borders, I had received for free.

"Were we born women merely to suffer?" asked the one who'd spoken previously.

She could not go on. Her question remained hanging in the air without a reply, and she began to weep. In her arms she held the child for whom she'd sold her dignity—a little boy of shocking thinness. In his case, the expression "skin and bones" was not just a figure of speech but the description of a harsh reality. And that thinness contrasted grotesquely with the roundness of his swollen belly. I was no doctor, but I was probably right in thinking that the child had reached an irreversible stage of malnutrition. In a few weeks, more likely in a few days, he would surely be dead. And still the woman clung tenaciously to her little son, enveloping him tenderly in her maternal love even though the battle was already lost.

I looked at Katelijne and tried to gauge her emotions, wondering if she, a European, could identify with the sufferings of these women as closely as someone from India or Afghanistan, or a Palestinian or a Somalian. I think she could. Weren't we all human? Any person can understand and share the pain of another, if only he or she makes the effort to do so. Katelijne, like Birgit and Tanisha, had made the effort.

Chapter Twenty-nine

Laokolé

A rumor that the president of the republic was coming to visit the camp began making the rounds first thing in the morning. Soldiers soon appeared everywhere, telling us to clean up our tents in case the president passed through and, as an extra incentive, promising us double rations if we gave that august personage an enthusiastic reception. We could count on getting a bit of meat or fish, and perhaps even some sugar. They selected a few children and issued them new clothes and shoes for the welcoming ceremony. They asked us to make ourselves look our best, as if we had deliberately taken pains to be in such a deplorable condition.

For me, the most important thing was to find out whether this visit by the head of state would preclude all other visits. If so, it meant that humanitarian organizations were barred from the camp and Birgit wouldn't be able to get me out till the next day. A real disappointment, since I was already celebrating the fact that I'd spent my last night there.

Three hours before the president arrived, we were told to go and stand behind the line of soldiers guarding the podium where he would be speaking. We were thoroughly searched beforehand, as if poor refugees like us could possibly have weapons that could be used to kill the head of state. On the dais, one of the six children chosen for the welcoming committee—all of whom had likewise been standing there for hours waiting—collapsed headlong, doubtless from fatigue and hunger. He was removed with all possible speed.

At last we heard the surveillance helicopter that always preceded the head of state on his travels; then the motorcycle escort; then the ululations of the women, as prescribed by etiquette. The women spread their pagnes on the ground for the president to walk on, so his illustrious boots wouldn't be soiled before they reached the red carpet that had been laid out for him in the dust. The soldiers were getting more and more nervous, their fingers poised over the triggers of their weapons. This was no time to scratch your nose or make any sudden movement, for they'd shoot you instantly without a second thought. As members of the president's bodyguard, they were above the law and, like him, could act with total impunity. A few of them were wearing dark glasses, as if they were in some American movie.

After acknowledging the cheers of the crowd, the president stepped onto the platform. Perhaps for reasons of security, no one had told us that he would be accompanied by his wife. But I understood why her presence was necessary: the sacks of food waiting to be distributed had been donated by her—they were all labeled with the name of her organization, Children's Solidarity. A discreet signal was given, and the selected children began to sing. When the songs of praise were finished, the president's wife picked up one of the kids—a little girl of about five, who was so thin she was practically swimming in the new clothes she'd been decked out in. Her hair was the reddish color you see on children suffering from kwashiorkor. The woman hugged her, then handed her some vitamin-enriched biscuits while the crowd applauded and the cameras rolled. The little girl was obviously hungry, for she couldn't wait. No sooner had the president's wife set her down, out of camera range, than she began tearing open the packet of biscuits. One of the soldiers admonished her, unobtrusively but firmly rapping her on the wrist. The box fell and its contents scattered all over the ground, while the little girl looked in dismay at the biscuits she was forbidden to pick up and cram into her mouth.

The president began to speak. I retained only one thing from his address—namely, that France had donated shovels and lime. I think these were meant to be used for digging up and reinterring all the hastily buried bodies throughout the city so that an epidemic could be averted, the way you sprinkled lime in the pits when burying the bodies of animals that had died of anthrax. Then the ceremony was over. The president, his wife, the motorcycles, and the helicopter all left. The head of state hadn't bothered to tour the camp.

We'd been told that the food would be distributed after the president's departure, but, curiously, the soldiers began carrying sacks of it to the trucks they'd parked at the camp's front entrance. The refugees began to protest—weakly at first, for fear of the guns. But soon their empty stomachs persuaded them to throw caution to the winds, and they tried to grab their share. Sacks of rice and of beans were ripped open, and women hurried to fill their pagnes; the stronger men tried to lift entire sacks or to carry away large containers of cooking oil. The result was a free-for-all.

The little girl who'd been embraced by the president's wife was now abandoned on the dais, in the midst of the melee. Where was her mother? Or was she one of the countless orphans in the camp, left to fend for themselves? Yes, this was clearly what she was. Scanning the platform and seeing no sign of the soldier who'd reprimanded her, she dropped to her knees and began to stuff her mouth hungrily with the biscuits scattered about. Then she caught sight of the rest of the packet, stretched out her hand, and . . . *wham!* With shocking violence, a soldier's belt descended on her, just missing her hand and breaking open a box of powdered milk that had fallen to the boards in the confusion. I looked around. The vicious disciplinarian was standing near me, preparing to inflict another blow. I caught hold of the belt; I think I even snatched it out of his hand. He glared at me and knit his brows threateningly—an absurd, histrionic expression.

And I recognized him. It was Mad Dog, the militiaman who had ruthlessly gunned down the little fruit-seller in the street and whom I'd later seen in the HCR compound. He was a beast. He was getting ready to strike the child again. Calling him every foul name I knew, I quickly bent down and shielded her body with mine. He rained down blows like a demon, each lash searing my flesh and shredding my T-shirt even further. If the little girl herself had received that beating, she would have been reduced to a bloody mess. The pain was becoming unbearable—I didn't know how much longer I could hold out before I'd have to scream and let go of the child. I braced myself for the next biting lash of the belt. But it never came. Surprised, I looked up.

Mad Dog was on the ground, being pummeled from every side. A riot had broken out. The mothers in the camp, many of whom had sunk into apathy as a result of the humiliations they'd endured, had recovered their spirit and were attacking the soldiers with anything they could lay their hands on. The defeated, discouraged men who were ashamed of being unable to protect their families in adversity seemed likewise to be taking their revenge. After all, there were about a thousand of them, whereas there were only about a hundred soldiers. Unfortunately, though, the latter had guns, and were more than willing to use them . . .

After the riot had been quelled, the soldiers punished everyone by announcing that no food would be distributed for forty-eight hours. Then they made a sweep through the camp. They systematically rounded up all the men of fighting age, and, as usual, took some women along. I was preparing to go back to my tent with the little girl in my arms when Mad Dog forcibly stopped me. He was still boiling with anger. Two of his fellow soldiers picked me up and threw me into one of the trucks. If the child hadn't been holding tight to me, I would have dropped her.

The trucks made stops at two or three military camps, each time unloading some men. I was sure their wives would never see them again. At each stop, too, the soldiers unloaded the women they had picked out—for the pleasure of raping them, I suppose. Brave warriors. When, at the last stop, I was transferred to a Toyota Hi-Lux and Mad Dog took the wheel, I understood that my future lay in his paws. He drove at an insane speed, honking loudly, barreling through intersections without slowing down, and at last coming to a halt before a house in one of the western districts of the city. He got out first and went to unlock the front door and turn on the exterior light, since it was after dark. He came back to the vehicle and in a hoarse voice ordered me to get out.

As I stood there with the child in my arms and watched that killer put the car in the garage, I knew that this was the moment of reckoning. I'd seen and lived through so much in this rotten country that nothing could surprise me any longer. I knew that he would order me into the house, and that of course I'd refuse and try to resist. He would strike me with his fists or with his gun, he would torment the child, and eventually I'd have to yield to his brute strength. I'd be dragged into the house, and what happened after that would be anybody's guess. Well, it would be good to keep my wits about me, in any case. The familiar expression "to meet one's fate" occurred to me. So I decided to really go and meet my fate—to take the initiative and not simply wait until he gave me an order.

With a determination that was part bravado, part movie gesture, I opened the unlocked door and entered the beast's lair. It was like walking into Ali Baba's cave. Televisions, CD players, computers, refrigerators, gas cookers, medical supplies, and on and on. More surprising was that he'd also stolen books. I never would have thought an animal like him would steal books, since they weren't worth anything on the local market. I chose the handsomest armchair, sat down, turned out the light, and waited for him—waited for him in the darkness. One thing was sure: I wouldn't just give up. I'd fight tooth and nail until the end. There was only one thing I regretted, namely that I couldn't save the child sitting on my lap—the child who no doubt thought I could protect her from the rest of the world.

Chapter Thirty

Johnny, Known as Mad Dog

Strange woman, strange girl. No one—certainly no woman—had ever given me such an impression before. When I got out of the car after stowing it in the garage, she'd vanished. I thought she had run away, and I was angry at myself for not keeping an eye on her. Well, she couldn't have gotten far in this unfamiliar neighborhood, especially hauling a child around, and I'd catch her without difficulty as soon as I went after her. To see if she might be somewhere near the house, I took a walk around it. I looked in the clumps of lantana and hibiscus that bordered the property, but she wasn't there. I even looked behind the fencing that surrounded the cesspool, thinking she might have been able to bear the nauseating stench, but I didn't find her there, either. There was nothing left to do but put away the two tins of cooking oil and the sack of beans I'd taken, and head off in pursuit. This time I wouldn't go lightly on her—she'd feel the full brunt of my anger.

* * *

I went into the house. I thought I'd turned on all the lights a few minutes before, but evidently I hadn't, because the living room was completely dark. I flipped the switch. The light came on—and I nearly had a heart attack! A ghost had sprung from the darkness: it was sitting in an armchair with a child on its lap. Turn around! Run! But no, my fear passed. I got hold of myself just in time. What the devil—it was her!

Strange woman, strange girl. She looked at me fearlessly, as if waiting with curiosity to see what I was going to do to her. She wasn't stupid. She must have noticed that I'd gone haywire for a moment when I'd seen her. So I immediately had to reestablish the natural order of things—had to make her understand right away that I was in control here.

"Who . . . who gave you permission to enter my house?" I said foolishly.

"Who gave you permission to kidnap me?"

"What? I do as I please—I don't take orders from anyone!"

"I don't either! I do as I please—nobody gives me orders!"

"What's your name?"

"You really think I'm going to tell you?"

The cunt! What did she take me for?

"What do you take me for?" I shouted.

"For what you are—a murderer!"

The insult hit me like a blow.

"I'm not a murderer, for your information! I fight wars! In war, you kill, you burn buildings, you rape women. That's normal. That's what war is all about—killing is natural. But that doesn't mean I'm a common murderer!"

"Why don't you just go ahead and rape me, Mad Dog?"

Wham! No shit, I was speechless. She knew me! She knew my name! Who on earth was she, this plain-looking girl in the ragged T-shirt? This girl who still defied me, in spite of the beating I'd given her? Who had no fear of the gun in my belt? Maybe I'd brought a witch into my house! I confess I was scared. In my country, you've got to watch out for women. There are certain women called *mamiwatas* who live in rivers and streams and can cast an evil spell on a man with their beauty and sensuality. Maybe she was one of them. Or a succubus who had waited for nightfall so she could lure me into an orgy and drain me of all my virility by taking my thing into her mouth! . . . No, she was neither of these, because *mamiwatas* and succubi appeared only in the dead of night or at dawn. She was nothing but a shabby refugee I'd picked up in a camp. I touched my pistol. Force was my weapon, and guns were my instruments of terror. Yet what could I do when someone had no fear of force or guns? I was lost. I could kill her easily. But if I killed her without making her afraid, without humiliating her, she would have won. "Why don't you just go ahead and rape me?" she'd asked sarcastically. But who could get a hard-on and feel like committing rape after such mockery, in the face of such contempt?

"You're wrong—I don't even want to touch you. Look at you," I sneered. "You're filthy. That rat's nest on your head—it's like the hair of a grieving widow. And you're a whore. I bet you don't even know the name of your child's father. How do I know you don't have AIDS? Who'd want to fuck a woman like you? I'd a million times rather masturbate."

No, she wasn't incensed. My insults hadn't driven her into a rage. She continued to look at me coldly, exasperatingly, all the while tenderly holding her child.

"Answer me!" I shouted. "When I speak, people answer me!"

Still she said nothing.

"You think I do nothing in life but kill people? Come look!" I said angrily.

I opened the door to the bedroom and went in. She set the child down in the chair and followed me. Remaining on her guard, though, she halted on the threshold.

I threw open the closet with a furious jerk. It contained everything I'd looted and purchased in my life. Before joining the militia, I'd been a member of the Society of Ambiancers and Persons of Elegance, one of the kings of SAPE—those nightclub patrons and arbiters of taste, always dressed in the height of fashion. Hot with anger, I pulled out a suit by my favorite London tailor, Old River: navy blue pants, always worn with the hand-sewn Versace belt that I kept looped around the waistband, and a slim-fitting three-button jacket, in super-100 fabric, likewise navy blue, with piping around the pockets. I flung them down on the bed. On a handmade Yves Saint Laurent shirt of yellow cotton piqué I placed a tie of solid yellow, the same shade as the shirt, to illustrate what we, the new generation of *sapeurs*, called "tone on tone" dressing. I had replaced the traditional cuff links with what we termed "snowballs," imported directly from Italy. As for shoes, I showed her my Westons, my Salamanders, my John Lobbs. What else? My little Gucci parasol, for protection against the sun. Cologne? Giorgio Armani. So—would a common murderer ever dress like that?

From the bundles of pagnes I'd found at Mr. Ibara's house, I took out the ones I'd set aside for my late darling Lovelita, and of these I picked out the most beautiful. It was a Dutch superwax adorned with proud cocks showing off their plumage against a flowered background.

"Here—you can have it. See? Mad Dog is no vicious beast."

She wasn't impressed in the slightest and showed no interest at all, returning to the living room before I'd even finished displaying all of my treasures. She sat down next to the child. I didn't know what else to do to intimidate her, impress her, make her react. Shit. I went into the living room and said:

"I'm not just a king of SAPE. I'm also an intellectual."

At this, she was genuinely surprised. She stared at me as if I'd dropped from the moon. Maybe she didn't know what an intellectual was!

"That means someone who's been to school and whose brain keeps working even at night while he's sleeping. He can figure out the surface of a cube and of a sphere, he's studied grammatology and stroboscopy, he has beautiful books in his library," I explained all in one breath. She probably didn't believe me—I was talking to a brick wall. I reached toward the bookshelf to my right and pulled out a large hardcover volume bound in leather. It was the first book in my collection—the blood-spattered Bible I'd taken from the home of that old mystic in Kandahar. It was even heavier than I thought. I tossed it to her.

"Here's the first book I got for my library. A Bible."

It landed in her lap, which the child was no longer sitting in. She picked it up with both hands and held it in her left, so she could defend herself with her right hand if she needed to. An old fox like me knew that trick. She made no move to open the book. And still refused to say anything, which irritated me more and more.

"When I speak, people answer! Answer me!"

Still that look of contempt and that disdainful curl of the

lips. It was too much. And to be chattering away in front of a woman was a sign of weakness. It was time for action. A man must act. Deliver a good slap, for example.

"Okay, you don't want to speak? Fine. I'll make you scream."

I moved toward her. I didn't see the Bible coming.

Thrown with her left hand, the heavy book struck me full in the face, right between the eyes, with incredible force. Why hadn't it occurred to me that the witch must be left-handed? I fell over backward from the blow. The nape of my neck smashed against the edge of the table, and I landed on the floor, stunned, bleeding profusely from my nose and neck. I was dead, killed by a Bible. People had always told me to beware of women and books! The room was swimming around me. I had to get up, I had to kill her. My hand reached instinctively for the gun at my hip, but a heavy object came smashing down on my fingers. And then a fury began giving me relentless, repeated blows between my legs. The pain was unbearable. I screamed, I pleaded for it to stop—but the fury didn't know what pity was, and continued to strike, to strike. I began pissing blood, my testicles burst, my balls were pulp. I was castrated. But the fury still didn't stop. Now the pain filled my entire body . . . I was in agony . . . I was dying . . . I was dead . . . I . . . I . . .

Chapter Thirty-one

Laokolé

He was petrified when the light came on and he saw me there, sitting in an armchair with my child. I'd shaken him out of his preening arrogance and had chalked up a solid point against him. On the one hand, that was a good thing because he'd be more afraid of me and more cautious about what he tried to do to me. On the other hand, it might also be a bad thing because it could make him more cruel. I had to stay one step ahead of him at all costs, had to maintain my psychological advantage. Now I knew that so long as I gave him no opportunity to use his gun, I'd be able to manage him.

I began by giving a quick, aggressive retort to everything he said, thus throwing him even further off balance. I don't think any of his victims had ever stood up to him like that. What completely disoriented him was my refusal to tell him my name, followed by my complete silence. The silence of the deep sea. To hide his disarray, he invited me to see the contents of his closet, which was stuffed with clothes from the finest London tailors and shoemakers, things that he'd looted from all over. In his stupidity and naivete, he went so far as to offer me some stolen pagnes. When I still refused to say anything, he came out with something truly astounding: he announced that he was an intellectual.

I confess that I myself was thrown off balance by this. I had never heard one of those looting, thieving, raping militiamen say he was an intellectual and fond of books. Life is certainly full of surprises. I almost broke my silence to ask him which books he had read and liked, but his stream of chatter saved me. Still talking away, he tossed me a large Bible, which landed in my lap. I picked up the book with my left hand, the one I normally used, while I made a show of keeping my right hand free, to make him think it was my dominant hand, the one I defended myself with. And thus I took advantage of his bias, the bias of a right-handed person.

While he got himself tangled up in a nonsensical definition of the word "intellectual," I was surreptitiously hefting the large book, grasping it firmly in my hand. I waited for the right moment, which fortunately came quite soon. After his thoroughly muddled description of what an intellectual was, he looked at me. I could see by his expression that he was desperately seeking validation of his status as an intellectual and a man of superior mind, wanting me to confirm this with some slight gesture, some small mark of admiration. I did just the opposite. I curled my lips to show my contempt, and this worked. He became furious and took a step forward, a step toward me.

The Bible hit him square in the face.

When despair is transformed into destructive energy, its

force is multiplied beyond belief. The blow sent him sprawling. He could have gotten up right away if luck hadn't been with me. It so happened that as he fell, the back of his neck collided sharply with the right angle formed by two sides of the rectangular table. From the sound of the impact, I thought his neck might be broken.

I jumped up immediately. When I saw him reaching for his gun, I smashed his fingers with a large bottle full of whiskey. Then I began stomping, crushing, kicking with all my might, aiming my blows at those genitals that had humiliated so many women. I thought of the twelve-year-old girl in the camp; I thought of my daughter, whom he'd nearly flayed alive with lashes from his belt; and I rammed him ceaselessly between the legs. I trampled, pounded, pulverized his groin. I struck him like a mad fury. By the time I calmed down, his body was still.

The child in the armchair was looking at me without saying a word. I took the new pagne he'd offered me, made a small rip in it with my teeth, and tore it into two large pieces. I nestled my daughter against my back with her feet at my sides, and tied her snugly to me with half of the pagne. Without even glancing at the motionless body lying in a pool of blood, I went out the door and began striding briskly down the street.

The fresh air was like a tonic, and I was filled with an all-encompassing joy. Joy at being alive. Joy at having survived. Joy at continuing to live. The fresh air revived the child, too, for she began to cry. And this was good—a child who's crying is a child who is alive. And I remembered that my little daughter had no name.

Now, everything that's ever existed in the universe began with a name. I sent my memory plunging into the rich heritage of my grandfather's language, and I came up with the purest word of the tribe, the most beautiful word, a perfect reflection of the moment: *Kiessé!* Joy! My child, I name you Kiessé!

And I looked up at the sky. There they were, those brilliant diamonds, crowning our heads. What would we do without the stars?